A Heron Books Collection

CHARLES DICKENS

COMPLETE
WORKS

CENTENNIAL EDITION

Charles Dickens

CHARLES DICKENS

THE POSTHUMOUS PAPERS
OF
THE PICKWICK CLUB
I

Introduction
by
Bernard Darwin

Illustrations
by Seymour and Phiz

HERON BOOKS

*The introduction to this book
was originally published for the
Oxford Illustrated Dickens,
published by
the Oxford University Press.*

INTRODUCTION

'There aint nobody like you, though I like you better than nothin' at all.' Thus Sam Weller, reading aloud his Valentine, and he added 'I thought it best to make that rayther strong.' His words express the sentiments of many lovers of Dickens in general towards Pickwick in particular. There is nothing like it. Some will agree with the statement only in a limited sense, since when setting down the books in order of their affections they begin by putting Pickwick on one side as being 'different'. There are obvious differences, to which I will return, but the intransigent Pickwickian will scarcely allow this shelving of the issue, and he is fortified by unquestionably the greatest critic of Dickens. Chesterton wrote that if he never again descended to the level of Sketches by Boz it was doubtful if to the level of Pickwick he ever again rose. There are qualities in which some of Dickens' later books excelled Pickwick, but they are those in which other writers equalled or excelled Dickens. Pickwick is richest in the qualities in which Dickens excelled all the other writers; and if that is rather strong I think it best to say so boldly and at once.

'I thought of Mr. Pickwick and wrote the first chapter.' So wrote Dickens in after years of the genesis of this unfading book, and *unless it be in* Veni, Vidi, Vici, *so great a feat has perhaps never been described in so few words. To have conceived the mere embryo Mr. Pickwick as we first meet him may have been no very wonderful thing; but to have produced him as we part from him sorrowfully at Dulwich, the great gentleman and the great romantic, the knight errant, the 'reglar thoroughbred angel in tights and gaiters', was an achievement unsurpassed in the domain of the lovable.*

To Sam Weller is historically due the first immense success of the book. He has, in Mr. Lowten's expressive phrase, 'the key of the street'; he is the ideal Cockney, shrewd, kindly, and undaunted, who can disconcert a Serjeant-at-law as easily as he can knock down a beadle, to whom all hearts are instantly given. It is an outstanding moment in literature when, at the beginning of Chapter X, the man in the white hat says 'Ask number twenty-two, whether he'll have 'em now or wait till he gets 'em'. From this instant the sales, which had comparatively speaking hung fire, began to soar, and the binders who had prepared four hundred copies of the first number in April 1836 were called on for forty thousand of the fifteenth. Sam must have all due credit, for Mr. Pickwick could not have done without him. Yet there are some who deem it a still greater moment, ten chapters later, when a hoarse voice emerging from a cloud of shawls and tobacco smoke utters the words 'Wy, Sammy!' If Sam himself could be consulted he would surely agree, for he appears so intuitively conscious of his father's overpowering qualities that in any scene between the two he lets him take the centre of the stage. He himself does little more than provide the cues which shall exhibit the philosopher in his richest and most oracular vein.

It is perhaps impious to make comparisons between the persons of a trinity: the book owes much to each of these three figures; but it is permissible to suggest that, judged in terms of the reader's affections, Mr. Pickwick holds the first place. It is noteworthy that when a few years ago the centenary of the book was celebrated by a banquet, it was Mr. Pickwick's name that was 'surrounded with a rich halo of enthusiastic cheering'; it was for him that we sang 'For he's a jolly good fellow'. It seemed so entirely natural a thing to do that it was hard not to believe him there in person; a little moved by the applause and privily wiping a tear from his round

INTRODUCTION

*and shining spectacles, but full of vigour and spirit ready to spring
on to the seat of his Windsor chair and address the gathering with
that plain eloquence of which he was the master. The love of Mr.
Pickwick is of a comparatively slow growth and comes gradually
with much re-reading, but it is the deepest of all.*

*The story of the book's origin has often been told and need not
be recapitulated, but the fact is perhaps worth emphasizing yet
again that when Chapman and Hall asked Dickens to undertake
it they thought of him as little more than a handy young man to
write round Seymour's pictures. They did not even think of him
first; they had asked two other men before him, and it is one of our
undying reasons for thankfulness to Providence that one did not
take the trouble to answer and the other refused. If either had
accepted we should assuredly have had Dickens, for nothing could
have held him back, but we should not have had* Pickwick *and to
many people nothing could have made up for that loss.*

*It has already been admitted that the book is to some extent
different in kind from its successors and it may now be suggested
that it is none the worse for that. There is for instance the absence
of plot. The book was probably written more from hand to mouth
than those which followed it, with the author scarcely knowing
from number to number what he was going to do with his characters
or his characters were going to do with him. An example of his
masterful casualness is that a few days after popular feeling at
Ipswich had subsided 'Consekens o' the boys having dispersed to
cricket' the Pickwickians were at Dingley Dell for a snowy Christmas. Nevertheless the simple structure of the book is not unskilful
and holds tolerably well together. To put it at its mildest, and with
all respect for those who believe that* Edwin Drood *would have
triumphantly proved the contrary, Dickens' plots were not his
strong point. Some of them at least are as unconvincing as they are
tedious. If they do no great harm it is because of Dickens' supreme
genius in other directions, and they do no good. In* Pickwick *we
are all the better without one.*

*It may be said that in some respects Dickens did not here aim so
high as he did later, that he left unscaled and unattempted some of
those difficult and slippery peaks which try the climber hardest.
This is true as regards any considerable presentation of a love*

affair. Arabella Allen with her archness and the fur round her boots is, as Mr. Pickwick said, 'a very amiable creature', and, like him, we don't know how it is but we have been very fond of her from the first. We may even in a profane moment reflect that it would be a far, far better thing to marry her than Agnes Wickfield; but we cannot take her and Mr. Winkle nor any of the other incidental pairs of lovers seriously. Dickens was here unambitious, avoiding both heights and pitfalls, but this is not so as regards genuine touchingness or sheer, stark power. In its perfect simplicity and dignity the scene between Sam and his father after Mrs. Weller's death is, to me at any rate, infinitely more moving than those deliberate death beds which made Dickens' contemporaries use, like Job Trotter, their pink pocket handkerchiefs. It has rather the unforced and pathetic charm of the scenes between Bella Wilfer and her father, and is in its way unsurpassable. Nearly as much may be said of every passage in which the mutual affection between Sam and his master is described, and the last few words in the book can hardly be read without tears.

It was only gradually as the book went on that Dickens rose to these heights, and, as we may assume, became conscious of the force that was in him. He would scarcely have dared the Fleet scenes when he began, not merely because the publisher might have told him that that was not what he was paid for, but because he would have felt incapable of them. He was like a boy who is growing so quickly in strength and stature that he can run perceptibly faster or jump perceptibly higher almost from day to day. By the time he came to the Fleet he was able to say confidently that those chapters would 'bang all the rest'. It may be argued that from a severely artistic point of view they are little out of keeping with the rest, but of their power there can be no question. He described life in a debtors' prison in other books and always superbly well, but he never excelled the dreadful restlessness, the broken misery side by side with the noisy, hollow roistering of the Fleet. He was very young (in his mid-twenties), very happy, very confident, when he wrote Pickwick; *he took everything without toil or agony in his triumphant stride; if we except parts of* David Copperfield *he was more utterly spontaneous than ever again. That sudden wonderful springtime was the best.*

X

INTRODUCTION

There is one point on which the fervid Pickwickian will uphold the book with special assurance; with an exception to which I will come back, there is nothing to skip. When re-reading the very greatest of Dickens' other books with an experienced eye for country, we instinctively avoid certain tracts, in particular those which are a little swampy with sentiment, and pass on to the firm and glorious uplands beyond. There are no such tracts in Pickwick. *The first chapter begins laboriously but is redeemed by the mutual concessions of Mr. Pickwick and Mr. Blotton of Aldgate, and after that the book goes with an unbroken rush, shedding the clumsy machinery of the club and Mr. Snodgrass' note-book as it goes. There is no temptation to miss a single word except the inter-polated stories. Dickens was fond of the principle of a story within a story, and the whole design of* Master Humphrey's Clock *was originally founded upon it. Most of these stories in* Pickwick *are tiresome and some are crudely melodramatic, for Dickens had not yet acquired his touch for melodrama and for an atmosphere char-ged with terrific events to come. But there are two exceptions to this exception, two stories which must be read, those of Gabriel Grub and Tom Smart.*

Gabriel Grub may not be great in itself but it is historically important as the germ of A Christmas Carol. *The idea underlying both stories, as well as to a large extent the machinery for carrying it out, is the same, though the author used it with far greater skill, power, and humour in the* Carol. *The 'Bagman's Story' of Tom Smart no one will ever skip if he reads* Pickwick *a thousand times. Dickens was supreme in depicting snugness, the contrast between the wild wind and weather without and the crackling fire within. He did it many times afterwards and always to admiration, as witness the scene in this very book where Mr. Pickwick, surveying the Christmas revels at Dingley Dell, exclaims in the fullness of his heart 'This is indeed comfort'. But he never did it better than in the moment at which Tom Smart, alighting from his gig at the little inn beyond the Marlborough Downs, sees the ruddy light in the window and the green bottles with gold labels in the bar. There never was such hot punch as that. He never did it better because it could not be better done.*

It is a commonplace that Dickens is unequalled in his minor

characters, some of whom, like the young man in Our Mutual
Friend *who said 'Esker', flash across the stage for an instant and
impress themselves for ever on the memory.* Pickwick *is at least
as rich in them as any of the other books, as the reader will discover
who plays at the agreeably childish game of choosing an eleven from
it. He will find that some of the chief characters have no chance of
a place. They are crowded out by the apparently lesser but in truth
gigantic figures of Mr. Tom Roker, Mr. Solomon Pell, Mr. Jack
Hopkins, and one who has no name but is palpably of the immor-
tals, the small boy in the hairy cap who gave 'several chaste and
extremely correct imitations of a drover's whistle'. Not merely
George Yard, but, in a Pickwickian sense at least, the whole world
has echoed with him ever since. If this appears an excessive statement I must plead that these words are written near Christmas
time, a season at which gratitude for all the happiness and solace
of* Pickwick *overpowers the critical faculties. And so, in Mr.
Weller's words, 'Now, gen'l'men, fall on, as the English said to
the French when they fixed bagginets'.*

Bernard Darwin

March 1947

PREFACE.

It was observed, in the Preface to the original Edition of the "Posthumous Papers of the Pickwick Club," that they were designed for the introduction of diverting characters and incidents; that no ingenuity of plot was attempted, or even at that time considered very feasible by the author in connexion with the desultory mode of publication adopted; and that the machinery of the Club, proving cumbrous in the management, was gradually abandoned as the work progressed. Although, on one of these points, experience and study afterwards taught me something, and I could perhaps wish now that these chapters were strung together on a stronger thread of general interest, still, what they are they were designed to be.

I have seen various accounts of the origin of these Pickwick Papers, which have, at all events, possessed—for me— the charm of perfect novelty. As I may infer, from the occasional appearance of such histories, that my readers have an interest in the matter, I will relate how they came into existence.

I was a young man of two or three-and-twenty, when MESSRS. CHAPMAN and HALL, attracted by some pieces I was at that time writing in the Morning Chronicle newspaper, or had just written in the Old Monthly Magazine (of which one series had lately been collected and published in two volumes, illustrated by MR. GEORGE CRUIKSHANK), waited upon me to propose a something that should be published in shilling numbers—then only known to me, or, I believe, to anybody else, by a dim recollection of certain interminable novels in that form, which used to be carried about the country by pedlars, and over some of which I remember to have shed innumerable tears before I had served my apprenticeship to Life.

When I opened my door in Furnival's Inn to the partner who represented the firm, I recognised in him the person from whose hands I had bought, two or three years previously, and whom I had never seen before or since, my first copy of the Magazine in which my first effusion—a paper in the "Sketches," called MR. MINNS AND HIS COUSIN—dropped stealthily one evening at twilight, with fear and trembling, into a dark letter-box, in a dark office, up a dark court in Fleet Street—appeared in all the glory of print; on which occasion I walked down to Westminster Hall, and turned into it for half-an-hour, because my eyes were so dimmed with joy and pride, that they could not bear the street, and were not fit to be seen there. I told my visitor of the coincidence, which we both hailed as a good omen; and so fell to business.

The idea propounded to me, was, that the monthly something should be a vehicle for certain plates to be executed by MR. SEYMOUR; and there was a notion, either on the part of that admirable humorous artist, or of my visitor, that a "NIMROD Club," the members of which were to go out shooting, fishing, and so forth, and getting themselves into difficulties through their want of dexterity, would be the best means

PREFACE.

of introducing these. I objected, on consideration, that although born and partly bred in the country I was no great sportsman, except in regard of all kinds of locomotion; that the idea was not novel, and had been already much used; that it would be infinitely better for the plates to arise naturally out of the text; and that I would like to take my own way, with a freer range of English scenes and people, and was afraid I should ultimately do so in any case, whatever course I might prescribe to myself at starting. My views being deferred to, I thought of Mr. Pickwick, and wrote the first number; from the proof sheets of which, MR. SEYMOUR made his drawing of the Club, and his happy portrait of its founder :—the latter on MR. EDWARD CHAPMAN's description of the dress and bearing of a real personage whom he had often seen. I connected Mr. Pickwick with a club, because of the original suggestion, and I put in Mr. Winkle expressly for the use of MR. SEYMOUR. We started with a number of twenty-four pages instead of thirty-two, and four illustrations in lieu of a couple. MR. SEYMOUR's sudden and lamented death before the second number was published, brought about a quick decision upon a point already in agitation; the number became one of thirty-two pages with only two illustrations, and remained so to the end.

It is with great unwillingness that I notice some intangible and incoherent assertions which have been made, professedly on behalf of MR. SEYMOUR, to the effect that he had some share in the invention of this book, or of anything in it, not faithfully described in the foregoing paragraph. With the moderation that is due equally to my respect for the memory of a brother-artist, and to my self-respect, I confine myself to placing on record here the facts:

PREFACE.

That, MR. SEYMOUR never originated or suggested an incident, a phrase, or a word, to be found in this book. That, MR. SEYMOUR died when only twenty-four pages of this book were published, and when assuredly not forty-eight were written. That, I believe I never saw MR. SEYMOUR's hand-writing in my life. That, I never saw MR. SEYMOUR but once in my life, and that was on the night but one before his death, when he certainly offered no suggestion whatsoever. That I saw him then in the presence of two persons, both living, perfectly acquainted with all these facts, and whose written testimony to them I possess. Lastly, that MR. EDWARD CHAPMAN (the survivor of the original firm of CHAPMAN and HALL) has set down in writing, for similar preservation, his personal knowledge of the origin and progress of this book, of the monstrosity of the baseless assertions in question, and (tested by details) even of the self-evident impossibility of there being any truth in them. In the exercise of the forbearance on which I have resolved, I do not quote MR. EDWARD CHAPMAN's account of his deceased partner's reception, on a certain occasion, of the pretences in question.

"Boz," my signature in the Morning Chronicle, and in the Old Monthly Magazine, appended to the monthly cover of this book, and retained long afterwards, was the nickname of a pet child, a younger brother, whom I had dubbed Moses, in honour of the Vicar of Wakefield; which being facetiously pronounced through the nose, became Boses, and being shortened, became Boz. Boz was a very familiar household word to me, long before I was an author, and so I came to adopt it.

It has been observed of Mr. Pickwick, that there is a decided change in his character, as these pages proceed, and that he becomes more good and more sensible. I do not think this change will appear forced or unnatural to my readers, if they will reflect that in real life the peculiarities and oddities of a man who has anything whimsical about him, generally impress us first, and that it is not until we are better acquainted with him that we usually begin to look below these superficial traits, and to know the better part of him.

Lest there should be any well-intentioned persons who do not perceive the difference (as some such could not, when OLD MORTALITY was newly published), between religion and the cant of religion, piety and the pretence of piety, a humble reverence for the great truths of Scripture and an audacious and offensive obtrusion of its letter and not its spirit in the commonest dissensions and meanest affairs of life, to the extraordinary confusion of ignorant minds, let them understand that it is always the latter, and never the former, which is satirized here. Further, that the latter is here satirized as being, according to all experience, inconsistent with the former, impossible of union with it, and one of the most evil and mischievous falsehoods existent in society— whether it establish its head-quarters, for the time being, in Exeter Hall, or Ebenezer Chapel, or both. It may appear unnecessary to offer a word of observation on so plain a head. But it is never out of season to protest against that coarse familiarity with sacred things which is busy on the lip, and idle in the heart; or against the confounding of Christianity with any class of persons who, in the words of SWIFT, have just enough religion to make them hate, and not enough to make them love, one another.

I have found it curious and interesting, looking over the sheets of this reprint, to mark what important social

PREFACE.

improvements have taken place about us, almost imperceptibly, since they were originally written. The licence of Counsel, and the degree to which Juries are ingeniously bewildered, are yet susceptible of moderation; while an improvement in the mode of conducting Parliamentary Elections (and even Parliaments too, perhaps) is still within the bounds of possibility. But legal reforms have pared the claws of Messrs. Dodson and Fogg; a spirit of self-respect, mutual forbearance, education, and co-operation for such good ends, has diffused itself among their clerks; places far apart are brought together, to the present convenience and advantage of the Public, and to the certain destruction, in time, of a host of petty jealousies, blindnesses, and prejudices, by which the Public alone have always been the sufferers; the laws relating to imprisonment for debt are altered; and the Fleet Prison is pulled down!

Who knows, but by the time the series reaches its conclusion, it may be discovered that there are even magistrates in town and country, who should be taught to shake hands every day with Common-sense and Justice; that even Poor Laws may have mercy on the weak, the aged, and unfortunate; that Schools, on the broad principles of Christianity, are the best adornment for the length and breadth of this civilised land; that Prison-doors should be barred on the outside, no less heavily and carefully than they are barred within; that the universal diffusion of common means of decency and health is as much the right of the poorest of the poor, as it is indispensable to the safety of the rich, and of the State, that a few petty boards and bodies—less than drops in the great ocean of humanity, which roars around them—are not for ever to let loose Fever and Consumption on God's creatures at their will, or always to keep their jobbing little fiddles going, for a Dance of Death.

CONTENTS OF VOL. I.

CHAPTER I.

The Pickwickians 1

CHAPTER II.

The first Day's Journey, and the first Evening's Adventures; with
their Consequences 7

CHAPTER III.

A new Acquaintance. The Stroller's Tale. A disagreeable Interruption; and an unpleasant Rencontre 39

CHAPTER IV.

A Field-day and Bivouac. More new Friends; and an Invitation
to the Country 53

CHAPTER V.

A short one—showing, among other Matters, how Mr. Pickwick
undertook to drive, and Mr. Winkle to ride; and how they
both did it 68

CHAPTER VI.

An old-fashioned Card Party. The Clergyman's Verses. The
Story of the Convict's Return 80

CONTENTS.

CHAPTER VII.

How Mr. Winkle, instead of shooting at the Pigeon and killing the Crow, shot at the Crow and wounded the Pigeon ; how the Dingley Dell Cricket Club played All Muggleton, and how All Muggleton dined at the Dingley Dell expense : with other interesting and instructive Matters 98

CHAPTER VIII.

Strongly illustrative of the Position, that the Course of True Love is not a Railway 115

CHAPTER IX.

A Discovery and a Chase 131

CHAPTER X.

Clearing up all Doubts (if any existed) of the Disinterestedness of Mr. Jingle's Character 142

CHAPTER XI.

Involving another Journey, and an Antiquarian Discovery. Recording Mr. Pickwick's Determination to be present at an Election ; and containing a Manuscript of the old Clergyman's 159

CHAPTER XII.

Descriptive of a very important Proceeding on the Part of Mr. Pickwick ; no less an Epoch in his Life, than in this History 181

CHAPTER XIII.

Some Account of Eatanswill ; of the State of Parties therein ; and of the Election of a Member to serve in Parliament for that ancient, loyal, and patriotic Borough 189

CHAPTER XIV.

Comprising a brief Description of the Company at the Peacock assembled ; and a Tale told by a Bagman 211

CONTENTS.

CHAPTER XV.

In which is given a faithful Portraiture of two distinguished Persons ; and an accurate Description of a Public Breakfast in their House and Grounds ; which Public Breakfast leads to the Recognition of an old Acquaintance, and the commencement of another Chapter 232

CHAPTER XVI.

Too full of Adventure to be briefly described 249

CHAPTER XVII.

Showing that an Attack of Rheumatism, in some cases, acts as a Quickener to Inventive Genius 272

CHAPTER XVIII.

Briefly illustrative of two Points ;—first, the Power of Hysterics, and, secondly, the Force of Circumstances 283

CHAPTER XIX.

A pleasant Day, with an unpleasant Termination 296

CHAPTER XX.

Showing how Dodson and Fogg were Men of Business, and their Clerks Men of Pleasure ; and how an affecting Interview took place between Mr. Weller and his long-lost Parent ; showing also what Choice Spirits assembled at the Magpie and Stump, and what a capital Chapter the next one will be . . . 313

CHAPTER XXI.

In which the Old Man launches forth into his favourite Theme, and relates a Story about a queer Client 333

CHAPTER XXII.

Mr. Pickwick journeys to Ipswich, and meets with a romantic Adventure with a middle-aged Lady in Yellow Curl Papers . 354

CONTENTS.

CHAPTER XXIII.

In which Mr. Samuel Weller begins to devote his Energies to the Return Match between himself and Mr. Trotter . . . 374

CHAPTER XXIV.

Wherein Mr. Peter Magnus grows jealous, and the middle-aged Lady apprehensive, which brings the Pickwickians within the grasp of the Law 384

CHAPTER XXV.

Showing, among a variety of pleasant Matters, how majestic and impartial Mr. Nupkins was; and how Mr. Weller returned Mr. Job Trotter's Shuttlecock, as heavily as it came. With another Matter, which will be found in its Place . . . 403

CHAPTER XXVI.

Which contains a brief Account of the Progress of the Action of Bardell against Pickwick 426

CHAPTER XXVII.

Samuel Weller makes a Pilgrimage to Dorking, and beholds his Mother-in-law 434

CHAPTER XXVIII.

A good-humoured Christmas Chapter, containing an Account of a Wedding, and some other Sports beside: which although in their way, even as good Customs as Marriage itself, are not quite so religiously kept up, in these degenerate Times . . 446

CHAPTER XXIX.

The Story of the Goblins who stole a Sexton 472

LIST OF ILLUSTRATIONS

Mr. Pickwick Addresses the Club 4
The Pugnacious Cabman 10
The Sagacious Dog 14
Dr. Slammer's Defiance of Jingle 26
The Dying Clown 46
Mr. Pickwick in Chase of his Hat 60
Winkle Soothes the Refractory Mare 74
The Fat Boy Awake 118
Wardle and his Friends Under the Influence of
    "the Salmon" 120
The Break-Down 140
First Appearance of Mr. Samuel Weller 148
Mrs. Bardell Faints in Mr. Pickwick's Arms 184
The Election at Eatanswill 208
Mrs. Leo Hunter's Fancy-Dress Dejeune 240
The Unexpected "Breaking-up" of the Seminary for
    Young Ladies 268
Mr. Pickwick in the Pound 312
Mr. Pickwick and Sam in the Attorney's Office . . 318
The Last Visit of Heyling to the Old Man 352
The Middle-Aged Lady in the Double-Bedded Room 368
Mr. Weller Attacks the Executive of Ipswich . . . 402
Job Trotter Encounters Sam in Mr. Muzzle's Kitchen 420
Christmas Eve at Mr. Wardle's 468
The Goblin and the Sexton 476

LIST OF ILLUSTRATIONS

CHAPTER I.

THE PICKWICKIANS.

THE first ray of light which illumines the gloom, and converts into a dazzling brilliancy that obscurity in which the earlier history of the public career of the immortal Pickwick would appear to be involved, is derived from the perusal of the following entry in the Transactions of the Pickwick Club, which the editor of these papers feels the highest pleasure in laying before his readers, as a proof of the careful attention, indefatigable assiduity, and nice discrimination, with which his search among the multifarious documents confided to him has been conducted.

"May 12, 1827. Joseph Smiggers, Esq., P.V.P.M.P.C.,* presiding. The following resolutions unanimously agreed to :—

"That this Association has heard read, with feelings of unmingled satisfaction, and unqualified approval, the paper communicated by Samuel Pickwick, Esq., G.C.M.P.C.,† entitled 'Speculations on the Source of the Hampstead Ponds, with some Observations on the Theory of Tittlebats;' and that this Association does hereby return its warmest thanks to the said Samuel Pickwick, Esq., G.C.M.P.C., for the same.

* Perpetual Vice-President—Member Pickwick Club.
† General Chairman—Member Pickwick Club.

"That while this Association is deeply sensible of the advantages which must accrue to the cause of science from the production to which they have just adverted,—no less than from the unwearied researches of Samuel Pickwick, Esq., G.C.M.P.C., in Hornsey, Highgate, Brixton, and Camberwell, —they cannot but entertain a lively sense of the inestimable benefits which must inevitably result from carrying the speculations of that learned man into a wider field, from extending his travels, and consequently enlarging his sphere of observation, to the advancement of knowledge, and the diffusion of learning.

"That, with the view just mentioned, this Association has taken into its serious consideration a proposal, emanating from the aforesaid Samuel Pickwick, Esq., G.C.M.P.C., and three other Pickwickians hereinafter named, for forming a new branch of United Pickwickians, under the title of The Corresponding Society of the Pickwick Club.

"That the said proposal has received the sanction and approval of this Association.

"That the Corresponding Society of the Pickwick Club is therefore hereby constituted; and that Samuel Pickwick, Esq., G.C.M.P.C., Tracy Tupman, Esq., M.P.C., Augustus Snodgrass, Esq., M.P.C., and Nathaniel Winkle, Esq., M.P.C., are hereby nominated and appointed members of the same; and that they be requested to forward, from time to time, authenticated accounts of their journeys and investigations, of their observations of character and manners, and of the whole of their adventures, together with all tales and papers to which local scenery or associations may give rise, to the Pickwick Club, stationed in London.

"That this Association cordially recognises the principle of every member of the Corresponding Society defraying his own travelling expenses; and that it sees no objection whatever to the members of the said society pursuing their inquiries for any length of time they please, upon the same terms.

"That the members of the aforesaid Corresponding Society

2

be, and are, hereby informed, that their proposal to pay the postage of their letters, and the carriage of their parcels, has been deliberated upon by this Association: that this Association considers such proposal worthy of the great minds from which it emanated, and that it hereby signifies its perfect acquiescence therein."

A casual observer, adds the secretary, to whose notes we are indebted for the following account—a casual observer might possibly have remarked nothing extraordinary in the bald head, and circular spectacles, which were intently turned towards his (the secretary's) face, during the reading of the above resolutions: to those who knew that the gigantic brain of Pickwick was working beneath that forehead, and that the beaming eyes of Pickwick were twinkling behind those glasses, the sight was indeed an interesting one. There sat the man who had traced to their source the mighty ponds of Hampstead, and agitated the scientific world with his Theory of Tittlebats, as calm and unmoved as the deep waters of the one on a frosty day, or as a solitary specimen of the other in the inmost recesses of an earthen jar. And how much more interesting did the spectacle become, when, starting into full life and animation, as a simultaneous call for "Pickwick" burst from his followers, that illustrious man slowly mounted into the Windsor chair, on which he had been previously seated, and addressed the club himself had founded. What a study for an artist did that exciting scene present! The eloquent Pickwick, with one hand gracefully concealed behind his coat tails, and the other waving in air, to assist his glowing declamation; his elevated position revealing those tights and gaiters, which, had they clothed an ordinary man, might have passed without observation, but which, when Pickwick clothed them —if we may use the expression—inspired voluntary awe and respect; surrounded by the men who had volunteered to share the perils of his travels, and who were destined to participate in the glories of his discoveries. On his right hand sat Mr. Tracy Tupman—the too susceptible Tupman, who to the wisdom and experience of maturer years superadded the enthusiasm and ardour of a boy, in the most interesting and pardonable of human weaknesses—love. Time and feeding had expanded that once romantic form; the black silk waistcoat had become more and more developed; inch by inch had the gold watch-chain beneath it disappeared from within the range of Tupman's vision; and gradually had the capacious chin encroached upon the borders of the white cravat: but the soul of Tupman had known no change— admiration of the fair sex was still its ruling passion. On the left of his great leader sat the poetic Snodgrass, and near him again the sporting Winkle, the former poetically enveloped in a mysterious blue cloak with a canine-skin collar, and the latter communicating additional lustre to a new green shooting coat, plaid neckerchief, and closely-fitted drabs.

Mr. Pickwick's oration upon this occasion, together with the debate thereon, is entered on the Transactions of the Club. Both bear a strong affinity to the discussions of other celebrated bodies; and, as it is always interesting to trace a resemblance between the proceedings of great men, we transfer the entry to these pages.

"Mr. Pickwick observed (says the Secretary) that fame was dear to the heart of every man. Poetic fame was dear to the heart of his friend Snodgrass; the fame of conquest was equally dear to his friend Tupman; and the desire of earning fame in the sports of the field, the air, and the water, was uppermost in the breast of his friend Winkle. He (Mr. Pickwick) would not deny that he was influenced by human passions, and human feelings (cheers)—possibly by human weaknesses—(loud cries of 'No'); but this he would say, that if ever the fire of self-importance broke out in his bosom, the desire to benefit the human race in preference effectually quenched it. The praise of mankind was his Swing; philanthropy was his insurance office. (Vehement cheering.) He had felt some pride—he acknowledged it freely,

Mr. Pickwick Addresses the Club

and let his enemies make the most of it—he had felt some pride when he presented his Tittlebatian Theory to the world; it might be celebrated or it might not. (A cry of 'It is,' and great cheering.) He would take the assertion of that honourable Pickwickian whose voice he had just heard—it was celebrated; but if the fame of that treatise were to extend to the furthest confines of the known world, the pride with which he should reflect on the authorship of that production would be as nothing compared with the pride with which he looked around him, on this, the proudest moment of his existence. (Cheers.) He was a humble individual. (No, no.) Still he could not but feel that they had selected him for a service of great honour, and of some danger. Travelling was in a troubled state, and the minds of coachmen were unsettled. Let them look abroad and contemplate the scenes which were enacting around them. Stage coaches were upsetting in all directions, horses were bolting, boats were overturning, and boilers were bursting. (Cheers—a voice 'No.') No! (Cheers.) Let that honourable Pickwickian who cried 'No' so loudly come forward and deny it, if he could. (Cheers.) Who was it that cried 'No?' (Enthusiastic cheering.) Was it some vain and disappointed man—he would not say haberdasher—(loud cheers)—who, jealous of the praise which had been—perhaps undeservedly—bestowed on his (Mr. Pickwick's) researches, and smarting under the censure which had been heaped upon his own feeble attempts at rivalry, now took this vile and calumnious mode of——

"Mr. BLOTTON (of Aldgate) rose to order. Did the honourable Pickwickian allude to him? (Cries of 'Order,' 'Chair,' 'Yes,' 'No,' 'Go on,' 'Leave off,' &c.)

"Mr. PICKWICK would not put up to be put down by clamour. He *had* alluded to the honourable gentleman. (Great excitement.)

"Mr. BLOTTON would only say then, that he repelled the hon. gent.'s false and scurrilous accusation, with profound

5

contempt. (Great cheering.) The hon. gent. was a humbug. (Immense confusion, and loud cries of 'Chair' and 'Order.')

"Mr. A. SNODGRASS rose to order. He threw himself upon the chair. (Hear.) He wished to know whether this disgraceful contest between two members of that club should be allowed to continue. (Hear, hear.)

"The CHAIRMAN was quite sure the hon. Pickwickian would withdraw the expression he had just made use of.

"Mr. BLOTTON, with all possible respect for the chair, was quite sure he would not.

"The CHAIRMAN felt it his imperative duty to demand of the honourable gentleman, whether he had used the expression which had just escaped him in a common sense.

"Mr. BLOTTON had no hesitation in saying that he had not—he had used the word in its Pickwickian sense. (Hear, hear.) He was bound to acknowledge that, personally, he entertained the highest regard and esteem for the honourable gentleman; he had merely considered him a humbug in a Pickwickian point of view. (Hear, hear.)

"Mr. PICKWICK felt much gratified by the fair, candid, and full explanation of his honourable friend. He begged it to be at once understood, that his own observations had been merely intended to bear a Pickwickian construction. (Cheers.)"

Here the entry terminates, as we have no doubt the debate did also, after arriving at such a highly satisfactory and intelligible point. We have no official statement of the facts which the reader will find recorded in the next chapter, but they have been carefully collated from letters and other MS. authorities, so unquestionably genuine as to justify their narration in a connected form.

CHAPTER II.

THAT punctual servant of all work, the sun, had just risen,
and begun to strike a light on the morning of the thirteenth
of May, one thousand eight hundred and twenty-seven,
when Mr. Samuel Pickwick burst like another sun from his
slumbers, threw open his chamber window, and looked out
upon the world beneath. Goswell Street was at his feet,
Goswell Street was on his right hand—as far as the eye could
reach, Goswell Street extended on his left; and the opposite
side of Goswell Street was over the way. "Such," thought
Mr. Pickwick, "are the narrow views of those philosophers
who, content with examining the things that lie before them,
look not to the truths which are hidden beyond. As well
might I be content to gaze on Goswell Street for ever, without
one effort to penetrate to the hidden countries which on every
side surround it." And having given vent to this beautiful
reflection, Mr. Pickwick proceeded to put himself into his
clothes, and his clothes into his portmanteau. Great men
are seldom over scrupulous in the arrangement of their attire;
the operation of shaving, dressing, and coffee-imbibing was
soon performed: and in another hour, Mr. Pickwick, with his
portmanteau in his hand, his telescope in his great-coat
pocket, and his note-book in his waistcoat, ready for the
reception of any discoveries worthy of being noted down, had
arrived at the coach stand in St. Martin's-le-Grand.

"Cab!" said Mr. Pickwick.

"Here you are, sir," shouted a strange specimen of the human race, in a sackcloth coat, and apron of the same, who with a brass label and number round his neck, looked as if he were catalogued in some collection of rarities. This was the waterman. "Here you are, sir. Now, then, fust cab!" And the first cab having been fetched from the public-house, where he had been smoking his first pipe, Mr. Pickwick and his portmanteau were thrown into the vehicle.

"Golden Cross," said Mr. Pickwick.

"Only a bob's vorth, Tommy," cried the driver, sulkily, for the information of his friend the waterman, as the cab drove off.

"How old is that horse, my friend?" inquired Mr. Pickwick, rubbing his nose with the shilling he had reserved for the fare.

"Forty-two," replied the driver, eyeing him askant.

"What!" ejaculated Mr. Pickwick, laying his hand upon his note-book. The driver reiterated his former statement. Mr. Pickwick looked very hard at the man's face, but his features were immovable, so he noted down the fact forthwith.

"And how long do you keep him out at a time?" inquired Mr. Pickwick, searching for further information.

"Two or three veeks," replied the man.

"Weeks!" said Mr. Pickwick in astonishment—and out came the note-book again.

"He lives at Pentonwil when he's at home," observed the driver, coolly, "but we seldom takes him home, on account of his veakness."

"On account of his weakness!" reiterated the perplexed Mr. Pickwick.

"He always falls down when he's took out o' the cab," continued the driver, "but when he's in it, we bears him up werry tight, and takes him in werry short, so as he can't werry well fall down; and we've got a pair o' precious large wheels on, so ven he *does* move, they run after him, and he must go on—he can't help it."

THE CABMAN AND HIS HORSE.

Mr. Pickwick entered every word of this statement in his note-book, with the view of communicating it to the club, as a singular instance of the tenacity of life in horses, under trying circumstances. The entry was scarcely completed when they reached the Golden Cross. Down jumped the driver, and out got Mr. Pickwick. Mr. Tupman, Mr. Snodgrass, and Mr. Winkle, who had been anxiously waiting the arrival of their illustrious leader, crowded to welcome him.

"Here's your fare," said Mr. Pickwick, holding out the shilling to the driver.

What was the learned man's astonishment, when that unaccountable person flung the money on the pavement, and requested in figurative terms to be allowed the pleasure of fighting him (Mr. Pickwick) for the amount!

"You are mad," said Mr. Snodgrass.

"Or drunk," said Mr. Winkle.

"Or both," said Mr. Tupman.

"Come on!" said the cab-driver, sparring away like clock-work. "Come on—all four on you."

"Here's a lark!" shouted half-a-dozen hackney coachmen. "Go to vork, Sam,"—and they crowded with great glee round the party.

"What's the row, Sam?" inquired one gentleman in black calico sleeves.

"Row!" replied the cabman, "what did he want my number for?"

"I didn't want your number," said the astonished Mr. Pickwick.

"What did you take it for, then?" inquired the cabman.

"I didn't take it," said Mr. Pickwick, indignantly.

"Would any body believe," continued the cab-driver, appealing to the crowd, "would any body believe as an informer 'ud go about in a man's cab, not only takin' down his number, but ev'ry word he says into the bargain" (a light flashed upon Mr. Pickwick—it was the note-book).

"Did he though?" inquired another cabman.

9

"Yes, did he," replied the first; "and then arter aggera-watin' me to assault him, gets three witnesses here to prove it. But I'll give it him, if I've six months for it. Come on!" and the cabman dashed his hat upon the ground, with a reckless disregard of his own private property, and knocked Mr. Pickwick's spectacles off, and followed up the attack with a blow on Mr. Pickwick's nose, and another on Mr. Pickwick's chest, and a third in Mr. Snodgrass's eye, and a fourth, by way of variety, in Mr. Tupman's waistcoat, and then danced into the road, and then back again to the pavement, and finally dashed the whole temporary supply of breath out of Mr. Winkle's body; and all in half-a-dozen seconds.

"Where's an officer?" said Mr. Snodgrass.

"Put 'em under the pump," suggested a hot-pieman.

"You shall smart for this," gasped Mr. Pickwick.

"Informers!" shouted the crowd.

"Come on," cried the cabman, who had been sparring without cessation the whole time.

The mob had hitherto been passive spectators of the scene, but as the intelligence of the Pickwickians being informers was spread among them, they began to canvass with considerable vivacity the propriety of enforcing the heated pastry-vendor's proposition; and there is no saying what acts of personal aggression they might have committed had not the affray been unexpectedly terminated by the interposition of a new comer.

"What's the fun?" said a rather tall thin young man, in a green coat, emerging suddenly from the coach yard.

"Informers!" shouted the crowd again.

"We are not," roared Mr. Pickwick, in a tone which, to any dispassionate listener, carried conviction with it.

"Ain't you, though,—ain't you?" said the young man, appealing to Mr. Pickwick, and making his way through the crowd by the infallible process of elbowing the countenances of its component members.

The Pugnacious Cabman

THE LIVELY STRANGER.

That learned man in a few hurried words explained the real state of the case.

"Come along, then," said he of the green coat, lugging Mr. Pickwick after him by main force, and talking the whole way. "Here, No. 924, take your fare, and take yourself off —respectable gentleman,—know him well—none of your nonsense—this way, sir,—where's your friends?—all a mistake, I see—never mind—accidents will happen—best regulated families—never say die—down upon your luck—pull him up —put that in his pipe—like the flavour—damned rascals." And with a lengthened string of similar broken sentences, delivered with extraordinary volubility, the stranger led the way to the travellers' waiting-room, whither he was closely followed by Mr. Pickwick and his disciples.

"Here, waiter!" shouted the stranger, ringing the bell with tremendous violence, "glasses round,—brandy and water, hot and strong, and sweet, and plenty,—eye damaged, sir? Waiter! raw beef-steak for the gentleman's eye,—nothing like raw beef-steak for a bruise, sir; cold lamp-post very good, but lamp-post inconvenient—damned odd standing in the open street half-an-hour, with your eye against a lamp-post—eh,—very good—ha! ha!" And the stranger, without stopping to take breath, swallowed at a draught full half-a-pint of the reeking brandy and water, and flung himself into a chair with as much ease as if nothing uncommon had occurred.

While his three companions were busily engaged in proffering their thanks to their new acquaintance, Mr. Pickwick had leisure to examine his costume and appearance.

He was about the middle height, but the thinness of his body, and the length of his legs, gave him the appearance of being much taller. The green coat had been a smart dress garment in the days of swallow-tails, but had evidently in those times adorned a much shorter man than the stranger, for the soiled and faded sleeves scarcely reached to his wrists. It was buttoned closely up to his chin, at the imminent hazard of splitting the back; and an old stock, without a vestige of shirt collar, ornamented his neck. His scanty black trousers displayed here and there those shiny patches which bespeak long service, and were strapped very tightly over a pair of patched and mended shoes, as if to conceal the dirty white stockings, which were nevertheless distinctly visible. His long black hair escaped in negligent waves from beneath each side of his old pinched up hat; and glimpses of his bare wrists might be observed between the tops of his gloves, and the cuffs of his coat sleeves. His face was thin and haggard; but an indescribable air of jaunty impudence and perfect self-possession pervaded the whole man.

Such was the individual on whom Mr. Pickwick gazed through his spectacles (which he had fortunately recovered), and to whom he proceeded, when his friends had exhausted themselves, to return in chosen terms his warmest thanks for his recent assistance.

"Never mind," said the stranger, cutting the address very short, "said enough,—no more; smart chap that cabman—handled his fives well; but if I'd been your friend in the green jemmy—damn me—punch his head,—'cod I would,—pig's whisper—pieman too,—no gammon."

This coherent speech was interrupted by the entrance of the Rochester coachman, to announce that "The Commodore" was on the point of starting.

"Commodore!" said the stranger, starting up, "my coach,—place booked,—one outside—leave you to pay for the brandy and water,—want change for a five,—bad silver—Brummagem buttons—won't do—no go—eh?" and he shook his head most knowingly.

Now it so happened that Mr. Pickwick and his three companions had resolved to make Rochester their first halting place too; and having intimated to their new-found acquaintance that they were journeying to the same city, they agreed to occupy the seat at the back of the coach, where they could all sit together.

12

A TRAVELLING COMPANION.

"Up with you," said the stranger, assisting Mr. Pickwick on to the roof with so much precipitation as to impair the gravity of that gentleman's deportment very materially.

"Any luggage, sir?" inquired the coachman.

"Who—I? Brown paper parcel here, that's all,—other luggage gone by water,—packing cases, nailed up—big as houses—heavy, heavy, damned heavy," replied the stranger, as he forced into his pocket as much as he could of the brown paper parcel, which presented most suspicious indications of containing one shirt and a handkerchief.

"Heads, heads—take care of your heads!" cried the loquacious stranger, as they came out under the low archway, which in those days formed the entrance to the coach-yard. "Terrible place—dangerous work—other day—five children—mother—tall lady, eating sandwiches—forgot the arch—crash—knock—children look round—mother's head off—sandwich in her hand—no mouth to put it in—head of a family off—shocking, shocking! Looking at Whitehall, sir?—fine place—little window—somebody else's head off there, eh, sir? —he didn't keep a sharp look-out enough either—eh, sir, eh?"

"I am ruminating," said Mr. Pickwick, "on the strange mutability of human affairs."

"Ah! I see—in at the palace door one day, out at the window the next. Philosopher, sir?"

"An observer of human nature, sir," said Mr. Pickwick.

"Ah, so am I. Most people are when they've little to do and less to get. Poet, sir?"

"My friend Mr. Snodgrass has a strong poetic turn," said Mr. Pickwick.

"So have I," said the stranger. "Epic poem,—ten thousand lines—revolution of July—composed it on the spot—Mars by day, Apollo by night,—bang the field-piece, twang the lyre."

"You were present at that glorious scene, sir?" said Mr. Snodgrass.

"Present! think I was;* fired a musket,—fired with an idea,—rushed into wine shop—wrote it down—back again—whiz, bang—another idea—wine shop again—pen and ink—back again—cut and slash—noble time, sir. Sportsman, sir?" abruptly turning to Mr. Winkle.

"A little, sir," replied that gentleman.

"Fine pursuit, sir,—fine pursuit.—Dogs, sir?"

"Not just now," said Mr. Winkle.

"Ah! you should keep dogs—fine animals—sagacious creatures—dog of my own once—Pointer—surprising instinct—out shooting one day—entering enclosure—whistled—dog stopped—whistled again—Ponto—no go; stock still—called him—Ponto, Ponto—wouldn't move—dog transfixed—staring at a board—looked up, saw an inscription—'Gamekeeper has orders to shoot all dogs found in this enclosure'—wouldn't pass it—wonderful dog—valuable dog that—very."

"Singular circumstance that," said Mr. Pickwick. "Will you allow me to make a note of it?"

"Certainly, sir, certainly—hundred more anecdotes of the same animal.—Fine girl, sir" (to Mr. Tracy Tupman, who had been bestowing sundry anti-Pickwickian glances on a young lady by the roadside).

"Very!" said Mr. Tupman.

"English girls not so fine as Spanish—noble creatures—jet hair—black eyes—lovely forms—sweet creatures—beautiful."

"You have been in Spain, sir?" said Mr. Tracy Tupman.

"Lived there—ages."

"Many conquests, sir?" inquired Mr. Tupman.

"Conquests! Thousands. Don Bolaro Fizzgig—Grandee—only daughter—Donna Christina—splendid creature—loved me to distraction—jealous father—high-souled daughter—handsome Englishman—Donna Christina in despair—prussic acid—stomach pump in my portmanteau—operation performed—old Bolaro in ecstasies—consent to our union—join hands and floods of tears—romantic story—very."

* A remarkable instance of the prophetic force of Mr. Jingle's imagination; this dialogue occurring in the year 1827, and the Revolution in 1830.

14

NOTICE
THE
GAMEKEEPER
HAS ORDERS
TO SHOOT ALL
DOGS
FOUND IN
THIS
INCLOSURE

The Sagacious Dog

THE ANCIENT CITY OF ROCHESTER.

"Is the lady in England now, sir?" inquired Mr. Tupman, on whom the description of her charms had produced a powerful impression.

"Dead, sir—dead," said the stranger, applying to his right eye the brief remnant of a very old cambric handkerchief. "Never recovered the stomach pump—undermined constitution —fell a victim."

"And her father?" inquired the poetic Snodgrass.

"Remorse and misery," replied the stranger. "Sudden disappearance—talk of the whole city—search made everywhere—without success—public fountain in the great square suddenly ceased playing—weeks elapsed—still a stoppage—workmen employed to clean it—water drawn off—father-in-law discovered sticking head first in the main pipe, with a full confession in his right boot—took him out, and the fountain played away again, as well as ever."

"Will you allow me to note that little romance down, sir?" said Mr. Snodgrass, deeply affected.

"Certainly, sir, certainly,—fifty more if you like to hear 'em—strange life mine—rather curious history—not extraordinary, but singular."

In this strain, with an occasional glass of ale, by way of parenthesis, when the coach changed horses, did the stranger proceed, until they reached Rochester bridge, by which time the note-books, both of Mr. Pickwick and Mr. Snodgrass, were completely filled with selections from his adventures.

"Magnificent ruin!" said Mr. Augustus Snodgrass, with all the poetic fervour that distinguished him, when they came in sight of the fine old castle.

"What a study for an antiquarian!" were the very words which fell from Mr. Pickwick's mouth, as he applied his telescope to his eye.

"Ah! fine place," said the stranger, "glorious pile—frowning walls—tottering arches—dark nooks—crumbling staircases—Old cathedral too—earthy smell—pilgrims' feet worn away

15

the old steps—little Saxon doors—confessionals like money-takers' boxes at theatres—queer customers those monks—Popes, and Lord Treasurers, and all sorts of old fellows, with great red faces, and broken noses, turning up every day—buff jerkins too—match-locks—Sarcophagus—fine place—old legends too—strange stories: capital;" and the stranger continued to soliloquise until they reached the Bull Inn, in the High Street, where the coach stopped.

"Do you remain here, sir?" inquired Mr. Nathaniel Winkle.

"Here—not I—but you'd better—good house—nice beds—Wright's next house, dear—very dear—half-a-crown in the bill if you look at the waiter—charge you more if you dine at a friend's than they would if you dined in the coffee-room—rum fellows—very."

Mr. Winkle turned to Mr. Pickwick, and murmured a few words; a whisper passed from Mr. Pickwick to Mr. Snodgrass, from Mr. Snodgrass to Mr. Tupman, and nods of assent were exchanged. Mr. Pickwick addressed the stranger.

"You rendered us a very important service this morning, sir," said he, "will you allow us to offer a slight mark of our gratitude by begging the favour of your company at dinner?"

"Great pleasure—not presume to dictate, but broiled fowl and mushrooms—capital thing! what time?"

"Let me see," replied Mr. Pickwick, referring to his watch, "it is now nearly three. Shall we say five?"

"Suit me excellently," said the stranger, "five precisely—till then—care of yourselves;" and lifting the pinched-up hat a few inches from his head, and carelessly replacing it very much on one side, the stranger, with half the brown paper parcel sticking out of his pocket, walked briskly up the yard, and turned into the High Street.

"Evidently a traveller in many countries, and a close observer of men and things," said Mr. Pickwick.

"I should like to see his poem," said Mr. Snodgrass.

"I should like to have seen that dog," said Mr. Winkle.

Mr. Tupman said nothing; but he thought of Donna

Christina, the stomach pump, and the fountain; and his eyes filled with tears.

A private sitting-room having been engaged, bed-rooms inspected, and dinner ordered, the party walked out to view the city and adjoining neigbourhood.

We do not find, from a careful perusal of Mr. Pickwick's notes on the four towns, Stroud, Rochester, Chatham, and Brompton, that his impressions of their appearance differ in any material point from those of other travellers who have gone over the same ground. His general description is easily abridged.

"The principal productions of these towns," says Mr. Pickwick, "appear to be soldiers, sailors, Jews, chalk, shrimps, officers, and dockyard men. The commodities chiefly exposed for sale in the public streets are marine stores, hardbake, apples, flat-fish, and oysters. The streets present a lively and animated appearance, occasioned chiefly by the conviviality of the military. It is truly delightful to a philanthropic mind, to see these gallant men staggering along under the influence of an overflow, both of animal and ardent spirits; more especially when we remember that the following them about, and jesting with them, affords a cheap and innocent amusement for the boy population. Nothing (adds Mr. Pickwick) can exceed their good humour. It was but the day before my arrival that one of them had been most grossly insulted in the house of a publican. The bar-maid had positively refused to draw him any more liquor; in return for which he had (merely in playfulness) drawn his bayonet, and wounded the girl in the shoulder. And yet this fine fellow was the very first to go down to the house next morning, and express his readiness to overlook the matter, and forget what had occurred.

"The consumption of tobacco in these towns (continues Mr. Pickwick) must be very great: and the smell which pervades the streets must be exceedingly delicious to those who are extremely fond of smoking. A superficial traveller

17

might object to the dirt which is their leading characteristic; but to those who view it as an indication of traffic and commercial prosperity, it is truly gratifying."

Punctual to five o'clock came the stranger, and shortly afterwards the dinner. He had divested himself of his brown paper parcel, but had made no alteration in his attire; and was, if possible, more loquacious than ever.

"What's that?" he inquired, as the waiter removed one of the covers.

"Soles, sir."

"Soles—ah!—capital fish—all come from London—stage-coach proprietors get up political dinners—carriage of soles—dozens of baskets—cunning fellows. Glass of wine, sir."

"With pleasure," said Mr. Pickwick; and the stranger took wine, first with him, and then with Mr. Snodgrass, and then with Mr. Tupman, and then with Mr. Winkle, and then with the whole party together, almost as rapidly as he talked.

"Devil of a mess on the staircase, waiter," said the stranger. "Forms going up—carpenters coming down—lamps, glasses, harps. What's going forward?"

"Ball, sir," said the waiter.

"Assembly, eh?"

"No, sir, not Assembly, sir. Ball for the benefit of a charity, sir."

"Many fine women in this town, do you know, sir?" inquired Mr. Tupman, with great interest.

"Splendid—capital. Kent, sir—everybody knows Kent—apples, cherries, hops, and women. Glass of wine, sir?"

"With great pleasure," replied Mr. Tupman. The stranger filled, and emptied.

"I should very much like to go," said Mr. Tupman, resuming the subject of the ball, "very much."

"Tickets at the bar, sir," interposed the waiter; "half-a-guinea each, sir."

Mr. Tupman again expressed an earnest wish to be present at the festivity; but meeting with no response in the darkened eye of Mr. Snodgrass, or the abstracted gaze of Mr. Pickwick, he applied himself with great interest to the port wine and dessert, which had just been placed on the table. The waiter withdrew, and the party were left to enjoy the cosy couple of hours succeeding dinner.

"Beg your pardon, sir," said the stranger, "bottle stands—pass it round—way of the sun—through the button-hole—no heeltaps," and he emptied his glass, which he had filled about two minutes before, and poured out another, with the air of a man who was used to it

The wine was passed, and a fresh supply ordered. The visitor talked, the Pickwickians listened. Mr. Tupman felt every moment more disposed for the ball. Mr. Pickwick's countenance glowed with an expression of universal philanthropy; and Mr. Winkle and Mr. Snodgrass fell fast asleep.

"They're beginning up-stairs," said the stranger—"hear the company—fiddles tuning—now the harp—there they go." The various sounds which found their way down-stairs announced the commencement of the first quadrille.

"How I should like to go," said Mr. Tupman, again.

"So should I," said the stranger,—"confounded luggage—heavy smacks—nothing to go in—odd, ain't it?"

Now general benevolence was one of the leading features of the Pickwickian theory, and no one was more remarkable for the zealous manner in which he observed so noble a principle than Mr. Tracy Tupman. The number of instances, recorded on the Transactions of the Society, in which that excellent man referred objects of charity to the houses of other members for left-off garments or pecuniary relief is almost incredible.

"I should be very happy to lend you a change of apparel for the purpose," said Mr. Tracy Tupman, "but you are rather slim, and I am—"

"Rather fat—grown up Bacchus—cut the leaves—dismounted from the tub, and adopted kersey, eh?—not double distilled, but double milled—ha! ha! pass the wine."

19

Whether Mr. Tupman was somewhat indignant at the peremptory tone in which he was desired to pass the wine which the stranger passed so quickly away; or whether he felt very properly scandalised, at an influential member of the Pickwick club being ignominiously compared to a dismounted Bacchus, is a fact not yet completely ascertained. He passed the wine, coughed twice, and looked at the stranger for several seconds with a stern intensity; as that individual, however, appeared perfectly collected, and quite calm under his searching glance, he gradually relaxed, and reverted to the subject of the ball.

"I was about to observe, sir," he said, "that though my apparel would be too large, a suit of my friend Mr. Winkle's would perhaps fit you better."

The stranger took Mr. Winkle's measure with his eye; and that feature glistened with satisfaction as he said—"just the thing."

Mr. Tupman looked round him. The wine, which had exerted its somniferous influence over Mr. Snodgrass and Mr. Winkle, had stolen upon the senses of Mr. Pickwick. That gentleman had gradually passed through the various stages which precede the lethargy produced by dinner, and its consequences. He had undergone the ordinary transitions from the height of conviviality to the depth of misery, and from the depth of misery to the height of conviviality. Like a gas lamp in the street, with the wind in the pipe, he had exhibited for a moment an unnatural brilliancy; then sunk so low as to be scarcely discernible: after a short interval he had burst out again, to enlighten for a moment, then flickered with an uncertain, staggering sort of light, and then gone out altogether. His head was sunk upon his bosom; and perpetual snoring, with a partial choke occasionally, were the only audible indications of the great man's presence.

The temptation to be present at the ball, and to form his first impressions of the beauty of the Kentish ladies, was strong upon Mr. Tupman. The temptation to take the stranger with him was equally great. He was wholly unacquainted with the place, and its inhabitants; and the stranger seemed to possess as great a knowledge of both as if he had lived there from his infancy. Mr. Winkle was asleep, and Mr. Tupman had had sufficient experience in such matters to know, that the moment he awoke he would, in the ordinary course of nature, roll heavily to bed. He was undecided. "Fill your glass, and pass the wine," said the indefatigable visitor.

Mr. Tupman did as he was requested; and the additional stimulus of the last glass settled his determination.

"Winkle's bed-room is inside mine," said Mr. Tupman; "I couldn't make him understand what I wanted, if I woke him now, but I know he has a dress suit, in a carpet-bag, and supposing you wore it to the ball, and took it off when we returned, I could replace it without troubling him at all about the matter."

"Capital," said the stranger, "famous plan—damned odd situation—fourteen coats in the packing cases, and obliged to wear another man's—very good notion, that—very."

"We must purchase our tickets," said Mr. Tupman.

"Not worth while splitting a guinea," said the stranger, "toss who shall pay for both—I call; you spin—first time—woman—woman—bewitching woman," and down came the sovereign, with the Dragon (called by courtesy a woman) uppermost.

Mr. Tupman rang the bell, purchased the tickets, and ordered chamber candlesticks. In another quarter of an hour the stranger was completely arrayed in a full suit of Mr. Nathaniel Winkle's.

"It's a new coat," said Mr. Tupman, as the stranger surveyed himself with great complacency in a cheval glass; "the first that's been made with our club button," and he called his companion's attention to the large gilt button which displayed a bust of Mr. Pickwick in the centre, and the letters "P. C." on either side.

"P. C.," said the stranger—"queer set out—old fellow's likeness, and 'P. C.'—What does 'P. C.' stand for—Peculiar coat, eh?"

Mr. Tupman, with rising indignation and great importance, explained the mystic device.

"Rather short in the waist, an't it?" said the stranger, screwing himself round to catch a glimpse in the glass of the waist buttons, which were half way up his back. "Like a general postman's coat—queer coats those—made by contract—no measuring—mysterious dispensations of Providence —all the short men get long coats—all the long men short ones." Running on in this way, Mr. Tupman's new companion adjusted his dress, or rather the dress of Mr. Winkle; and, accompanied by Mr. Tupman, ascended the staircase leading to the ball-room.

"What names, sir?" said the man at the door. Mr. Tracy Tupman was stepping forward to announce his own titles, when the stranger prevented him.

"No names at all;" and then he whispered Mr. Tupman, "Names won't do—not known—very good names in their way, but not great ones—capital names for a small party, but won't make an impression in public assemblies—*incog.* the thing— Gentlemen from London—distinguished foreigners—anything." The door was thrown open; and Mr. Tracy Tupman, and the stranger, entered the ball-room.

It was a long room, with crimson-covered benches, and wax candles in glass chandeliers. The musicians were securely confined in an elevated den, and quadrilles were being systematically got through by two or three sets of dancers. Two card-tables were made up in the adjoining card-room, and two pair of old ladies, and a corresponding number of stout gentlemen, were executing whist therein.

The finale concluded, the dancers promenaded the room, and Mr. Tupman and his companion stationed themselves in a corner, to observe the company.

"Wait a minute," said the stranger, "fun presently—nobs

not come yet—queer place—Dock-yard people of upper rank don't know Dock-yard people of lower rank—Dock-yard people of lower rank don't know small gentry—small gentry don't know tradespeople—Commissioner don't know anybody."

"Who's that little boy with the light hair and pink eyes, in a fancy dress?" inquired Mr. Tupman.

"Hush, pray—pink eyes—fancy dress—little boy—nonsense —Ensign 97th—Honourable Wilmot Snipe—great family— Snipes—very."

"Sir Thomas Clubber, Lady Clubber, and the Miss Clubbers!" shouted the man at the door in a stentorian voice. A great sensation was created throughout the room by the entrance of a tall gentleman in a blue coat and bright buttons, a large lady in blue satin, and two young ladies, on a similar scale, in fashionably-made dresses of the same hue.

"Commissioner—head of the yard—great man—remarkably great man," whispered the stranger in Mr. Tupman's ear, as the charitable committee ushered Sir Thomas Clubber and family to the top of the room. The Honourable Wilmot Snipe, and other distinguished gentlemen crowded to render homage to the Miss Clubbers; and Sir Thomas Clubber stood bolt upright, and looked majestically over his black neckerchief at the assembled company.

"Mr. Smithie, Mrs. Smithie, and the Misses Smithie," was the next announcement.

"What's Mr. Smithie?" inquired Mr. Tracy Tupman.

"Something in the yard," replied the stranger. Mr. Smithie bowed deferentially to Sir Thomas Clubber ; and Sir Thomas Clubber acknowledged the salute with conscious condescension. Lady Clubber took a telescopic view of Mrs. Smithie and family through her eye-glass, and Mrs. Smithie stared in her turn at Mrs. Somebody else, whose husband was not in the Dock-yard at all.

"Colonel Bulder, Mrs. Colonel Bulder, and Miss Bulder," were the next arrivals.

"Head of the Garrison," said the stranger, in reply to Mr. Tupman's inquiring look.

Miss Bulder was warmly welcomed by the Miss Clubbers; the greeting between Mrs. Colonel Bulder and Lady Clubber was of the most affectionate description; Colonel Bulder and Sir Thomas Clubber exchanged snuff-boxes, and looked very much like a pair of Alexander Selkirks—"Monarchs of all they surveyed."

While the aristocracy of the place—the Bulders, and Clubbers, and Snipes—were thus preserving their dignity at the upper end of the room, the other classes of society were imitating their example in other parts of it. The less aristocratic officers of the 97th devoted themselves to the families of the less important functionaries from the Dockyard. The solicitors' wives, and the wine-merchant's wife, headed another grade (the brewer's wife visited the Bulders); and Mrs. Tomlinson, the post-office keeper, seemed by mutual consent to have been chosen the leader of the trade party.

One of the most popular personages, in his own circle, present was a little fat man, with a ring of upright black hair round his head, and an extensive bald plain on the top of it —Doctor Slammer, surgeon to the 97th. The Doctor took snuff with everybody, chatted with everybody, laughed, danced, made jokes, played whist, did everything, and was everywhere. To these pursuits, multifarious as they were, the little Doctor added a more important one than any—he was indefatigable in paying the most unremitting and devoted attention to a little old widow, whose rich dress and profusion of ornament bespoke her a most desirable addition to a limited income.

Upon the Doctor, and the widow, the eyes of both Mr. Tupman and his companion had been fixed for some time, when the stranger broke silence.

"Lots of money—old girl—pompous Doctor—not a bad idea—good fun," were the intelligible sentences which issued from his lips. Mr. Tupman looked inquisitively in his face.

"I'll dance with the widow," said the stranger.

AT THE BALL.

"Who is she?" inquired Mr. Tupman.

"Don't know—never saw her in all my life—cut out the Doctor—here goes." And the stranger forthwith crossed the room; and, leaning against a mantel-piece, commenced gazing with an air of respectful and melancholy admiration on the fat countenance of the little old lady. Mr. Tupman looked on, in mute astonishment. The stranger progressed rapidly; the little Doctor danced with another lady; the widow dropped her fan, the stranger picked it up and pre-sented it,—a smile—a bow—a curtsey—a few words of conversation. The stranger walked boldly up to, and returned with, the master of the ceremonies; a little in-troductory pantomime; and the stranger and Mrs. Budger took their places in a quadrille.

The surprise of Mr. Tupman at this summary proceeding, great as it was, was immeasurably exceeded by the astonishment of the Doctor. The stranger was young, and the widow was flattered. The Doctor's attentions were unheeded by the widow; and the Doctor's indignation was wholly lost on his imperturbable rival. Doctor Slammer was paralysed. He, Doctor Slammer, of the 97th, to be extinguished in a moment, by a man whom nobody had ever seen before, and whom nobody knew even now! Doctor Slammer—Doctor Slammer of the 97th rejected! Impossible! It could not be! Yes, it was; there they were. What! introducing his friend! Could he believe his eyes! He looked again, and was under the painful necessity of admitting the veracity of his optics; Mrs. Budger was dancing with Mr. Tracy Tupman, there was no mistaking the fact. There was the widow before him, bouncing bodily, here and there, with unwonted vigour; and Mr. Tracy Tupman hopping about, with a face expressive of the most intense solemnity, dancing (as a good many people do) as if a quadrille were not a thing to be laughed at, but a severe trial to the feelings, which it requires inflexible resolution to encounter.

Silently and patiently did the Doctor bear all this, and all the handings of negus, and watching for glasses, and darting for biscuits, and coquetting, that ensued; but, a few seconds after the stranger had disappeared to lead Mrs. Budger to her carriage, he darted swiftly from the room with every particle of his hitherto-bottled-up indignation effervescing, from all parts of his countenance, in a perspiration of passion.

The stranger was returning, and Mr. Tupman was beside him. He spoke in a low tone, and laughed. The little Doctor thirsted for his life. He was exulting. He had triumphed.

"Sir!" said the Doctor, in an awful voice, producing a card, and retiring into an angle of the passage, "my name is Slammer, Doctor Slammer, sir—97th Regiment—Chatham Barracks—my card, sir, my card." He would have added more, but his indignation choked him.

"Ah!" replied the stranger, coolly, "Slammer—much obliged —polite attention—not ill now, Slammer—but when I am— knock you up."

"You—you're a shuffler! sir," gasped the furious Doctor, "a poltroon—a coward—a liar—a—a—will nothing induce you to give me your card, sir!"

"Oh! I see," said the stranger, half aside, "negus too strong here—liberal landlord—very foolish—very—lemonade much better—hot rooms—elderly gentlemen—suffer for it in the morning—cruel—cruel;" and he moved on a step or two.

"You are stopping in this house, sir," said the indignant little man; "you are intoxicated now, sir; you shall hear from me in the morning, sir. I shall find you out, sir; I shall find you out."

"Rather you found me out than found me at home," replied the unmoved stranger.

Doctor Slammer looked unutterable ferocity, as he fixed his hat on his head with an indignant knock; and the stranger and Mr. Tupman ascended to the bedroom of the latter to restore the borrowed plumage to the unconscious Winkle.

That gentleman was fast asleep; the restoration was soon made. The stranger was extremely jocose; and Mr. Tracy

Dr. Slammer's Defiance of Jingle

MR. WINKLE IS WANTED.

Tupman, being quite bewildered with wine, negus, lights, and ladies, thought the whole affair an exquisite joke. His new friend departed; and, after experiencing some slight difficulty in finding the orifice in his night-cap, originally intended for the reception of his head, and finally overturning his candlestick in his struggles to put it on, Mr. Tracy Tupman managed to get into bed by a series of complicated evolutions, and shortly afterwards sank into repose.

Seven o'clock had hardly ceased striking on the following morning when Mr. Pickwick's comprehensive mind was aroused from the state of unconsciousness, in which slumber had plunged it, by a loud knocking at his chamber door.

"Who's there?" said Mr. Pickwick, starting up in bed.

"Boots, sir."

"What do you want?"

"Please, sir, can you tell me, which gentleman of your party wears a bright blue dress coat, with a gilt button with P. C. on it?"

"It's been given out to brush," thought Mr. Pickwick, "and the man has forgotten whom it belongs to.—Mr. Winkle," he called out, "next room but two, on the right hand."

"Thank'ee, sir," said the Boots, and away he went.

"What's the matter?" cried Mr. Tupman, as a loud knocking at *his* door roused *him* from his oblivious repose.

"Can I speak to Mr. Winkle, sir?" replied the Boots from the outside.

"Winkle—Winkle!" shouted Mr. Tupman, calling into the inner room.

"Hallo!" replied a faint voice from within the bed-clothes.

"You're wanted—some one at the door—" and having exerted himself to articulate thus much, Mr. Tracy Tupman turned round and fell fast asleep again.

"Wanted!" said Mr. Winkle, hastily jumping out of bed, and putting on a few articles of clothing: "wanted! at this distance from town—who on earth can want me?"

"Gentleman in the coffee-room, sir," replied the Boots, as Mr. Winkle opened the door, and confronted him; "gentleman says he'll not detain you a moment, sir, but he can take no denial."

"Very odd!" said Mr. Winkle; "I'll be down directly."

He hurriedly wrapped himself in a travelling-shawl and dressing-gown, and proceeded down-stairs. An old woman and a couple of waiters were cleaning the coffee-room, and an officer in undress uniform was looking out of the window. He turned round as Mr. Winkle entered, and made a stiff inclination of the head. Having ordered the attendants to retire, and closed the door very carefully, he said, "Mr. Winkle, I presume?"

"My name *is* Winkle, sir."

"You will not be surprised, sir, when I inform you, that I have called here this morning on behalf of my friend, Dr. Slammer, of the Ninety-seventh."

"Doctor Slammer!" said Mr. Winkle.

"Doctor Slammer. He begged me to express his opinion that your conduct of last evening was of a description which no gentleman could endure: and (he added) which no one gentleman would pursue towards another."

Mr. Winkle's astonishment was too real, and too evident, to escape the observation of Dr. Slammer's friend; he therefore proceeded—"My friend, Doctor Slammer, requested me to add, that he was firmly persuaded you were intoxicated during a portion of the evening, and possibly unconscious of the extent of the insult you were guilty of. He commissioned me to say, that should this be pleaded as an excuse for your behaviour, he will consent to accept a written apology, to be penned by you, from my dictation."

"A written apology!" repeated Mr. Winkle, in the most emphatic tone of amazement possible.

"Of course you know the alternative," replied the visitor, coolly.

"Were you entrusted with this message to me, by name?"

inquired Mr. Winkle, whose intellects were hopelessly confused by this extraordinary conversation.

"I was not present myself," replied the visitor, "and in consequence of your firm refusal to give your card to Doctor Slammer, I was desired by that gentleman to identify the wearer of a very uncommon coat—a bright blue dress coat, with a gilt button displaying a bust, and the letters 'P. C.'"

Mr. Winkle actually staggered with astonishment as he heard his own costume thus minutely described. Dr. Slammer's friend proceeded:—"From the inquiries I made at the bar, just now, I was convinced that the owner of the coat in question arrived here, with three gentlemen, yesterday afternoon. I immediately sent up to the gentleman who was described as appearing the head of the party, and he at once referred me to you."

If the principal tower of Rochester Castle had suddenly walked from its foundation, and stationed itself opposite the coffee-room window, Mr. Winkle's surprise would have been as nothing compared with the profound astonishment with which he had heard this address. His first impression was, that his coat had been stolen. "Will you allow me to detain you one moment?" said he.

"Certainly," replied the unwelcome visitor.

Mr. Winkle ran hastily up-stairs, and with a trembling hand opened the bag. There was the coat in its usual place, but exhibiting, on a close inspection, evident tokens of having been worn on the preceding night.

"It must be so," said Mr. Winkle, letting the coat fall from his hands. "I took too much wine after dinner, and have a very vague recollection of walking about the streets and smoking a cigar afterwards. The fact is, I was very drunk;—I must have changed my coat—gone somewhere—and insulted somebody—I have no doubt of it; and this message is the terrible consequence." Saying which, Mr. Winkle retraced his steps in the direction of the coffee-room, with the gloomy and dreadful resolve of accepting the challenge of the warlike Doctor Slammer, and abiding by the worst consequences that might ensue.

To this determination Mr. Winkle was urged by a variety of considerations; the first of which was, his reputation with the club. He had always been looked up to as a high authority on all matters of amusement and dexterity, whether offensive, defensive, or inoffensive; and if, on this very first occasion of being put to the test, he shrunk back from the trial, beneath his leader's eye, his name and standing were lost for ever. Besides, he remembered to have heard it frequently surmised by the uninitiated in such matters, that by an understood arrangement between the seconds, the pistols were seldom loaded with ball; and, furthermore, he reflected that if he applied to Mr. Snodgrass to act as his second, and depicted the danger in glowing terms, that gentleman might possibly communicate the intelligence to Mr. Pickwick, who would certainly lose no time in transmitting it to the local authorities, and thus prevent the killing or maiming of his follower.

Such were his thoughts when he returned to the coffee-room, and intimated his intention of accepting the Doctor's challenge.

"Will you refer me to a friend, to arrange the time and place of meeting?" said the officer.

"Quite unnecessary," replied Mr. Winkle; "name them to me, and I can procure the attendance of a friend afterwards."

"Shall we say—sunset this evening?" inquired the officer, in a careless tone.

"Very good," replied Mr. Winkle; thinking in his heart it was very bad.

"You know Fort Pitt?"

"Yes; I saw it yesterday."

"If you will take the trouble to turn into the field which borders the trench, take the foot-path to the left when you arrive at an angle of the fortification, and keep straight on

MR. WINKLE CONFIDES A SECRET.

'till you see me, I will precede you to a secluded place, where the affair can be conducted without fear of interruption."

"*Fear* of interruption!" thought Mr. Winkle.

"Nothing more to arrange, I think," said the officer.

"I am not aware of anything more," replied Mr. Winkle. "Good morning."

"Good morning:" and the officer whistled a lively air as he strode away.

That morning's breakfast passed heavily off. Mr. Tupman was not in a condition to rise, after the unwonted dissipation of the previous night; Mr. Snodgrass appeared to labour under a poetical depression of spirits; and even Mr. Pickwick evinced an unusual attachment to silence and soda-water. Mr. Winkle eagerly watched his opportunity: it was not long wanting. Mr. Snodgrass proposed a visit to the castle, and as Mr. Winkle was the only other member of the party disposed to walk, they went out together.

"Snodgrass," said Mr. Winkle, when they had turned out of the public street, "Snodgrass, my dear fellow, can I rely upon your secrecy?" As he said this, he most devoutly and earnestly hoped he could not.

"You can," replied Mr. Snodgrass. "Hear me swear—"

"No, no," interrupted Winkle, terrified at the idea of his companion's unconsciously pledging himself not to give information; "don't swear, don't swear; it's quite unnecessary."

Mr. Snodgrass dropped the hand which he had, in the spirit of poesy, raised towards the clouds as he made the above appeal, and assumed an attitude of attention.

"I want your assistance, my dear fellow, in an affair of honour," said Mr. Winkle.

"You shall have it," replied Mr. Snodgrass, clasping his friend's hand.

"With a Doctor—Doctor Slammer, of the Ninety-seventh," said Mr. Winkle, wishing to make the matter appear as solemn as possible; "an affair with an officer, seconded by

31

another officer, at sunset this evening, in a lonely field beyond Fort Pitt."

"I will attend you," said Mr. Snodgrass.

He was astonished, but by no means dismayed. It is extraordinary how cool any party but the principal can be in such cases. Mr. Winkle had forgotten this. He had judged of his friend's feelings by his own.

"The consequences may be dreadful," said Mr. Winkle.

"I hope not," said Mr. Snodgrass.

"The Doctor, I believe, is a very good shot," said Mr. Winkle.

"Most of these military men are," observed Mr. Snodgrass, calmly; "but so are you, an't you?"

Mr. Winkle replied in the affirmative; and perceiving that he had not alarmed his companion sufficiently, changed his ground.

"Snodgrass," he said, in a voice tremulous with emotion, "if I fall, you will find in a packet which I shall place in your hands a note for my—for my father."

This attack was a failure also. Mr. Snodgrass was affected, but he undertook the delivery of the note as readily as if he had been a Twopenny Postman.

"If I fall," said Mr. Winkle, "or if the Doctor falls, you, my dear friend, will be tried as an accessory before the fact. Shall I involve my friend in transportation—possibly for life!"

Mr. Snodgrass winced a little at this, but his heroism was invincible. "In the cause of friendship," he fervently exclaimed, "I would brave all dangers."

How Mr. Winkle cursed his companion's devoted friendship internally, as they walked silently along, side by side, for some minutes, each immersed in his own meditations! The morning was wearing away; he grew desperate.

"Snodgrass," he said, stopping suddenly, "do *not* let me be baulked in this matter—do *not* give information to the local authorities—do *not* obtain the assistance of several peace officers, to take either me or Doctor Slammer, of the Ninety-seventh Regiment, at present quartered in Chatham Barracks, into custody, and thus prevent this duel;—I say, do *not*."

Mr. Snodgrass seized his friend's hand warmly, as he enthusiastically replied, "Not for worlds!"

A thrill passed over Mr. Winkle's frame as the conviction that he had nothing to hope from his friend's fears, and that he was destined to become an animated target, rushed forcibly upon him.

The state of the case having been formally explained to Mr. Snodgrass, and a case of satisfaction pistols, with the satisfactory accompaniments of powder, ball, and caps, having been hired from a manufacturer in Rochester, the two friends returned to their inn; Mr. Winkle to ruminate on the approaching struggle, and Mr. Snodgrass to arrange the weapons of war, and put them into proper order for immediate use.

It was a dull and heavy evening when they again sallied forth on their awkward errand. Mr. Winkle was muffled up in a huge cloak to escape observation, and Mr. Snodgrass bore under his the instruments of destruction.

"Have you got everything?" said Mr. Winkle, in an agitated tone.

"Ev'rything," replied Mr. Snodgrass; "plenty of ammunition, in case the shots don't take effect. There's a quarter of a pound of powder in the case, and I have got two newspapers in my pocket for the loadings."

These were instances of friendship for which any man might reasonably feel most grateful. The presumption is, that the gratitude of Mr. Winkle was too powerful for utterance, as he said nothing, but continued to walk on—' rather slowly.

"We are in excellent time," said Mr. Snodgrass, as they climbed the fence of the first field; "the sun is just going down." Mr. Winkle looked up at the declining orb, and painfully thought of the probability of his "going down" himself, before long.

"There's the officer," exclaimed Mr. Winkle, after a few minutes' walking.

"Where?" said Mr. Snodgrass.

"There;—the gentleman in the blue cloak." Mr. Snodgrass looked in the direction indicated by the forefinger of his friend, and observed a figure, muffled up, as he had described. The officer evinced his consciousness of their presence by slightly beckoning with his hand; and the two friends followed him at a little distance, as he walked away.

The evening grew more dull every moment, and a melancholy wind sounded through the deserted fields, like a distant giant whistling for his house-dog. The sadness of the scene imparted a sombre tinge to the feelings of Mr. Winkle. He started as they passed the angle of the trench—it looked like a colossal grave.

The officer turned suddenly from the path, and after climbing a paling, and scaling a hedge, entered a secluded field. Two gentlemen were waiting in it; one was a little fat man, with black hair; and the other—a portly personage in a braided surtout—was sitting with perfect equanimity on a camp-stool.

"The other party, and a surgeon, I suppose," said Mr. Snodgrass; "take a drop of brandy." Mr. Winkle seized the wicker bottle which his friend proffered, and took a lengthened pull at the exhilarating liquid.

"My friend, sir, Mr. Snodgrass," said Mr. Winkle, as the officer approached. Doctor Slammer's friend bowed, and produced a case similar to that which Mr. Snodgrass carried.

"We have nothing farther to say, sir, I think," he coldly remarked, as he opened the case; "an apology has been resolutely declined."

"Nothing, sir," said Mr. Snodgrass, who began to feel rather uncomfortable himself.

"Will you step forward?" said the officer.

"Certainly," replied Mr. Snodgrass. The ground was measured, and preliminaries arranged.

"You will find these better than your own," said the opposite second, producing his pistols. "You saw me load them. Do you object to use them?"

"Certainly not," replied Mr. Snodgrass. The offer relieved him from considerable embarrassment, for his previous notions of loading a pistol were rather vague and undefined.

"We may place our men, then, I think," observed the officer, with as much indifference as if the principals were chess-men, and the seconds players.

"I think we may," replied Mr. Snodgrass; who would have assented to any proposition, because he knew nothing about the matter. The officer crossed to Doctor Slammer, and Mr. Snodgrass went up to Mr. Winkle.

"It's all ready," he said, offering the pistol. "Give me your cloak."

"You have got the packet, my dear fellow," said poor Winkle.

"All right," said Mr. Snodgrass. "Be steady, and wing him."

It occurred to Mr. Winkle that this advice was very like that which bystanders invariably give to the smallest boy in a street fight, namely, "Go in, and win:"—an admirable thing to recommend, if you only know how to do it. He took off his cloak, however, in silence—it always took a long time to undo, that cloak—and accepted the pistol. The seconds retired, the gentleman on the camp-stool did the same, and the belligerents approached each other.

Mr. Winkle was always remarkable for extreme humanity. It is conjectured that his unwillingness to hurt a fellow-creature intentionally was the cause of his shutting his eyes when he arrived at the fatal spot; and that the circumstance of his eyes being closed, prevented his observing the very extraordinary and unaccountable demeanour of Doctor Slammer. That gentleman started, stared, retreated, rubbed his eyes, stared again; and, finally, shouted "Stop, stop!"

"What's all this?" said Doctor Slammer, as his friend

and Mr. Snodgrass came running up; "That's not the man."

"Not the man!" said Dr. Slammer's second.

"Not the man!" said Mr. Snodgrass.

"Not the man!" said the gentleman with the camp-stool in his hand.

"Certainly not," replied the little Doctor. "That's not the person who insulted me last night."

"Very extraordinary!" exclaimed the officer.

"Very," said the gentleman with the camp-stool. "The only question is, whether the gentleman, being on the ground, must not be considered, as a matter of form, to be the individual who insulted our friend, Doctor Slammer, yesterday evening, whether he is really that individual or not:" and having delivered this suggestion, with a very sage and mysterious air, the man with the camp-stool took a large pinch of snuff, and looked profoundly round, with the air of an authority in such matters.

Now Mr. Winkle had opened his eyes, and his ears too, when he heard his adversary call out for a cessation of hostilities; and perceiving by what he had afterwards said, that there was, beyond all question, some mistake in the matter, he at once foresaw the increase of reputation he should inevitably acquire by concealing the real motive of his coming out: he therefore stepped boldly forward, and said—

"I am not the person. I know it."

"Then, that," said the man with the camp-stool, "is an affront to Dr. Slammer, and a sufficient reason for proceeding immediately."

"Pray be quiet, Payne," said the Doctor's second. "Why did you not communicate this fact to me this morning, sir?"

"To be sure—to be sure," said the man with the camp-stool, indignantly.

"I entreat you to be quiet, Payne," said the other. "May I repeat my question, sir?"

"Because, sir," replied Mr. Winkle, who had had time to

deliberate upon his answer, "because, sir, you described an intoxicated and ungentlemanly person as wearing a coat which I have the honour, not only to wear, but to have invented —the proposed uniform, sir, of the Pickwick Club in London. The honour of that uniform I feel bound to maintain, and I therefore, without inquiry, accepted the challenge which you offered me."

"My dear sir," said the good-humoured little Doctor, advancing with extended hand, "I honour your gallantry. Permit me to say, sir, that I highly admire your conduct, and extremely regret having caused you the inconvenience of this meeting, to no purpose."

"I beg you won't mention it, sir," said Mr. Winkle.

"I shall feel proud of your acquaintance, sir," said the little Doctor.

"It will afford me the greatest pleasure to know you, sir," replied Mr. Winkle. Thereupon the Doctor and Mr. Winkle shook hands, and then Mr. Winkle and Lieutenant Tappleton (the Doctor's second), and then Mr. Winkle and the man with the camp-stool, and, finally, Mr. Winkle and Mr. Snodgrass —the last-named gentleman in an excess of admiration at the noble conduct of his heroic friend.

"I think we may adjourn," said Lieutenant Tappleton.

"Certainly," added the Doctor.

"Unless," interposed the man with the camp-stool, "unless Mr. Winkle feels himself aggrieved by the challenge; in which case, I submit, he has a right to satisfaction."

Mr. Winkle, with great self-denial, expressed himself quite satisfied already.

"Or possibly," said the man with the camp-stool, "the gentleman's second may feel himself affronted with some observations which fell from me at an early period of this meeting: if so, I shall be happy to give *him* satisfaction immediately."

Mr. Snodgrass hastily professed himself very much obliged with the handsome offer of the gentleman who had spoken last, which he was only induced to decline by his entire contentment with the whole proceedings. The two seconds adjusted the cases, and the whole party left the ground in a much more lively manner than they had proceeded to it.

"Do you remain long here?" inquired Dr. Slammer of Mr. Winkle, as they walked on most amicably together.

"I think we shall leave here the day after to-morrow," was the reply.

"I trust I shall have the pleasure of seeing you and your friend at my rooms, and of spending a pleasant evening with you, after this awkward mistake," said the little Doctor; "are you disengaged this evening?"

"We have some friends here," replied Mr. Winkle, "and I should not like to leave them to-night. Perhaps you and your friend will join us at the Bull."

"With great pleasure," said the little Doctor; "will ten o'clock be too late to look in for half an hour?"

"Oh dear, no," said Mr. Winkle. "I shall be most happy to introduce you to my friends, Mr. Pickwick and Mr. Tupman."

"It will give me great pleasure, I am sure," replied Doctor Slammer, little suspecting who Mr. Tupman was.

"You will be sure to come?" said Mr. Snodgrass.

"Oh, certainly."

By this time they had reached the road. Cordial farewells were exchanged, and the party separated. Doctor Slammer and his friends repaired to the barracks, and Mr. Winkle, accompanied by his friend, Mr. Snodgrass, returned to their inn.

CHAPTER III.

A NEW ACQUAINTANCE. THE STROLLER'S TALE. A DISAGREEABLE
INTERRUPTION, AND AN UNPLEASANT ENCOUNTER.

MR. PICKWICK had felt some apprehensions in consequence of
the unusual absence of his two friends, which their mysterious
behaviour during the whole morning had by no means tended
to diminish. It was, therefore, with more than ordinary
pleasure that he rose to greet them when they again entered;
and with more than ordinary interest that he inquired what
had occurred to detain them from his society. In reply to
his questions on this point, Mr. Snodgrass was about to offer
an historical account of the circumstances just now detailed,
when he was suddenly checked by observing that there were
present, not only Mr. Tupman and their stage-coach companion
of the preceding day, but another stranger of equally singular
appearance. It was a care-worn looking man, whose sallow
face, and deeply sunken eyes, were rendered still more striking
than nature had made them, by the straight black hair which
hung in matted disorder half way down his face. His eyes
were almost unnaturally bright and piercing; his cheek-bones
were high and prominent; and his jaws were so long and
lank, that an observer would have supposed that he was
drawing the flesh of his face in, for a moment, by some
contraction of the muscles, if his half-opened mouth and
immovable expression had not announced that it was his
ordinary appearance. Round his neck he wore a green shawl,
with the large ends straggling over his chest, and making

39

their appearance occasionally beneath the worn button-holes
of his old waistcoat. His upper garment was a long black
surtout; and below it he wore wide drab trousers, and large
boots, running rapidly to seed.

It was on this uncouth-looking person that Mr. Winkle's
eye rested, and it was towards him that Mr. Pickwick extended
his hand, when he said " A friend of our friend's here. We
discovered this morning that our friend was connected with
the theatre in this place, though he is not desirous to have
it generally known, and this gentleman is a member of the
same profession. He was about to favour us with a little
anecdote connected with it, when you entered."

" Lots of anecdote," said the green-coated stranger of the
day before, advancing to Mr. Winkle and speaking in a low
and confidential tone. " Rum fellow—does the heavy business
—no actor—strange man—all sorts of miseries—Dismal
Jemmy, we call him on the circuit." Mr. Winkle and Mr.
Snodgrass politely welcomed the gentleman, elegantly
designated as " Dismal Jemmy;" and calling for brandy and
water, in imitation of the remainder of the company, seated
themselves at the table.

" Now, sir," said Mr. Pickwick, " will you oblige us by
proceeding with what you were going to relate?"

The dismal individual took a dirty roll of paper from his
pocket, and turning to Mr. Snodgrass, who had just taken
out his note-book, said in a hollow voice perfectly in keeping
with his outward man—" Are you the poet?"

" I—I do a little in that way," replied Mr. Snodgrass,
rather taken aback by the abruptness of the question.

" Ah! poetry makes life what lights and music do the
stage—strip the one of its false embellishments, and the
other of its illusions, and what is there real in either to live
or care for?"

" Very true, sir," replied Mr. Snodgrass.

" To be before the footlights," continued the dismal man,
" is like sitting at a grand court show, and admiring the

THE STROLLER'S TALE.

silken dresses of the gaudy throng—to be behind them is to be the people who make that finery, uncared for and unknown, and left to sink or swim, to starve or live, as fortune wills it."

"Certainly," said Mr. Snodgrass: for the sunken eye of the dismal man rested on him, and he felt it necessary to say something.

"Go on, Jemmy," said the Spanish traveller, "like black-eyed Susan—all in the Downs—no croaking—speak out—look lively."

"Will you make another glass before you begin, sir?" said Mr. Pickwick.

The dismal man took the hint, and having mixed a glass of brandy and water, and slowly swallowed half of it, opened the roll of paper and proceeded, partly to read, and partly to relate, the following incident, which we find recorded on the Transactions of the club as "The Stroller's Tale."

THE STROLLER'S TALE.

"THERE is nothing of the marvellous in what I am going to relate," said the dismal man; "there is nothing even uncommon in it. Want and sickness are too common in many stations of life, to deserve more notice than is usually bestowed on the most ordinary vicissitudes of human nature. I have thrown these few notes together, because the subject of them was well known to me for many years. I traced his progress downwards, step by step, until at last he reached that excess of destitution from which he never rose again.

"The man of whom I speak was a low pantomime actor; and, like many people of his class, an habitual drunkard. In his better days, before he had become enfeebled by dissipation and emaciated by disease, he had been in the receipt of a good salary, which, if he had been careful and prudent, he might have continued to receive for some years —not many; because these men either die early, or, by unnaturally taxing their bodily energies, lose, prematurely,

41

those physical powers on which alone they can depend for subsistence. His besetting sin gained so fast upon him, however, that it was found impossible to employ him in the situations in which he really was useful to the theatre. The public-house had a fascination for him which he could not resist. Neglected disease and hopeless poverty were as certain to be his portion as death itself, if he persevered in the same course; yet he *did* persevere, and the result may be guessed. He could obtain no engagement, and he wanted bread.

"Everybody who is at all acquainted with theatrical matters knows what a host of shabby, poverty-stricken men hang about the stage of a large establishment—not regularly engaged actors, but ballet people, procession men, tumblers, and so forth, who are taken on during the run of a pantomime, or an Easter piece, and are then discharged, until the production of some heavy spectacle occasions a new demand for their services. To this mode of life the man was compelled to resort; and taking the chair every night, at some low theatrical house, at once put him in possession of a few more shillings weekly, and enabled him to gratify his old propensity. Even this resource shortly failed him; his irregularities were too great to admit of his earning the wretched pittance he might thus have procured, and he was actually reduced to a state bordering on starvation, only procuring a trifle occasionally by borrowing it of some old companion, or by obtaining an appearance at one or other of the commonest of the minor theatres; and when he did earn anything, it was spent in the old way.

"About this time, and when he had been existing for upwards of a year no one knew how, I had a short engagement at one of the theatres on the Surrey side of the water, and here I saw this man whom I had lost sight of for some time; for I had been travelling in the provinces, and he had been skulking in the lanes and alleys of London. I was dressed to leave the house, and was crossing the stage on my way out, when he tapped me on the shoulder. Never shall I forget

42

the repulsive sight that met my eye when I turned round. He was dressed for the pantomime, in all the absurdity of a clown's costume. The spectral figures in the Dance of Death, the most frightful shapes that the ablest painter ever portrayed on canvas, never presented an appearance half so ghastly. His bloated body and shrunken legs—their deformity enhanced a hundred fold by the fantastic dress—the glassy eyes, contrasting fearfully with the thick white paint with which the face was besmeared; the grotesquely ornamented head, trembling with paralysis, and the long, skinny hands, rubbed with white chalk—all gave him a hideous and unnatural appearance, of which no description could convey an adequate idea, and which, to this day, I shudder to think of. His voice was hollow and tremulous, as he took me aside, and in broken words recounted a long catalogue of sickness and privations, terminating as usual with an urgent request for the loan of a trifling sum of money. I put a few shillings in his hand, and as I turned away I heard the roar of laughter which followed his first tumble on to the stage.

" A few nights afterwards, a boy put a dirty scrap of paper in my hand, on which were scrawled a few words in pencil, intimating that the man was dangerously ill, and begging me, after the performance, to see him at his lodging in some street—I forget the name of it now—at no great distance from the theatre. I promised to comply, as soon as I could get away; and, after the curtain fell, sallied forth on my melancholy errand.

" It was late, for I had been playing in the last piece; and as it was a benefit night, the performances had been protracted to an unusual length. It was a dark cold night, with a chill damp wind, which blew the rain heavily against the windows and house fronts. Pools of water had collected in the narrow and little-frequented streets, and as many of the thinly-scattered oil-lamps had been blown out by the violence of the wind, the walk was not only a comfortless, but most uncertain one. I had fortunately taken the right course, however, and succeeded, after a little difficulty, in finding the house to which I had been directed—a coal-shed, with one story above it, in the back room of which lay the object of my search.

"A wretched-looking woman, the man's wife, met me on the stairs, and, telling me that he had just fallen into a kind of doze, led me softly in, and placed a chair for me at the bedside. The sick man was lying with his face turned towards the wall; and as he took no heed of my presence, I had leisure to observe the place in which I found myself.

"He was lying on an old bedstead, which turned up during the day. The tattered remains of a checked curtain were drawn round the bed's head, to exclude the wind, which however made its way into the comfortless room through the numerous chinks in the door, and blew it to and fro every instant. There was a low cinder fire in a rusty unfixed grate; and an old three-cornered stained table, with some medicine bottles, a broken glass, and a few other domestic articles, was drawn out before it. A little child was sleeping on a temporary bed which had been made for it on the floor, and the woman sat on a chair by its side. There were a couple of shelves, with a few plates and cups and saucers: and a pair of stage shoes and a couple of foils hung beneath them. With the exception of little heaps of rags and bundles which had been carelessly thrown into the corners of the room, these were the only things in the apartment.

"I had had time to note these little particulars, and to mark the heavy breathing and feverish startings of the sick man, before he was aware of my presence. In his restless attempts to procure some easy resting-place for his head, he tossed his hand out of the bed, and it fell on mine. He started up, and stared eagerly in my face.

"'Mr. Hutley, John,' said his wife; 'Mr. Hutley, that you sent for to-night, you know.'

"'Ah!' said the invalid, passing his hand across his forehead; 'Hutley—Hutley—let me see.' He seemed endeavouring

44

to collect his thoughts for a few seconds, and then grasping me tightly by the wrist said, "Don't leave me—don't leave me, old fellow. She'll murder me; I know she will.'

"'Has he been long so?' said I, addressing his weeping wife.

"'Since yesterday night,' she replied. 'John, John, don't you know me?'

"'Don't let her come near me,' said the man, with a shudder, as she stooped over him. 'Drive her away; I can't bear her near me.' He stared wildly at her, with a look of deadly apprehension, and then whispered in my ear, 'I beat her, Jem; I beat her yesterday, and many times before. I have starved her and the boy too; and now I am weak and helpless, Jem, she'll murder me for it; I know she will. If you'd seen her cry, as I have, you'd know it too. Keep her off.' He relaxed his grasp, and sank back exhausted on the pillow.

"I knew but too well what all this meant. If I could have entertained any doubt of it, for an instant, one glance at the woman's pale face and wasted form would have sufficiently explained the real state of the case. 'You had better stand aside,' said I to the poor creature. 'You can do him no good. Perhaps he will be calmer, if he does not see you.' She retired out of the man's sight. He opened his eyes, after a few seconds, and looked anxiously round.

"'Is she gone?' he eagerly inquired.

"'Yes—yes,' said I; 'she shall not hurt you.'

"'I'll tell you what, Jem,' said the man, in a low voice, 'she *does* hurt me. There's something in her eyes wakes such a dreadful fear in my heart, that it drives me mad. All last night, her large staring eyes and pale face were close to mine; wherever I turned, they turned; and whenever I started up from my sleep, she was at the bedside looking at me.' He drew me closer to him, as he said in a deep, alarmed whisper—'Jem, she must be an evil spirit—a devil! Hush! I know she is. If she had been a woman she would have died long ago. No woman could have borne what she has.'

45

" I sickened at the thought of the long course of cruelty and neglect which must have occurred to produce such an impression on such a man. I could say nothing in reply; for who could offer hope, or consolation, to the abject being before me ?

" I sat there for upwards of two hours, during which time he tossed about, murmuring exclamations of pain or impatience, restlessly throwing his arms here and there, and turning constantly from side to side. At length he fell into that state of partial unconsciousness, in which the mind wanders uneasily from scene to scene, and from place to place, without the control of reason, but still without being able to divest itself of an indescribable sense of present suffering. Finding from his incoherent wanderings that this was the case, and knowing that in all probability the fever would not grow immediately worse, I left him, promising his miserable wife that I would repeat my visit next evening, and, if necessary, sit up with the patient during the night.

" I kept my promise. The last four-and-twenty hours had produced a frightful alteration. The eyes, though deeply sunk and heavy, shone with a lustre frightful to behold. The lips were parched, and cracked in many places : the dry hard skin glowed with a burning heat, and there was an almost unearthly air of wild anxiety in the man's face, indicating even more strongly the ravages of the disease. The fever was at its height.

" I took the seat I had occupied the night before, and there I sat for hours, listening to sounds which must strike deep to the heart of the most callous among human beings —the awful ravings of a dying man. From what I had heard of the medical attendant's opinion, I knew there was no hope for him : I was sitting by his death-bed. I saw the wasted limbs, which a few hours before had been distorted for the amusement of a boisterous gallery, writhing under the tortures of a burning fever—I heard the clown's shrill laugh, blending with the low murmurings of the dying man.

The Dying Clown

THE DYING MAN'S WANDERINGS.

"It is a touching thing to hear the mind reverting to the ordinary occupations and pursuits of health, when the body lies before you weak and helpless; but when those occupations are of a character the most strongly opposed to anything we associate with grave or solemn ideas, the impression produced is infinitely more powerful. The theatre, and the public-house, were the chief themes of the wretched man's wanderings. It was evening, he fancied; he had a part to play that night; it was late, and he must leave home instantly. Why did they hold him, and prevent his going?—he should lose the money —he must go. No! they would not let him. He hid his face in his burning hands, and feebly bemoaned his own weakness, and the cruelty of his persecutors. A short pause, and he shouted out a few doggrel rhymes—the last he had ever learnt. He rose in bed, drew up his withered limbs, and rolled about in uncouth positions; he was acting—he was at the theatre. A minute's silence, and he murmured the burden of some roaring song. He had reached the old house at last: how hot the room was. He had been ill, very ill, but he was well now, and happy. Fill up his glass. Who was that, that dashed it from his lips? It was the same persecutor that had followed him before. He fell back upon his pillow and moaned aloud. A short period of oblivion, and he was wandering through a tedious maze of low arched-rooms—so low, sometimes, that he must creep upon his hands and knees to make his way along; it was close and dark, and every way he turned, some obstacle impeded his progress. There were insects too, hideous crawling things with eyes that stared upon him, and filled the very air around: glistening horribly amidst the thick darkness of the place. The walls and ceiling were alive with reptiles—the vault expanded to an enormous size—frightful figures flitted to and fro—and the faces of men he knew, rendered hideous by gibing and mouthing, peered out from among them; they were searing him with heated irons, and binding his head with cords till the blood started; and he struggled madly for life.

47

"At the close of one of these paroxysms, when I had with great difficulty held him down in his bed, he sank into what appeared to be a slumber. Overpowered with watching and exertion, I had closed my eyes for a few minutes, when I felt a violent clutch on my shoulder. I awoke instantly. He had raised himself up, so as to seat himself in bed—a dreadful change had come over his face, but consciousness had returned, for he evidently knew me. The child who had been long since disturbed by his ravings, rose from its little bed, and ran towards its father, screaming with fright—the mother hastily caught it in her arms, lest he should injure it in the violence of his insanity; but, terrified by the alteration of his features, stood transfixed by the bed-side. He grasped my shoulder convulsively, and, striking his breast with the other hand, made a desperate attempt to articulate. It was unavailing—he extended his arm towards them, and made another violent effort. There was a rattling noise in the throat—a glare of the eye—a short stifled groan—and he fell back—dead!"

It would afford us the highest gratification to be enabled to record Mr. Pickwick's opinion of the foregoing anecdote. We have little doubt that we should have been enabled to present it to our readers, but for a most unfortunate occurrence.

Mr. Pickwick had replaced on the table the glass which, during the last few sentences of the tale, he had retained in his hand, and had just made up his mind to speak—indeed, we have the authority of Mr. Snodgrass's note-book for stating, that he had actually opened his mouth—when the waiter entered the room, and said—

"Some gentlemen, sir."

It has been conjectured that Mr. Pickwick was on the point of delivering some remarks which would have enlightened the world, if not the Thames, when he was thus interrupted: for he gazed sternly on the waiter's countenance, and then looked round on the company generally, as if seeking for information relative to the new comers.

"Oh!" said Mr. Winkle, rising, "some friends of mine—show them in. Very pleasant fellows," added Mr. Winkle, after the waiter had retired—"Officers of the 97th, whose acquaintance I made rather oddly this morning. You will like them very much."

Mr. Pickwick's equanimity was at once restored. The waiter returned, and ushered three gentlemen into the room.

"Lieutenant Tappleton," said Mr. Winkle, "Lieutenant Tappleton, Mr. Pickwick—Doctor Payne, Mr. Pickwick—Mr. Snodgrass, you have seen before: my friend Mr. Tupman, Doctor Payne—Dr. Slammer, Mr. Pickwick—Mr. Tupman, Doctor Slam—."

Here Mr. Winkle suddenly paused; for strong emotion was visible on the countenance both of Mr. Tupman and the Doctor.

"I have met *this* gentleman before," said the Doctor, with marked emphasis.

"Indeed!" said Mr. Winkle.

"And—and that person, too, if I am not mistaken," said the Doctor, bestowing a scrutinising glance on the green-coated stranger. "I think I gave that person a very pressing invitation last night, which he thought proper to decline." Saying which the Doctor scowled magnanimously on the stranger, and whispered his friend Lieutenant Tappleton.

"You don't say so," said that gentleman, at the conclusion of the whisper.

"I do, indeed," replied Doctor Slammer.

"You are bound to kick him on the spot," murmured the owner of the camp-stool with great importance.

"*Do* be quiet, Payne," interposed the Lieutenant. "Will you allow me to ask you, sir," he said, addressing Mr. Pickwick, who was considerably mystified by this very unpolite by-play, "will you allow me to ask you, sir, whether that person belongs to your party?"

"No, sir," replied Mr. Pickwick, "he is a guest of ours."

"He is a member of your club, or I am mistaken?" said the Lieutenant, inquiringly.

"Certainly not," responded Mr. Pickwick.

"And never wears your club-button?" said the Lieutenant.

"No—never!" replied the astonished Mr. Pickwick.

Lieutenant Tappleton turned round to his friend Doctor Slammer, with a scarcely perceptible shrug of the shoulder, as if implying some doubt of the accuracy of his recollection. The little Doctor looked wrathful, but confounded; and Mr. Payne gazed with a ferocious aspect on the beaming countenance of the unconscious Pickwick.

"Sir," said the Doctor, suddenly addressing Mr. Tupman, in a tone which made that gentleman start as perceptibly as if a pin had been cunningly inserted in the calf of his leg, "you were at the ball here last night!"

Mr. Tupman gasped a faint affirmative, looking very hard at Mr. Pickwick all the while.

"That person was your companion," said the Doctor, pointing to the still unmoved stranger.

Mr. Tupman admitted the fact.

"Now, sir," said the Doctor to the stranger, "I ask you once again, in the presence of these gentlemen, whether you choose to give me your card, and to receive the treatment of a gentleman; or whether you impose upon me the necessity of personally chastising you on the spot?"

"Stay, sir," said Mr. Pickwick, "I really cannot allow this matter to go any further without some explanation. Tupman, recount the circumstances."

Mr. Tupman, thus solemnly abjured, stated the case in a few words; touched slightly on the borrowing of the coat; expatiated largely on its having been done "after dinner;" wound up with a little penitence on his own account; and left the stranger to clear himself as he best could.

He was apparently about to proceed to do so, when Lieutenant Tappleton, who had been eyeing him with great curiosity, said with considerable scorn—"Haven't I seen you at the theatre, sir?"

"Certainly," replied the unabashed stranger.

"He is a strolling actor," said the Lieutenant, contemptuously; turning to Dr. Slammer—"He acts in the piece that the Officers of the 52nd get up at the Rochester Theatre to-morrow night. You cannot proceed in this affair, Slammer—impossible!"

"Quite!" said the dignified Payne.

"Sorry to have placed you in this disagreeable situation," said Lieutenant Tappleton, addressing Mr. Pickwick; "allow me to suggest, that the best way of avoiding a recurrence of such scenes in future, will be to be more select in the choice of your companions. Good evening, sir!" and the Lieutenant bounced out of the room.

"And allow *me* to say, sir," said the irascible Doctor Payne, "that if I had been Tappleton, or if I had been Slammer, I would have pulled your nose, sir, and the nose of every man in this company. I would, sir, every man. Payne is my name, sir—Doctor Payne of the 43rd. Good evening, sir." Having concluded this speech, and uttered the three last words in a loud key, he stalked majestically after his friend, closely followed by Doctor Slammer, who said nothing, but contented himself by withering the company with a look.

Rising rage and extreme bewilderment had swelled the noble breast of Mr. Pickwick, almost to the bursting of his waistcoat, during the delivery of the above defiance. He stood transfixed to the spot, gazing on vacancy. The closing of the door recalled him to himself. He rushed forward with fury in his looks, and fire in his eye. His hand was upon the lock of the door; in another instant it would have been on the throat of Doctor Payne of the 43rd, had not Mr. Snodgrass seized his revered leader by the coat tail, and dragged him backwards.

"Restrain him," cried Mr. Snodgrass, "Winkle, Tupman—he must not peril his distinguished life in such a cause as this."

"Let me go," said Mr. Pickwick.

"Hold him tight," shouted Mr. Snodgrass; and by the united efforts of the whole company, Mr. Pickwick was forced into an arm-chair.

"Leave him alone," said the green-coated stranger—"brandy and water—jolly old gentleman—lots of pluck—swallow this —ah!—capital stuff." Having previously tested the virtues of a bumper, which had been mixed by the dismal man, the stranger applied the glass to Mr. Pickwick's mouth; and the remainder of its contents rapidly disappeared.

There was a short pause; the brandy and water had done its work; the amiable countenance of Mr. Pickwick was fast recovering its customary expression.

"They are not worth your notice," said the dismal man.

"You are right, sir," replied Mr. Pickwick, "they are not. I am ashamed to have been betrayed into this warmth of feeling. Draw your chair up to the table, sir."

The dismal man readily complied: a circle was again formed round the table, and harmony once more prevailed. Some lingering irritability appeared to find a resting-place in Mr. Winkle's bosom, occasioned possibly by the temporary abstraction of his coat—though it is scarcely reasonable to suppose that so slight a circumstance can have excited even a passing feeling of anger in a Pickwickian breast. With this exception, their good humour was completely restored; and the evening concluded with the conviviality with which it had begun.

CHAPTER IV.

A FIELD-DAY AND BIVOUAC. MORE NEW FRIENDS. AN INVITATION
TO THE COUNTRY.

MANY authors entertain, not only a foolish, but a really
dishonest objection to acknowledge the sources from whence
they derive much valuable information. We have no such
feeling. We are merely endeavouring to discharge, in an upright manner, the responsible duties of our editorial functions;
and whatever ambition we might have felt under other circumstances to lay claim to the authorship of these adventures, a
regard for truth forbids us to do more than claim the merit
of their judicious arrangement and impartial narration. The
Pickwick papers are our New River Head; and we may be
compared to the New River Company. The labours of others
have raised for us an immense reservoir of important facts.
We merely lay them on, and communicate them, in a clear
and gentle stream, through the medium of these numbers, to
a world thirsting for Pickwickian knowledge.

Acting in this spirit, and resolutely proceeding on our
determination to avow our obligations to the authorities we
have consulted, we frankly say, that to the note-book of Mr.
Snodgrass are we indebted for the particulars recorded in
this, and the succeeding chapter—particulars which, now that
we have disburdened our conscience, we shall proceed to detail
without further comment.

The whole population of Rochester and the adjoining towns
rose from their beds at an early hour of the following morning,

53

in a state of the utmost bustle and excitement. A grand review was to take place upon the Lines. The manœuvres of half-a-dozen regiments were to be inspected by the eagle eye of the commander-in-chief; temporary fortifications had been erected, the citadel was to be attacked and taken, and a mine was to be sprung.

Mr. Pickwick was, as our readers may have gathered from the slight extract we gave from his description of Chatham, an enthusiastic admirer of the army. Nothing could have been more delightful to him—nothing could have harmonised so well with the peculiar feeling of each of his companions —as this sight. Accordingly they were soon a-foot, and walking in the direction of the scene of action, towards which crowds of people were already pouring from a variety of quarters.

The appearance of everything on the Lines denoted that the approaching ceremony was one of the utmost grandeur and importance. There were sentries posted to keep the ground for the troops, and servants on the batteries keeping places for the ladies, and sergeants running to and fro, with vellum-covered books under their arms, and Colonel Bulder, in full military uniform, on horseback, galloping first to one place and then to another, and backing his horse among the people, and prancing, and curvetting, and shouting in a most alarming manner, and making himself very hoarse in the voice, and very red in the face, without any assignable cause or reason whatever. Officers were running backwards and forwards, first communicating with Colonel Bulder, and then ordering the sergeants, and then running away altogether; and even the very privates themselves looked from behind their glazed stocks with an air of mysterious solemnity, which sufficiently bespoke the special nature of the occasion.

Mr. Pickwick and his three companions stationed themselves in the front rank of the crowd, and patiently awaited the commencement of the proceedings. The throng was increasing every moment; and the efforts they were compelled to make, to retain the position they had gained, sufficiently occupied their attention during the two hours that ensued. At one time there was a sudden pressure from behind; and then Mr. Pickwick was jerked forward for several yards, with a degree of speed and elasticity highly inconsistent with the general gravity of his demeanour; at another moment there was a request to "keep back" from the front, and then the butt-end of a musket was either dropped upon Mr. Pickwick's toe, to remind him of the demand, or thrust into his chest, to ensure its being complied with. Then some facetious gentlemen on the left, after pressing sideways in a body, and squeezing Mr. Snodgrass into the very last extreme of human torture, would request to know "vere he vos a shovin' to;" and when Mr. Winkle had done expressing his excessive indignation at witnessing this unprovoked assault, some person behind would knock his hat over his eyes, and beg the favour of his putting his head in his pocket. These, and other practical witticisms, coupled with the unaccountable absence of Mr. Tupman (who had suddenly disappeared, and was nowhere to be found), rendered their situation upon the whole rather more uncomfortable than pleasing or desirable.

At length that low roar of many voices ran through the crowd, which usually announces the arrival of whatever they have been waiting for. All eyes were turned in the direction of the sally-port. A few moments of eager expectation, and colours were seen fluttering gaily in the air, arms glistened brightly in the sun, column after column poured on to the plain. The troops halted and formed; the word of command rung through the line, there was a general clash of muskets as arms were presented; and the commander-in-chief, attended by Colonel Bulder and numerous officers, cantered to the front. The military bands struck up altogether; the horses stood upon two legs each, cantered backwards, and whisked their tails about in all directions: the dogs barked, the mob screamed, the troops recovered, and nothing was to be seen on either side, as far as the eye could reach, but a long perspective of red coats and white trousers, fixed and motionless.

Mr. Pickwick had been so fully occupied in falling about, and disentangling himself, miraculously, from between the legs of horses, that he had not enjoyed sufficient leisure to observe the scene before him, until it assumed the appearance we have just described. When he was at last enabled to stand firmly on his legs, his gratification and delight were unbounded.

"Can anything be finer or more delightful?" he inquired of Mr. Winkle.

"Nothing," replied that gentleman, who had had a short man standing on each of his feet for the quarter of an hour immediately preceding.

"It is indeed a noble and a brilliant sight," said Mr. Snodgrass, in whose bosom a blaze of poetry was rapidly bursting forth, "to see the gallant defenders of their country drawn up in brilliant array before its peaceful citizens; their faces beaming—not with warlike ferocity, but with civilised gentleness; their eyes flashing—not with the rude fire of rapine or revenge, but with the soft light of humanity and intelligence."

Mr. Pickwick fully entered into the spirit of this eulogium, but he could not exactly re-echo its terms; for the soft light of intelligence burnt rather feebly in the eyes of the warriors, inasmuch as the command "eyes front" had been given, and all the spectator saw before him was several thousand pairs of optics, staring straight forward, wholly divested of any expression whatever.

"We are in a capital situation now," said Mr. Pickwick, looking round him. The crowd had gradually dispersed in their immediate vicinity, and they were nearly alone.

"Capital!" echoed both Mr. Snodgrass and Mr. Winkle.

"What are they doing now?" inquired Mr. Pickwick, adjusting his spectacles.

"I—I—rather think," said Mr. Winkle, changing colour —"I rather think they're going to fire."

A TRYING SITUATION.

"Nonsense," said Mr. Pickwick, hastily.

"I—I—really think they are," urged Mr. Snodgrass, somewhat alarmed.

"Impossible," replied Mr. Pickwick. He had hardly uttered the word, when the whole half-dozen regiments levelled their muskets as if they had but one common object, and that object the Pickwickians, and burst forth with the most awful and tremendous discharge that ever shook the earth to its centre, or an elderly gentleman off his.

It was in this trying situation, exposed to a galling fire of blank cartridges, and harassed by the operations of the military, a fresh body of whom had begun to fall in on the opposite side, that Mr. Pickwick displayed that perfect coolness and self-possession, which are the indispensable accompaniments of a great mind. He seized Mr. Winkle by the arm, and placing himself between that gentleman and Mr. Snodgrass, earnestly besought them to remember that beyond the possibility of being rendered deaf by the noise, there was no immediate danger to be apprehended from the firing.

"But—but—suppose some of the men should happen to have ball cartridges by mistake," remonstrated Mr. Winkle, pallid at the supposition he was himself conjuring up. "I heard something whistle through the air just now—so sharp; close to my ear."

"We had better throw ourselves on our faces, hadn't we?" said Mr. Snodgrass.

"No, no—it's over now," said Mr. Pickwick. His lip might quiver, and his cheek might blanch, but no expression of fear or concern escaped the lips of that immortal man.

Mr. Pickwick was right: the firing ceased; but he had scarcely time to congratulate himself on the accuracy of his opinion, when a quick movement was visible in the line: the hoarse shout of the word of command ran along it, and before either of the party could form a guess at the meaning of this new manœuvre, the whole of the half-dozen regiments, with fixed bayonets, charged at double quick time down upon

57

the very spot on which Mr. Pickwick and his friends were stationed.

Man is but mortal: and there is a point beyond which human courage cannot extend. Mr. Pickwick gazed through his spectacles for an instant on the advancing mass, and then fairly turned his back and—we will not say fled; firstly, because it is an ignoble term, and, secondly, because Mr. Pickwick's figure was by no means adapted for that mode of retreat—he trotted away, at as quick a rate as his legs would convey him; so quickly, indeed, that he did not perceive the awkwardness of his situation, to the full extent, until too late.

The opposite troops, whose falling-in had perplexed Mr. Pickwick a few seconds before, were drawn up to repel the mimic attack of the sham besiegers of the citadel; and the consequence was that Mr. Pickwick and his two companions found themselves suddenly inclosed between two lines of great length, the one advancing at a rapid pace, and the other firmly waiting the collision in hostile array.

"Hoi!" shouted the officers of the advancing line.

"Get out of the way," cried the officers of the stationary one.

"Where are we to go to?" screamed the agitated Pickwickians.

"Hoi—hoi—hoi!" was the only reply. There was a moment of intense bewilderment, a heavy tramp of footsteps, a violent concussion, a smothered laugh; the half-dozen regiments were half a thousand yards off, and the soles of Mr. Pickwick's boots were elevated in air.

Mr. Snodgrass and Mr. Winkle had each performed a compulsory somerset with remarkable agility, when the first object that met the eyes of the latter as he sat on the ground, staunching with a yellow silk handkerchief the stream of life which issued from his nose, was his venerated leader at some distance off, running after his own hat, which was gamboling playfully away in perspective.

There are very few moments in a man's existence when he

experiences so much ludicrous distress, or meets with so little charitable commiseration, as when he is in pursuit of his own hat. A vast deal of coolness, and a peculiar degree of judgment, are requisite in catching a hat. A man must not be precipitate, or he runs over it; he must not rush into the opposite extreme, or he loses it altogether. The best way is, to keep gently up with the object of pursuit, to be wary and cautious, to watch your opportunity well, get gradually before it, then make a rapid dive, seize it by the crown, and stick it firmly on your head: smiling pleasantly all the time, as if you thought it as good a joke as anybody else.

There was a fine gentle wind, and Mr. Pickwick's hat rolled sportively before it. The wind puffed, and Mr. Pickwick puffed, and the hat rolled over and over as merrily as a lively porpoise in a strong tide; and on it might have rolled, far beyond Mr. Pickwick's reach, had not its course been providentially stopped, just as that gentleman was on the point of resigning it to its fate.

Mr. Pickwick, we say, was completely exhausted, and about to give up the chase, when the hat was blown with some violence against the wheel of a carriage, which was drawn up in a line with half-a-dozen other vehicles on the spot to which his steps had been directed. Mr. Pickwick, perceiving his advantage, darted briskly forward, secured his property, planted it on his head, and paused to take breath. He had not been stationary half a minute, when he heard his own name eagerly pronounced by a voice, which he at once recognised as Mr. Tupman's, and, looking upwards, he beheld a sight which filled him with surprise and pleasure.

In an open barouche, the horses of which had been taken out, the better to accommodate it to the crowded place, stood a stout old gentleman, in a blue coat and bright buttons, corduroy breeches and top boots, two young ladies in scarfs and feathers, a young gentleman apparently enamoured of one of the young ladies in scarfs and feathers, a lady of doubtful age, probably the aunt of the aforesaid, and Mr.

Tupman, as easy and unconcerned as if he had belonged to the family from the first moments of his infancy. Fastened up behind the barouche was a hamper of spacious dimensions —one of those hampers which always awakens in a contemplative mind associations connected with cold fowls, tongues, and bottles of wine—and on the box sat a fat and red-faced boy, in a state of somnolency, whom no speculative observer could have regarded for an instant without setting down as the official dispenser of the contents of the before-mentioned hamper, when the proper time for their consumption should arrive.

Mr. Pickwick had bestowed a hasty glance on these interesting objects, when he was again greeted by his faithful disciple.

" Pickwick—Pickwick," said Mr. Tupman : " come up here. Make haste."

" Come along, sir. Pray, come up," said the stout gentleman. " Joe !—damn that boy, he's gone to sleep again.— Joe, let down the steps." The fat boy rolled slowly off the box, let down the steps, and held the carriage door invitingly open. Mr. Snodgrass and Mr. Winkle came up at the moment.

" Room for you all, gentlemen," said the stout man. " Two inside, and one out. Joe, make room for one of these gentlemen on the box. Now, sir, come along ; " and the stout gentleman extended his arm, and pulled first Mr. Pickwick, and then Mr. Snodgrass, into the barouche by main force. Mr. Winkle mounted to the box, the fat boy waddled to the same perch, and fell fast asleep instantly.

" Well, gentlemen," said the stout man, " very glad to see you. Know you very well, gentlemen, though you mayn't remember me. I spent some ev'nins at your club last winter —picked up my friend Mr. Tupman here this morning, and very glad I was to see him. Well, sir, and how are you ? You do look uncommon well, to be sure."

Mr. Pickwick acknowledged the compliment, and cordially shook hands with the stout gentleman in the top boots.

Mr. Pickwick in Chase of his Hat

ASTOUNDING EVOLUTIONS.

"Well, and how are you, sir?" said the stout gentleman, addressing Mr Snodgrass with paternal anxiety. "Charming, eh? Well, that's right—that's right. And how are you, sir (to Mr. Winkle)? Well, I am glad to hear you say you are well; very glad I am, to be sure. My daughters, gentlemen —my gals these are; and that's my sister, Miss Rachael Wardle. She's a Miss, she is; and yet she an't a Miss—eh, sir, eh?" And the stout gentleman playfully inserted his elbow between the ribs of Mr. Pickwick, and laughed very heartily.

"Lor, brother?" said Miss Wardle, with a deprecating smile.

"True, true," said the stout gentleman; "no one can deny it. Gentlemen, I beg your pardon; this is my friend Mr. Trundle. And now you all know each other, let's be comfortable and happy, and see what's going forward; that's what I say." So the stout gentleman put on his spectacles, and Mr. Pickwick pulled out his glass, and everybody stood up in the carriage, and looked over somebody else's shoulder at the evolutions of the military.

Astounding evolutions they were, one rank firing over the heads of another rank, and then running away; and then the other rank firing over the heads of another rank, and running away in their turn; and then forming squares, with officers in the centre; and then descending the trench on one side with scaling ladders, and ascending it on the other again by the same means; and knocking down barricades of baskets, and behaving in the most gallant manner possible. Then there was such a ramming down of the contents of enormous guns on the battery, with instruments like magnified mops; such a preparation before they were let off, and such an awful noise when they did go, that the air resounded with the screams of ladies. The young Miss Wardles were so frightened, that Mr. Trundle was actually obliged to hold one of them up in the carriage, while Mr. Snodgrass supported the other, and Mr. Wardle's sister suffered under such a dreadful state of nervous alarm, that Mr. Tupman found it indispensably necessary to put his arm round her waist, to keep her up at all. Everybody was excited, except the fat boy, and he slept as soundly as if the roaring of cannon were his ordinary lullaby.

"Joe, Joe!" said the stout gentleman, when the citadel was taken, and the besiegers and besieged sat down to dinner. "Damn that boy, he's gone to sleep again. Be good enough to pinch him, sir—in the leg, if you please; nothing else wakes him—thank you. Undo the hamper, Joe."

The fat boy, who had been effectually roused by the compression of a portion of his leg between the finger and thumb of Mr. Winkle, rolled off the box once again, and proceeded to unpack the hamper, with more expedition than could have been expected from his previous inactivity.

"Now, we must sit close," said the stout gentleman. After a great many jokes about squeezing the ladies' sleeves, and a vast quantity of blushing at sundry jocose proposals, that the ladies should sit in the gentlemen's laps, the whole party were stowed down in the barouche; and the stout gentleman proceeded to hand the things from the fat boy (who had mounted up behind for the purpose) into the carriage.

"Now, Joe, knives and forks." The knives and forks were handed in, and the ladies and gentlemen inside, and Mr. Winkle on the box, were each furnished with those useful instruments.

"Plates, Joe, plates." A similiar process employed in the distribution of the crockery.

"Now, Joe, the fowls. Damn that boy; he's gone to sleep again. Joe! Joe!" (Sundry taps on the head with a stick, and the fat boy, with some difficulty, roused from his lethargy). "Come, hand in the eatables."

There was something in the sound of the last word which roused the unctuous boy. He jumped up: and the leaden eyes, which twinkled behind his mountainous cheeks, leered horribly upon the food as he unpacked it from the basket.

"Now make haste," said Mr. Wardle; for the fat boy was hanging fondly over a capon, which he seemed wholly unable to part with. The boy sighed deeply, and, bestowing an ardent gaze upon its plumpness, unwillingly consigned it to his master.

"That's right—look sharp. Now the tongue—now the pigeon-pie. Take care of that veal and ham—mind the lobsters—take the salad out of the cloth—give me the dressing." Such were the hurried orders which issued from the lips of Mr. Wardle, as he handed in the different articles described, and placed dishes in everybody's hands, and on everybody's knees, in endless number.

"Now, an't this capital?" inquired that jolly personage, when the work of destruction had commenced.

"Capital!" said Mr. Winkle, who was carving a fowl on the box.

"Glass of wine?"

"With the greatest pleasure."

"You'd better have a bottle to yourself, up there, hadn't you?"

"You're very good."

"Joe!"

"Yes, sir." (He wasn't asleep this time, having just succeeded in abstracting a veal patty).

"Bottle of wine to the gentleman on the box. Glad to see you, sir."

"Thankee." Mr. Winkle emptied his glass, and placed the bottle on the coach-box, by his side.

"Will you permit me to have the pleasure, sir?" said Mr. Trundle to Mr. Winkle.

"With great pleasure," replied Mr. Winkle to Mr. Trundle: and then the two gentlemen took wine, after which they took a glass of wine round, ladies and all.

"How dear Emily is flirting with the stranger gentleman,"

whispered the spinster aunt, with true spinster-aunt-like envy, to her brother Mr. Wardle.

"Oh! I don't know," said the jolly old gentleman; "all very natural, I dare say—nothing unusual. Mr. Pickwick, some wine, sir?" Mr. Pickwick, who had been deeply investigating the interior of the pigeon-pie, readily assented.

"Emily, my dear," said the spinster aunt, with a patronising air, "don't talk so loud, love."

"Lor, aunt!"

"Aunt and the little old gentleman want to have it all to themselves, I think," whispered Miss Isabella Wardle to her sister Emily. The young ladies laughed very heartily, and the old one tried to look amiable, but couldn't manage it.

"Young girls have *such* spirits," said Miss Wardle to Mr. Tupman, with an air of gentle commiseration, as if animal spirits were contraband, and their possession without a permit, a high crime and misdemeanour.

"Oh, they have," replied Mr. Tupman, not exactly making the sort of reply that was expected from him. "It's quite delightful."

"Hem!" said Miss Wardle, rather dubiously.

"Will you permit me," said Mr. Tupman, in his blandest manner, touching the enchanting Rachael's wrist with one hand, and gently elevating the bottle with the other. "Will you permit me?"

"Oh, sir!" Mr. Tupman looked most impressive; and Rachael expressed her fear that more guns were going off, in which case, of course, she would have required support again.

"Do you think my dear nieces pretty?" whispered their affectionate aunt to Mr. Tupman.

"I should, if their aunt wasn't here," replied the ready Pickwickian, with a passionate glance.

"Oh, you naughty man—but really, if their complexions were a little *little* better, don't you think they would be nice-looking girls—by candle-light?"

THE AMIABLE AUNT.

"Yes; I think they would;" said Mr. Tupman, with an air of indifference.

"Oh, you quiz—I know what you were going to say."

"What?" inquired Mr. Tupman, who had not precisely made up his mind to say anything at all.

"You were going to say, that Isabel stoops—I know you were—you men are such observers. Well, so she does; it can't be denied; and, certainly, if there is one thing more than another that makes a girl look ugly, it is stooping. I often tell her, that when she gets a little older, she'll be quite frightful. Well, you *are* a quiz!"

Mr. Tupman had no objection to earning the reputation at so cheap a rate: so he looked very knowing, and smiled mysteriously.

"What a sarcastic smile," said the admiring Rachael; "I declare I'm quite afraid of you."

"Afraid of me!"

"Oh, you can't disguise anything from me—I know what that smile means, very well."

"What?" said Mr. Tupman, who had not the slightest notion himself.

"You mean," said the amiable aunt, sinking her voice still lower—"You mean, that you don't think Isabella's stooping is as bad as Emily's boldness. Well, she *is* bold! You cannot think how wretched it makes me sometimes. I'm sure I cry about it for hours together—my dear brother is *so* good, and *so* unsuspicious, that he never sees it; if he did, I'm quite certain it would break his heart. I wish I could think it was only manner—I hope it may be—" (here the affectionate relative heaved a deep sigh, and shook her head despondingly.)

"I'm sure aunt's talking about us," whispered Miss Emily Wardle to her sister—"I'm quite certain of it—she looks so malicious."

"Is she?" replied Isabella—"Hem! aunt dear!"

"Yes, my dear love!"

"I'm *so* afraid you'll catch cold, aunt—have a silk handkerchief to tie round your dear old head—you really should take care of yourself—consider your age!"

However well deserved this piece of retaliation might have been, it was as vindictive a one as could well have been resorted to. There is no guessing in what form of reply the aunt's indignation would have vented itself, had not Mr. Wardle unconsciously changed the subject, by calling emphatically for Joe.

"Damn that boy," said the old gentleman, "he's gone to sleep again."

"Very extraordinary boy, that," said Mr. Pickwick, "does he always sleep in this way!"

"Sleep!" said the old gentleman, "he's always asleep. Goes on errands fast asleep, and snores as he waits at table."

"How very odd!" said Mr. Pickwick.

"Ah! odd indeed," returned the old gentleman; "I'm proud of that boy—wouldn't part with him on any account —he's a natural curiosity! Here, Joe—Joe—take these things away, and open another bottle—d'ye hear?"

The fat boy rose, opened his eyes, swallowed the huge piece of pie he had been in the act of masticating when he last fell asleep, and slowly obeyed his master's orders—gloating languidly over the remains of the feast, as he removed the plates, and deposited them in the hamper. The fresh bottle was produced, and speedily emptied: the hamper was made fast in its old place—the fat boy once more mounted the box —the spectacles and pocket-glass were again adjusted and the evolutions of the military recommenced. There was a great fizzing and banging of guns, and starting of ladies—and then a mine was sprung, to the gratification of everybody—and when the mine had gone off, the military and the company followed its example, and went off too.

"Now, mind," said the old gentleman, as he shook hands with Mr. Pickwick at the conclusion of a conversation which had been carried on at intervals, during the conclusion of the proceedings—"we shall see you all to-morrow."

"Most certainly," replied Mr. Pickwick.

"You have got the address."

"Manor Farm, Dingley Dell," said Mr. Pickwick, consulting his pocket-book.

"That's it," said the old gentleman. "I don't let you off, mind, under a week; and undertake that you shall see everything worth seeing. If you've come down for a country life, come to me, and I'll give you plenty of it. Joe—damn that boy, he's gone to sleep again—Joe, help Tom put in the horses."

The horses were put in—the driver mounted—the fat boy clambered up by his side—farewells were exchanged—and the carriage rattled off. As the Pickwickians turned round to take a last glimpse of it, the setting sun cast a rich glow on the faces of their entertainers, and fell upon the form of the fat boy. His head was sunk upon his bosom; and he slumbered again.

CHAPTER V.

A SHORT ONE. SHOWING, AMONG OTHER MATTERS, HOW MR. PICK-
WICK UNDERTOOK TO DRIVE, AND MR. WINKLE TO RIDE ; AND
HOW THEY BOTH DID IT.

BRIGHT and pleasant was the sky, balmy the air, and beautiful
the appearance of every object around, as Mr. Pickwick leant
over the balustrades of Rochester Bridge, contemplating nature,
and waiting for breakfast. The scene was indeed one which
might well have charmed a far less reflective mind, than that
to which it was presented.

On the left of the spectator lay the ruined wall, broken in
many places, and in some, overhanging the narrow beach below
in rude and heavy masses. Huge knots of sea-weed hung
upon the jagged and pointed stones, trembling in every breath
of wind ; and the green ivy clung mournfully round the dark
and ruined battlements. Behind it rose the ancient castle,
its towers roofless, and its massive walls crumbling away, but
telling us proudly of its own might and strength, as when,
seven hundred years ago, it rang with the clash of arms, or
resounded with the noise of feasting and revelry. On either
side, the banks of the Medway, covered with corn-fields and
pastures, with here and there a windmill, or a distant church,
stretched away as far as the eye could see, presenting a rich
and varied landscape, rendered more beautiful by the changing shadows which passed swiftly across it, as the thin and
half-formed clouds skimmed away in the light of the morning
sun. The river, reflecting the clear blue of the sky, glistened

and sparkled as it flowed noiselessly on; and the oars of the fishermen dipped into the water with a clear and liquid sound, as the heavy but picturesque boats glided slowly down the stream.

Mr. Pickwick was roused from the agreeable reverie into which he had been led by the objects before him, by a deep sigh, and a touch on his shoulder. He turned round: and the dismal man was at his side.

"Contemplating the scene?" inquired the dismal man.

"I was," said Mr. Pickwick.

"And congratulating yourself on being up so soon?" Mr. Pickwick nodded assent.

"Ah! people need to rise early, to see the sun in all his splendour, for his brightness seldom lasts the day through. The morning of day and the morning of life are but too much alike."

"You speak truly, sir," said Mr. Pickwick.

"How common the saying," continued the dismal man, "'The morning's too fine to last.' How well might it be applied to our every-day existence. God! what would I forfeit to have the days of my childhood restored, or to be able to forget them for ever!"

"You have seen much trouble, sir," said Mr. Pickwick, compassionately.

"I have," said the dismal man, hurriedly; "I have. More than those who see me now would believe possible." He paused for an instant, and then said, abruptly—

"Did it ever strike you, on such a morning as this, that drowning would be happiness and peace?"

"God bless me, no!" replied Mr. Pickwick, edging a little from the balustrade, as the possibility of the dismal man's tipping him over, by way of experiment, occurred to him rather forcibly.

"*I* have thought so, often," said the dismal man, without noticing the action. "The calm, cool water seems to me to murmur an invitation to repose and rest. A bound, a splash, a brief struggle; there is an eddy for an instant, it gradually subsides into a gentle ripple; the waters have closed above your head, and the world has closed upon your miseries and misfortunes for ever." The sunken eye of the dismal man flashed brightly as he spoke, but the momentary excitement quickly subsided; and he turned calmly away, as he said—

"There—enough of that. I wish to see you on another subject. You invited me to read that paper, the night before last, and listened attentively while I did so."

"I did," replied Mr. Pickwick; "and I certainly thought——"

"I asked for no opinion," said the dismal man, interrupting him, "and I want none. You are travelling for amusement and instruction. Suppose I forwarded you a curious manuscript—observe, not curious because wild or improbable, but curious as a leaf from the romance of real life. Would you communicate it to the club, of which you have spoken so frequently?"

"Certainly," replied Mr. Pickwick, "if you wished it; and it would be entered on their transactions."

"You shall have it," replied the dismal man. "Your address;" and, Mr. Pickwick having communicated their probable route, the dismal man carefully noted it down in a greasy pocket-book, and, resisting Mr. Pickwick's pressing invitation to breakfast, left that gentleman at his inn, and walked slowly away.

Mr. Pickwick found that his three companions had risen, and were waiting his arrival to commence breakfast, which was ready laid in tempting display. They sat down to the meal; and broiled ham, eggs, tea, coffee, and sundries, began to disappear with a rapidity which at once bore testimony to the excellence of the fare, and the appetites of its consumers.

"Now, about Manor Farm," said Mr. Pickwick. "How shall we go?"

"We had better consult the waiter, perhaps," said Mr. Tupman, and the waiter was summoned accordingly.

TRAVELLING ARRANGEMENTS.

" Dingley Dell, gentlemen—fifteen miles, gentlemen—cross road—post-chaise, sir ? "

" Post-chaise won't hold more than two," said Mr. Pickwick.

" True, sir—beg your pardon, sir.—Very nice four-wheeled chaise, sir—seat for two behind—one in front for the gentleman that drives—oh ! beg your pardon, sir—that'll only hold three."

" What's to be done ? " said Mr. Snodgrass.

" Perhaps one of the gentlemen would like to ride, sir ? " suggested the waiter, looking towards Mr. Winkle; " very good saddle horses, sir—any of Mr. Wardle's men coming to Rochester bring 'em back, sir."

" The very thing," said Mr. Pickwick. " Winkle, will you go on horseback ? "

Mr. Winkle did entertain considerable misgivings in the very lowest recesses of his own heart, relative to his equestrian skill; but, as he would not have them even suspected on any account, he at once replied with great hardihood, " Certainly. I should enjoy it, of all things."

Mr. Winkle had rushed upon his fate; there was no resource. " Let them be at the door by eleven," said Mr. Pickwick.

" Very well, sir," replied the waiter.

The waiter retired; the breakfast concluded; and the travellers ascended to their respective bed-rooms, to prepare a change of clothing, to take with them on their approaching expedition.

Mr. Pickwick had made his preliminary arrangements, and was looking over the coffee-room blinds at the passengers in the street, when the waiter entered, and announced that the chaise was ready—an announcement which the vehicle itself confirmed, by forthwith appearing before the coffee-room blinds aforesaid.

It was a curious little green box on four wheels, with a low place like a wine-bin for two behind, and an elevated perch for one in front, drawn by an immense brown horse, displaying great symmetry of bone. An hostler stood near, holding

71

by the bridle another immense horse—apparently a near relative of the animal in the chaise—ready saddled for Mr. Winkle.

"Bless my soul!" said Mr. Pickwick, as they stood upon the pavement while the coats were being put in. "Bless my soul! who's to drive? I never thought of that."

"Oh! you, of course," said Mr. Tupman.

"Of course," said Mr. Snodgrass.

"I!" exclaimed Mr. Pickwick.

"Not the slightest fear, sir," interposed the hostler. "Warrant him quiet, sir; a hinfant in arms might drive him."

"He don't shy, does he?" inquired Mr. Pickwick.

"Shy, sir?—He wouldn't shy if he was to meet a vaggin-load of monkeys with their tails burnt off."

The last recommendation was indisputable. Mr. Tupman and Mr. Snodgrass got into the bin; Mr. Pickwick ascended to his perch, and deposited his feet on a floor-clothed shelf, erected beneath it for that purpose.

"Now, shiny Villiam," said the hostler to the deputy hostler, "give the gen'lm'n the ribbins." "Shiny Villiam" —so called, probably, from his sleek hair and oily countenance—placed the reins in Mr. Pickwick's left hand; and the upper hostler thrust a whip into his right.

"Wo—o!" cried Mr. Pickwick, as the tall quadruped evinced a decided inclination to back into the coffee-room window.

"Wo—o!" echoed Mr. Tupman and Mr. Snodgrass, from the bin.

"Only his playfulness, gen'lm'n," said the head hostler encouragingly; "jist kitch hold on him, Villiam." The deputy restrained the animal's impetuosity, and the principal ran to assist Mr. Winkle in mounting.

"T'other side, sir, if you please."

"Blowed if the gen'lm'n worn't a gettin' up on the wrong side," whispered a grinning post-boy to the inexpressibly gratified waiter.

EQUINE PECULIARITIES.

Mr. Winkle, thus instructed, climbed into his saddle, with about as much difficulty as he would have experienced in getting up the side of a first-rate man-of-war.

"All right?" inquired Mr. Pickwick, with an inward presentiment that it was all wrong.

"All right," replied Mr. Winkle faintly.

"Let 'em go," cried the hostler,—"Hold him in, sir," and away went the chaise, and the saddle-horse, with Mr. Pickwick on the box of the one, and Mr. Winkle on the back of the other, to the delight and gratification of the whole inn yard.

"What makes him go sideways?" said Mr. Snodgrass in the bin, to Mr. Winkle in the saddle.

"I can't imagine," replied Mr. Winkle. His horse was drifting up the street in the most mysterious manner—side first, with his head towards one side of the way, and his tail towards the other.

Mr. Pickwick had no leisure to observe either this or any other particular, the whole of his faculties being concentrated in the management of the animal attached to the chaise, who displayed various peculiarities, highly interesting to a by-stander, but by no means equally amusing to any one seated behind him. Besides constantly jerking his head up, in a very unpleasant and uncomfortable manner, and tugging at the reins to an extent which rendered it a matter of great difficulty for Mr. Pickwick to hold them, he had a singular propensity for darting suddenly every now and then to the side of the road, then stopping short, and then rushing forward for some minutes, at a speed which it was wholly impossible to control.

"What *can* he mean by this?" said Mr. Snodgrass, when the horse had executed this manœuvre for the twentieth time.

"I don't know," replied Mr. Tupman; "it *looks* very like shying, don't it?" Mr. Snodgrass was about to reply, when he was interrupted by a shout from Mr. Pickwick.

"Woo!" said that gentleman; "I have dropped my whip."

"Winkle," said Mr. Snodgrass, as the equestrian came trotting up on the tall horse, with his hat over his ears, and shaking all over, as if he would shake to pieces, with the violence of the exercise, "pick up the whip, there's a good fellow." Mr. Winkle pulled at the bridle of the tall horse till he was black in the face; and having at length succeeded in stopping him, dismounted, handed the whip to Mr. Pickwick, and grasping the reins, prepared to remount.

Now whether the tall horse, in the natural playfulness of his disposition, was desirous of having a little innocent recreation with Mr. Winkle, or whether it occurred to him that he could perform the journey as much to his own satisfaction without a rider as with one, are points upon which, of course, we can arrive at no definite and distinct conclusion. By whatever motives the animal was actuated, certain it is that Mr. Winkle had no sooner touched the reins, than he slipped them over his head, and darted backwards to their full length.

"Poor fellow," said Mr. Winkle, soothingly,—"poor fellow—good old horse." The "poor fellow" was proof against flattery: the more Mr. Winkle tried to get nearer him, the more he sidled away; and, notwithstanding all kinds of coaxing and wheedling, there were Mr. Winkle and the horse going round and round each other for ten minutes, at the end of which time each was at precisely the same distance from the other as when they first commenced—an unsatisfactory sort of thing under any circumstances, but particularly so in a lonely road, where no assistance can be procured.

"What am I to do?" shouted Mr. Winkle, after the dodging had been prolonged for a considerable time. "What am I to do? I can't get on him."

"You had better lead him till we come to a turnpike," replied Mr. Pickwick from the chaise.

"But he won't come!" roared Mr. Winkle. "Do come, and hold him."

Mr. Pickwick was the very personation of kindness and

Winkle Soothes the Refractory Mare

humanity : he threw the reins on the horse's back, and having descended from his seat, carefully drew the chaise into the hedge, lest anything should come along the road, and stepped back to the assistance of his distressed companion, leaving Mr. Tupman and Mr. Snodgrass in the vehicle.

The horse no sooner beheld Mr. Pickwick advancing towards him with the chaise whip in his hand, than he exchanged the rotatory motion in which he had previously indulged, for a retrograde movement of so very determined a character, that it at once drew Mr. Winkle, who was still at the end of the bridle, at a rather quicker rate than fast walking, in the direction from which they had just come. Mr. Pickwick ran to his assistance, but the faster Mr. Pickwick ran forward, the faster the horse ran backward. There was a great scraping of feet, and kicking up of the dust; and at last Mr. Winkle, his arms being nearly pulled out of their sockets, fairly let go his hold. The horse paused, stared, shook his head, turned round, and quietly trotted home to Rochester, leaving Mr. Winkle and Mr. Pickwick gazing on each other with countenances of blank dismay. A rattling noise at a little distance attracted their attention. They looked up.

"Bless my soul!" exclaimed the agonized Mr. Pickwick, "there's the other horse running away!"

It was but too true. The animal was startled by the noise, and the reins were on his back. The result may be guessed. He tore off with the four-wheeled chaise behind him, and Mr. Tupman and Mr. Snodgrass in the four-wheeled chaise. The heat was a short one. Mr. Tupman threw himself into the hedge, Mr. Snodgrass followed his example, the horse dashed the four-wheeled chaise against a wooden bridge, separated the wheels from the body, and the bin from the perch : and finally stood stock still to gaze upon the ruin he had made.

The first care of the two unspilt friends was to extricate their unfortunate companions from their bed of quickset—a process which gave them the unspeakable satisfaction of discovering that they had sustained no injury, beyond sundry rents in their garments, and various lacerations from the brambles. The next thing to be done was, to unharness the horse. This complicated process having been effected, the party walked slowly forward, leading the horse among them, and abandoning the chaise to its fate.

An hour's walking brought the travellers to a little road-side public-house, with two elm trees, a horse trough, and a sign-post, in front; one or two deformed hay-ricks behind, a kitchen garden at the side, and rotten sheds and mouldering out-houses jumbled in strange confusion all about it. A red-headed man was working in the garden; and to him Mr. Pickwick called lustily—"Hallo there!"

The red-headed man raised his body, shaded his eyes with his hand, and stared, long and coolly, at Mr. Pickwick and his companions.

"Hallo there!" repeated Mr. Pickwick.

"Hallo!" was the red-headed man's reply.

"How far is it to Dingley Dell?"

"Better er seven mile."

"Is it a good road?"

"No, t'ant." Having uttered this brief reply, and apparently satisfied himself with another scrutiny, the red-headed man resumed his work.

"We want to put this horse up here," said Mr. Pickwick; "I suppose we can, can't we?"

"Want to put that ere horse up, do ee?" repeated the red-headed man, leaning on his spade.

"Of course," replied Mr. Pickwick, who had by this time advanced, horse in hand, to the garden rails.

"Missus"—roared the man with the red head, emerging from the garden, and looking very hard at the horse— "Missus!"

A tall bony woman—straight all the way down—in a coarse blue pelisse, with the waist an inch or two below her arm-pits, responded to the call.

"Can we put this horse up here, my good woman?" said

MR. PICKWICK INDIGNANT.

Mr. Tupman, advancing, and speaking in his most seductive tones. The woman looked very hard at the whole party; and the red-headed man whispered something in her ear.

"No," replied the woman, after a little consideration, "I'm afeerd on it."

"Afraid!" exclaimed Mr. Pickwick, "what's the woman afraid of?"

"It got us in trouble last time," said the woman, turning into the house; "I woant have nothin' to say to 'un."

"Most extraordinary thing I ever met with in my life," said the astonished Mr. Pickwick.

"I—I—really believe," whispered Mr. Winkle, as his friends gathered round him, "that they think we have come by this horse in some dishonest manner."

"What!" exclaimed Mr. Pickwick, in a storm of indignation. Mr. Winkle modestly repeated his suggestion.

"Hallo, you fellow!" said the angry Mr. Pickwick, "do you think we stole this horse?"

"I'm sure ye did," replied the red-headed man, with a grin which agitated his countenance from one auricular organ to the other. Saying which, he turned into the house, and banged the door after him.

"It's like a dream," ejaculated Mr. Pickwick, "a hideous dream. The idea of a man's walking about, all day, with a dreadful horse that he can't get rid of!" The depressed Pickwickians turned moodily away, with the tall quadruped, for which they all felt the most unmitigated disgust, following slowly at their heels.

It was late in the afternoon when the four friends and their four-footed companion turned into the lane leading to Manor Farm: and even when they were so near their place of destination, the pleasure they would otherwise have experienced was materially damped as they reflected on the singularity of their appearance, and the absurdity of their situation. Torn clothes, lacerated faces, dusty shoes, exhausted looks, and, above all, the horse. Oh, how Mr. Pickwick

cursed that horse: he had eyed the noble animal from time
to time with looks expressive of hatred and revenge; more
than once he had calculated the probable amount of the
expense he would incur by cutting his throat; and now the
temptation to destroy him, or to cast him loose upon the
world, rushed upon his mind with tenfold force. He was
roused from a meditation on these dire imaginings, by the
sudden appearance of two figures at a turn of the lane. It
was Mr. Wardle, and his faithful attendant, the fat boy.

"Why, where *have* you been?" said the hospitable old
gentleman; "I've been waiting for you all day. Well, you
do look tired. What! Scratches! Not hurt, I hope—eh?
Well, I *am* glad to hear that—very. So you've been spilt,
eh? Never mind. Common accident in these parts. Joe—
he's asleep again!—Joe, take that horse from the gentleman,
and lead it into the stable."

The fat boy sauntered heavily behind them with the
animal; and the old gentleman, condoling with his guests
in homely phrase on so much of the day's adventures as they
thought proper to communicate, led the way to the kitchen.

"We'll have you put to rights here," said the old gentleman,
"and then I'll introduce you to the people in the parlour.
Emma, bring out the cherry brandy; now, Jane, a needle
and thread here; towels and water, Mary. Come, girls, bustle
about."

Three or four buxom girls speedily dispersed in search of
the different articles in requisition, while a couple of large-
headed, circular-visaged males rose from their seats in the
chimney-corner (for although it was a May evening, their
attachment to the wood fire appeared as cordial as if it were
Christmas), and dived into some obscure recesses, from which
they speedily produced a bottle of blacking, and some half-
dozen brushes.

"Bustle!" said the old gentleman again, but the admonition
was quite unnecessary, for one of the girls poured out the
cherry brandy, and another brought in the towels, and one

of the men suddenly seizing Mr. Pickwick by the leg, at imminent hazard of throwing him off his balance, brushed away at his boot, till his corns were red-hot; while the other shampoo'd Mr. Winkle with a heavy clothes-brush, indulging, during the operation, in that hissing sound which hostlers are wont to produce when engaged in rubbing down a horse.

Mr. Snodgrass, having concluded his ablutions, took a survey of the room, while standing with his back to the fire, sipping his cherry brandy with heartfelt satisfaction. He describes it as a large apartment, with a red brick floor and a capacious chimney; the ceiling garnished with hams, sides of bacon, and ropes of onions. The walls were decorated with several hunting-whips, two or three bridles, a saddle and an old rusty blunderbuss, with an inscription below it, intimating that it was " Loaded "—as it had been, on the same authority, for half a century at least. An old eight-day clock, of solemn and sedate demeanour, ticked gravely in one corner; and a silver watch, of equal antiquity, dangled from one of the many hooks which ornamented the dresser.

" Ready ? " said the old gentleman inquiringly, when his guests had been washed, mended, brushed, and brandied.

" Quite," replied Mr. Pickwick.

" Come along, then," and the party having traversed several dark passages, and being joined by Mr. Tupman, who had lingered behind to snatch a kiss from Emma, for which he had been duly rewarded with sundry pushings and scratchings, arrived at the parlour door.

" Welcome," said their hospitable host, throwing it open and stepping forward to announce them, " Welcome, gentlemen, to Manor Farm."

CHAPTER VI.

AN OLD-FASHIONED CARD-PARTY. THE CLERGYMAN'S VERSES.
THE STORY OF THE CONVICT'S RETURN.

SEVERAL guests who were assembled in the old parlour rose
to greet Mr. Pickwick and his friends upon their entrance;
and during the performance of the ceremony of introduction,
with all due formalities, Mr. Pickwick had leisure to observe
the appearance, and speculate upon the characters and pursuits,
of the persons by whom he was surrounded—a habit in which
he in common with many other great men delighted to indulge.

A very old lady, in a lofty cap and faded silk gown—no
less a personage than Mr. Wardle's mother—occupied the
post of honour on the right-hand corner of the chimney-piece;
and various certificates of her having been brought up in the
way she should go when young, and of her not having departed
from it when old, ornamented the walls, in the form of
samplers of ancient date, worsted landscapes of equal antiquity,
and crimson silk tea-kettle holders of a more modern period.
The aunt, the two young ladies, and Mr. Wardle, each vying
with the other in paying zealous and unremitting attentions
to the old lady, crowded round her easy-chair, one holding
her ear-trumpet, another an orange, and a third a smelling-
bottle, while a fourth was busily engaged in patting and
punching the pillows which were arranged for her support.
On the opposite side sat a bald-headed old gentleman, with
a good-humoured benevolent face—the clergyman of Dingley
Dell; and next him sat his wife, a stout blooming old lady,

80

who looked as if she were well skilled, not only in the art and mystery of manufacturing home-made cordials greatly to other people's satisfaction, but of tasting them occasionally very much to her own. A little hard-headed, Ribston-pippin-faced man, was conversing with a fat old gentleman in one corner; and two or three more old gentlemen, and two or three more old ladies, sat bolt upright and motionless on their chairs, staring very hard at Mr. Pickwick and his fellow-voyagers.

"Mr. Pickwick, mother," said Mr. Wardle, at the very top of his voice.

"Ah!" said the old lady, shaking her head; "I can't hear you."

"Mr. Pickwick, grandma!" screamed both the young ladies together.

"Ah!" exclaimed the old lady. "Well; it don't much matter. He don't care for an old 'ooman like me, I dare say."

"I assure you, ma'am," said Mr. Pickwick, grasping the old lady's hand, and speaking so loud that the exertion imparted a crimson hue to his benevolent countenance, "I assure you, ma'am, that nothing delights me more than to see a lady of your time of life heading so fine a family, and looking so young and well."

"Ah!" said the old lady, after a short pause; "it's all very fine, I dare say; but I can't hear him."

"Grandma's rather put out now," said Miss Isabella Wardle, in a low tone; "but she'll talk to you presently."

Mr. Pickwick nodded his readiness to humour the infirmities of age, and entered into a general conversation with the other members of the circle.

"Delightful situation this," said Mr. Pickwick.

"Delightful!" echoed Messrs. Snodgrass, Tupman, and Winkle.

"Well, I think it is," said Mr. Wardle.

"There an't a better spot o' ground in all Kent, sir," said

the hard-headed man with the pippin-face; "there an't indeed, sir—I'm sure there an't, sir." The hard-headed man looked triumphantly round, as if he had been very much contradicted by somebody, but had got the better of him at last.

"There an't a better spot o' ground in all Kent," said the hard-headed man again, after a pause.

"'Cept Mullins's Meadows," observed the fat man solemnly.

"Mullins's Meadows!" ejaculated the other, with profound contempt.

"Ah, Mullins's Meadows," repeated the fat man.

"Reg'lar good land that," interposed another fat man.

"And so it is, sure-ly," said a third fat man.

"Everybody knows that," said the corpulent host.

The hard-headed man looked dubiously round, but finding himself in a minority, assumed a compassionate air, and said no more.

"What are they talking about?" inquired the old lady of one of her grand-daughters, in a very audible voice; for, like many deaf people, she never seemed to calculate on the possibility of other persons hearing what she said herself.

"About the land, grandma."

"What about the land?—Nothing the matter, is there?"

"No, no. Mr. Miller was saying our land was better than Mullins's Meadows."

"How should he know anything about it?" inquired the old lady indignantly. "Miller's a conceited coxcomb, and you may tell him I said so." Saying which, the old lady, quite unconscious that she had spoken above a whisper, drew herself up, and looked carving-knives at the hard-headed delinquent.

"Come, come," said the bustling host, with a natural anxiety to change the conversation,—"What say you to a rubber, Mr. Pickwick?"

"I should like it of all things," replied that gentleman; "but pray don't make up one on my account."

"Oh, I assure you, mother's very fond of a rubber," said Mr. Wardle; "an't you, mother?"

A CARD-PARTY.

The old lady, who was much less deaf on this subject than on any other, replied in the affirmative.

"Joe, Joe!" said the old gentleman; "Joe—damn that—oh, here he is; put out the card-tables."

The lethargic youth contrived without any additional rousing to set out two card-tables; the one for Pope Joan, and the other for whist. The whist-players were Mr. Pickwick and the old lady; Mr. Miller and the fat gentleman. The round game comprised the rest of the company.

The rubber was conducted with all that gravity of deportment and sedateness of demeanour which befit the pursuit entitled "whist"—a solemn observance, to which, as it appears to us, the title of "game" has been very irreverently and ignominiously applied. The round-game table, on the other hand, was so boisterously merry as materially to interrupt the contemplations of Mr. Miller, who, not being quite so much absorbed as he ought to have been, contrived to commit various high crimes and misdemeanours, which excited the wrath of the fat gentleman to a very great extent, and called forth the good-humour of the old lady in a proportionate degree.

"There!" said the criminal Miller triumphantly, as he took up the odd trick at the conclusion of a hand; "that could not have been played better, I flatter myself;—impossible to have made another trick!"

"Miller ought to have trumped the diamond, oughtn't he, sir?" said the old lady.

Mr. Pickwick nodded assent.

"Ought I, though?" said the unfortunate, with a doubtful appeal to his partner.

"You ought, sir," said the fat gentleman, in an awful voice.

"Very sorry," said the crest-fallen Miller.

"Much use that," growled the fat gentleman.

"Two by honours makes us eight," said Mr. Pickwick.

Another hand. "Can you one?" inquired the old lady.

"I can," replied Mr. Pickwick. "Double, single, and the rub."

"Never was such luck," said Mr. Miller.

"Never was such cards," said the fat gentleman.

A solemn silence: Mr. Pickwick humorous, the old lady serious, the fat gentleman captious, and Mr. Miller timorous.

"Another double," said the old lady: triumphantly making a memorandum of the circumstance, by placing one sixpence and a battered halfpenny under the candlestick.

"A double, sir," said Mr. Pickwick.

"Quite aware of the fact, sir," replied the fat gentleman, sharply.

Another game, with a similar result, was followed by a revoke from the unlucky Miller; on which the fat gentleman burst into a state of high personal excitement which lasted until the conclusion of the game, when he retired into a corner, and remained perfectly mute for one hour and twenty-seven minutes; at the end of which time he emerged from his retirement, and offered Mr. Pickwick a pinch of snuff with the air of a man who had made up his mind to a Christian forgiveness of injuries sustained. The old lady's hearing decidedly improved, and the unlucky Miller felt as much out of his element as a dolphin in a sentry-box.

Meanwhile the round game proceeded right merrily. Isabella Wardle and Mr. Trundle "went partners," and Emily Wardle and Mr. Snodgrass did the same; and even Mr. Tupman and the spinster aunt established a joint-stock company of fish and flattery. Old Mr. Wardle was in the very height of his jollity; and he was *so* funny in his management of the board, and the old ladies were *so* sharp after their winnings, that the whole table was in a perpetual roar of merriment and laughter. There was one old lady who always had about half a dozen cards to pay for, at which everybody laughed, regularly every round; and when the old lady looked cross at having to pay, they laughed louder than ever; on which the old lady's face gradually brightened up, till at last she laughed louder than any of them. Then, when the spinster aunt got "matrimony," the young ladies laughed afresh, and the spinster aunt seemed disposed to be pettish; till, feeling Mr. Tupman squeezing her hand under the table, *she* brightened up too, and looked rather knowing, as if matrimony in reality were not quite so far off as some people thought for; whereupon everybody laughed again, and especially old Mr. Wardle, who enjoyed a joke as much as the youngest. As to Mr. Snodgrass, he did nothing but whisper poetical sentiments into his partner's ear, which made one old gentleman facetiously sly, about partnerships at cards and partnerships for life, and caused the aforesaid old gentleman to make some remarks thereupon, accompanied with divers winks and chuckles, which made the company very merry and the old gentleman's wife especially so. And Mr. Winkle came out with jokes which are very well known in town, but are not at all known in the country : and as everybody laughed at them very heartily, and said they were very capital, Mr. Winkle was in a state of great honour and glory. And the benevolent clergyman looked pleasantly on ; for the happy faces which surrounded the table made the good old man feel happy too ; and though the merriment was rather boisterous, still it came from the heart and not from the lips : and this is the right sort of merriment, after all.

The evening glided swiftly away, in these cheerful recreations ; and when the substantial though homely supper had been despatched, and the little party formed a social circle round the fire, Mr. Pickwick thought he had never felt so happy in his life, and at no time so much disposed to enjoy, and make the most of, the passing moment.

"Now this," said the hospitable host, who was sitting in great state next the old lady's arm-chair, with her hand fast clasped in his—"This is just what I like—the happiest moments of my life have been passed at this old fire-side : and I am so attached to it, that I keep up a blazing fire here every evening, until it actually grows too hot to bear it. Why, my poor old mother, here, used to sit before this fire-place upon that little stool when she was a girl; didn't you, mother?"

The tear which starts unbidden to the eye when the recollection of old times and the happiness of many years ago is suddenly recalled, stole down the old lady's face as she shook her head with a melancholy smile.

"You must excuse my talking about this old place, Mr. Pickwick," resumed the host, after a short pause, "for I love it dearly, and know no other—the old houses and fields seem like living friends to me: and so does our little church with the ivy,—about which, by-the-bye, our excellent friend there made a song when he first came amongst us. Mr. Snodgrass, have you anything in your glass?"

"Plenty, thank you," replied that gentleman, whose poetic curiosity had been greatly excited by the last observations of his entertainer. "I beg your pardon, but you were talking about the song of the Ivy."

"You must ask our friend opposite about that," said the host knowingly: indicating the clergyman by a nod of his head.

"May I say that I should like to hear you repeat it, sir?" said Mr. Snodgrass.

"Why really," replied the clergyman, "it's a very slight affair; and the only excuse I have for having ever perpetrated it is, that I was a young man at the time. Such as it is, however, you shall hear it if you wish."

A murmur of curiosity was of course the reply; and the old gentleman proceeded to recite, with the aid of sundry promptings from his wife, the lines in question. "I call them," said he,

THE IVY GREEN.

OH, a dainty plant is the Ivy green,
That creepeth o'er ruins old!
Of right choice food are his meals I ween,
In his cell so lone and cold.
The wall must be crumbled, the stone decayed,
To pleasure his dainty whim:

> And the mouldering dust that years have made
> Is a merry meal for him.
> > Creeping where no life is seen,
> > A rare old plant is the Ivy green.
>
> Fast he stealeth on, though he wears no wings,
> And a staunch old heart has he.
> How closely he twineth, how tight he clings
> To his friend the huge Oak Tree!
> And slily he traileth along the ground,
> And his leaves he gently waves,
> As he joyously hugs and crawleth round
> The rich mould of dead men's graves.
> > Creeping where grim death has been,
> > A rare old plant is the Ivy green.
>
> Whole ages have fled and their works decayed,
> And nations have scattered been;
> But the stout old Ivy shall never fade,
> From its hale and hearty green.
> The brave old plant in its lonely days,
> Shall fatten upon the past:
> For the stateliest building man can raise,
> Is the Ivy's food at last.
> > Creeping on, where time has been,
> > A rare old plant is the Ivy green.

While the old gentleman repeated these lines a second time, to enable Mr. Snodgrass to note them down, Mr. Pickwick perused the lineaments of his face with an expression of great interest. The old gentleman having concluded his dictation, and Mr. Snodgrass having returned his note-book to his pocket, Mr. Pickwick said:

"Excuse me, sir, for making the remark on so short an acquaintance; but a gentleman like yourself cannot fail, I should think, to have observed many scenes and incidents worth recording, in the course of your experience as a minister of the Gospel."

"I have witnessed some certainly," replied the old gentleman; "but the incidents and characters have been of a homely and ordinary nature, my sphere of action being so very limited."

"You *did* make some notes, I think, about John Edmunds, did you not?" inquired Mr. Wardle, who appeared very desirous to draw his friend out, for the edification of his new visitors.

The old gentleman slightly nodded his head in token of assent, and was proceeding to change the subject, when Mr. Pickwick said—

"I beg your pardon, sir; but pray, if I may venture to inquire, who was John Edmunds?"

"The very thing I was about to ask," said Mr. Snodgrass, eagerly.

"You are fairly in for it," said the jolly host. "You must satisfy the curiosity of these gentlemen, sooner or later; so you had better take advantage of this favourable opportunity, and do so at once."

The old gentleman smiled good-humouredly as he drew his chair forward;—the remainder of the party drew their chairs closer together, especially Mr. Tupman and the spinster aunt, who were possibly rather hard of hearing; and the old lady's ear trumpet having been duly adjusted, and Mr. Miller (who had fallen asleep during the recital of the verses) roused from his slumbers by an admonitory pinch, administered beneath the table by his ex-partner the solemn fat man, the old gentleman, without farther preface, commenced the following tale, to which we have taken the liberty of prefixing the title of

THE CONVICT'S RETURN.

"WHEN I first settled in this village," said the old gentleman, "which is now just five-and-twenty years ago, the most notorious person among my parishioners was a man of the name of Edmunds, who leased a small farm near this spot. He was a morose, savage-hearted, bad man: idle and dissolute in his habits; cruel and ferocious in his disposition. Beyond the few lazy and reckless vagabonds with whom he sauntered away his time in the fields, or sotted in the ale-house, he had not a single friend or acquaintance; no one cared to speak to the man whom many feared, and every one detested—and Edmunds was shunned by all.

"This man had a wife and one son, who, when I first

came here, was about twelve years old. Of the acuteness of that woman's sufferings, of the gentle and enduring manner in which she bore them, of the agony of solicitude with which she reared that boy, no one can form an adequate conception. Heaven forgive me the supposition, if it be an uncharitable one, but I do firmly and in my soul believe, that the man systematically tried for many years to break her heart; but she bore it all for her child's sake, and, however strange it may seem to many, for his father's too; for brute as he was and cruelly as he had treated her, she had loved him once; and the recollection of what he had been to her, awakened feelings of forbearance and meekness under suffering in her bosom, to which all God's creatures, but women, are strangers.

"They were poor—they could not be otherwise when the man pursued such courses; but the woman's unceasing and unwearied exertions, early and late, morning, noon, and night, kept them above actual want. Those exertions were but ill repaid. People who passed the spot in the evening—sometimes at a late hour of the night—reported that they had heard the moans and sobs of a woman in distress, and the sound of blows: and more than once, when it was past midnight, the boy knocked softly at the door of a neighbour's house, whither he had been sent, to escape the drunken fury of his unnatural father.

"During the whole of this time, and when the poor creature often bore about her marks of ill-usage and violence which she could not wholly conceal, she was a constant attendant at our little church. Regularly every Sunday, morning and afternoon, she occupied the same seat with the boy at her side; and though they were both poorly dressed—much more so than many of their neighbours who were in a lower station —they were always neat and clean. Every one had a friendly nod and a kind word for ' poor Mrs. Edmunds; ' and sometimes, when she stopped to exchange a few words with a neighbour at the conclusion of the service in the little row of elm trees which leads to the church porch, or lingered behind to gaze with a mother's pride and fondness upon her healthy boy, as he sported before her with some little companions, her care-worn face would lighten up with an expression of heartfelt gratitude; and she would look, if not cheerful and happy, at least tranquil and contented.

"Five or six years passed away; the boy had become a robust and well-grown youth. The time that had strengthened the child's slight frame and knit his weak limbs into the strength of manhood had bowed his mother's form, and enfeebled her steps; but the arm that should have supported her was no longer locked in hers; the face that should have cheered her, no more looked upon her own. She occupied her old seat, but there was a vacant one beside her. The Bible was kept as carefully as ever, the places were found and folded down as they used to be: but there was no one to read it with her; and the tears fell thick and fast upon the book, and blotted the words from her eyes. Neighbours were as kind as they were wont to be of old, but she shunned their greetings with averted head. There was no lingering among the old elm trees now—no cheering anticipations of happiness yet in store. The desolate woman drew her bonnet closer over her face, and walked hurriedly away.

"Shall I tell you, that the young man, who, looking back to the earliest of his childhood's days to which memory and consciousness extended, and carrying his recollection down to that moment, could remember nothing which was not in some way connected with a long series of voluntary privations suffered by his mother for his sake, with ill-usage, and insult, and violence, and all endured for him;—shall I tell you, that he, with a reckless disregard of her breaking heart, and a sullen wilful forgetfulness of all she had done and borne for him, had linked himself with depraved and abandoned men, and was madly pursuing a headlong career, which must bring death to him, and shame to her? Alas for human nature! You have anticipated it long since.

"The measure of the unhappy woman's misery and

misfortune was about to be completed. Numerous offences had been committed in the neighbourhood; the perpetrators remained undiscovered, and their boldness increased. A robbery of a daring and aggravated nature occasioned a vigilance of pursuit, and a strictness of search, they had not calculated on. Young Edmunds was suspected with three companions. He was apprehended—committed—tried—condemned—to die.

"The wild and piercing shriek from a woman's voice, which resounded through the court when the solemn sentence was pronounced, rings in my ears at this moment. That cry struck a terror to the culprit's heart, which trial, condemnation—the approach of death itself, had failed to awaken. The lips which had been compressed in dogged sullenness throughout, quivered and parted involuntarily; the face turned ashy pale as the cold perspiration broke forth from every pore; the sturdy limbs of the felon trembled, and he staggered in the dock.

"In the first transports of her mental anguish, the suffering mother threw herself upon her knees at my feet, and fervently besought the Almighty Being who had hitherto supported her in all her troubles, to release her from a world of woe and misery, and to spare the life of her only child. A burst of grief, and a violent struggle, such as I hope I may never have to witness again, succeeded. I knew that her heart was breaking from that hour; but I never once heard complaint or murmur escape her lips.

"It was a piteous spectacle to see that woman in the prison yard from day to day, eagerly and fervently attempting, by affection and entreaty, to soften the hard heart of her obdurate son. It was in vain. He remained moody, obstinate, and unmoved. Not even the unlooked-for commutation of his sentence to transportation for fourteen years, softened for an instant the sullen hardihood of his demeanour.

"But the spirit of resignation and endurance that had so long upheld her, was unable to contend against bodily weakness and infirmity. She fell sick. She dragged her tottering limbs from the bed to visit her son once more, but her strength failed her, and she sunk powerless on the ground.

"And now the boasted coldness and indifference of the young man were tested indeed;˙and the retribution that fell heavily upon him, nearly drove him mad. A day passed away and his mother was not there; another flew by, and she came not near him; a third evening arrived, and yet he had not seen her; and in four-and-twenty hours he was to be separated from her—perhaps for ever. Oh! how the long-forgotten thoughts of former days rushed upon his mind, as he almost ran up and down the narrow yard—as if intelligence would arrive the sooner for *his* hurrying—and how bitterly a sense of his helplessness and desolation rushed upon him, when he heard the truth! His mother, the only parent he had ever known, lay ill—it might be, dying—within one mile of the ground he stood on: were he free and unfettered, a few minutes would place him by her side. He rushed to the gate, and grasping the iron rails with the energy of desperation, shook it till it rang again, and threw himself against the thick wall as if to force a passage through the stone; but the strong building mocked his feeble efforts, and he beat his hands together and wept like a child.

"I bore the mother's forgiveness and blessing to her son in prison; and I carried his solemn assurance of repentance, and his fervent supplication for pardon, to her sick bed. I heard, with pity and compassion, the repentant man devise a thousand little plans for her comfort and support when he returned; but I knew that many months before he could reach his place of destination, his mother would be no longer of this world.

"He was removed by night. A few weeks afterwards the poor woman's soul took its flight, I confidently hope, and solemnly believe, to a place of eternal happiness and rest. I performed the burial service over her remains. She lies in

our little churchyard.   There is no stone at her grave's head.
Her sorrows were known to man ; her virtues to God.

" It had been arranged previously to the convict's departure,
that he should write to his mother as soon as he could
obtain permission, and that the letter should be addressed
to me.   The father had positively refused to see his son from
the moment of his apprehension ; and it was a matter of
indifference to him whether he lived or died.   Many years
passed over without any intelligence of him ; and when more
than half his term of transportation had expired, and I had
received no letter, I concluded him to be dead, as indeed, I
almost hoped he might be.

" Edmunds, however, had been sent a considerable distance
up the country on his arrival at the settlement ; and to this
circumstance, perhaps, may be attributed the fact, that
though several letters were despatched, none of them ever
reached my hands.   He remained in the same place during the
whole fourteen years.   At the expiration of the term, steadily
adhering to his old resolution and the pledge he gave his
mother, he made his way back to England amidst innumerable
difficulties, and returned, on foot, to his native place.

" On a fine Sunday evening, in the month of August, John
Edmunds set foot in the village he had left with shame and
disgrace seventeen years before.   His nearest way lay through
the churchyard.   The man's heart swelled as he crossed the
stile.   The tall old elms, through whose branches the declining sun cast here and there a rich ray of light upon the shady
path, awakened the associations of his earliest days.   He
pictured himself as he was then, clinging to his mother's hand,
and walking peacefully to church.   He remembered how he
used to look up into her pale face ; and how her eyes would
sometimes fill with tears as she gazed upon his features—tears
which fell hot upon his forehead as she stooped to kiss him,
and made him weep too, although he little knew then what
bitter tears hers were.   He thought, how often he had run
merrily down that path with some childish playfellow, looking

back, ever and again, to catch his mother's smile, or hear her gentle voice; and then a veil seemed lifted from his memory, and words of kindness unrequited, and warnings despised, and promises broken, thronged upon his recollection till his heart failed him, and he could bear it no longer.

"He entered the church. The evening service was concluded and the congregation had dispersed, but it was not yet closed. His steps echoed through the low building with a hollow sound, and he almost feared to be alone, it was so still and quiet. He looked round him. Nothing was changed. The place seemed smaller than it used to be, but there were the old monuments on which he had gazed with childish awe a thousand times; the little pulpit with its faded cushion; the Communion-table before which he had so often repeated the Commandments he had reverenced as a child, and forgotten as a man. He approached the old seat; it looked cold and desolate. The cushion had been removed, and the Bible was not there. Perhaps his mother now occupied a poorer seat, or possibly she had grown infirm and could not reach the church alone. He dared not think of what he feared. A cold feeling crept over him, and he trembled violently as he turned away.

"An old man entered the porch just as he reached it. Edmunds started back, for he knew him well; many a time he had watched him digging graves in the churchyard. What would *he* say to the returned convict?

"The old man raised his eyes to the stranger's face, bid him 'good evening,' and walked slowly on. He had forgotten him.

"He walked down the hill, and through the village. The weather was warm, and the people were sitting at their doors, or strolling in their little gardens as he passed, enjoying the serenity of the evening, and their rest from labour. Many a look was turned towards him, and many a doubtful glance he cast on either side to see whether any knew and shunned him. There were strange faces in almost every house; in

94

some he recognised the burly form of some old schoolfellow
—a boy when he last saw him—surrounded by a troop of
merry children; in others he saw, seated in an easy-chair at
a cottage door, a feeble and infirm old man, whom he only
remembered as a hale and hearty labourer; but they had all
forgotten him, and he passed on unknown.

"The last soft light of the setting sun had fallen on the
earth, casting a rich glow on the yellow corn sheaves, and
lengthening the shadows of the orchard trees, as he stood
before the old house—the home of his infancy—to which
his heart had yearned with an intensity of affection not
to be described, through long and weary years of captivity
and sorrow. The paling was low, though he well remembered the time when it had seemed a high wall to him:
and he looked over into the old garden. There were more
seeds and gayer flowers than there used to be, but there
were the old trees still—the very tree, under which he had
lain a thousand times when tired of playing in the sun, and
felt the soft mild sleep of happy boyhood steal gently upon
him. There were voices within the house. He listened, but
they fell strangely upon his ear; he knew them not. They
were merry too; and he well knew that his poor old mother
could not be cheerful, and he away. The door opened, and
a group of little children bounded out, shouting and romping.
The father, with a little boy in his arms, appeared at the door,
and they crowded round him, clapping their tiny hands, and
dragging him out, to join their joyous sports. The convict
thought on the many times he had shrunk from his father's
sight in that very place. He remembered how often he had
buried his trembling head beneath the bed-clothes, and heard
the harsh word, and the hard stripe, and his mother's wailing;
and though the man sobbed aloud with agony of mind as he
left the spot, his fist was clenched, and his teeth were set, in
fierce and deadly passion.

"And such was the return to which he had looked through
the weary perspective of many years, and for which he had

undergone so much suffering! No face of welcome, no look of forgiveness, no house to receive, no hand to help him—and this too in the old village. What was his loneliness in the wild thick woods, where man was never seen, to this!

" He felt that in the distant land of his bondage and infamy, he had thought of his native place as it was when he left it; not as it would be when he returned. The sad reality struck coldly at his heart, and his spirit sank within him. He had not courage to make inquiries, or to present himself to the only person who was likely to receive him with kindness and compassion. He walked slowly on; and shunning the road-side like a guilty man, turned into a meadow he well remembered; and covering his face with his hands, threw himself upon the grass.

" He had not observed that a man was lying on the bank beside him; his garments rustled as he turned round to steal a look at the new-comer; and Edmunds raised his head.

" The man had moved into a sitting posture. His body was much bent, and his face was wrinkled and yellow. His dress denoted him an inmate of the workhouse: he had the appearance of being very old, but it looked more the effect of dissipation or disease, than length of years. He was staring hard at the stranger, and though his eyes were lustreless and heavy at first, they appeared to glow with an unnatural and alarmed expression after they had been fixed upon him for a short time, until they seemed to be starting from their sockets. Edmunds gradually raised himself to his knees, and looked more and more earnestly upon the old man's face. They gazed upon each other in silence.

" The old man was ghastly pale. He shuddered and tottered to his feet. Edmunds sprang to his. He stepped back a pace or two. Edmunds advanced.

" ' Let me hear you speak,' said the convict, in a thick broken voice.

" ' Stand off!' cried the old man, with a dreadful oath. The convict drew closer to him.

THE TALE CONCLUDED.

"'Stand off!' shrieked the old man. Furious with terror he raised his stick, and struck Edmunds a heavy blow across the face.

"'Father—devil!' murmured the convict, between his set teeth. He rushed wildly forward, and clenched the old man by the throat—but he was his father; and his arm fell powerless by his side.

"The old man uttered a loud yell which rang through the lonely fields like the howl of an evil spirit. His face turned black: the gore rushed from his mouth and nose, and dyed the grass a deep dark red, as he staggered and fell. He had ruptured a blood-vessel: and he was a dead man before his son could raise him.

"In that corner of the churchyard," said the old gentleman, after a silence of a few moments, "in that corner of the churchyard of which I have before spoken, there lies buried a man, who was in my employment for three years after this event: and who was truly contrite, penitent, and humbled, if ever man was. No one save myself knew in that man's life-time who he was, or whence he came:—it was John Edmunds the returned convict."

CHAPTER VII.

HOW MR. WINKLE, INSTEAD OF SHOOTING AT THE PIGEON AND
KILLING THE CROW, SHOT AT THE CROW AND WOUNDED THE
PIGEON; HOW THE DINGLEY DELL CRICKET CLUB PLAYED
ALL-MUGGLETON, AND HOW ALL-MUGGLETON DINED AT THE
DINGLEY DELL EXPENSE : WITH OTHER INTERESTING AND
INSTRUCTIVE MATTERS.

THE fatiguing adventures of the day or the somniferous
influence of the clergyman's tale operated so strongly on the
drowsy tendencies of Mr. Pickwick, that in less than five
minutes after he had been shown to his comfortable bed-
room, he fell into a sound and dreamless sleep, from which
he was only awakened by the morning sun darting his bright
beams reproachfully into the apartment. Mr. Pickwick was
no sluggard; and he sprang like an ardent warrior from his
tent—bedstead.

"Pleasant, pleasant country," sighed the enthusiastic
gentleman, as he opened his lattice window. "Who could
live to gaze from day to day on bricks and slates, who had
once felt the influence of a scene like this? Who could
continue to exist, where there are no cows but the cows on
the chimney-pots; nothing redolent of Pan but pan-tiles;
no crop but stone crop? Who could bear to drag out a
life in such a spot? Who I ask could endure it?" and,
having cross-examined solitude after the most approved
precedents, at considerable length, Mr. Pickwick thrust his
head out of the lattice, and looked around him.

PREPARATIONS FOR ROOK-SHOOTING.

The rich, sweet smell of the hayricks rose to his chamber window; the hundred perfumes of the little flower-garden beneath scented the air around; the deep-green meadows shone in the morning dew that glistened on every leaf as it trembled in the gentle air; and the birds sang as if every sparkling drop were a fountain of inspiration to them. Mr. Pickwick fell into an enchanting and delicious reverie.

"Hallo!" was the sound that roused him.

He looked to the right, but he saw nobody; his eyes wandered to the left, and pierced the prospect; he stared into the sky, but he wasn't wanted there; and then he did what a common mind would have done at once—looked into the garden, and there saw Mr. Wardle.

"How are you?" said that good-humoured individual, out of breath with his own anticipations of pleasure. "Beautiful morning, an't it? Glad to see you up so early. Make haste down, and come out. I'll wait for you here."

Mr. Pickwick needed no second invitation. Ten minutes sufficed for the completion of his toilet, and at the expiration of that time he was by the old gentleman's side.

"Hallo!" said Mr. Pickwick in his turn: seeing that his companion was armed with a gun, and that another lay ready on the grass. "What's going forward?"

"Why, your friend and I," replied the host, "are going out rook-shooting before breakfast. He's a very good shot, an't he?"

"I've heard him say he's a capital one," replied Mr. Pickwick; "but I never saw him aim at anything."

"Well," said the host, "I wish he'd come. Joe—Joe!"

The fat boy, who under the exciting influence of the morning did not appear to be more than three parts and a fraction asleep, emerged from the house.

"Go up, and call the gentleman, and tell him he'll find me and Mr. Pickwick in the rookery. Show the gentleman the way there; d'ye hear?"

The boy departed to execute his commission; and the host,

carrying both guns like a second Robinson Crusoe, led the way from the garden.

"This is the place," said the old gentleman, pausing after a few minutes' walking, in an avenue of trees. The information was unnecessary; for the incessant cawing of the unconscious rooks sufficiently indicated their whereabout.

The old gentleman laid one gun on the ground, and loaded the other.

"Here they are," said Mr. Pickwick; and as he spoke, the forms of Mr. Tupman, Mr. Snodgrass, and Mr. Winkle appeared in the distance. The fat boy, not being quite certain which gentleman he was directed to call, had with peculiar sagacity, and to prevent the possibility of any mistake, called them all.

"Come along," shouted the old gentleman, addressing Mr. Winkle; "a keen hand like you ought to have been up long ago, even to such poor work as this."

Mr. Winkle responded with a forced smile, and took up the spare gun with an expression of countenance which a metaphysical rook, impressed with a foreboding of his approaching death by violence, may be supposed to assume. It might have been keenness, but it looked remarkably like misery.

The old gentleman nodded; and two ragged boys who had been marshalled to the spot under the direction of the infant Lambert, forthwith commenced climbing up two of the trees.

"What are those lads for?" inquired Mr. Pickwick abruptly. He was rather alarmed; for he was not quite certain but that the distress of the agricultural interest, about which he had often heard a great deal, might have compelled the small boys attached to the soil to earn a precarious and hazardous subsistence by making marks of themselves for inexperienced sportsmen.

"Only to start the game," replied Mr. Wardle, laughing.

"To what?" inquired Mr. Pickwick.

"Why, in plain English to frighten the rooks."

"Oh! is that all?"

A WELL-INTENDED SHOT.

" You are satisfied ? "

" Quite."

" Very well.   Shall I begin ? "

" If you please," said Mr. Winkle, glad of any respite.

" Stand aside, then.   Now for it."

The boy shouted, and shook a branch with a nest on it. Half a dozen young rooks in violent conversation, flew out to ask what the matter was.   The old gentleman fired by way of reply.   Down fell one bird, and off flew the others.

" Take him up, Joe," said the old gentleman.

There was a smile upon the youth's face as he advanced. Indistinct visions of rook-pie floated through his imagination. He laughed as he retired with the bird—it was a plump one.

" Now, Mr. Winkle," said the host, reloading his own gun. " Fire away."

Mr. Winkle advanced, and levelled his gun.   Mr. Pickwick and his friends cowered involuntarily to escape damage from the heavy fall of rooks, which they felt quite certain would be occasioned by the devastating barrel of their friend. There was a solemn pause—a shout—a flapping of wings—a faint click.

" Hallo ! " said the old gentleman.

" Won't it go ? " inquired Mr. Pickwick.

" Missed fire," said Mr. Winkle, who was very pale : probably from disappointment.

" Odd," said the old gentleman, taking the gun.   " Never knew one of them miss fire before.   Why, I don't see anything of the cap."

" Bless my soul," said Mr. Winkle.   " I declare I forgot the cap ! "

The slight omission was rectified.   Mr. Pickwick crouched again.   Mr. Winkle stepped forward with an air of determination and resolution ; and Mr. Tupman looked out from behind a tree.   The boy shouted ; four birds flew out.   Mr. Winkle fired.   There was a scream as of an individual—not a rook— in corporeal anguish.   Mr. Tupman had saved the lives of innumerable unoffending birds by receiving a portion of the charge in his left arm.

To describe the confusion that ensued would be impossible. To tell how Mr. Pickwick in the first transports of his emotion called Mr. Winkle "Wretch!" how Mr. Tupman lay prostrate on the ground; and how Mr. Winkle knelt horror-stricken beside him; how Mr. Tupman called distractedly upon some feminine Christian name, and then opened first one eye, and then the other, and then fell back and shut them both;—all this would be as difficult to describe in detail, as it would be to depict the gradual recovering of the unfortunate individual, the binding up of his arm with pocket-handkerchiefs, and the conveying him back by slow degrees supported by the arms of his anxious friends.

They drew near the house. The ladies were at the garden-gate, waiting for their arrival and their breakfast. The spinster aunt appeared; she smiled, and beckoned them to walk quicker. 'Twas evident she knew not of the disaster. Poor thing! there are times when ignorance is bliss indeed.

They approached nearer.

"Why, what *is* the matter with the little old gentleman?" said Isabella Wardle. The spinster aunt heeded not the remark; she thought it applied to Mr. Pickwick. In her eyes Tracy Tupman was a youth; she viewed his years through a diminishing glass.

"Don't be frightened," called out the old host, fearful of alarming his daughters. The little party had crowded so completely round Mr. Tupman, that they could not yet clearly discern the nature of the accident.

"Don't be frightened," said the host.

"What's the matter?" screamed the ladies.

"Mr. Tupman has met with a little accident; that's all."

The spinster aunt uttered a piercing scream, burst into an hysteric laugh, and fell backwards in the arms of her nieces.

"Throw some cold water over her," said the old gentleman.

"No, no," murmured the spinster aunt; "I am better now.

ACCIDENT TO MR. TUPMAN.

Bella, Emily—a surgeon! Is he wounded?—Is he dead?
—Is he——ha, ha, ha!" Here the spinster aunt burst into
fit number two, of hysteric laughter interspersed with screams.

"Calm yourself," said Mr. Tupman, affected almost to tears
by this expression of sympathy with his sufferings. "Dear,
dear madam, calm yourself."

"It is his voice!" exclaimed the spinster aunt; and strong
symptoms of fit number three developed themselves forthwith.

"Do not agitate yourself, I entreat you, dearest madam,"
said Mr. Tupman soothingly. "I am very little hurt, I assure
you."

"Then you are not dead!" ejaculated the hysterical lady.
"Oh, say you are not dead!"

"Don't be a fool, Rachael," interposed Mr. Wardle, rather
more roughly than was quite consistent with the poetic nature
of the scene. "What the devil's the use of his *saying* he
isn't dead?"

"No, no, I am not," said Mr. Tupman. "I require no
assistance but yours. Let me lean on your arm." He added,
in a whisper, "Oh, Miss Rachael!" The agitated female
advanced, and offered her arm. They turned into the breakfast parlour. Mr. Tracy Tupman gently pressed her hand to
his lips, and sank upon the sofa.

"Are you faint?" inquired the anxious Rachael.

"No," said Mr. Tupman. "It is nothing. I shall be
better presently." He closed his eyes.

"He sleeps," murmured the spinster aunt. (His organs of
vision had been closed nearly twenty seconds). "Dear—dear
—Mr. Tupman!"

Mr. Tupman jumped up—"Oh, say those words again!"
he exclaimed.

The lady started. "Surely you did not hear them!" she
said, bashfully.

"Oh yes, I did!" replied Mr. Tupman; "repeat them. If
you would have me recover, repeat them."

"Hush!" said the lady. "My brother."

Mr. Tracy Tupman resumed his former position; and Mr. Wardle, accompanied by a surgeon, entered the room.

The arm was examined, the wound dressed, and pronounced to be a very slight one; and the minds of the company having been thus satisfied, they proceeded to satisfy their appetites with countenances to which an expression of cheerfulness was again restored. Mr. Pickwick alone was silent and reserved. Doubt and distrust were exhibited in his countenance. His confidence in Mr. Winkle had been shaken—greatly shaken —by the proceedings of the morning.

"Are you a cricketer?" inquired Mr. Wardle of the marksman.

At any other time, Mr. Winkle would have replied in the affirmative. He felt the delicacy of his situation, and modestly replied, "No."

"Are you, sir?" inquired Mr. Snodgrass.

"I was once upon a time," replied the host; "but I have given it up now. I subscribe to the club here, but I don't play."

"The grand match is played to-day, I believe," said Mr. Pickwick.

"It is," replied the host. "Of course you would like to see it."

"I, sir," replied Mr. Pickwick, "am delighted to view any sports which may be safely indulged in, and in which the impotent effects of unskilful people do not endanger human life." Mr. Pickwick paused, and looked steadily on Mr. Winkle, who quailed beneath his leader's searching glance. The great man withdrew his eyes after a few minutes, and added: "Shall we be justified in leaving our wounded friend to the care of the ladies?"

"You cannot leave me in better hands," said Mr. Tupman.

"Quite impossible," said Mr. Snodgrass.

It was therefore settled that Mr. Tupman should be left at home in charge of the females; and that the remainder of the guests, under the guidance of Mr. Wardle, should proceed to the spot where was to be held that trial of skill, which had roused all Muggleton from its torpor, and inoculated Dingley Dell with a fever of excitement.

As their walk, which was not above two miles long, lay through shady lanes, and sequestered footpaths, and as their conversation turned upon the delightful scenery by which they were on every side surrounded, Mr. Pickwick was almost inclined to regret the expedition they had used, when he found himself in the main street of the town of Muggleton.

Everybody whose genius has a topographical bent knows perfectly well that Muggleton is a corporate town, with a mayor, burgesses, and freemen; and anybody who has consulted the addresses of the mayor to the freemen, or the freemen to the mayor, or both to the corporation, or all three to Parliament, will learn from thence what they ought to have known before, that Muggleton is an ancient and loyal borough, mingling a zealous advocacy of Christian principles with a devoted attachment to commercial rights; in demonstration whereof, the mayor, corporation, and other inhabitants, have presented at divers times, no fewer than one thousand four hundred and twenty petitions against the continuance of negro slavery abroad, and an equal number against any interference with the factory system at home; sixty-eight in favour of the sale of livings in the Church, and eighty-six for abolishing Sunday trading in the street.

Mr. Pickwick stood in the principal street of this illustrious town, and gazed with an air of curiosity, not unmixed with interest, on the objects around him. There was an open square for the market-place; and in the centre of it, a large inn with a sign-post in front, displaying an object very common in art, but rarely met with in nature—to wit, a blue lion, with three bow legs in the air, balancing himself on the extreme point of the centre claw of his fourth foot. There were, within sight, an auctioneer's and fire-agency office, a corn-factor's, a linen-draper's, a saddler's, a distiller's, a grocer's, and a shoe-shop—the last-mentioned warehouse being also

105

appropriated to the diffusion of hats, bonnets, wearing apparel, cotton umbrellas, and useful knowledge. There was a red brick house with a small paved court-yard in front, which anybody might have known belonged to the attorney; and there was, moreover, another red brick house with Venetian blinds, and a large brass door-plate, with a very legible announcement that it belonged to the surgeon. A few boys were making their way to the cricket-field; and two or three shop-keepers who were standing at their doors, looked as if they should like to be making their way to the same spot, as indeed to all appearance they might have done, without losing any great amount of custom thereby. Mr. Pickwick having paused to make these observations, to be noted down at a more convenient period, hastened to rejoin his friends, who had turned out of the main street, and were already within sight of the field of battle.

The wickets were pitched, and so were a couple of marquees for the rest and refreshment of the contending parties. The game had not yet commenced. Two or three Dingley Dellers, and All-Muggletonians, were amusing themselves with a majestic air by throwing the ball carelessly from hand to hand; and several other gentlemen dressed like them, in straw hats, flannel jackets, and white trousers—a costume in which they looked very much like amateur stone-masons— were sprinkled about the tents, towards one of which Mr. Wardle conducted the party.

Several dozen of "How-are-you's?" hailed the old gentleman's arrival; and a general raising of the straw hats, and bending forward of the flannel jackets, followed his introduction of his guests as gentlemen from London, who were extremely anxious to witness the proceedings of the day, with which, he had no doubt, they would be greatly delighted.

"You had better step into the marquee, I think, sir," said one very stout gentleman, whose body and legs looked like half a gigantic roll of flannel, elevated on a couple of inflated pillow-cases.

THE MYSTERIOUS STRANGER AGAIN.

"You'll find it much pleasanter, sir," urged another stout gentleman, who strongly resembled the other half of the roll of flannel aforesaid.

"You're very good," said Mr. Pickwick

"This way," said the first speaker; "they notch in here —it's the best place in the whole field;" and the cricketer, panting on before, preceded them to the tent.

"Capital game—smart sport—fine exercise—very," were the words which fell upon Mr. Pickwick's ear as he entered the tent; and the first object that met his eyes was his green-coated friend of the Rochester coach, holding forth, to the no small delight and edification of a select circle of the chosen of All-Muggleton. His dress was slightly improved, and he wore boots; but there was no mistaking him.

The stranger recognised his friends immediately: and, dart-ing forward and seizing Mr. Pickwick by the hand, dragged him to a seat with his usual impetuosity, talking all the while as if the whole of the arrangements were under his especial patronage and direction.

"This way—this way—capital fun—lots of beer—hogs-heads; rounds of beef — bullocks; mustard — cart loads; glorious day—down with you—make yourself at home—glad to see you—very."

Mr. Pickwick sat down as he was bid, and Mr. Winkle and Mr. Snodgrass also complied with the directions of their mysterious friend. Mr. Wardle looked on, in silent wonder.

"Mr. Wardle—a friend of mine," said Mr. Pickwick.

"Friend of yours !—My dear sir, how are you ?—Friend of *my* friend's—give me your hand, sir "—and the stranger grasped Mr. Wardle's hand with all the fervour of a close intimacy of many years, and then stepped back a pace or two as if to take a full survey of his face and figure, and then shook hands with him again, if possible, more warmly than before.

"Well; and how came you here?" said Mr. Pickwick, with a smile in which benevolence struggled with surprise.

"Come," replied the stranger—"stopping at Crown—Crown

107

at Muggleton—met a party—flannel jackets—white trousers
—anchovy sandwiches—devilled kidneys—splendid fellows
—glorious."

Mr. Pickwick was sufficiently versed in the stranger's system
of stenography to infer from this rapid and disjointed communication that he had, somehow or other, contracted an
acquaintance with the All-Muggletons, which he had converted,
by a process peculiar to himself, into that extent of good
fellowship on which a general invitation may be easily founded.
His curiosity was therefore satisfied, and putting on his
spectacles he prepared himself to watch the play which was
just commencing.

All-Muggleton had the first innings; and the interest
became intense when Mr. Dumkins and Mr. Podder, two of
the most renowned members of that most distinguished club,
walked, bat in hand, to their respective wickets. Mr. Luffey,
the highest ornament of Dingley Dell, was pitched to bowl
against the redoubtable Dumkins, and Mr. Struggles was
selected to do the same kind office for the hitherto unconquered Podder. Several players were stationed, to "look
out," in different parts of the field, and each fixed himself
into the proper attitude by placing one hand on each knee,
and stooping very much as if he were "making a back" for
some beginner at leap-frog. All the regular players do this
sort of thing;—indeed it's generally supposed that it is quite
impossible to look out properly in any other position.

The umpires were stationed behind the wickets; the scorers
were prepared to notch the runs; a breathless silence ensued.
Mr. Luffey retired a few paces behind the wicket of the
passive Podder, and applied the ball to his right eye for
several seconds. Dumkins confidently awaited its coming
with his eyes fixed on the motions of Luffey.

"Play!" suddenly cried the bowler. The ball flew from
his hand straight and swift towards the centre stump of the
wicket. The wary Dumkins was on the alert; it fell upon
the tip of the bat, and bounded far away over the heads of

the scouts, who had just stooped low enough to let it fly over them.

"Run—run—another.—Now, then, throw her up—up with her—stop there—another—no—yes—no—throw her up, throw her up!"—Such were the shouts which followed the stroke; and, at the conclusion of which All-Muggleton had scored two. Nor was Podder behindhand in earning laurels wherewith to garnish himself and Muggleton. He blocked the doubtful balls, missed the bad ones, took the good ones, and sent them flying to all parts of the field. The scouts were hot and tired; the bowlers were changed and bowled till their arms ached; but Dumkins and Podder remained unconquered. Did an elderly gentleman essay to stop the progress of the ball, it rolled between his legs or slipped between his fingers. Did a slim gentleman try to catch it, it struck him on the nose, and bounded pleasantly off with redoubled violence, while the slim gentleman's eyes filled with water, and his form writhed with anguish. Was it thrown straight up to the wicket, Dumkins had reached it before the ball. In short, when Dumkins was caught out, and Podder stumped out, All-Muggleton had notched some fifty-four, while the score of the Dingley Dellers was as blank as their faces. The advantage was too great to be recovered. In vain did the eager Luffey, and the enthusiastic Struggles, do all that skill and experience could suggest, to regain the ground Dingley Dell had lost in the contest;—it was of no avail; and in an early period of the winning game Dingley Dell gave in, and allowed the superior prowess of All-Muggleton.

The stranger, meanwhile, had been eating, drinking, and talking, without cessation. At every good stroke he expressed his satisfaction and approval of the player in a most condescending and patronising manner, which could not fail to have been highly gratifying to the party concerned; while at every bad attempt at a catch, and every failure to stop the ball, he launched his personal displeasure at the head of the devoted

individual in such denunciations—as "Ah, ah!—stupid"—
"Now, butter-fingers"—"Muff"—"Humbug"—and so forth
—ejaculations which seemed to establish him in the opinion
of all around, as a most excellent and undeniable judge of the
whole art and mystery of the noble game of cricket.

"Capital game—well played—some strokes admirable," said
the stranger, as both sides crowded into the tent, at the
conclusion of the game.

"You have played it, sir?" inquired Mr. Wardle, who
had been much amused by his loquacity.

"Played it! Think I have—thousands of times—not here
—West Indies—exciting thing—hot work—very."

"It must be rather a warm pursuit in such a climate,"
observed Mr. Pickwick.

"Warm!—red hot—scorching—glowing. Played a match
once—single wicket—friend the Colonel—Sir Thomas Blazo
—who should get the greatest number of runs.—Won the
toss—first innings—seven o'clock A.M.—six natives to look
out—went in; kept in—heat intense—natives all fainted—
taken away—fresh half-dozen ordered—fainted also—Blazo
bowling—supported by two natives—couldn't bowl me out—
fainted too—cleared away the Colonel—wouldn't give in—
faithful attendant—Quanko Samba—last man left—sun so
hot, bat in blisters, ball scorched brown—five hundred and
seventy runs—rather exhausted—Quanko mustered up last
remaining strength—bowled me out—had a bath, and went
out to dinner."

"And what became of what's-his-name, sir?" inquired an
old gentleman.

"Blazo?"

"No—the other gentleman."

"Quanko Samba?"

"Yes, sir.

"Poor Quanko—never recovered it—bowled on, on my
account—bowled off, on his own—died, sir." Here the stranger
buried his countenance in a brown jug, but whether to hide

his emotion or imbibe its contents, we cannot distinctly affirm. We only know that he paused suddenly, drew a long and deep breath, and looked anxiously on, as two of the principal members of the Dingley Dell club approached Mr. Pickwick, and said—

"We are about to partake of a plain dinner at the Blue Lion, sir; we hope you and your friends will join us."

"Of course," said Mr. Wardle, "among our friends we include Mr. ——;" and he looked towards the stranger.

"Jingle," said that versatile gentleman, taking the hint at once. "Jingle—Alfred Jingle, Esq., of No Hall, Nowhere."

"I shall be very happy, I am sure," said Mr. Pickwick.

"So shall I," said Mr. Alfred Jingle, drawing one arm through Mr. Pickwick's, and another through Mr. Wardle's, as he whispered confidentially in the ear of the former gentleman :—

"Devilish good dinner—cold, but capital—peeped into the room this morning—fowls and pies, and all that sort of thing—pleasant fellows these—well behaved, too—very."

There being no further preliminaries to arrange, the company straggled into the town in little knots of twos and threes; and within a quarter of an hour were all seated in the great room of the Blue Lion Inn, Muggleton—Mr. Dumkins acting as chairman, and Mr. Luffey officiating as vice.

There was a vast deal of talking and rattling of knives and forks, and plates : a great running about of three ponderous headed waiters, and a rapid disappearance of the substantial viands on the table; to each and every of which item of confusion, the facetious Mr. Jingle lent the aid of half-a-dozen ordinary men at least. When everybody had eaten as much as possible, the cloth was removed, bottles, glasses, and dessert were placed on the table; and the waiters withdrew to "clear away," or in other words, to appropriate to their own private use and emolument whatever remnants of the eatables and drinkables they could contrive to lay their hands on.

111

THE PICKWICK CLUB.

Amidst the general hum of mirth and conversation that ensued, there was a little man with a puffy Say-nothing-to-me,-or-I'll-contradict-you sort of countenance, who remained very quiet; occasionally looking round him when the conversation slackened, as if he contemplated putting in something very weighty; and now and then bursting into a short cough of inexpressible grandeur. At length, during a moment of comparative silence, the little man called out in a very loud, solemn voice—

"Mr. Luffey!"

Everybody was hushed into a profound stillness as the individual addressed, replied—

"Sir!"

"I wish to address a few words to you, sir, if you will entreat the gentlemen to fill their glasses."

Mr. Jingle uttered a patronising "hear, hear," which was responded to by the remainder of the company : and the glasses having been filled the Vice-President assumed an air of wisdom in a state of profound attention, and said—

"Mr. Staple."

"Sir," said the little man, rising, "I wish to address what I have to say to *you* and not to our worthy chairman, because our worthy chairman is in some measure—I may say in a great degree—the subject of what I have to say, or I may say—to—"

"State," suggested Mr. Jingle.

—"Yes, to state," said the little man. "I thank my honourable friend, if he will allow me to call him so—(four 'hears,' and one certainly from Mr. Jingle)—for the suggestion. Sir, I am a Deller—a Dingley Deller (cheers). I cannot lay claim to the honour of forming an item in the population of Muggleton; nor, sir, I will frankly admit, do I covet that honour : and I will tell you why, sir—(hear); to Muggleton I will readily concede all those honours and distinctions to which it can fairly lay claim—they are too numerous and too well known to require aid or recapitulation from me.

THE ANGLO-SAXON PROPENSITY.

But, sir, while we remember that Muggleton has given birth to a Dumkins and a Podder, let us never forget that Dingley Dell can boast a Luffey and a Struggles. (Vociferous cheering.) Let me not be considered as wishing to detract from the merits of the former gentlemen. Sir, I envy them the luxury of their own feelings on this occasion. (Cheers). Every gentleman who hears me, is probably acquainted with the reply made by an individual, who—to use an ordinary figure of speech—'hung out' in a tub, to the emperor Alexander:— 'If I were not Diogenes,' said he, 'I would be Alexander.' I can well imagine these gentlemen to say, 'If I were not Dumkins I would be Luffey; if I were not Podder I would be Struggles.' (Enthusiasm.) But, gentlemen of Muggleton, is it in cricket alone that your fellow-townsmen stand pre-eminent? Have you never heard of Dumkins and determination? Have you never been taught to associate Podder with property? (Great applause.) Have you never, when struggling for your rights, your liberties, and your privileges, been reduced, if only for an instant, to misgiving and despair? And when you have been thus depressed, has not the name of Dumkins laid afresh within your breast the fire which had just gone out; and has not a word from that man, lighted it again as brightly as if it had never expired? (Great cheering.) Gentlemen, I beg to surround with a rich halo of enthusiastic cheering the united names of 'Dumkins and Podder.'"

Here the little man ceased, and here the company commenced a raising of voices, and thumping of tables, which lasted with little intermission during the remainder of the evening. Other toasts were drunk. Mr. Luffey and Mr. Struggles, Mr. Pickwick and Mr. Jingle, were, each in his turn, the subject of unqualified eulogium; and each in due course returned thanks for the honour.

Enthusiastic as we are in the noble cause to which we have devoted ourselves, we should have felt a sensation of pride which we cannot express, and a consciousness of having done

113

something to merit immortality of which we are now deprived, could we have laid the faintest outline of these addresses before our ardent readers. Mr. Snodgrass, as usual, took a great mass of notes, which would no doubt have afforded most useful and valuable information, had not the burning eloquence of the words or the feverish influence of the wine made that gentleman's hand so extremely unsteady, as to render his writing nearly unintelligible, and his style wholly so. By dint of patient investigation, we have been enabled to trace some characters bearing a faint resemblance to the names of the speakers; and we can also discern an entry of a song (supposed to have been sung by Mr. Jingle), in which the words "bowl" "sparkling" "ruby" "bright," and "wine" are frequently repeated at short intervals. We fancy too, that we can discern at the very end of the notes, some indistinct reference to "broiled bones;" and then the words "cold" "without" occur: but as any hypothesis we could found upon them must necessarily rest upon mere conjecture, we are not disposed to indulge in any of the speculations to which they may give rise.

We will therefore return to Mr. Tupman; merely adding that within some few minutes before twelve o'clock that night, the convocation of worthies of Dingley Dell and Muggleton were heard to sing, with great feeling and emphasis, the beautiful and pathetic national air of

> We won't go home 'till morning,
> We won't go home 'till morning,
> We won't go home 'till morning,
> 'Till daylight doth appear.

CHAPTER VIII.

STRONGLY ILLUSTRATIVE OF THE POSITION, THAT THE COURSE OF TRUE LOVE IS NOT A RAILWAY.

THE quiet seclusion of Dingley Dell, the presence of so many of the gentler sex, and the solicitude and anxiety they evinced in his behalf, were all favourable to the growth and development of those softer feelings which nature had implanted deep in the bosom of Mr. Tracy Tupman, and which now appeared destined to centre in one lovely object. The young ladies were pretty, their manners winning, their dispositions unexceptionable; but there was a dignity in the air, a touch-me-not-ishness in the walk, a majesty in the eye of the spinster aunt, to which, at their time of life, they could lay no claim, which distinguished her from any female on whom Mr. Tupman had ever gazed. That there was something kindred in their nature, something congenial in their souls, something mysteriously sympathetic in their bosoms, was evident. Her name was the first that rose to Mr. Tupman's lips as he lay wounded on the grass; and her hysteric laughter was the first sound that fell upon his ear when he was supported to the house. But had her agitation arisen from an amiable and feminine sensibility which would have been equally irrepressible in any case; or had it been called forth by a more ardent and passionate feeling, which he, of all men living, could alone awaken? These were the doubts which racked his brain as he lay extended on the sofa : these were the doubts which he determined should be at once and for ever resolved.

It was evening. Isabella and Emily had strolled out with Mr. Trundle; the deaf old lady had fallen asleep in her chair; the snoring of the fat boy, penetrated in a low and monotonous sound from the distant kitchen; the buxom servants were lounging at the side-door, enjoying the pleasantness of the hour, and the delights of a flirtation, on first principles, with certain unwieldy animals attached to the farm; and there sat the interesting pair, uncared for by all, caring for none, and dreaming only of themselves; there they sat, in short, like a pair of carefully-folded kid-gloves—bound up in each other.

" I have forgotten my flowers," said the spinster aunt.

" Water them now," said Mr. Tupman in accents of persuasion.

" You will take cold in the evening air," urged the spinster aunt, affectionately.

" No, no," said Mr. Tupman rising; " it will do me good. Let me accompany you."

The lady paused to adjust the sling in which the left arm of the youth was placed, and taking his right arm led him to the garden.

There was a bower at the further end, with honeysuckle, jessamine, and creeping plants—one of those sweet retreats which humane men erect for the accommodation of spiders.

The spinster aunt took up a large watering-pot which lay in one corner, and was about to leave the arbour. Mr. Tupman detained her, and drew her to a seat beside him.

" Miss Wardle !" said he.

The spinster aunt trembled, till some pebbles which had accidentally found their way into the large watering-pot shook like an infant's rattle.

" Miss Wardle," said Mr. Tupman, " you are an angel."

" Mr. Tupman !" exclaimed Rachael, blushing as red as the watering-pot itself.

"Nay," said the eloquent Pickwickian—"I know it but too well."

"All women are angels, they say," murmured the lady, playfully.

"Then what can *you* be; or to what, without presumption, can I compare you?" replied Mr. Tupman. "Where was the woman ever seen who resembled you? Where else could I hope to find so rare a combination of excellence and beauty? Where else could I seek to——Oh!" Here Mr. Tupman paused, and pressed the hand which clasped the handle of the happy watering-pot.

The lady turned aside her head. "Men are such deceivers," she softly whispered.

"They are, they are," ejaculated Mr. Tupman; "but not all men. There lives at least one being who can never change—one being who would be content to devote his whole existence to your happiness—who lives but in your eyes—who breathes but in your smiles—who bears the heavy burden of life itself only for you."

"Could such an individual be found," said the lady——

"But he *can* be found," said the ardent Mr. Tupman, interposing. "He *is* found. He is here, Miss Wardle." And ere the lady was aware of his intention, Mr. Tupman had sunk upon his knees at her feet.

"Mr. Tupman, rise," said Rachael.

"Never!" was the valorous reply. "Oh, Rachael!"—He seized her passive hand, and the watering-pot fell to the ground as he pressed it to his lips.—"Oh, Rachael! say you love me."

"Mr. Tupman," said the spinster aunt, with averted head —"I can hardly speak the words; but—but—you are not wholly indifferent to me."

Mr. Tupman no sooner heard this avowal, than he proceeded to do what his enthusiastic emotions prompted, and what, for aught we know (for we are but little acquainted with such matters), people so circumstanced always do. He jumped

117

up, and, throwing his arm round the neck of the spinster aunt, imprinted upon her lips numerous kisses, which after a due show of struggling and resistance, she received so passively, that there is no telling how many more Mr. Tupman might have bestowed, if the lady had not given a very unaffected start and exclaimed in an affrighted tone—

"Mr. Tupman, we are observed!—we are discovered!"

Mr. Tupman looked round. There was the fat boy, perfectly motionless, with his large circular eyes staring into the arbour, but without the slightest expression on his face that the most expert physiognomist could have referred to astonishment, curiosity, or any other known passion that agitates the human breast. Mr. Tupman gazed on the fat boy, and the fat boy stared at him; and the longer Mr. Tupman observed the utter vacancy of the fat boy's countenance, the more convinced he became that he either did not know, or did not understand, anything that had been going forward. Under this impression, he said with great firmness—

"What do you want here, sir?"

"Supper's ready, sir," was the prompt reply.

"Have you just come here, sir?" inquired Mr. Tupman, with a piercing look.

"Just," replied the fat boy.

Mr. Tupman looked at him very hard again; but there was not a wink in his eye, or a curve in his face.

Mr. Tupman took the arm of the spinster aunt, and walked towards the house; the fat boy followed behind.

"He knows nothing of what has happened," he whispered.

"Nothing," said the spinster aunt.

There was a sound behind them, as of an imperfectly suppressed chuckle. Mr. Tupman turned sharply round. No; it could not have been the fat boy; there was not a gleam of mirth, or anything but feeding in his whole visage.

"He must have been fast asleep," whispered Mr. Tupman.

"I have not the least doubt of it," replied the spinster aunt.

The Fat Boy Awake

THE GENTLEMEN RETURN.

They both laughed heartily.

Mr. Tupman was wrong. The fat boy, for once, had not been fast asleep. He was awake—wide awake—to what had been going forward.

The supper passed off without any attempt at a general conversation. The old lady had gone to bed; Isabella Wardle devoted herself exclusively to Mr. Trundle; the spinster's attentions were reserved for Mr. Tupman; and Emily's thoughts appeared to be engrossed by some distant object—possibly they were with the absent Snodgrass.

Eleven—twelve—one o'clock had struck, and the gentlemen had not arrived. Consternation sat on every face. Could they have been waylaid and robbed? Should they send men and lanterns in every direction by which they could be supposed likely to have travelled home? or should they——Hark! there they were. What could have made them so late? A strange voice, too! To whom could it belong? They rushed into the kitchen whither the truants had repaired, and at once obtained rather more than a glimmering of the real state of the case.

Mr. Pickwick, with his hands in his pockets and his hat cocked completely over his left eye, was leaning against the dresser, shaking his head from side to side, and producing a constant succession of the blandest and most benevolent smiles without being moved thereunto by any discernible cause or pretence whatsoever; old Mr. Wardle, with a highly-inflamed countenance, was grasping the hand of a strange gentleman muttering protestations of eternal friendship; Mr. Winkle, supporting himself by the eight-day clock, was feebly invoking destruction upon the head of any member of the family who should suggest the propriety of his retiring for the night; and Mr. Snodgrass had sunk into a chair, with an expression of the most abject and hopeless misery that the human mind can imagine, portrayed in every lineament of his expressive face.

"Is anything the matter?" inquired the three ladies.

"Nothing the matter," replied Mr. Pickwick. "We—we're—all right.—I say, Wardle, we're all right, an't we?"

"I should think so," replied the jolly host.—"My dears, here's my friend, Mr. Jingle—Mr. Pickwick's friend, Mr. Jingle, come 'pon—little visit."

"Is anything the matter with Mr. Snodgrass, sir?" inquired Emily, with great anxiety.

"Nothing the matter, ma'am," replied the stranger. "Cricket dinner—glorious party—capital songs—old port —claret—good—very good—wine, ma'am—wine."

"It wasn't the wine," murmured Mr. Snodgrass, in a broken voice. "It was the salmon." (Somehow or other, it never *is* the wine, in these cases.)

"Hadn't they better go to bed, ma'am?" inquired Emma. "Two of the boys will carry the gentlemen up stairs."

"I won't go to bed," said Mr. Winkle, firmly.

"No living boy shall carry me," said Mr. Pickwick, stoutly; —and he went on smiling as before.

"Hurrah!" gasped Mr. Winkle, faintly.

"Hurrah!" echoed Mr. Pickwick, taking off his hat and dashing it on the floor, and insanely casting his spectacles into the middle of the kitchen.—At this humorous feat he laughed outright.

"Let's — have — 'nother — bottle," cried Mr. Winkle, commencing in a very loud key, and ending in a very faint one. His head dropped upon his breast; and, muttering his invincible determination not to go to his bed, and a sanguinary regret that he had not "done for old Tupman" in the morning, he fell fast asleep; in which condition he was borne to his apartment by two young giants under the personal superintendence of the fat boy, to whose protecting care Mr. Snodgrass shortly afterwards confided his own person. Mr. Pickwick accepted the proffered arm of Mr. Tupman and quietly disappeared, smiling more than ever; and Mr. Wardle, after taking as affectionate a leave of the whole family as if he were ordered for immediate execution, consigned to Mr.

Wardle and his Friends Under the Influence of the "Salmon"

Trundle the honour of conveying him up-stairs, and retired, with a very futile attempt to look impressively solemn and dignified.

"What a shocking scene!" said the spinster aunt.

"Dis—gusting!" ejaculated both the young ladies.

"Dreadful—dreadful!" said Jingle, looking very grave: he was about a bottle and a half ahead of any of his companions. "Horrid spectacle—very!"

"What a nice man!" whispered the spinster aunt to Mr. Tupman.

"Good-looking, too!" whispered Emily Wardle.

"Oh, decidedly," observed the spinster aunt.

Mr. Tupman thought of the widow at Rochester: and his mind was troubled. The succeeding half-hour's conversation was not of a nature to calm his perturbed spirit. The new visitor was very talkative, and the number of his anecdotes was only to be exceeded by the extent of his politeness. Mr. Tupman felt that as Jingle's popularity increased, he (Tupman) retired further into the shade. His laughter was forced—his merriment feigned; and when at last he laid his aching temples between the sheets, he thought, with horrid delight, on the satisfaction it would afford him to have Jingle's head at that moment between the feather bed and the mattress.

The indefatigable stranger rose betimes next morning, and, although his companions remained in bed overpowered with the dissipation of the previous night, exerted himself most successfully to promote the hilarity of the breakfast-table. So successful were his efforts, that even the deaf old lady insisted on having one or two of his best jokes retailed through the trumpet; and even she condescended to observe to the spinster aunt, that "he" (meaning Jingle) "was an impudent young fellow:" a sentiment in which all her relations then and there present thoroughly coincided.

It was the old lady's habit on the fine summer mornings to repair to the arbour in which Mr. Tupman had already signalised himself, in form and manner following: first, the fat boy fetched from a peg behind the old lady's bed-room door, a close black satin bonnet, a warm cotton shawl, and a thick stick with a capacious handle; and the old lady having put on the bonnet and shawl at her leisure, would lean one hand on the stick and the other on the fat boy's shoulder, and walk leisurely to the arbour, where the fat boy would leave her to enjoy the fresh air for the space of half an hour; at the expiration of which time he would return and reconduct her to the house.

The old lady was very precise and very particular; and as this ceremony had been observed for three successive summers without the slightest deviation from the accustomed form, she was not a little surprised on this particular morning, to see the fat boy, instead of leaving the arbour, walk a few paces out of it, look carefully round him in every direction, and return towards her with great stealth and an air of the most profound mystery.

The old lady was timorous—most old ladies are—and her first impression was that the bloated lad was about to do her some grievous bodily harm with the view of possessing himself of her loose coin. She would have cried for assistance, but age and infirmity had long ago deprived her of the power of screaming; she, therefore, watched his motions with feelings of intense terror, which were in no degree diminished by his coming close up to her, and shouting in her ear in an agitated, and as it seemed to her, a threatening tone—

"Missus!"

Now it so happened that Mr. Jingle was walking in the garden close to the arbour at this moment. He too heard the shout of "Missus," and stopped to hear more. There were three reasons for his doing so. In the first place, he was idle and curious; secondly, he was by no means scrupulous; thirdly, and lastly, he was concealed from view by some flowering shrubs. So there he stood, and there he listened.

"Missus!" shouted the fat boy.

A SNAKE IN THE GRASS.

"Well, Joe," said the trembling old lady. "I'm sure I have been a good mistress to you, Joe. You have invariably been treated very kindly. You have never had too much to do; and you have always had enough to eat."

This last was an appeal to the fat boy's most sensitive feelings. He seemed touched, as he replied, emphatically—

"I knows I has."

"Then what can you want to do now?" said the old lady, gaining courage.

"I wants to make your flesh creep," replied the boy.

This sounded like a very bloodthirsty mode of showing one's gratitude; and as the old lady did not precisely understand the process by which such a result was to be attained, all her former horrors returned.

"What do you think I see in this very arbour last night?" inquired the boy.

"Bless us! What?" exclaimed the old lady, alarmed at the solemn manner of the corpulent youth.

"The strange gentleman—him as had his arm hurt—a kissin' and huggin'——"

"Who, Joe? None of the servants, I hope."

"Worser than that," roared the fat boy, in the old lady's ear.

"Not one of my grand-da'aters?"

"Worser than that."

"Worse than *that*, Joe!" said the old lady, who had thought this the extreme limit of human atrocity. "Who was it, Joe? I insist upon knowing."

The fat boy looked cautiously round, and having concluded his survey, shouted in the old lady's ear:

"Miss Rachael."

"What!" said the old lady, in a shrill tone. "Speak louder."

"Miss Rachael," roared the fat boy.

"My da'ater!"

The train of nods which the fat boy gave by way of

123

assent, communicated a *blanc-mange* like motion to his fat cheeks.

"And she suffered him!" exclaimed the old lady.

A grin stole over the fat boy's features as he said:

"I see her a kissin' of him agin."

If Mr. Jingle, from his place of concealment, could have beheld the expression which the old lady's face assumed at this communication, the probability is that a sudden burst of laughter would have betrayed his close vicinity to the summer-house. He listened attentively. Fragments of angry sentences such as, "Without my permission!"—"At her time of life"—"Miserable old 'ooman like me"—"Might have waited till I was dead," and so forth, reached his ears; and then he heard the heels of the fat boy's boots crunching the gravel, as he retired and left the old lady alone.

It was a remarkable coincidence perhaps, but it was nevertheless a fact, that Mr. Jingle within five minutes after his arrival at Manor Farm on the preceding night, had inwardly resolved to lay siege to the heart of the spinster aunt, without delay. He had observation enough to see, that his off-hand manner was by no means disagreeable to the fair object of his attack; and he had more than a strong suspicion that she possessed that most desirable of all requisites, a small independence. The imperative necessity of ousting his rival by some means or other, flashed quickly upon him, and he immediately resolved to adopt certain proceedings tending to that end and object, without a moment's delay. Fielding tells us that man is fire, and woman tow, and the Prince of Darkness sets a light to 'em. Mr. Jingle knew that young men, to spinster aunts, are as lighted gas to gunpowder, and he determined to essay the effect of an explosion without loss of time.

Full of reflections upon this important decision, he crept from his place of concealment, and, under cover of the shrubs before mentioned, approached the house. Fortune seemed determined to favour his design. Mr. Tupman and the rest of the gentlemen left the garden by the side gate just as he obtained a view of it; and the young ladies, he knew, had walked out alone, soon after breakfast. The coast was clear.

The breakfast-parlour door was partially open. He peeped in. The spinster aunt was knitting. He coughed; she looked up and smiled. Hesitation formed no part of Mr. Alfred Jingle's character. He laid his finger on his lips mysteriously, walked in, and closed the door.

"Miss Wardle," said Mr. Jingle, with affected earnestness, "forgive intrusion—short acquaintance—no time for ceremony—all discovered."

"Sir!" said the spinster aunt, rather astonished by the unexpected apparition and somewhat doubtful of Mr. Jingle's sanity.

"Hush!" said Mr. Jingle, in a stage whisper;—"large boy—dumpling face—round eyes—rascal!" Here he shook his head expressively, and the spinster aunt trembled with agitation.

"I presume you allude to Joseph, sir?" said the lady, making an effort to appear composed.

"Yes, ma'am—damn that Joe!—treacherous dog, Joe— told the old lady—old lady furious—wild—raving—arbour— Tupman—kissing and hugging—all that sort of thing—eh, ma'am—eh?"

"Mr. Jingle," said the spinster aunt, "if you come here, sir, to insult me——"

"Not at all—by no means," replied the unabashed Mr. Jingle;—"overheard the tale—came to warn you of your danger—tender my services—prevent the hubbub. Never mind—think it an insult—leave the room"—and he turned, as if to carry the threat into execution.

"What *shall* I do!" said the poor spinster, bursting into tears. "My brother will be furious."

"Of course he will," said Mr. Jingle pausing—"outrageous."

"Oh, Mr. Jingle, what *can* I say!" exclaimed the spinster aunt, in another flood of despair.

"Say he dreamt it," replied Mr. Jingle, coolly.

A ray of comfort darted across the mind of the spinster aunt at this suggestion. Mr. Jingle perceived it, and followed up his advantage.

"Pooh, pooh!—nothing more easy—blackguard boy—lovely woman—fat boy horsewhipped—you believed—end of the matter—all comfortable."

Whether the probability of escaping from the consequences of this ill-timed discovery was delightful to the spinster's feelings, or whether the hearing herself described as a "lovely woman" softened the asperity of her grief, we know not. She blushed slightly, and cast a grateful look on Mr. Jingle.

That insinuating gentleman sighed deeply, fixed his eyes on the spinster aunt's face for a couple of minutes, started melo-dramatically, and suddenly withdrew them.

"You seem unhappy, Mr. Jingle," said the lady, in a plaintive voice. "May I show my gratitude for your kind interference, by inquiring into the cause, with a view, if possible, to its removal?"

"Ha!" exclaimed Mr. Jingle, with another start—"removal! remove *my* unhappiness, and your love bestowed upon a man who is insensible to the blessing—who even now contemplates a design upon the affections of the niece of the creature who —but no; he is my friend; I will not expose his vices. Miss Wardle—farewell!" At the conclusion of this address, the most consecutive he was ever known to utter, Mr. Jingle applied to his eyes the remnant of a handkerchief before noticed, and turned towards the door.

"Stay, Mr. Jingle!" said the spinster aunt emphatically. "You have made an allusion to Mr. Tupman—explain it."

"Never!" exclaimed Jingle, with a professional (*i.e.* theatrical) air. "Never!" and, by way of showing that he had no desire to be questioned further, he drew a chair close to that of the spinster aunt and sat down.

"Mr. Jingle," said the aunt, "I entreat—I implore you,

if there is any dreadful mystery connected with Mr. Tupman, reveal it."

"Can I," said Mr. Jingle, fixing his eyes on the aunt's face —"can I see—lovely creature—sacrificed at the shrine— heartless avarice !" He appeared to be struggling with various conflicting emotions for a few seconds, and then said in a low deep voice—

"Tupman only wants your money."

"The wretch !" exclaimed the spinster, with energetic indignation. (Mr. Jingle's doubts were resolved. She *had* money).

"More than that," said Jingle—"loves another."

"Another !" ejaculated the spinster. "Who ?"

"Short girl—black eyes—niece Emily."

There was a pause.

Now, if there were one individual in the whole world, of whom the spinster aunt entertained a mortal and deeply-rooted jealousy, it was this identical niece. The colour rushed over her face and neck, and she tossed her head in silence with an air of ineffable contempt. At last, biting her thin lips, and bridling up, she said—

"It can't be. I won't believe it."

"Watch 'em," said Jingle.

"I will," said the aunt.

"Watch his looks."

"I will."

"His whispers."

"I will."

"He'll sit next her at table."

"Let him."

"He'll flatter her."

"Let him."

"He'll pay her every possible attention."

"Let him."

"And he'll cut you."

"Cut *me* !" screamed the spinster aunt. "*He* cut *me* ;— *will* he !" and she trembled with rage and disappointment.

" You will convince yourself?" said Jingle.

" I will."

" You'll show your spirit?"

" I will."

" You'll not have him afterwards?"

" Never."

" You'll take somebody else?"

" Yes."

" You shall."

Mr. Jingle fell on his knees, remained thereupon for five minutes thereafter: and rose the accepted lover of the spinster aunt: conditionally upon Mr. Tupman's perjury being made clear and manifest.

The burden of proof lay with Mr. Alfred Jingle; and he produced his evidence that very day at dinner. The spinster aunt could hardly believe her eyes. Mr. Tracy Tupman was established at Emily's side, ogling, whispering, and smiling, in opposition to Mr. Snodgrass. Not a word, not a look, not a glance, did he bestow upon his heart's pride of the evening before.

" Damn that boy!" thought old Mr. Wardle to himself. —He had heard the story from his mother. " Damn that boy! He *must* have been asleep. It's all imagination."

" Traitor!" thought the spinster aunt. " Dear Mr. Jingle was not deceiving me. Ugh! how I hate the wretch!"

The following conversation may serve to explain to our readers this apparently unaccountable alteration of deportment on the part of Mr. Tracy Tupman.

The time was evening; the scene the garden. There were two figures walking in a side path; one was rather short and stout; the other rather tall and slim. They were Mr. Tupman and Mr. Jingle. The stout figure commenced the dialogue.

" How did I do it?" he inquired.

" Splendid—capital—couldn't act better myself—you must repeat the part to-morrow—every evening, till further notice."

" Does Rachael still wish it?"

THE SNAKE VICTORIOUS.

"Of course—she don't like it—but must be done—avert suspicion—afraid of her brother—says there's no help for it —only a few days more—when old folks blinded—crown your happiness."

"Any message?"

"Love—best love—kindest regards—unalterable affection. Can I say anything for you?"

"My dear fellow," replied the unsuspicious Mr. Tupman, fervently grasping his "friend's" hand—"carry my best love —say how hard I find it to dissemble—say anything that's kind; but add how sensible I am of the necessity of the suggestion she made to me, through you, this morning. Say I applaud her wisdom and admire her discretion."

"I will. Anything more?"

"Nothing; only add how ardently I long for the time when I may call her mine, and all dissimulation may be unnecessary."

"Certainly, certainly. Anything more?"

"Oh, my friend!" said poor Mr. Tupman, again grasping the hand of his companion, "receive my warmest thanks for your disinterested kindness; and forgive me if I have ever, even in thought, done you the injustice of supposing that you *could* stand in my way. My dear friend, can I ever repay you?"

"Don't talk of it," replied Mr. Jingle. He stopped short, as if suddenly recollecting something, and said—"By-the-bye —can't spare ten pounds, can you?—very particular purpose —pay you in three days."

"I dare say I can," replied Mr. Tupman, in the fulness of his heart. "Three days, you say?"

"Only three days—all over then—no more difficulties."

Mr. Tupman counted the money into his companion's hand, and he dropped it piece by piece into his pocket, as they walked towards the house.

"Be careful," said Mr. Jingle—"not a look."

"Not a wink," said Mr. Tupman.

"Not a syllable."

"Not a whisper."

"All your attentions to the niece—rather rude, than otherwise, to the aunt—only way of deceiving the old ones."

"I'll take care," said Mr. Tupman aloud.

"And *I*'ll take care," said Mr. Jingle internally; and they entered the house.

The scene of that afternoon was repeated that evening, and on the three afternoons and evenings next ensuing. On the fourth, the host was in high spirits, for he had satisfied himself that there was no ground for the charge against Mr. Tupman. So was Mr. Tupman, for Mr. Jingle had told him that his affair would soon be brought to a crisis. So was Mr. Pickwick, for he was seldom otherwise. So was not Mr. Snodgrass, for he had grown jealous of Mr. Tupman. So was the old lady, for she had been winning at whist. So were Mr. Jingle and Miss Wardle, for reasons of sufficient importance in this eventful history to be narrated in another chapter.

CHAPTER IX.

THE supper was ready laid, the chairs were drawn round the table, bottles, jugs, and glasses were arranged upon the sideboard, and everything betokened the approach of the most convivial period in the whole four-and-twenty hours.

"Where's Rachael?" said Mr. Wardle.

"Ay, and Jingle?" added Mr. Pickwick.

"Dear me," said the host, "I wonder I haven't missed him before. Why, I don't think I've heard his voice for two hours at least. Emily, my dear, ring the bell."

The bell was rung, and the fat boy appeared.

"Where's Miss Rachael?" He couldn't say.

"Where's Mr. Jingle, then?" He didn't know.

Everybody looked surprised. It was late—past eleven o'clock. Mr. Tupman laughed in his sleeve. They were loitering somewhere, talking about *him*. Ha, ha! capital notion that—funny.

"Never mind," said Wardle, after a short pause, "they'll turn up presently, I dare say. I never wait supper for anybody."

"Excellent rule, that," said Mr. Pickwick, "admirable."

"Pray, sit down," said the host.

"Certainly," said Mr. Pickwick: and down they sat.

There was a gigantic round of cold beef on the table, and

Mr. Pickwick was supplied with a plentiful portion of it. He had raised his fork to his lips, and was on the very point of opening his mouth for the reception of a piece of beef, when the hum of many voices suddenly arose in the kitchen. He paused, and laid down his fork. Mr. Wardle paused too, and insensibly released his hold of the carving-knife, which remained inserted in the beef. He looked at Mr. Pickwick. Mr. Pickwick looked at him.

Heavy footsteps were heard in the passage; the parlour door was suddenly burst open; and the man who had cleaned Mr. Pickwick's boots on his first arrival, rushed into the room, followed by the fat boy, and all the domestics.

"What the devil's the meaning of this?" exclaimed the host.

"The kitchen chimney ain't a-fire, is it, Emma?" inquired the old lady.

"Lor grandma! No," screamed both the young ladies.

"What's the matter?" roared the master of the house.

The man gasped for breath, and faintly ejaculated—

"They ha' gone, Mas'r!—gone right clean off, sir!" (At this juncture Mr. Tupman was observed to lay down his knife and fork, and to turn very pale.)

"Who's gone?" said Mr. Wardle, fiercely.

"Mus'r Jingle and Miss Rachael, in a po'-chay, from Blue Lion, Muggleton. I was there; but I couldn't stop 'em; so I run off to tell'ee."

"I paid his expenses!" said Mr. Tupman, jumping up frantically. "He's got ten pounds of mine!—stop him!— he's swindled me!—I won't bear it!—I'll have justice, Pickwick! —I won't stand it!" and with sundry incoherent exclamations of the like nature, the unhappy gentleman spun round and round the apartment, in a transport of frenzy.

"Lord preserve us!" ejaculated Mr. Pickwick, eyeing the extraordinary gestures of his friend with terrified surprise. "He's gone mad! What shall we do!"

"Do!" said the stout old host, who regarded only the last

words of the sentence. "Put the horse in the gig! I'll get a chaise at the Lion, and follow 'em instantly. Where"—he exclaimed, as the man ran out to execute the commission—"Where's that villain Joe?"

"Here I am; but I han't a willin," replied a voice. It was the fat boy's.

"Let me get at him, Pickwick," cried Wardle, as he rushed at the ill-starred youth. "He was bribed by that scoundrel, Jingle, to put me on a wrong scent, by telling a cock-and-a-bull story of my sister and your friend Tupman!" (Here Mr. Tupman sunk into a chair.) "Let me get at him!"

"Don't let him!" screamed all the women, above whose exclamations the blubbering of the fat boy was distinctly audible.

"I won't be held!" cried the old man. "Mr. Winkle, take your hands off. Mr. Pickwick, let me go, sir!"

It was a beautiful sight, in that moment of turmoil and confusion, to behold the placid and philosophical expression of Mr. Pickwick's face, albeit somewhat flushed with exertion, as he stood with his arms firmly clasped round the extensive waist of their corpulent host, thus restraining the impetuosity of his passion, while the fat boy was scratched, and pulled, and pushed from the room by all the females congregated therein. He had no sooner released his hold, than the man entered to announce that the gig was ready.

"Don't let him go alone!" screamed the females. "He'll kill somebody!"

"I'll go with him," said Mr. Pickwick.

"You're a good fellow, Pickwick," said the host, grasping his hand. "Emma, give Mr. Pickwick a shawl to tie round his neck—make haste. Look after your grandmother, girls; she has fainted away. Now then, are you ready?"

Mr. Pickwick's mouth and chin having been hastily enveloped in a large shawl: his hat having been put on his head, and his great coat thrown over his arm, he replied in the affirmative.

They jumped into the gig. "Give her her head, Tom,"

cried the host; and away they went, down the narrow lanes: jolting in and out of the cart-ruts, and bumping up against the hedges on either side, as if they would go to pieces every moment.

"How much are they a-head?" shouted Wardle, as they drove up to the door of the Blue Lion, round which a little crowd had collected, late as it was.

"Not above three-quarters of an hour," was everybody's reply.

"Chaise and four directly!—out with 'em! Put up the gig afterwards."

"Now, boys!" cried the landlord—"chaise and four out—make haste—look alive there!"

Away ran the hostlers, and the boys. The lanterns glimmered, as the men ran to and fro; the horses' hoofs clattered on the uneven paving of the yard; the chaise rumbled as it was drawn out of the coach-house; and all was noise and bustle.

"Now then!—is that chaise coming out to-night?" cried Wardle.

"Coming down the yard now, sir," replied the hostler.

Out came the chaise—in went the horses—on sprung the boys—in got the travellers.

"Mind—the seven-mile stage in less than half an hour!" shouted Wardle.

"Off with you!"

The boys applied whip and spur, the waiters shouted, the hostlers cheered, and away they went, fast and furiously.

"Pretty situation," thought Mr. Pickwick, when he had had a moment's time for reflection. "Pretty situation for the General Chairman of the Pickwick Club. Damp chaise—strange horses—fifteen miles an hour—and twelve o'clock at night!"

For the first three or four miles, not a word was spoken by either of the gentlemen, each being too much immersed in his own reflections to address any observations to his companion. When they had gone over that much ground, however, and the horses getting thoroughly warmed began to do their work in really good style, Mr. Pickwick became too much exhilarated with the rapidity of the motion, to remain any longer perfectly mute.

"We're sure to catch them, I think," said he.

"Hope so," replied his companion.

"Fine night," said Mr. Pickwick, looking up at the moon, which was shining brightly.

"So much the worse," returned Wardle; "for they'll have had all the advantage of the moonlight to get the start of us, and we shall lose it. It will have gone down in another hour."

"It will be rather unpleasant going at this rate in the dark, won't it?" inquired Mr. Pickwick.

"I dare say it will," replied his friend drily.

Mr. Pickwick's temporary excitement began to sober down a little, as he reflected upon the inconveniences and dangers of the expedition in which he had so thoughtlessly embarked. He was roused by a loud shouting of the post-boy on the leader.

"Yo—yo—yo—yo—yoe," went the first boy.

"Yo—yo—yo—yoe!" went the second.

"Yo—yo—yo—yoe!" chimed in old Wardle himself, most lustily, with his head and half his body out of the coach window.

"Yo—yo—yo—yoe!" shouted Mr. Pickwick, taking up the burden of the cry, though he had not the slightest notion of its meaning or object. And amidst the yo—yoing of the whole four, the chaise stopped.

"What's the matter?" inquired Mr. Pickwick.

"There's a gate here," replied old Wardle. "We shall hear something of the fugitives."

After a lapse of five minutes, consumed in incessant knocking and shouting, an old man in his shirt and trousers emerged from the turnpike-house, and opened the gate.

"How long is it since a post-chaise went through here?" inquired Mr. Wardle.

"How long?"

"Ah!"

"Why, I don't rightly know. It worn't a long time ago, nor it worn't a short time ago—just between the two, perhaps."

"Has any chaise been by at all?"

"Oh yes, there's been a shay by."

"How long ago, my friend," interposed Mr. Pickwick, "an hour?"

"Ah, I daresay it might be," replied the man.

"Or two hours?" inquired the post-boy on the wheeler.

"Well, I shouldn't wonder if it was," returned the old man doubtfully.

"Drive on, boys," cried the testy old gentleman; "don't waste any more time with that old idiot!"

"Idiot!" exclaimed the old man with a grin, as he stood in the middle of the road with the gate half-closed, watching the chaise which rapidly diminished in the increasing distance. "No—not much o' that either; you've lost ten minutes here, and gone away as wise as you came, arter all. If every man on the line as has a guinea give him, earns it half as well, you won't catch t'other shay this side Mich'lmas, old short-and-fat." And with another prolonged grin, the old man closed the gate, re-entered his house, and bolted the door after him.

Meanwhile the chaise proceeded, without any slackening of pace, towards the conclusion of the stage. The moon, as Wardle had foretold, was rapidly on the wane; large tiers of dark heavy clouds, which had been gradually overspreading the sky for some time past, now formed one black mass over head; and large drops of rain which pattered every now and then against the windows of the chaise, seemed to warn the travellers of the rapid approach of a stormy night. The wind, too, which was directly against them, swept in furious gusts down the narrow road, and howled dismally through the trees which skirted the pathway. Mr. Pickwick drew his coat closer about him, coiled himself more snugly up into the corner of the chaise, and fell into a sound sleep, from which he was only awakened by the stopping of the vehicle, the sound of the hostler's bell, and a loud cry of "Horses on directly!"

But here another delay occurred. The boys were sleeping with such mysterious soundness, that it took five minutes a-piece to wake them. The hostler had somehow or other mislaid the key of the stable, and even when that was found, two sleepy helpers put the wrong harness on the wrong horses, and the whole process of harnessing had to be gone through afresh. Had Mr. Pickwick been alone, these multiplied obstacles would have completely put an end to the pursuit at once, but old Wardle was not to be so easily daunted; and he laid about him with such hearty good-will, cuffing this man, and pushing that; strapping a buckle here, and taking in a link there, that the chaise was ready in a much shorter time than could reasonably have been expected, under so many difficulties.

They resumed their journey; and certainly the prospect before them was by no means encouraging. The stage was fifteen miles long, the night was dark, the wind high, and the rain pouring in torrents. It was impossible to make any great way against such obstacles united: it was hard upon one o'clock already; and nearly two hours were consumed in getting to the end of the stage. Here, however, an object presented itself, which rekindled their hopes, and re-animated their drooping spirits.

"When did this chaise come in?" cried old Wardle, leaping out of his own vehicle, and pointing to one covered with wet mud, which was standing in the yard.

"Not a quarter of an hour ago, sir;" replied the hostler, to whom the question was addressed.

"Lady and gentleman?" inquired Wardle, almost breathless with impatience.

" Yes, sir."

" Tall gentleman—dress coat—long legs—thin body ? "

" Yes, sir."

" Elderly lady—thin face—rather skinny—eh ? "

" Yes, sir."

" By heavens, it's the couple, Pickwick," exclaimed the old gentleman.

" Would have been here before," said the hostler, " but they broke a trace."

" It is ! " said Wardle, " it is by Jove ! Chaise and four instantly ! We shall catch them yet, before they reach the next stage. A guinea a-piece, boys—be alive there—bustle about—there's good fellows."

And with such admonitions as these, the old gentleman ran up and down the yard, and bustled to and fro, in a state of excitement which communicated itself to Mr. Pickwick also; and under the influence of which, that gentleman got himself into complicated entanglements with harness, and mixed up with horses and wheels of chaises, in the most surprising manner, firmly believing that by so doing he was materially forwarding the preparations for their resuming their journey.

" Jump in—jump in ! " cried old Wardle, climbing into the chaise, pulling up the steps, and slamming the door after him. " Come along ! Make haste ! " And before Mr. Pickwick knew precisely what he was about, he felt himself forced in at the other door, by one pull from the old gentleman, and one push from the hostler; and off they were again.

" Ah ! we *are* moving now," said the old gentleman exultingly. They were indeed, as was sufficiently testified to Mr. Pickwick, by his constant collisions either with the hard woodwork of the chaise, or the body of his companion.

" Hold up ! " said the stout old Mr. Wardle, as Mr. Pickwick dived head foremost into his capacious waistcoat.

" I never did feel such a jolting in my life," said Mr. Pickwick.

"Never mind," replied his companion, "it will soon be over. Steady, steady."

Mr. Pickwick planted himself into his own corner, as firmly as he could; and on whirled the chaise faster than ever.

They had travelled in this way about three miles, when Mr. Wardle, who had been looking out of the window for two or three minutes, suddenly drew in his face, covered with splashes, and exclaimed in breathless eagerness—

"Here they are!"

Mr. Pickwick thrust his head out of his window. Yes: there was a chaise and four, a short distance before them, dashing along at full gallop.

"Go on, go on," almost shrieked the old gentleman. "Two guineas a-piece, boys—don't let 'em gain on us—keep it up—keep it up."

The horses in the first chaise started on at their utmost speed; and those in Mr. Wardle's galloped furiously behind them.

"I see his head," exclaimed the choleric old man. "Damme, I see his head."

"So do I," said Mr. Pickwick, "that's he."

Mr. Pickwick was not mistaken. The countenance of Mr. Jingle, completely coated with the mud thrown up by the wheels, was plainly discernible at the window of his chaise; and the motion of his arm, which he was waving violently towards the postilions, denoted that he was encouraging them to increased exertion.

The interest was intense. Fields, trees, and hedges, seemed to rush past them with the velocity of a whirlwind, so rapid was the pace at which they tore along. They were close by the side of the first chaise. Jingle's voice could be plainly heard, even above the din of the wheels, urging on the boys. Old Mr. Wardle foamed with rage and excitement. He roared out scoundrels and villains by the dozen, clenched his fist and shook it expressively at the object of his indignation; but Mr. Jingle only answered with a contemptuous smile, and replied to his menaces by a shout of triumph, as his horses, answering the increased application of whip and spur, broke into a faster gallop, and left the pursuers behind.

Mr. Pickwick had just drawn in his head, and Mr. Wardle, exhausted with shouting, had done the same, when a tremendous jolt threw them forward against the front of the vehicle. There was a sudden bump—a loud crash—away rolled a wheel, and over went the chaise.

After a very few seconds of bewilderment and confusion, in which nothing but the plunging of horses and breaking of glass could be made out, Mr. Pickwick felt himself violently pulled out from among the ruins of the chaise; and as soon as he had gained his feet, and extricated his head from the skirts of his great coat, which materially impeded the usefulness of his spectacles, the full disaster of the case met his view.

Old Mr. Wardle without a hat, and his clothes torn in several places, stood by his side, and the fragments of the chaise lay scattered at their feet. The post-boys, who had succeeded in cutting the traces, were standing, disfigured with mud and disordered by hard riding, by the horses' heads. About a hundred yards in advance was the other chaise, which had pulled up on hearing the crash. The postilions, each with a broad grin convulsing his countenance, were viewing the adverse party from their saddles, and Mr. Jingle was contemplating the wreck from the coach-window, with evident satisfaction. The day was just breaking, and the whole scene was rendered perfectly visible by the grey light of the morning.

"Hallo!" shouted the shameless Jingle, "anybody damaged? —elderly gentlemen—no light weights—dangerous work— very."

"You're a rascal!" roared Wardle.

"Ha! ha!" replied Jingle; and then he added, with a knowing wink, and a jerk of the thumb towards the interior of the chaise—"I say—she's very well—desires her compliments

The Break-Down

—begs you won't trouble yourself—love to *Tuppy*—won't you get up behind?—drive on, boys."

The postilions resumed their proper attitudes, and away rattled the chaise, Mr. Jingle fluttering in derision a white handkerchief from the coach-window.

Nothing in the whole adventure, not even the upset, had disturbed the calm and equable current of Mr. Pickwick's temper. The villany, however, which could first borrow money of his faithful follower, and then abbreviate his name to "Tuppy," was more than he could patiently bear. He drew his breath hard, and coloured up to the very tips of his spectacles, as he said, slowly and emphatically—

"If ever I meet that man again, I'll——"

"Yes, yes," interrupted Wardle, "that's all very well: but while we stand talking here, they'll get their licence, and be married in London."

Mr. Pickwick paused, bottled up his vengeance, and corked it down.

"How far is it to the next stage?" inquired Mr. Wardle, of one of the boys.

"Six mile, an't it, Tom?"

"Rayther better."

"Rayther better nor six mile, sir."

"Can't be helped," said Wardle, "we must walk it, Pickwick."

"No help for it," replied that truly great man.

So sending forward one of the boys on horseback, to procure a fresh chaise and horses, and leaving the other behind to take care of the broken one, Mr. Pickwick and Mr. Wardle set manfully forward on the walk, first tying their shawls round their necks, and slouching down their hats to escape as much as possible from the deluge of rain, which after a slight cessation had again begun to pour heavily down.

CHAPTER X.

THERE are in London several old inns, once the head-quarters of celebrated coaches in the days when coaches performed their journeys in a graver and more solemn manner than they do in these times; but which have now degenerated into little more than the abiding and booking places of country waggons. The reader would look in vain for any of these ancient hostelries, among the Golden Crosses and Bull and Mouths, which rear their stately fronts in the improved streets of London. If he would light upon any of these old places, he must direct his steps to the obscurer quarters of the town; and there in some secluded nooks he will find several, still standing with a kind of gloomy sturdiness, amidst the modern innovations which surround them.

In the Borough especially, there still remain some half dozen old inns, which have preserved their external features unchanged, and which have escaped alike the rage for public improvement, and the encroachments of private speculation. Great, rambling, queer, old places they are, with galleries, and passages, and staircases, wide enough and antiquated enough to furnish materials for a hundred ghost stories, sup- posing we should ever be reduced to the lamentable necessity of inventing any, and that the world should exist long enough to exhaust the innumerable veracious legends connected with old London Bridge, and its adjacent neighbourhood on the Surrey side.

It was in the yard of one of these inns—of no less celebrated a one than the White Hart—that a man was busily employed in brushing the dirt off a pair of boots, early on the morning succeeding the events narrated in the last chapter. He was habited in a coarse-striped waistcoat, with black calico sleeves, and blue glass buttons; drab breeches and leggings. A bright red handkerchief was wound in a very loose and unstudied style round his neck, and an old white hat was carelessly thrown on one side of his head. There were two rows of boots before him, one cleaned and the other dirty, and at every addition he made to the clean row, he paused from his work, and contemplated its results with evident satisfaction.

The yard presented none of that bustle and activity which are the usual characteristics of a large coach inn. Three or four lumbering waggons, each with a pile of goods beneath its ample canopy, about the height of the second-floor window of an ordinary house, were stowed away beneath a lofty roof which extended over one end of the yard; and another, which was probably to commence its journey that morning, was drawn out into the open space. A double tier of bed-room galleries, with old clumsy balustrades, ran round two sides of the straggling area, and a double row of bells to correspond, sheltered from the weather by a little sloping roof, hung over the door leading to the bar and coffee-room. Two or three gigs and chaise-carts were wheeled up under different little sheds and pent-houses; and the occasional heavy tread of a cart-horse, or rattling of a chain at the further end of the yard, announced to anybody who cared about the matter, that the stable lay in that direction. When we add that a few boys in smock frocks were lying asleep on heavy packages, woolpacks, and other articles that were scattered about on heaps of straw, we have described as fully as need be the general appearance of the yard of the White Hart Inn, High Street, Borough, on the particular morning in question.

A loud ringing of one of the bells, was followed by the appearance of a smart chambermaid in the upper sleeping gallery, who, after tapping at one of the doors, and receiving a request from within, called over the balustrades—

"Sam!"

"Hallo," replied the man with the white hat.

"Number twenty-two wants his boots."

"Ask number twenty-two, wether he'll have 'em now, or wait till he gets 'em," was the reply.

"Come, don't be a fool, Sam," said the girl, coaxingly, "the gentleman wants his boots directly."

"Well, you *are* a nice young 'ooman for a musical party, you are," said the boot-cleaner. "Look at these here boots —eleven pair o' boots; and one shoe as b'longs to number six, with the wooden leg. The eleven boots is to be called at half-past eight and the shoe at nine. Who's number twenty-two, that's to put all the others out? No, no; reg'lar rotation, as Jack Ketch said, wen he tied the men up. Sorry to keep you a waitin', sir, but I'll attend to you directly."

Saying which, the man in the white hat set to work upon a top-boot with increased assiduity.

There was another loud ring; and the bustling old landlady of the White Hart made her appearance in the opposite gallery.

"Sam," cried the landlady, "where's that lazy, idle—why, Sam—oh, there you are; why don't you answer?"

"Wouldn't be gen-teel to answer, 'till you'd done talking," replied Sam, gruffly.

"Here, clean them shoes for number seventeen directly, and take 'em to private sitting-room, number five, first floor."

The landlady flung a pair of lady's shoes into the yard, and bustled away.

"Number 5," said Sam, as he picked up the shoes, and

taking a piece of chalk from his pocket, made a memorandum of their destination on the soles—" Lady's shoes
and private sittin' room! I suppose *she* didn't come in the
waggin."

"She came in early this morning," cried the girl, who was
still leaning over the railing of the gallery, " with a gentleman
in a hackney-coach, and it's him as wants his boots, and
you'd better do 'em, that's all about it."

"Vy didn't you say so before?" said Sam, with great indignation, singling out the boots in question from the heap
before him. "For all I know'd he vas one o' the regular
three-pennies. Private room! and a lady too! If he's
anything of a gen'lm'n, he's vorth a shillin' a day, let alone
the arrands."

Stimulated by this inspiring reflection, Mr. Samuel brushed
way with such hearty good will, that in a few minutes the
boots and shoes, with a polish which would have struck envy
to the soul of the amiable Mr. Warren (for they used Day
and Martin at the White Hart), had arrived at the door of
number five.

"Come in," said a man's voice, in reply to Sam's rap at
the door.

Sam made his best bow, and stepped into the presence of
a lady and gentleman seated at breakfast. Having officiously
deposited the gentleman's boots right and left at his feet,
and the lady's shoes right and left at hers, he backed towards
the door.

"Boots," said the gentleman.

"Sir," said Sam, closing the door, and keeping his hand
on the knob of the lock.

"Do you know—what's a-name—Doctors' Commons?"

"Yes, sir."

"Where is it?"

"Paul's Church-yard, sir; low archway on the carriage-side,
bookseller's at one corner, hot-el on the other, and two porters
in the middle as touts for licences."

"Touts for licences!" said the gentleman.

"Touts for licences," replied Sam. "Two coves in vhite aprons—touches their hats wen you walk in—'Licence, sir, licence?' Queer sort, them, and their mas'rs too, sir—Old Baily Proctors—and no mistake."

"What do they do?" inquired the gentleman.

"Do! You, sir! That a'nt the wost on it, neither. They puts things into old gen'lm'n's heads as they never dreamed of. My father, sir, wos a coachman. A widower he wos, and fat enough for anything—uncommon fat, to be sure. His missus dies, and leaves him four hundred pound. Down he goes to the Commons, to see the lawyer and draw the blunt—wery smart—top boots on—nosegay in his button-hole—broad-brimmed tile—green shawl—quite the gen'lm'n. Goes through the archvay, thinking how he should inwest the money—up comes the touter, touches his hat—'Licence, sir, licence?'—'What's that?' says my father.—'Licence, sir,' says he.—'What licence?' says my father.—'Marriage licence,' says the touter.—'Dash my veskit,' says my father, 'I never thought o' that.'—'I think you wants one, sir,' says the touter. My father pulls up, and thinks abit—'No,' says he, 'damme, I'm too old, b'sides I'm a many sizes too large,' says he.—'Not a bit on it, sir,' says the touter.—'Think not?' says my father.—'I'm sure not,' says he; 'we married a gen'lm'n twice your size, last Monday.'—'Did you, though,' said my father.—'To be sure we did,' says the touter, 'you're a babby to him—this way, sir—this way!'—and sure enough my father walks arter him, like a tame monkey behind a horgan, into a little back office, vere a feller sat among dirty papers and tin boxes, making believe he was busy. 'Pray take a seat, vile I makes out the affidavit, sir,' says the lawyer. —'Thankee, sir,' says my father, and down he sat, and stared with all his eyes, and his mouth vide open, at the names on the boxes. 'What's your name, sir,' says the lawyer.—'Tony Weller,' says my father.—'Parish?' says the lawyer.—'Belle Savage,' says my father; for he stopped there wen he drove up, and he know'd nothing about parishes, *he* didn't.—'And what's the lady's name?' says the lawyer. My father was struck all of a heap. 'Blessed if I know,' says he.—'Not know!' says the lawyer.—'No more nor you do,' says my father, 'can't I put that in arterwards?'—'Impossible!' says the lawyer.—'Wery well,' says my father, after he'd thought a moment, 'put down Mrs. Clarke.'—'What Clarke?' says the lawyer, dipping his pen in the ink.—'Susan Clarke, Markis o' Granby, Dorking,' says my father; 'she'll have me, if I ask, I des-say—I never said nothing to her, but she'll have me, I know.' The licence was made out, and she *did* have him, and what's more she's got him now; and *I* never had any of the four hundred pound, worse luck. Beg your pardon, sir," said Sam, when he had concluded, "but wen I gets on this here grievance, I runs on like a new barrow vith the wheel greased." Having said which, and having paused for an instant to see whether he was wanted for anything more, Sam left the room.

"Half-past nine—just the time—off at once;" said the gentleman, whom we need hardly introduce as Mr. Jingle.

"Time—for what?" said the spinster aunt, coquettishly.

"Licence, dearest of angels—give notice at the church— call you mine, to-morrow"—said Mr. Jingle, and he squeezed the spinster aunt's hand.

"The licence!" said Rachael, blushing.

"The licence," repeated Mr. Jingle—

> "In hurry, post-haste for a licence,
> In hurry, ding dong I come back."

"How you run on," said Rachael.

"Run on—nothing to the hours, days, weeks, months, years, when we're united—*run* on—they'll fly on—bolt—mizzle —steam-engine—thousand-horse power—nothing to it."

"Can't—can't we be married before to-morrow morning?" inquired Rachael.

"Impossible—can't be—notice at the church—leave the licence to-day—ceremony come off to-morrow."

"I am so terrified, lest my brother should discover us!" said Rachael.

"Discover—nonsense—too much shaken by the break-down—besides—extreme caution—gave up the post-chaise—walked on—took a hackney coach—came to the Borough—last place in the world that he'd look in—ha! ha!—capital notion that—very."

"Don't be long," said the spinster, affectionately, as Mr. Jingle stuck the pinched-up hat on his head.

"Long away from *you?*—Cruel charmer," and Mr. Jingle skipped playfully up to the spinster aunt, imprinted a chaste kiss upon her lips, and danced out of the room.

"Dear man!" said the spinster as the door closed after him.

"Rum old girl," said Mr. Jingle, as he walked down the passage.

It is painful to reflect upon the perfidy of our species; and we will not, therefore, pursue the thread of Mr. Jingle's meditations, as he wended his way to Doctors' Commons. It will be sufficient for our purpose to relate, that escaping the snares of the dragons in white aprons, who guard the entrance to that enchanted region, he reached the Vicar General's office in safety, and having procured a highly flattering address on parchment, from the Archbishop of Canterbury, to his "trusty and well-beloved Alfred Jingle and Rachael Wardle, greeting," he carefully deposited the mystic document in his pocket, and retraced his steps in triumph to the Borough.

He was yet on his way to the White Hart, when two plump gentlemen and one thin one entered the yard, and looked round in search of some authorised person of whom they could make a few inquiries. Mr. Samuel Weller happened to be at that moment engaged in burnishing a pair of painted tops, the personal property of a farmer who was refreshing himself with a slight lunch of two or three pounds of cold beef and a pot or two of porter, after the fatigues of the

First Appearance of Mr. Samuel Weller

Borough market; and to him the thin gentleman straightway advanced.

"My friend," said the thin gentleman.

"You're one o' the adwice gratis order," thought Sam, "or you wouldn't be so werry fond o' me all at once." But he only said—"Well, sir."

"My friend," said the thin gentleman, with a conciliatory hem—"Have you got many people stopping here, now? Pretty busy. Eh?"

Sam stole a look at the inquirer. He was a little high-dried man, with a dark squeezed-up face, and small restless black eyes, that kept winking and twinkling on each side of his little inquisitive nose, as if they were playing a perpetual game of peep-bo with that feature. He was dressed all in black, with boots as shiny as his eyes, a low white neckcloth, and a clean shirt with a frill to it. A gold watch-chain, and seals, depended from his fob. He carried his black kid gloves *in* his hands, not *on* them; and as he spoke, thrust his wrists beneath his coat-tails, with the air of a man who was in the habit of propounding some regular posers.

"Pretty busy, eh?" said the little man.

"Oh, werry well, sir," replied Sam, "we shan't be bankrupts, and we shan't make our fort'ns. We eats our biled mutton without capers, and don't care for horse-radish wen ve can get beef."

"Ah," said the little man, "you're a wag, a'nt you?"

"My eldest brother was troubled with that complaint," said Sam; "it may be catching—I used to sleep with him."

"This is a curious old house of yours," said the little man, looking round him.

"If you'd sent word you was a coming, we'd ha' had it repaired;" replied the imperturbable Sam.

The little man seemed rather baffled by these several repulses, and a short consultation took place between him and the two plump gentlemen. At its conclusion, the little man took a pinch of snuff from an oblong silver box, and was apparently on the point of renewing the conversation, when one of the plump gentlemen, who in additon to a benevolent countenance, possessed a pair of spectacles, and a pair of black gaiters, interfered—

"The fact of the matter is," said the benevolent gentleman, "that my friend here (pointing to the other plump gentleman) will give you half a guinea, if you'll answer one or two—"

"Now, my dear sir—my dear sir," said the little man, "pray, allow me—my dear sir, the very first principle to be observed in these cases, is this : if you place a matter in the hands of a professional man, you must in no way interfere in the progress of the business ; you must repose implicit confidence in him. Really, Mr. (he turned to the other plump gentleman, and said)—I forget your friend's name."

"Pickwick," said Mr. Wardle, for it was no other than that jolly personage.

"Ah, Pickwick—really Mr. Pickwick, my dear sir, excuse me—I shall be happy to receive any private suggestions of yours, as *amicus curiœ*, but you must see the impropriety of your interfering with my conduct in this case, with such an *ad captandum* argument as the offer of half a guinea. Really, my dear sir, really ; " and the little man took an argumentative pinch of snuff, and looked very profound.

"My only wish, sir," said Mr. Pickwick. "was to bring this very unpleasant matter to as speedy a close as possible."

"Quite right—quite right," said the little man.

"With which view," continued Mr. Pickwick, "I made use of the argument which my experience of men has taught me is the most likely to succeed in any case."

"Ay, ay," said the little man, "very good, very good, indeed ; but you should have suggested it to *me*. My dear sir, I'm quite certain you cannot be ignorant of the extent of confidence which must be placed in professional men. If any authority can be necessary on such a point, my dear sir, let me refer you to the well-known case in Barnwell and—"

"Never mind George Barnwell," interrupted Sam, who had

remained a wondering listener during this short colloquy; "every body knows vhat sort of a case his was, tho' it's always been my opinion, mind you, that the young 'ooman deserved scragging a precious sight more than he did. Hows'ever, that's neither here nor there. You want me to except of half a guinea. Werry well, I'm agreeable: I can't say no fairer than that, can I, sir? (Mr. Pickwick smiled.) Then the next question is, what the devil do you want with me, as the man said wen he see the ghost?"

"We want to know——" said Mr. Wardle.

"Now, my dear sir—my dear sir," interposed the busy little man.

Mr. Wardle shrugged his shoulders, and was silent.

"We want to know," said the little man, solemnly; "and we ask the question of you, in order that we may not awaken apprehensions inside—we want to know who you've got in this house, at present?"

"Who there is in the house!" said Sam, in whose mind the inmates were always represented by that particular article of their costume, which came under his immediate superintendence. "There's a wooden leg in number six; there's a pair of Hessians in thirteen; there's two pair of halves in the commercial; there's these here painted tops in the snuggery inside the bar; and five more tops in the coffee-room."

"Nothing more?" said the little man.

"Stop a bit," replied Sam, suddenly recollecting himself. "Yes; there's a pair of Wellingtons a good deal worn, and a pair o' lady's shoes, in number five."

"What sort of shoes?" hastily inquired Wardle, who, together with Mr. Pickwick, had been lost in bewilderment at the singular catalogue of visitors.

"Country make," replied Sam.

"Any maker's name?"

"Brown."

"Where of?"

"Muggleton.

"It *is* them," exclaimed Wardle. "By Heavens, we've found them."

"Hush!" said Sam. "The Wellingtons has gone to Doctors' Commons."

"No," said the little man.

"Yes, for a licence."

"We're in time," exclaimed Wardle. "Show us the room; not a moment is to be lost."

"Pray, my dear sir—pray," said the little man; "caution, caution." He drew from his pocket a red silk purse, and looked very hard at Sam as he drew out a sovereign.

Sam grinned expressively.

"Show us into the room at once, without announcing us," said the little man, "and it's yours."

Sam threw the painted tops into a corner, and led the way through a dark passage, and up a wide staircase. He paused at the end of a second passage, and held out his hand.

"Here it is," whispered the attorney, as he deposited the money in the hand of their guide.

The man stepped forward for a few paces, followed by the two friends and their legal adviser. He stopped at a door.

"Is this the room?" murmured the little gentleman.

Sam nodded assent.

Old Wardle opened the door; and the whole three walked into the room just as Mr. Jingle, who had that moment returned, had produced the licence to the spinster aunt.

The spinster uttered a loud shriek, and, throwing herself in a chair, covered her face with her hands. Mr. Jingle crumpled up the licence, and thrust it into his coat-pocket. The unwelcome visitors advanced into the middle of the room.

"You—you are a nice rascal, arn't you?" exclaimed Wardle, breathless with passion.

"My dear sir, my dear sir," said the little man, laying his hat on the table. "Pray, consider—pray. Defamation of character: action for damages. Calm yourself, my dear sir, pray—"

MR. WARDLE AND THE FUGITIVES.

"How dare you drag my sister from my house?" said the old man.

"Ay—ay—very good," said the little gentleman, "you may ask that. How dare you, sir?—eh, sir?"

"Who the devil are you?" inquired Mr. Jingle, in so fierce a tone, that the little gentleman involuntarily fell back a step or two.

"Who is he, you scoundrel," interposed Wardle. "He's my lawyer, Mr. Perker, of Gray's Inn. Perker, I'll have this fellow prosecuted—indicted—I'll—I'll—I'll ruin him. And you," continued Mr. Wardle, turning abruptly round to his sister, "you, Rachael, at a time of life when you ought to know better, what do *you* mean by running away with a vagabond, disgracing your family, and making yourself miserable. Get on your bonnet, and come back. Call a hackney-coach there, directly, and bring this lady's bill, d'ye hear—d'ye hear?"

"Cert'nly, sir," replied Sam, who had answered Wardle's violent ringing of the bell with a degree of celerity which must have appeared marvellous to anybody who didn't know that his eye had been applied to the outside of the keyhole during the whole interview.

"Get on your bonnet," repeated Wardle.

"Do nothing of the kind," said Jingle. "Leave the room, sir—no business here—lady's free to act as she pleases—more than one-and-twenty."

"More than one-and-twenty!" ejaculated Wardle, contemptuously. "More than one-and-forty!"

"I a'nt," said the spinster aunt, her indignation getting the better of her determination to faint.

"You are," replied Wardle, "you're fifty if you're an hour."

Here the spinster aunt uttered a loud shriek, and became senseless.

"A glass of water," said the humane Mr. Pickwick, summoning the landlady.

"A *glass* of water!" said the passionate Wardle. "Bring

a bucket, and throw it all over her; it'll do her good, and she richly deserves it."

"Ugh, you brute!" ejaculated the kind-hearted landlady. "Poor dear." And with sundry ejaculations, of "Come now, there's a dear—drink a little of this—it'll do you good—don't give way so—there's a love," &c., &c., the landlady, assisted by a chamber-maid, proceeded to vinegar the fore-head, beat the hands, titillate the nose, and unlace the stays of the spinster aunt, and to administer such other restoratives as are usually applied by compassionate females to ladies who are endeavouring to ferment themselves into hysterics.

"Coach is ready, sir," said Sam, appearing at the door.

"Come along," cried Wardle. "I'll carry her down stairs."

At this proposition, the hysterics came on with redoubled violence.

The landlady was about to enter a very violent protest against this proceeding, and had already given vent to an indignant inquiry whether Mr. Wardle considered himself a lord of the creation, when Mr. Jingle interposed—

"Boots," said he, "get me an officer."

"Stay, stay," said little Mr. Perker. "Consider, sir, consider."

"I'll *not* consider," replied Jingle. "She's her own mistress —see who dares to take her away—unless she wishes it."

"I *won't* be taken away," murmured the spinster aunt. "I *don't* wish it." (Here there was a frightful relapse.)

"My dear sir," said the little man, in a low tone, taking Mr. Wardle and Mr. Pickwick apart: "My dear sir, we're in a very awkward situation. It's a distressing case—very; I never knew one more so; but really, my dear sir, really we have no power to control this lady's actions. I warned you before we came, my dear sir, that there was nothing to look to but a compromise."

There was a short pause.

"What kind of compromise would you recommend?" inquired Mr. Pickwick.

154

MAKING A COMPROMISE.

"Why, my dear sir, our friend's in an unpleasant position —very much so. We must be content to suffer some pecuniary loss."

"I'll suffer any, rather than submit to this disgrace, and let her, fool as she is, be made miserable for life," said Wardle.

"I rather think it can be done," said the bustling little man. "Mr. Jingle, will you step with us into the next room for a moment?"

Mr. Jingle assented, and the quartette walked into an empty apartment.

"Now, sir," said the little man, as he carefully closed the door, "is there no way of accommodating this matter—step this way, sir, for a moment—into this window, sir, where we can be alone—there, sir, there, pray sit down, sir. Now, my dear sir, between you and I, we know very well, my dear sir, that you have run off with this lady for the sake of her money. Don't frown, sir, don't frown; I say, between you and I, *we* know it. We are both men of the world, and *we* know very well that our friends here, are not—eh?"

Mr. Jingle's face gradually relaxed; and something distantly resembling a wink quivered for an instant in his left eye.

"Very good, very good," said the little man, observing the impression he had made. "Now the fact is, that beyond a few hundreds, the lady has little or nothing till the death of her mother—fine old lady, my dear sir."

"*Old*," said Mr. Jingle, briefly but emphatically.

"Why, yes," said the attorney with a slight cough. "You are right, my dear sir, she is *rather* old. She comes of an old family though, my dear sir; old in every sense of the word. The founder of that family came into Kent, when Julius Cæsar invaded Britain;—only one member of it, since, who hasn't lived to eighty-five, and *he* was beheaded by one of the Henrys. The old lady is not seventy-three now, my dear sir." The little man paused, and took a pinch of snuff.

"Well," cried Mr. Jingle.

"Well, my dear sir—you don't take snuff!—ah! so much the

better—expensive habit—well, my dear sir, you're a fine young man, man of the world—able to push your fortune, if you had capital, eh?"

"Well," said Mr. Jingle again.

"Do you comprehend me?"

"Not quite."

"Don't you think—now, my dear sir, I put it to you, *don't* you think—that fifty pounds and liberty, would be better than Miss Wardle and expectation?"

"Won't do—not half enough!" said Mr. Jingle rising.

"Nay, nay, my dear sir," remonstrated the little attorney, seizing him by the button. "Good round sum—a man like you could treble it in no time—great deal to be done with fifty pounds, my dear sir."

"More to be done with a hundred and fifty," replied Mr. Jingle, coolly.

"Well, my dear sir, we won't waste time in splitting straws," resumed the little man, "say—say—seventy."

"Won't do," said Mr. Jingle

"Don't go away, my dear sir—pray don't hurry," said the little man. "Eighty; come: I'll write you a cheque at once."

"Won't do," said Mr. Jingle.

"Well, my dear sir, well," said the little man, still detaining him; "just tell me what *will* do."

"Expensive affair," said Mr. Jingle. "Money out of pocket—posting, nine pounds; licence, three—that's twelve—compensation, a hundred—hundred and twelve—Breach of honour—and loss of the lady—"

"Yes, my dear sir, yes," said the little man, with a knowing look, "never mind the last two items. That's a hundred and twelve—say a hundred—come."

"And twenty," said Mr. Jingle.

"Come, come, I'll write you a cheque," said the little man; and down he sat at the table for that purpose.

"I'll make it payable the day after to-morrow," said the little man, with a look towards Mr. Wardle; "and we can get the lady away, meanwhile." Mr. Wardle sullenly nodded assent.

"A hundred," said the little man.

"And twenty," said Mr. Jingle.

"My dear sir," remonstrated the little man.

"Give it him," interposed Mr. Wardle, "and let him go." The cheque was written by the little gentleman, and pocketed by Mr. Jingle.

"Now, leave this house instantly!" said Wardle, starting up.

"My dear sir," urged the little man.

"And mind," said Mr. Wardle, "that nothing should have induced me to make this compromise—not even a regard for my family—if I had not known that the moment you got any money in that pocket of yours, you'd go to the devil faster, if possible, than you would without it—"

"My dear sir," urged the little man again.

"Be quiet, Perker," resumed Wardle. "Leave the room, sir."

"Off directly," said the unabashed Jingle. "Bye bye, Pickwick."

If any dispassionate spectator could have beheld the countenance of the illustrious man, whose name forms the leading feature of the title of this work, during the latter part of this conversation, he would have been almost induced to wonder that the indignant fire which flashed from his eyes, did not melt the glasses of his spectacles—so majestic was his wrath. His nostrils dilated, and his fists clenched involuntarily, as he heard himself addressed by the villain. But he restrained himself again—he did *not* pulverise him.

"Here," continued the hardened traitor, tossing the licence at Mr. Pickwick's feet; "get the name altered—take home the lady—do for Tuppy."

Mr. Pickwick was a philosopher, but philosophers are only men in armour, after all. The shaft had reached him, penetrated through his philosophical harness, to his very heart.

In the frenzy of his rage he hurled the inkstand madly forward, and followed it up himself. But Mr. Jingle had disappeared, and he found himself caught in the arms of Sam.

"Hallo," said that eccentric functionary, "furniter's cheap where you come from, sir. Self-acting ink, that 'ere; it's wrote your mark upon the wall, old gen'lm'n. Hold still, sir; wot's the use o' runnin' arter a man as has made his lucky, and got to t' other end of the Borough by this time."

Mr. Pickwick's mind, like those of all truly great men, was open to conviction. He was a quick and powerful reasoner; and a moment's reflection sufficed to remind him of the impotency of his rage. It subsided as quickly as it had been roused. He panted for breath, and looked benignantly round upon his friends.

Shall we tell the lamentations that ensued, when Miss Wardle found herself deserted by the faithless Jingle? Shall we extract Mr. Pickwick's masterly description of that heart-rending scene? His note-book, blotted with the tears of sympathising humanity, lies open before us; one word, and it is in the printer's hands. But, no! we will be resolute! We will not wring the public bosom, with the delineation of such suffering!

Slowly and sadly did the two friends and the deserted lady, return next day in the Muggleton heavy coach. Dimly and darkly had the sombre shadows of a summer's night fallen upon all around, when they again reached Dingley Dell, and stood within the entrance to Manor Farm.

CHAPTER XI.

INVOLVING ANOTHER JOURNEY, AND AN ANTIQUARIAN DISCOVERY.
RECORDING MR. PICKWICK'S DETERMINATION TO BE PRESENT
AT AN ELECTION; AND CONTAINING A MANUSCRIPT OF THE
OLD CLERGYMAN'S.

A NIGHT of quiet and repose in the profound silence of Dingley
Dell, and an hour's breathing of its fresh and fragrant air on
the ensuing morning, completely recovered Mr. Pickwick from
the effects of his late fatigue of body and anxiety of mind.
That illustrious man had been separated from his friends and
followers, for two whole days; and it was with a degree of
pleasure and delight, which no common imagination can
adequately conceive, that he stepped forward to greet Mr.
Winkle and Mr. Snodgrass, as he encountered those gentlemen
on his return from his early walk. The pleasure was mutual;
for who could ever gaze on Mr. Pickwick's beaming face
without experiencing the sensation? But still a cloud seemed
to hang over his companions which that great man could not
but be sensible of, and was wholly at a loss to account for.
There was a mysterious air about them both, as unusual as it
was alarming.

"And how," said Mr. Pickwick, when he had grasped his
followers by the hand, and exchanged warm salutations of
welcome; "how is Tupman?"

Mr. Winkle, to whom the question was more peculiarly
addressed, made no reply. He turned away his head, and
appeared absorbed in melancholy reflections.

"Snodgrass," said Mr. Pickwick, earnestly, "How is our friend—he is not ill?"

"No," replied Mr. Snodgrass; and a tear trembled on his sentimental eye-lid, like a rain-drop on a window-frame. "No; he is not ill."

Mr. Pickwick stopped, and gazed on each of his friends in turn.

"Winkle—Snodgrass," said Mr. Pickwick: "what does this mean? Where is our friend? What has happened? Speak —I conjure, I entreat—nay, I command you, speak."

There was a solemnity—a dignity—in Mr. Pickwick's manner, not to be withstood.

"He is gone," said Mr. Snodgrass.

"Gone!" exclaimed Mr. Pickwick. "Gone!"

"Gone," repeated Mr. Snodgrass.

"Where!" ejaculated Mr. Pickwick.

"We can only guess, from that communication," replied Mr Snodgrass, taking a letter from his pocket, and placing it in his friend's hand. "Yesterday morning, when a letter was received from Mr. Wardle, stating that you would be home with his sister at night, the melancholy which had hung over our friend during the whole of the previous day, was observed to increase. He shortly afterwards disappeared: he was missing during the whole day, and in the evening this letter was brought by the hostler from the Crown, at Muggleton. It had been left in his charge in the morning, with a strict injunction that it should not be delivered until night."

Mr. Pickwick opened the epistle. It was in his friend's handwriting, and these were its contents:—

"My dear Pickwick,

"You, my dear friend, are placed far beyond the reach of many mortal frailties and weaknesses which ordinary people cannot overcome. You do not know what it is, at one blow, to be deserted by a lovely and fascinating creature, and to fall a victim to the artifices of a villain, who hid the grin of cunning, beneath the mask of friendship. I hope you never may.

"Any letter, addressed to me at the Leather Bottle, Cobham, Kent, will be forwarded—supposing I still exist. I hasten from the sight of that world, which has become odious to me. Should I hasten from it altogether, pity—forgive me. Life, my dear Pickwick, has become insupportable to me. The spirit which burns within us, is a porter's knot, on which to rest the heavy load of worldly cares and troubles; and when that spirit fails us, the burden is too heavy to be borne. We sink beneath it. You may tell Rachael—Ah, that name!—

"TRACY TUPMAN."

"We must leave this place, directly," said Mr. Pickwick, as he refolded the note. "It would not have been decent for us to remain here, under any circumstances, after what has happened; and now we are bound to follow in search of our friend. And so saying, he led the way to the house.

His intention was rapidly communicated. The entreaties to remain were pressing, but Mr. Pickwick was inflexible. Business, he said, required his immediate attendance.

The old clergyman was present.

"You are not really going?" said he, taking Mr. Pickwick aside.

Mr. Pickwick reiterated his former determination.

"Then here," said the old gentleman, "is a little manuscript, which I had hoped to have the pleasure of reading to you myself. I found it on the death of a friend of mine —a medical man, engaged in our County Lunatic Asylum —among a variety of papers, which I had the option of destroying or preserving, as I thought proper. I can hardly believe that the manuscript is genuine, though it certainly is not in my friend's hand. However, whether it be the genuine production of a maniac, or founded upon the ravings of some unhappy being (which I think more probable), read it, and judge for yourself."

Mr. Pickwick received the manuscript, and parted from the benevolent old gentleman with many expressions of good-will and esteem.

It was a more difficult task to take leave of the inmates of Manor Farm, from whom they had received so much hospitality and kindness. Mr. Pickwick kissed the young ladies—we were going to say, as if they were his own daughters, only as he might possibly have infused a little more warmth into the salutation, the comparison would not be quite appropriate—hugged the old lady with filial cordiality : and patted the rosy cheeks of the female servants in a most patriarchal manner, as he slipped into the hands of each, some more substantial expression of his approval. The exchange of cordialities with their fine old host and Mr. Trundle, were even more hearty and prolonged; and it was not until Mr. Snodgrass had been several times called for, and at last emerged from a dark passage followed soon after by Emily (whose bright eyes looked unusually dim), that the three friends were enabled to tear themselves from their friendly entertainers. Many a backward look they gave at the Farm, as they walked slowly away : and many a kiss did Mr. Snodgrass waft in the air, in acknowledgment of something very like a lady's handkerchief, which was waved from one of the upper windows, until a turn of the lane hid the old house from their sight.

At Muggleton they procured a conveyance to Rochester. By the time they reached the last-named place, the violence of their grief had sufficiently abated to admit of their making a very excellent early dinner; and having procured the necessary information relative to the road, the three friends set forward again in the afternoon to walk to Cobham.

A delightful walk it was: for it was a pleasant afternoon in June, and their way lay through a deep and shady wood, cooled by the light wind which gently rustled the thick foliage, and enlivened by the songs of the birds that perched upon the boughs. The ivy and the moss crept in thick clusters over the old trees, and the soft green turf overspread the ground like a silken mat. They emerged upon an open park, with an ancient hall, displaying the quaint and picturesque architecture of Elizabeth's time. Long vistas of stately oaks and elm trees appeared on every side : large herds of deer were cropping the fresh grass; and occasionally a startled hare scoured along the ground, with the speed of the shadows thrown by the light clouds which swept across a sunny landscape like a passing breath of summer.

"If this," said Mr. Pickwick, looking about him, "if this were the place to which all who are troubled with our friend's complaint came, I fancy their old attachment to this world would very soon return."

"I think so too," said Mr. Winkle.

"And really," added Mr. Pickwick, after half an hour's walking had brought them to the village, "really, for a misanthrope's choice, this is one of the prettiest and most desirable places of residence I ever met with."

In this opinion also, both Mr. Winkle and Mr. Snodgrass expressed their concurrence ; and having been directed to the Leathern Bottle, a clean and commodious village ale-house, the three travellers entered, and at once inquired for a gentleman of the name of Tupman.

"Show the gentlemen into the parlour, Tom," said the landlady.

A stout country lad opened a door at the end of the passage, and the three friends entered a long, low-roofed room, furnished with a large number of high-backed leather-cushioned chairs of fantastic shapes, and embellished with a great variety of old portraits and roughly-coloured prints of some antiquity. At the upper end of the room was a table, with a white cloth upon it, well covered with a roast fowl, bacon, ale, and et ceteras ; and at the table sat Mr. Tupman, looking as unlike a man who had taken his leave of the world, as possible.

On the entrance of his friends, that gentleman laid down his knife and fork, and with a mournful air advanced to meet them.

"I did not expect to see you here," he said, as he grasped Mr. Pickwick's hand. "It's very kind."

"Ah!" said Mr. Pickwick, sitting down, and wiping from his forehead the perspiration which the walk had engendered. "Finish your dinner, and walk out with me. I wish to speak to you alone."

Mr. Tupman did as he was desired; and Mr. Pickwick having refreshed himself with a copious draught of ale, waited his friend's leisure. The dinner was quickly despatched, and they walked out together.

For half an hour, their forms might have been seen pacing the churchyard to and fro, while Mr. Pickwick was engaged in combatting his companion's resolution. Any repetition of his arguments would be useless; for what language could convey to them that energy and force which their great originator's manner communicated? Whether Mr. Tupman was already tired of retirement, or whether he was wholly unable to resist the eloquent appeal which was made to him, matters not, he did *not* resist it at last.

"It mattered little to him," he said, "where he dragged out the miserable remainder of his days : and since his friend laid so much stress upon his humble companionship, he was willing to share his adventures."

Mr. Pickwick smiled; they shook hands; and walked back to re-join their companions.

It was at this moment that Mr. Pickwick made that immortal discovery, which has been the pride and boast of his friends, and the envy of every antiquarian in this or any other country. They had passed the door of their inn, and walked a little way down the village, before they recollected the precise spot in which it stood. As they turned back, Mr. Pickwick's eye fell upon a small broken stone, partially buried in the ground, in front of a cottage door. He paused.

"This is very strange," said Mr. Pickwick.

"What is strange?" inquired Mr. Tupman, staring eagerly at every object near him, but the right one. "God bless me, what's the matter?"

This last was an ejaculation of irrepressible astonishment, occasioned by seeing Mr. Pickwick, in his enthusiasm for discovery, fall on his knees before the little stone, and commence wiping the dust off it with his pocket-handkerchief.

"There is an inscription here," said Mr. Pickwick.

"Is it possible?" said Mr. Tupman.

"I can discern," continued Mr. Pickwick, rubbing away with all his might, and gazing intently through his spectacles: "I can discern a cross, and a B, and then a T. This is important," continued Mr. Pickwick, starting up. "This is some very old inscription, existing perhaps long before the ancient alms-houses in this place. It must not be lost."

He tapped at the cottage door. A labouring man opened it.

"Do you know how this stone came here, my friend?" inquired the benevolent Mr. Pickwick.

"No, I doan't sir," replied the man civilly. "It was here long afore I war born, or any on us."

Mr. Pickwick glanced triumphantly at his companion.

"You—you—are not particularly attached to it, I dare say," said Mr. Pickwick, trembling with anxiety. "You wouldn't mind selling it, now?"

"Ah! but who'd buy it?" inquired the man, with an expression of face which he probably meant to be very cunning.

"I'll give you ten shillings for it, at once," said Mr Pickwick, "if you would take it up for me."

The astonishment of the village may be easily imagined, when (the little stone having been raised with one wrench of a spade), Mr. Pickwick, by dint of great personal exertion, bore it with his own hands to the inn, and after having carefully washed it, deposited it on the table.

The exultation and joy of the Pickwickians knew no bounds, when their patience and assiduity, their washing and scraping, were crowned with success. The stone was uneven and broken, and the letters were straggling and irregular, but the following fragment of an inscription was clearly to be deciphered:

+
B I L S T
U M
P S H I
S. M.
A R K

Mr. Pickwick's eyes sparkled with delight, as he sat and gloated over the treasure he had discovered. He had attained one of the greatest objects of his ambition. In a county known to abound in remains of the early ages; in a village in which there still existed some memorials of the olden time, he—he, the Chairman of the Pickwick Club—had discovered a strange and curious inscription of unquestionable antiquity, which had wholly escaped the observation of the many learned men who had preceded him. He could hardly trust the evidence of his senses.

"This—this," said he, "determines me. We return to town, to-morrow."

"To-morrow!" exclaimed his admiring followers.

"To-morrow," said Mr. Pickwick. "This treasure must be at once deposited where it can be thoroughly investigated, and properly understood. I have another reason for this step. In a few days, an election is to take place for the borough of Eatanswill, at which Mr. Perker, a gentleman whom I lately met, is the agent of one of the candidates. We will behold, and minutely examine, a scene so interesting to every Englishman."

"We will," was the animated cry of three voices.

Mr. Pickwick looked round him. The attachment and fervour of his followers, lighted up a glow of enthusiasm within him. He was their leader, and he felt it.

THE DAY MARKED BY A STONE.

"Let us celebrate this happy meeting with a convivial glass," said he. This proposition, like the other, was received with unanimous applause. Having himself deposited the important stone in a small deal box, purchased from the landlady for the purpose, he placed himself in an arm-chair at the head of the table; and the evening was devoted to festivity and conversation.

It was past eleven o'clock—a late hour for the little village of Cobham—when Mr. Pickwick retired to the bed-room which had been prepared for his reception. He threw open the lattice-window, and setting his light upon the table, fell into a train of meditation on the hurried events of the two preceding days.

The hour and the place were both favourable to contemplation; Mr. Pickwick was roused by the church-clock striking twelve. The first stroke of the hour sounded solemnly in his ear, but when the bell ceased the stillness seemed insupportable;—he almost felt as if he had lost a companion. He was nervous and excited; and hastily undressing himself and placing his light in the chimney, got into bed.

Every one has experienced that disagreeable state of mind, in which a sensation of bodily weariness in vain contends against an inability to sleep. It was Mr. Pickwick's condition at this moment: he tossed first on one side and then on the other; and perseveringly closed his eyes as if to coax himself to slumber. It was of no use. Whether it was the unwonted exertion he had undergone, or the heat, or the brandy and water, or the strange bed—whatever it was, his thoughts kept reverting very uncomfortably to the grim pictures down stairs, and the old stories to which they had given rise in the course of the evening. After half an hour's tumbling about, he came to the unsatisfactory conclusion, that it was of no use trying to sleep; so he got up, and partially dressed himself. Anything, he thought, was better than lying there fancying all kinds of horrors. He looked out of the window—it was very dark. He walked about the room—it was very lonely.

He had taken a few turns from the door to the window, and from the window to the door, when the clergyman's manuscript for the first time entered his head. It was a good thought. If it failed to interest him, it might send him to sleep. He took it from his coat-pocket, and drawing a small table towards his bedside, trimmed the light, put on his spectacles, and composed himself to read. It was a strange hand-writing, and the paper was much soiled and blotted. The title gave him a sudden start, too; and he could not avoid casting a wistful glance round the room. Reflecting on the absurdity of giving way to such feelings, however, he trimmed the light again, and read as follows:

A MADMAN'S MANUSCRIPT.

"Yes!—a madman's! How that word would have struck to my heart, many years ago! How it would have roused the terror that used to come upon me sometimes; sending the blood hissing and tingling through my veins, till the cold dew of fear stood in large drops upon my skin, and my knees knocked together with fright! I like it now though. It's a fine name. Shew me the monarch whose angry frown was ever feared like the glare of a madman's eye—whose cord and axe were ever half so sure as a madman's grip. Ho! ho! It's a grand thing to be mad! to be peeped at like a wild lion through the iron bars—to gnash one's teeth and howl, through the long still night, to the merry ring of a heavy chain—and to roll and twine among the straw, transported with such brave music. Hurrah for the madhouse! Oh, it's a rare place!

"I remember days when I was *afraid* of being mad; when I used to start from my sleep, and fall upon my knees, and pray to be spared from the curse of my race; when I rushed from the sight of merriment or happiness, to hide myself in some lonely place, and spend the weary hours in watching the progress of the fever that was to consume my brain. I knew that madness was mixed up with my very blood, and the marrow of my bones; that one generation had passed away without the pestilence appearing among them, and that I was the first in whom it would revive. I knew it *must* be so: that so it always had been, and so it ever would be: and when I cowered in some obscure corner of a crowded room, and saw men whisper, and point, and turn their eyes towards me, I knew they were telling each other of the doomed madman; and I slunk away again to mope in solitude.

"I did this for years; long, long years they were. The nights here are long sometimes—very long; but they are nothing to the restless nights, and dreadful dreams I had at that time. It makes me cold to remember them. Large dusky forms with sly and jeering faces crouched in the corners of the room, and bent over my bed at night, tempting me to madness. They told me in low whispers, that the floor of the old house in which my father's father died, was stained with his own blood, shed by his own hand in raging madness. I drove my fingers into my ears, but they screamed into my head till the room rang with it, that in one generation before him the madness slumbered, but that his grandfather had lived for years with his hands fettered to the ground, to prevent his tearing himself to pieces. I knew they told the truth—I knew it well. I had found it out years before, though they had tried to keep it from me. Ha! ha! I was too cunning for them, madman as they thought me.

"At last it came upon me, and I wondered how I could ever have feared it. I could go into the world now, and laugh and shout with the best among them. I knew I was mad, but they did not even suspect it. How I used to hug myself with delight, when I thought of the fine trick I was playing them after their old pointing and leering, when I was not mad, but only dreading that I might one day become so! And how I used to laugh for joy, when I was alone, and thought how well I kept my secret, and how quickly my kind friends would have fallen from me, if they had known the truth. I could have screamed with ecstasy when I dined alone with some fine roaring fellow, to think how pale he would have turned, and how fast he would have run, if he had known that the dear friend who sat close to him, sharpening a bright glittering knife, was a madman with all the power, and half the will, to plunge it in his heart. Oh, it was a merry life!

"Riches became mine, wealth poured in upon me, and I rioted in pleasures enhanced a thousandfold to me by the consciousness of my well-kept secret. I inherited an estate. The law—the eagle-eyed law itself—had been deceived, and had handed over disputed thousands to a madman's hands. Where was the wit of the sharp-sighted men of sound mind? Where the dexterity of the lawyers, eager to discover a flaw? The madman's cunning had over-reached them all.

"I had money. How I was courted! I spent it profusely. How I was praised! How those three proud overbearing brothers humbled themselves before me! The old white-headed father, too—such deference—such respect—such devoted friendship—he worshipped me! The old man had a daughter, and the young men a sister; and all the five were poor. I was rich; and when I married the girl, I saw a smile of triumph play upon the faces of her needy relatives, as they thought of their well-planned scheme, and their fine prize. It was for me to smile. To smile! To laugh outright, and tear my hair, and roll upon the ground with shrieks of merriment. They little thought they had married her to a madman.

"Stay. If they had known it, would they have saved her? A sister's happiness against her husband's gold. The lightest feather I blow into the air, against the gay chain that ornaments my body!

"In one thing I was deceived with all my cunning. If I had not been mad—for though we madmen are sharp-witted enough, we get bewildered sometimes—I should have known that the girl would rather have been placed, stiff and cold in a dull leaden coffin, than borne an envied bride to my rich, glittering house. I should have known that her heart was with the dark-eyed boy whose name I once heard her breathe in her troubled sleep; and that she had been sacrificed to me, to relieve the poverty of the old white-headed man, and the haughty brothers.

"I don't remember forms or faces now, but I know the girl was beautiful. I *know* she was; for in the bright moonlight nights, when I start up from my sleep, and all is quiet about me, I see, standing still and motionless in one corner of this cell, a slight and wasted figure with long black hair, which streaming down her back, stirs with no earthly wind, and eyes that fix their gaze on me, and never wink or close. Hush! the blood chills at my heart as I write it down—that form is *her's;* the face is very pale, and the eyes are glassy bright; but I know them well. That figure never moves; it never frowns and mouths as others do, that fill this place sometimes; but it is much more dreadful to me, even than the spirits that tempted me many years ago—it comes fresh from the grave; and is so very death-like.

"For nearly a year I saw that face grow paler; for nearly a year I saw the tears steal down the mournful cheeks, and never knew the cause. I found it out at last though. They could not keep it from me long. She had never liked me; I had never thought she did: she despised my wealth, and hated the splendour in which she lived ;—I had not expected that. She loved another. This I had never thought of. Strange feelings came over me. and thoughts, forced upon me by some secret power, whirled round and round my brain. I did not hate her, though I hated the boy she still wept for. I pitied—yes, I pitied—the wretched life to which her cold and selfish relations had doomed her. I knew that she could not live long, but the thought that before her death she might give birth to some ill-fated being, destined to hand down madness to its offspring, determined me. I resolved to kill her.

171

"For many weeks I thought of poison, and then of drowning, and then of fire. A fine sight the grand house in flames, and the madman's wife smouldering away to cinders. Think of the jest of a large reward, too, and of some sane man swinging in the wind for a deed he never did, and all through a madman's cunning! I thought often of this, but I gave it up at last. Oh! the pleasure of stropping the razor day after day, feeling the sharp edge, and thinking of the gash one stroke of its thin bright edge would make!

"At last the old spirits who had been with me so often before whispered in my ear that the time was come, and thrust the open razor into my hand. I grasped it firmly, rose softly from the bed. and leaned over my sleeping wife. Her face was buried in her hands. I withdrew them softly, and they fell listlessly on her bosom. She had been weeping; for the traces of the tears were still wet upon her cheek. Her face was calm and placid; and even as I looked upon it, a tranquil smile lighted up her pale features. I laid my hand softly on her shoulder. She started—it was only a passing dream. I leant forward again. She screamed, and woke.

"One motion of my hand, and she would never again have uttered cry or sound. But I was startled, and drew back. Her eyes were fixed on mine. I know not how it was, but they cowed and frightened me; and I quailed beneath them. She rose from the bed, still gazing fixedly and steadily on me. I trembled; the razor was in my hand, but I could not move. She made towards the door. As she neared it, she turned, and withdrew her eyes from my face. The spell was broken. I bounded forward, and clutched her by the arm. Uttering shriek upon shriek, she sunk upon the ground.

"Now I could have killed her without a struggle; but the house was alarmed. I heard the tread of footsteps on the stairs. I replaced the razor in its usual drawer, unfastened the door, and called loudly for assistance.

"They came, and raised her, and placed her on the bed. She lay bereft of animation for hours; and when life, look, and speech returned, her senses had deserted her, and she raved wildly and furiously.

"Doctors were called in—great men who rolled up to my door in easy carriages, with fine horses and gaudy servants. They were at her bedside for weeks. They had a great meeting, and consulted together in low and solemn voices in another room. One, the cleverest and most celebrated among them, took me aside, and bidding me prepare for the worst, told me—me, the madman!—that my wife was mad. He stood close beside me at an open window, his eyes looking in my face, and his hand laid upon my arm. With one effort, I could have hurled him into the street beneath. It would have been rare sport to have done it; but my secret was at stake, and I let him go. A few days after, they told me I must place her under some restraint: I must provide a keeper for her. *I!* I went into the open fields where none could hear me, and laughed till the air resounded with my shouts!

"She died next day. The white-headed old man followed her to the grave, and the proud brothers dropped a tear over the insensible corpse of her whose sufferings they had regarded in her lifetime with muscles of iron. All this was food for my secret mirth, and I laughed behind the white handkerchief which I held up to my face, as we rode home, 'till the tears came into my eyes.

"But though I had carried my object and killed her, I was restless and disturbed, and I felt that before long my secret must be known. I could not hide the wild mirth and joy which boiled within me, and made me when I was alone, at home, jump up and beat my hands together, and dance round and round, and roar aloud. When I went out, and saw the busy crowds hurrying about the streets; or to the theatre, and heard the sound of music, and beheld the people dancing, I felt such glee, that I could have rushed among them, and torn them to pieces limb from limb, and howled in transport. But I ground my teeth, and struck my feet upon the floor, and drove my sharp nails into my hands. I kept it down; and no one knew I was a madman yet.

"I remember—though it's one of the last things I *can* remember: for now I mix up realities with my dreams, and having so much to do, and being always hurried here, have no time to separate the two, from some strange confusion in which they get involved—I remember how I let it out at last. Ha! ha! I think I see their frightened looks now, and feel the ease with which I flung them from me, and dashed my clenched fist into their white faces, and then flew like the wind, and left them screaming and shouting far behind. The strength of a giant comes upon me when I think of it. There —see how this iron bar bends beneath my furious wrench. I could snap it like a twig, only there are long galleries here with many doors—I don't think I could find my way along them; and even if I could, I know there are iron gates below which they keep locked and barred. They know what a clever madman I have been, and they are proud to have me here, to show.

"Let me see;—yes, I had been out. It was late at night when I reached home, and found the proudest of the three proud brothers waiting to see me—urgent business he said: I recollect it well. I hated that man with all a madman's hate. Many and many a time had my fingers longed to tear him. They told me he was there. I ran swiftly up-stairs. He had a word to say to me. I dismissed the servants. It was late, and we were alone together—*for the first time*.

"I kept my eyes carefully from him at first, for I knew what he little thought—and I gloried in the knowledge—that the light of madness gleamed from them like fire. We sat in silence for a few minutes. He spoke at last. My recent dissipation, and strange remarks, made so soon after his sister's death, were an insult to her memory. Coupling together many circumstances which had at first escaped his observation, he thought I had not treated her well. He wished to know whether he was right in inferring that I meant to cast a

174

reproach upon her memory, and a disrespect upon her family. It was due to the uniform he wore, to demand this explanation.

"This man had a commission in the army—a commission, purchased with my money, and his sister's misery! This was the man who had been foremost in the plot to ensnare me, and grasp my wealth. This was the man who had been the main instrument in forcing his sister to wed me; well knowing that her heart was given to that puling boy. Due to *his* uniform! The livery of his degradation! I turned my eyes upon him—I could not help it—but I spoke not a word.

"I saw the sudden change that came upon him beneath my gaze. He was a bold man, but the colour faded from his face, and he drew back his chair. I dragged mine nearer to him; and as I laughed—I was very merry then—I saw him shudder. I felt the madness rising within me. He was afraid of me.

"'You were very fond of your sister when she was alive'—I said—'Very.'

"He looked uneasily round him, and I saw his hand grasp the back of his chair: but he said nothing.

"'You villain,' said I, 'I found you out; I discovered your hellish plots against me; I know her heart was fixed on some one else before you compelled her to marry me. I know it —I know it.'

"He jumped suddenly from his chair, brandished it aloft, and bid me stand back—for I took care to be getting closer to him all the time I spoke.

"I screamed rather than talked, for I felt tumultuous passions eddying through my veins, and the old spirits whispering and taunting me to tear his heart out.

"'Damn you,' said I, starting up, and rushing upon him; 'I killed her. I am a madman. Down with you. Blood, blood! I will have it!'

"I turned aside with one blow the chair he hurled at me in his terror, and closed with him; and with a heavy crash we rolled upon the floor together.

"It was a fine struggle that; for he was a tall strong man, fighting for his life; and I, a powerful madman, thirsting to destroy him. I knew no strength could equal mine, and I was right. Right again, though a madman! His struggles grew fainter. I knelt upon his chest, and clasped his brawny throat firmly with both hands. His face grew purple; his eyes were starting from his head, and with protruded tongue, he seemed to mock me. I squeezed the tighter.

"The door was suddenly burst open with a loud noise, and a crowd of people rushed forward, crying aloud to each other to secure the madman.

"My secret was out; and my only struggle now was for liberty and freedom. I gained my feet before a hand was on me, threw myself among my assailants, and cleared my way with my strong arm, as if I bore a hatchet in my hand, and hewed them down before me. I gained the door, dropped over the banisters, and in an instant was in the street.

"Straight and swift I ran, and no one dared to stop me. I heard the noise of feet behind, and redoubled my speed. It grew fainter and fainter in the distance, and at length died away altogether: but on I bounded, through marsh and rivulet, over fence and wall, with a wild shout which was taken up by the strange beings that flocked around me on every side, and swelled the sound, till it pierced the air. I was borne upon the arms of demons who swept along upon the wind, and bore down bank and hedge before them, and spun me round and round with a rustle and a speed that made my head swim, until at last they threw me from them with a violent shock, and I fell heavily upon the earth. When I woke I found myself here—here in this gay cell where the sun-light seldom comes, and the moon steals in, in rays which only serve to show the dark shadows about me, and that silent figure in its old corner. When I lie awake, I can sometimes hear strange shrieks and cries from distant parts of this large place. What they are, I know not; but they neither come from that pale form, nor does it regard them. For from the first shades of dusk 'till the earliest light of morning, it still stands motionless in the same place, listening to the music of my iron chain, and watching my gambols on my straw bed."

At the end of the manuscript was written, in another hand, this note:

[The unhappy man whose ravings are recorded above, was a melancholy instance of the baneful results of energies misdirected in early life, and excesses prolonged until their consequences could never be repaired. The thoughtless riot, dissipation, and debauchery of his younger days, produced fever and delirium. The first effects of the latter was the strange delusion, founded upon a well-known medical theory, strongly contended for by some, and as strongly contested by others, that an hereditary madness existed in his family. This produced a settled gloom, which in time developed a morbid insanity, and finally terminated in raving madness. There is every reason to believe that the events he detailed, though distorted in the description by his diseased imagination, really happened. It is only matter of wonder to those who were acquainted with the vices of his early career, that his passions, when no longer controlled by reason, did not lead him to the commission of still more frightful deeds.]

Mr. Pickwick's candle was just expiring in the socket, as he concluded the perusal of the old clergyman's manuscript; and when the light went suddenly out, without any previous flicker by way of warning, it communicated a very considerable start to his excited frame. Hastily throwing off such articles of clothing as he had put on when he rose from his uneasy bed, and casting a fearful glance around, he once more scrambled hastily between the sheets, and soon fell fast asleep.

The sun was shining brilliantly into his chamber when he awoke, and the morning was far advanced. The gloom which had oppressed him on the previous night, had disappeared with the dark shadows which shrouded the landscape, and his thoughts and feelings were as light and gay as the morning itself. After a hearty breakfast, the four gentlemen sallied forth to walk to Gravesend, followed by a man bearing the stone in its deal box. They reached that town about one o'clock (their luggage they had directed to be forwarded to the City, from Rochester), and being fortunate enough to secure places on the outside of a coach, arrived in London in sound health and spirits, on that same afternoon.

The next three or four days were occupied with the preparations which were necessary for their journey to the borough of Eatanswill. As any reference to that most important undertaking demands a separate chapter, we may devote the few lines which remain at the close of this, to narrate, with great brevity, the history of the antiquarian discovery.

It appears from the Transactions of the Club, then, that Mr. Pickwick lectured upon the discovery at a General Club Meeting, convened on the night succeeding their return, and entered into a variety of ingenious and erudite speculations on the meaning of the inscription. It also appears that a skilful artist executed a faithful delineation of the curiosity, which was engraven on stone, and presented to the Royal Antiquarian Society, and other learned bodies—that heartburnings and jealousies without number, were created by rival controversies which were penned upon the subject—and that Mr. Pickwick himself wrote a Pamphlet, containing ninety-six pages of very small print, and twenty-seven different readings of the inscription. That three old gentlemen cut off their eldest sons with a shilling a-piece for presuming to doubt the antiquity of the fragment—and that one enthusiastic individual cut himself off prematurely, in despair at being unable to fathom its meaning. That Mr. Pickwick was elected an honorary member of seventeen native and foreign societies, for making the discovery; that none of the seventeen could make anything of it; but that all the seventeen agreed it was very extraordinary.

Mr. Blotton, indeed—and the name will be doomed to the undying contempt of those who cultivate the mysterious and the sublime—Mr. Blotton, we say, with the doubt and cavilling peculiar to vulgar minds, presumed to state a view of the case, as degrading as ridiculous.   Mr. Blotton, with a mean desire to tarnish the lustre of the immortal name of Pickwick, actually undertook a journey to Cobham in person, and on his return, sarcastically observed in an oration at the club, that he had seen the man from whom the stone was purchased ; that the man presumed the stone to be ancient, but solemnly denied the antiquity of the inscription—inasmuch as he repre- sented it to have been rudely carved by himself in an idle mood, and to display letters intended to bear neither more nor less than the simple construction of—" BILL STUMPS, HIS MARK ; " and that Mr. Stumps, being little in the habit of original composition, and more accustomed to be guided by the sound of words than by the strict rules of orthography, had omitted the concluding " L " of his christian name.

The Pickwick Club (as might have been expected from so enlightened an Institution) received this statement with the contempt it deserved, expelled the presumptuous and ill- conditioned Blotton, and voted Mr. Pickwick a pair of gold spectacles, in token of their confidence and approbation ; in return for which, Mr. Pickwick caused a portrait of himself to be painted, and hung up in the club room.

Mr. Blotton though ejected was not conquered. He also wrote a pamphlet, addressed to the seventeen learned societies, native and foreign, containing a repetition of the statement he had already made, and rather more than half intimating his opinion that the seventeen learned societies were so many " humbugs." Hereupon the virtuous indignation of the seven- teen learned societies, native and foreign, being roused, several fresh pamphlets appeared ; the foreign learned societies corre- sponded with the native learned societies ; the native learned societies translated the pamphlets of the foreign learned societies into English ; the foreign learned societies translated the pamphlets of the native learned societies into all sorts of languages; and thus commenced that celebrated scientific discussion so well known to all men, as the Pickwick controversy.

But this base attempt to injure Mr. Pickwick, recoiled upon the head of its calumnious author. The seventeen learned societies unanimously voted the presumptuous Blotton an ignorant meddler, and forthwith set to work upon more treatises than ever. And to this day the stone remains, an illegible monument of Mr. Pickwick's greatness, and a lasting trophy to the littleness of his enemies.

CHAPTER XII.

DESCRIPTIVE OF A VERY IMPORTANT PROCEEDING ON THE PART OF
MR. PICKWICK; NO LESS AN EPOCH IN HIS LIFE, THAN IN
THIS HISTORY.

MR. PICKWICK's apartments in Goswell Street, although on
a limited scale, were not only of a very neat and comfortable
description, but peculiarly adapted for the residence of a man
of his genius and observation. His sitting-room was the first
floor front, his bed-room the second floor front; and thus,
whether he were sitting at his desk in his parlour, or standing
before the dressing-glass in his dormitory, he had an equal
opportunity of contemplating human nature in all the numerous phases it exhibits, in that not more populous than popular
thoroughfare. His landlady, Mrs. Bardell—the relict and sole
executrix of a deceased custom-house officer—was a comely
woman of bustling manners and agreeable appearance, with
a natural genius for cooking, improved by study and long
practice, into an exquisite talent. There were no children, no
servants, no fowls. The only other inmates of the house were
a large man and a small boy; the first a lodger, the second a
production of Mrs. Bardell's. The large man was always home
precisely at ten o'clock at night, at which hour he regularly
condensed himself into the limits of a dwarfish French bedstead
in the back parlour; and the infantine sports and gymnastic
exercises of Master Bardell were exclusively confined to the
neighbouring pavements and gutters. Cleanliness and quiet

reigned throughout the house; and in it Mr. Pickwick's will was law.

To any one acquainted with these points of the domestic economy of the establishment, and conversant with the admirable regulation of Mr. Pickwick's mind, his appearance and behaviour on the morning previous to that which had been fixed upon for the journey to Eatanswill, would have been most mysterious and unaccountable. He paced the room to and fro with hurried steps, popped his head out of the window at intervals of about three minutes each, constantly referred to his watch, and exhibited many other manifestations of impatience very unusual with him. It was evident that something of great importance was in contemplation, but what that something was, not even Mrs. Bardell herself had been enabled to discover.

"Mrs. Bardell," said Mr. Pickwick, at last, as that amiable female approached the termination of a prolonged dusting of the apartment.

"Sir," said Mrs. Bardell.

"Your little boy is a very long time gone."

"Why it's a good long way to the Borough, sir," remonstrated Mrs. Bardell.

"Ah," said Mr. Pickwick, "very true; so it is."

Mr. Pickwick relapsed into silence, and Mrs. Bardell resumed her dusting.

"Mrs. Bardell," said Mr. Pickwick, at the expiration of a few minutes.

"Sir," said Mrs. Bardell again.

"Do you think it a much greater expense to keep two people, than to keep one?"

"La, Mr. Pickwick," said Mrs. Bardell, colouring up to the very border of her cap, as she fancied she observed a species of matrimonial twinkle in the eyes of her lodger; "La, Mr. Pickwick, what a question!"

"Well, but *do* you?" inquired Mr. Pickwick.

"That depends—" said Mrs. Bardell, approaching the duster very near to Mr. Pickwick's elbow, which was planted on the table—"that depends a good deal upon the person, you know, Mr. Pickwick; and whether it's a saving and careful person, sir."

"That's very true," said Mr. Pickwick, "but the person I have in my eye (here he looked very hard at Mrs. Bardell) I think possesses these qualities; and has, moreover, a considerable knowledge of the world, and a great deal of sharpness, Mrs. Bardell; which may be of material use to me."

"La, Mr. Pickwick," said Mrs. Bardell; the crimson rising to her cap-border again.

"I do," said Mr. Pickwick, growing energetic, as was his wont in speaking of a subject which interested him, "I do, indeed; and to tell you the truth, Mrs. Bardell, I have made up my mind."

"Dear me, sir," exclaimed Mrs. Bardell.

"You'll think it very strange now," said the amiable Mr. Pickwick, with a good-humoured glance at his companion, "that I never consulted you about this matter, and never even mentioned it, till I sent your little boy out this morning—eh?"

Mrs. Bardell could only reply by a look. She had long worshipped Mr. Pickwick at a distance, but here she was, all at once, raised to a pinnacle to which her wildest and most extravagant hopes had never dared to aspire. Mr. Pickwick was going to propose—a deliberate plan, too—sent her little boy to the Borough, to get him out of the way—how thoughtful—how considerate!

"Well," said Mr. Pickwick, "what do you think?"

"Oh, Mr. Pickwick," said Mrs. Bardell, trembling with agitation, "you're very kind, sir."

"It'll save you a good deal of trouble, won't it?" said Mr. Pickwick.

"Oh, I never thought anything of the trouble, sir," replied Mrs. Bardell; "and, of course, I should take more trouble to please you then, than ever; but it is so kind of you, Mr. Pickwick, to have so much consideration for my loneliness."

"Ah, to be sure," said Mr. Pickwick; "I never thought of that. When I am in town, you'll always have somebody to sit with you. To be sure, so you will."

"I'm sure I ought to be a very happy woman," said Mrs. Bardell.

"And your little boy——" said Mr. Pickwick.

"Bless his heart!" interposed Mrs. Bardell, with a maternal sob.

"He, too, will have a companion," resumed Mr. Pickwick, "a lively one, who'll teach him, I'll be bound, more tricks in a week than he would ever learn in a year." And Mr. Pickwick smiled placidly.

"Oh you dear——" said Mrs. Bardell.

Mr. Pickwick started.

"Oh you kind, good, playful dear," said Mrs. Bardell; and without more ado, she rose from her chair, and flung her arms round Mr. Pickwick's neck, with a cataract of tears and a chorus of sobs.

"Bless my soul," cried the astonished Mr. Pickwick;—"Mrs. Bardell my good woman—dear me, what a situation—pray consider.—Mrs. Bardell, don't—if anybody should come——"

"Oh, let them come," exclaimed Mrs. Bardell, frantically; "I'll never leave you—dear, kind, good, soul;" and, with these words, Mrs. Bardell clung the tighter.

"Mercy upon me," said Mr. Pickwick, struggling violently, "I hear somebody coming up the stairs. Don't, don't, there's a good creature, don't." But entreaty and remonstrance were alike unavailing: for Mrs. Bardell had fainted in Mr. Pickwick's arms; and before he could gain time to deposit her on a chair, Master Bardell entered the room, ushering in Mr. Tupman, Mr. Winkle, and Mr. Snodgrass.

Mr. Pickwick was struck motionless and speechless. He stood with his lovely burden in his arms, gazing vacantly on the countenances of his friends, without the slightest attempt at recognition or explanation. They, in their turn, stared at him; and Master Bardell, in his turn, stared at everybody.

Mrs. Bardell Faints in Mr. Pickwick's Arms

PERPLEXITY OF MR. PICKWICK.

The astonishment of the Pickwickians was so absorbing, and the perplexity of Mr. Pickwick was so extreme, that they might have remained in exactly the same relative situations until the suspended animation of the lady was restored, had it not been for a most beautiful and touching expression of filial affection on the part of her youthful son. Clad in a tight suit of corderoy, spangled with brass buttons of a very considerable size, he at first stood at the door astounded and uncertain; but by degrees, the impression that his mother must have suffered some personal damage, pervaded his partially developed mind, and considering Mr. Pickwick as the aggressor, he set up an appalling and semi-earthly kind of howling, and butting forward with his head, commenced assailing that immortal gentleman about the back and legs, with such blows and pinches as the strength of his arm, and the violence of his excitement, allowed.

"Take this little villain away," said the agonised Mr. Pickwick, "he's mad."

"What *is* the matter?" said the three tongue-tied Pickwickians.

"I don't know," replied Mr. Pickwick, pettishly. "Take away the boy" (here Mr. Winkle carried the interesting boy, screaming and struggling, to the further end of the apartment). "Now, help me, lead this woman down stairs."

"Oh, I am better now," said Mrs. Bardell, faintly.

"Let me lead you down stairs," said the ever gallant Mr. Tupman.

"Thank you, sir—thank you;" exclaimed Mrs. Bardell, hysterically. And down stairs she was led accordingly, accompanied by her affectionate son.

"I cannot conceive—" said Mr. Pickwick, when his friend returned—"I cannot conceive what has been the matter with that woman. I had merely announced to her my intention of keeping a man servant, when she fell into the extraordinary paroxysm in which you found her. Very extraordinary thing."

"Very," said his three friends.

"Placed me in such an extremely awkward situation," continued Mr. Pickwick.

"Very," was the reply of his followers, as they coughed slightly, and looked dubiously at each other.

This behaviour was not lost upon Mr. Pickwick. He remarked their incredulity. They evidently suspected him.

"There is a man in the passage now," said Mr. Tupman.

"It's the man I spoke to you about," said Mr. Pickwick, "I sent for him to the Borough this morning. Have the goodness to call him up, Snodgrass."

Mr. Snodgrass did as he was desired; and Mr. Samuel Weller forthwith presented himself.

"Oh—you remember me, I suppose?" said Mr. Pickwick.

"I should think so," replied Sam, with a patronising wink. "Queer start that 'ere, but he was one too many for you, warn't he? Up to snuff and a pinch or two over—eh?"

"Never mind that matter now," said Mr. Pickwick hastily, "I want to speak to you about something else. Sit down."

"Thank'ee, sir," said Sam. And down he sat without farther bidding, having previously deposited his old white hat on the landing outside the door. "Ta'nt a werry good 'un to look at," said Sam, "but it's an astonishin' 'un to wear; and afore the brim went, it was a werry handsome tile. Hows'ever it's lighter without it, that's one thing, and every hole lets in some air, that's another—wentilation gossamer I calls it." On the delivery of this sentiment, Mr. Weller smiled agreeably upon the assembled Pickwickians.

"Now with regard to the matter on which I, with the concurrence of these gentlemen, sent for you," said Mr. Pickwick

"That's the pint, sir," interposed Sam; "out vith it, as the father said to the child, wen he swallowed a farden."

"We want to know, in the first place," said Mr. Pickwick, "whether you have any reason to be discontented with your present situation."

"Afore I answers that 'ere question, gen'lm'm," replied Mr.

Weller, "*I* should like to know, in the first place, whether you're a goin' to purwide me with a better."

A sunbeam of placid benevolence played on Mr. Pickwick's features as he said, "I have half made up my mind to engage you myself."

"Have you, though?" said Sam.

Mr. Pickwick nodded in the affirmative.

"Wages?" inquired Sam.

"Twelve pounds a year," replied Mr. Pickwick.

"Clothes?"

"Two suits."

"Work?"

"To attend upon me; and travel about with me and these gentlemen here."

"Take the bill down," said Sam, emphatically. "I'm let to a single gentleman, and the terms is agreed upon."

"You accept the situation?" inquired Mr. Pickwick.

"Certn'ly," replied Sam. "If the clothes fits me half as well as the place, they'll do."

"You can get a character of course?" said Mr. Pickwick.

"Ask the landlady o' the White Hart about that, sir," replied Sam.

"Can you come this evening?"

"I'll get into the clothes this minute, if they're here," said Sam with great alacrity.

"Call at eight this evening," said Mr. Pickwick; "and if the inquiries are satisfactory, they shall be provided."

With the single exception of one amiable indiscretion, in which an assistant housemaid had equally participated, the history of Mr. Weller's conduct was so very blameless, that Mr. Pickwick felt fully justified in closing the engagement that very evening. With the promptness and energy which characterised not only the public proceedings, but all the private actions of this extraordinary man, he at once led his new attendant to one of those convenient emporiums where gentlemen's new and second-hand clothes are provided, and the troublesome and inconvenient formality of measurement dispensed with; and before night had closed in, Mr. Weller was furnished with a grey coat with the P. C. button, a black hat with a cockade to it, a pink striped waistcoat, light breeches and gaiters, and a variety of other necessaries, too numerous to recapitulate.

"Well," said that suddenly-transformed individual, as he took his seat on the outside of the Eatanswill coach next morning; "I wonder whether I'm meant to be a footman, or a groom, or a gamekeeper, or a seedsman. I looks like a sort of compo of every one on 'em. Never mind; there 's change of air, plenty to see, and little to do; and all this suits my complaint uncommon; so long life to the Pickvicks, says I!"

CHAPTER XIII.

SOME ACCOUNT OF EATANSWILL; OF THE STATE OF PARTIES THEREIN; AND OF THE ELECTION OF A MEMBER TO SERVE IN PARLIAMENT FOR THAT ANCIENT, LOYAL, AND PATRIOTIC BOROUGH.

WE will frankly acknowledge, that up to the period of our being first immersed in the voluminous papers of the Pickwick Club, we had never heard of Eatanswill; we will with equal candour admit, that we have in vain searched for proof of the actual existence of such a place at the present day. Knowing the deep reliance to be placed on every note and statement of Mr. Pickwick's, and not presuming to set up our recollection against the recorded declarations of that great man, we have consulted every authority, bearing upon the subject, to which we could possibly refer. We have traced every name in schedules A and B, without meeting with that of Eatanswill; we have minutely examined every corner of the Pocket County Maps issued for the benefit of society by our distinguished publishers, and the same result has attended our investigation. We are therefore led to believe, that Mr. Pickwick, with that anxious desire to abstain from giving offence to any, and with those delicate feelings for which all who knew him well know he was so eminently remarkable, purposely substituted a fictitious designation, for the real name of the place in which his observations were made. We are confirmed in this belief by a little circumstance, apparently slight and trivial in itself, but when considered in this point of view, not undeserving of notice. In Mr. Pickwick's note-book, we can just trace an entry of the fact, that the places of himself and followers were booked by the Norwich coach; but this entry was afterwards lined through, as if for the purpose of concealing even the direction in which the borough is situated. We will not, therefore, hazard a guess upon the subject, but will at once proceed with this history; content with the materials which its characters have provided for us.

It appears, then, that the Eatanswill people, like the people of many other small towns, considered themselves of the utmost and most mighty importance, and that every man in Eatanswill, conscious of the weight that attached to his example, felt himself bound to unite, heart and soul, with one of the two great parties that divided the town—the Blues and the Buffs. Now the Blues lost no opportunity of opposing the Buffs, and the Buffs lost no opportunity of opposing the Blues; and the consequence was, that whenever the Buffs and Blues met together at public meeting, Town-Hall, fair, or market, disputes and high words arose between them. With these dissensions it is almost superfluous to say that everything in Eatanswill was made a party question. If the Buffs proposed to new skylight the market-place, the Blues got up public meetings, and denounced the proceeding; if the Blues proposed the erection of an additional pump in the High Street, the Buffs rose as one man and stood aghast at the enormity. There were Blue shops and Buff shops, Blue inns and Buff inns;—there was a Blue aisle and a Buff aisle, in the very church itself.

Of course it was essentially and indispensably necessary that each of these powerful parties should have its chosen organ and representative: and, accordingly, there were two newspapers in the town—the Eatanswill Gazette and the Eatanswill Independent; the former advocating Blue principles, and the latter conducted on grounds decidedly Buff. Fine newspapers they were. Such leading articles, and such spirited attacks!—" Our worthless contemporary, the Gazette "—" That disgraceful and dastardly journal, the Independent "—" That false and scurrilous print, the Independent "—" That vile and slanderous calumniator, the Gazette ; " these, and other spirit-stirring denunciations were strewn plentifully over the columns of each, in every number, and excited feelings of the most intense delight and indignation in the bosoms of the towns-people.

Mr. Pickwick, with his usual foresight and sagacity, had chosen a peculiarly desirable moment for his visit to the borough. Never was such a contest known. The Honourable Samuel Slumkey, of Slumkey Hall, was the Blue candidate ; and Horatio Fizkin, Esq., of Fizkin Lodge, near Eatanswill, had been prevailed upon by his friends to stand forward on the Buff interest. The Gazette warned the electors of Eatan-swill that the eyes not only of England, but of the whole civilised world, were upon them ; and the Independent imperatively demanded to know, whether the constituency of Eatanswill were the grand fellows they had always taken them for, or base and servile tools, undeserving alike the name of Englishmen and the blessings of freedom. Never had such a commotion agitated the town before.

It was late in the evening, when Mr. Pickwick and his companions, assisted by Sam, dismounted from the roof of the Eatanswill coach. Large blue silk flags were flying from the windows of the Town Arms Inn, and bills were posted in every sash, intimating, in gigantic letters, that the honour-able Samuel Slumkey's Committee sat there daily. A crowd of idlers were assembled in the road, looking at a hoarse man in the balcony, who was apparently talking himself very red in the face in Mr. Slumkey's behalf ; but the force and point of whose arguments were somewhat impaired by the perpetual beating of four large drums which Mr. Fizkin's committee had stationed at the street corner. There was a busy little man beside him, though, who took off his hat at intervals and motioned to the people to cheer, which they regularly did, most enthusiastically; and as the red-faced gentleman went on talking till he was redder in the face than ever, it seemed to answer his purpose quite as well as if anybody had heard him.

The Pickwickians had no sooner dismounted, than they were surrounded by a branch mob of the honest and independent, who forthwith set up three deafening cheers, which being responded to by the main body (for it's not at all necessary for a crowd to know what they are cheering about) swelled into a tremendous roar of triumph, which stopped even the red-faced man in the balcony.

"Hurrah!" shouted the mob in conclusion.

"One cheer more," screamed the little fugleman in the balcony, and out shouted the mob again, as if lungs were cast iron, with steel works.

"Slumkey for ever!" roared the honest and independent.

"Slumkey for ever!" echoed Mr. Pickwick, taking off his hat.

"No Fizkin!" roared the crowd.

"Certainly not!" shouted Mr. Pickwick.

"Hurrah!" And then there was another roaring, like that of a whole menagerie when the elephant has rung the bell for the cold meat.

"Who is Slumkey?" whispered Mr. Tupman.

"I don't know," replied Mr. Pickwick in the same tone. "Hush. Don't ask any questions. It's always best on these occasions to do what the mob do."

"But suppose there are two mobs?" suggested Mr. Snodgrass.

"Shout with the largest," replied Mr. Pickwick.

Volumes could not have said more.

They entered the house, the crowd opening right and left to let them pass, and cheering vociferously. The first object of consideration was to secure quarters for the night.

"Can we have beds here?" inquired Mr. Pickwick, summoning the waiter.

A DIFFICULT QUESTION.

"Don't know, sir," replied the man; "afraid we're full, sir—I'll inquire, sir." Away he went for that purpose, and presently returned, to ask whether the gentlemen were "Blue."

As neither Mr. Pickwick nor his companions took any vital interest in the cause of either candidate, the question was rather a difficult one to answer. In this dilemma Mr. Pickwick bethought himself of his new friend, Mr. Perker.

"Do you know a gentleman of the name of Perker?" inquired Mr. Pickwick.

"Certainly, sir; honourable Mr. Samuel Slumkey's agent."

"He is Blue, I think?"

"Oh yes, sir."

"Then *we* are Blue," said Mr. Pickwick; but observing that the man looked rather doubtful at this accommodating announcement, he gave him his card, and desired him to present it to Mr. Perker forthwith, if he should happen to be in the house. The waiter retired; and re-appearing almost immediately with a request that Mr. Pickwick would follow him, led the way to a large room on the first floor, where, seated at a long table covered with books and papers, was Mr. Perker.

"Ah—ah, my dear sir," said the little man, advancing to meet him; "very happy to see you, my dear sir, very. Pray sit down. So you have carried your intention into effect. You have come down here to see an election—eh?"

Mr. Pickwick replied in the affirmative.

"Spirited contest, my dear sir," said the little man.

"I am delighted to hear it," said Mr. Pickwick, rubbing his hands. "I like to see sturdy patriotism, on whatever side it is called forth;—and so it's a spirited contest?"

"Oh yes," said the little man, "very much so indeed. We have opened all the public-houses in the place, and left our adversary nothing but the beer-shops—masterly stroke of policy that, my dear sir, eh?"—the little man smiled complacently, and took a large pinch of snuff.

"And what are the probabilities as to the result of the contest?" inquired Mr. Pickwick.

"Why doubtful, my dear sir; rather doubtful as yet," replied the little man. "Fizkin's people have got three-and-thirty voters in the lock-up coach-house at the White Hart."

"In the coach-house!" said Mr. Pickwick, considerably astonished by this second stroke of policy.

"They keep 'em locked up there till they want 'em," resumed the little man. "The effect of that is, you see, to prevent our getting at them; and even if we could, it would be of no use, for they keep them very drunk on purpose. Smart fellow Fizkin's agent—very smart fellow indeed."

Mr. Pickwick stared, but said nothing.

"We are pretty confident, though," said Mr. Perker, sinking his voice almost to a whisper. "We had a little tea-party here, last night—five-and-forty women, my dear sir—and gave every one of 'em a green parasol when she went away."

"A parasol!" said Mr. Pickwick.

"Fact, my dear sir, fact. Five-and-forty green parasols, at seven and sixpence a-piece. All women like finery,—extraordinary the effects of those parasols. Secured all their husbands, and half their brothers — beats stockings, and flannel, and all that sort of thing hollow. My idea, my dear sir, entirely. Hail, rain, or sunshine, you can't walk half a dozen yards up the street, without encountering half a dozen green parasols."

Here the little man indulged in a convulsion of mirth, which was only checked by the entrance of a third party.

This was a tall, thin man, with a sandy-coloured head inclined to baldness, and a face in which solemn importance was blended with a look of unfathomable profundity. He was dressed in a long brown surtout, with a black cloth waistcoat, and drab trousers. A double eye-glass dangled at his waistcoat: and on his head he wore a very low-crowned hat with a broad brim. The new-comer was introduced to Mr. Pickwick as Mr. Pott, the editor of the Eatanswill

Gazette. After a few preliminary remarks, Mr. Pott turned round to Mr. Pickwick, and said with solemnity—

"This contest excites great interest in the metropolis, sir?"

"I believe it does," said Mr. Pickwick.

"To which I have reason to know," said Pott, looking towards Mr. Perker for corroboration,—"to which I have reason to know that my article of last Saturday in some degree contributed."

"Not the least doubt of it," said the little man.

"The press is a mighty engine, sir," said Pott.

Mr. Pickwick yielded his fullest assent to the proposition.

"But I trust, sir," said Pott, "that I have never abused the enormous power I wield. I trust, sir, that I have never pointed the noble instrument which is placed in my hands, against the sacred bosom of private life, or the tender breast of individual reputation;—I trust, sir, that I have devoted my energies to—to endeavours—humble they may be, humble I know they are—to instil those principles of—which—are—"

Here the editor of the Eatanswill Gazette, appearing to ramble, Mr. Pickwick came to his relief, and said—

"Certainly."

"And what, sir"—said Pott—"what, sir, let me ask you as an impartial man, is the state of the public mind in London, with reference to my contest with the Independent?"

"Greatly excited, no doubt," interposed Mr. Perker, with a look of slyness which was very likely accidental.

"The contest," said Pott, "shall be prolonged so long as I have health and strength, and that portion of talent with which I am gifted. From that contest, sir, although it may unsettle men's minds and excite their feelings, and render them incapable for the discharge of the every-day duties of ordinary life; from that contest, sir, I will never shrink, till I have set my heel upon the Eatanswill Independent. I wish the people of London, and the people of this country to know, sir, that they may rely upon me;—that I will not desert them, that I am resolved to stand by them, sir, to the last."

"Your conduct is most noble, sir," said Mr. Pickwick; and he grasped the hand of the magnanimous Pott.

"You are, sir, I perceive, a man of sense and talent," said Mr. Pott, almost breathless with the vehemence of his patriotic declaration. "I am most happy, sir, to make the acquaintance of such a man."

"And I," said Mr. Pickwick, "feel deeply honoured by this expression of your opinion. Allow me, sir, to introduce you to my fellow-travellers, the other corresponding members of the club I am proud to have founded."

"I shall be delighted," said Mr. Pott.

Mr. Pickwick withdrew, and returning with his friends, presented them in due form to the editor of the Eatanswill Gazette.

"Now, my dear Pott," said little Mr. Perker, "the question is, what are we to do with our friends here?"

"We can stop in this house, I suppose," said Mr. Pickwick.

"Not a spare bed in the house, my dear sir—not a single bed."

"Extremely awkward," said Mr. Pickwick.

"Very;" said his fellow-voyagers.

"I have an idea upon this subject," said Mr. Pott, "which I think may be very successfully adopted. They have two beds at the Peacock, and I can boldly say, on behalf of Mrs. Pott, that she will be delighted to accommodate Mr. Pickwick and any of his friends, if the other two gentlemen and their servant do not object to shifting, as they best can, at the Peacock."

After repeated pressings on the part of Mr. Pott, and repeated protestations on that of Mr. Pickwick that he could not think of incommoding or troubling his amiable wife, it was decided that it was the only feasible arrangement that could be made. So it *was* made; and after dining together at the Town Arms, the friends separated, Mr. Tupman and Mr. Snodgrass repairing to the Peacock, and Mr. Pickwick and Mr. Winkle proceeding to the mansion of Mr. Pott; it having been previously arranged that they should all re-assemble at the Town Arms in the morning, and accompany the honourable Samuel Slumkey's procession to the place of nomination.

Mr. Pott's domestic circle was limited to himself and his wife. All men whom mighty genius has raised to a proud eminence in the world, have usually some little weakness which appears the more conspicuous from the contrast it presents to their general character. If Mr. Pott had a weakness, it was, perhaps, that he was *rather* too submissive to the somewhat contemptuous control and sway of his wife. We do not feel justified in laying any particular stress upon the fact, because on the present occasion all Mrs. Pott's most winning ways were brought into requisition to receive the two gentlemen.

"My dear," said Mr. Pott, "Mr. Pickwick—Mr. Pickwick of London."

Mrs. Pott received Mr. Pickwick's paternal grasp of the hand with enchanting sweetness : and Mr. Winkle, who had not been announced at all, slided and bowed, unnoticed, in an obscure corner.

"P. my dear—" said Mrs. Pott.

"My life," said Mr. Pott.

"Pray introduce the other gentleman."

"I beg a thousand pardons," said Mr. Pott. "Permit me, Mrs. Pott, Mr.—"

"Winkle," said Mr. Pickwick.

"Winkle," echoed Mr. Pott; and the ceremony of introduction was complete.

"We owe you many apologies, ma'am," said Mr. Pickwick, "for disturbing your domestic arrangements at so short a notice."

"I beg you won't mention it, sir," replied the feminine Pott, with vivacity. "It is a high treat to me, I assure you, to see any new faces; living as I do, from day to day, and week to week, in this dull place, and seeing nobody."

"Nobody, my dear!" exclaimed Mr. Pott, archly.

"Nobody but *you*," retorted Mrs. Pott, with asperity.

"You see, Mr. Pickwick," said the host in explanation of his wife's lament, "that we are in some measure cut off from many enjoyments and pleasures of which we might otherwise partake. My public station, as editor of the Eatanswill Gazette, the position which that paper holds in the country, my constant immersion in the vortex of politics—"

"P. my dear—" interposed Mrs. Pott.

"My life—" said the editor.

"I wish, my dear, you would endeavour to find some topic of conversation in which these gentlemen might take some rational interest."

"But my love," said Mr. Pott, with great humility, "Mr. Pickwick does take an interest in it."

"It's well for him if he can," said Mrs. Pott, emphatically; "I am wearied out of my life with your politics, and quarrels with the Independent, and nonsense. I am quite astonished P. at your making such an exhibition of your absurdity."

"But my dear—" said Mr. Pott.

"Oh, nonsense, don't talk to me;" said Mrs. Pott. "Do you play *ecarté*, sir?"

"I shall be very happy to learn under your tuition," replied Mr. Winkle.

"Well, then, draw that little table into this window, and let me get out of hearing of those prosy politics."

"Jane," said Mr. Pott, to the servant who brought in candles, "go down into the office, and bring me up the file of the Gazette for Eighteen Hundred and Twenty Eight. I'll read you—" added the editor, turning to Mr. Pickwick, "I'll just read you a few of the leaders I wrote at that time upon the Buff job of appointing a new tollman to the turnpike here; I rather think they'll amuse you."

"I should like to hear them very much, indeed," said Mr. Pickwick.

Up came the file, and down sat the editor, with Mr. Pickwick at his side.

"A DELIGHTFUL OLD DEAR."

We have in vain pored over the leaves of Mr. Pickwick's note-book, in the hope of meeting with a general summary of these beautiful compositions. We have every reason to believe that he was perfectly enraptured with the vigour and freshness of the style; indeed Mr. Winkle has recorded the fact that his eyes were closed, as if with excess of pleasure, during the whole time of their perusal.

The announcement of supper put a stop to the game at *ecarté*, and the recapitulation of the beauties of the Eatanswill Gazette. Mrs. Pott was in the highest spirits and the most agreeable humour. Mr. Winkle had already made considerable progress in her good opinion, and she did not hesitate to inform him, confidentially, that Mr. Pickwick was "a delightful old dear." These terms convey a familiarity of expression, in which few of those who were intimately acquainted with that colossal-minded man, would have presumed to indulge. We have preserved them, nevertheless, as affording at once a touching and a convincing proof of the estimation in which he was held by every class of society, and the ease with which he made his way to their hearts and feelings.

It was a late hour of the night—long after Mr. Tupman and Mr. Snodgrass had fallen asleep in the inmost recesses of the Peacock—when the two friends retired to rest. Slumber soon fell upon the senses of Mr. Winkle, but his feelings had been excited, and his admiration roused; and for many hours after sleep had rendered him insensible to earthly objects, the face and figure of the agreeable Mrs. Pott presented themselves again and again to his wandering imagination.

The noise and bustle which ushered in the morning, were sufficient to dispel from the mind of the most romantic visionary in existence, any associations but those which were immediately connected with the rapidly-approaching election. The beating of drums, the blowing of horns and trumpets, the shouting of men, and tramping of horses, echoed and re-echoed through the streets from the earliest dawn of day; and an occasional fight between the light skirmishers of either party at once enlivened the preparations and agreeably diversified their character.

"Well, Sam," said Mr. Pickwick, as his valet appeared at his bed-room door, just as he was concluding his toilet; "all alive to-day, I suppose?"

"Reg'lar game, sir," replied Mr. Weller; "our people's a col-lecting down at the Town Arms, and they're a hollering themselves hoarse already."

"Ah," said Mr. Pickwick, "do they seem devoted to their party, Sam?"

"Never see such dewotion in my life, sir."

"Energetic, eh?" said Mr. Pickwick.

"Uncommon," replied Sam; "I never see men eat and drink so much afore. I wonder they a'nt afeer'd o' bustin."

"That's the mistaken kindness of the gentry here," said Mr. Pickwick.

"Wery likely," replied Sam, briefly.

"Fine, fresh, hearty fellows they seem," said Mr. Pickwick, glancing from the window.

"Wery fresh," replied Sam; "me, and the two waiters at the Peacock, has been a pumpin' over the independent woters as supped there last night."

"Pumping over independent voters!" exclaimed Mr. Pickwick.

"Yes," said his attendant, "every man slept vere he fell down; we dragged 'em out, one by one, this mornin', and put 'em under the pump, and they're in reg'lar fine order, now. Shillin' a head the committee paid for that 'ere job."

"Can such things be!" exclaimed the astonished Mr. Pickwick.

"Lord bless your heart, sir," said Sam, "why where was you half baptized?—that's nothin', that a'nt."

"Nothing?" said Mr. Pickwick.

"Nothin' at all, sir," replied his attendant. "The night

afore the last day o' the last election here, the opposite party bribed the bar-maid at the Town Arms, to hocus the brandy and water of fourteen unpolled electors as was a stoppin' in the house."

" What do you mean by 'hocussing' brandy and water?" inquired Mr. Pickwick.

" Puttin' laud'num in it," replied Sam. " Blessed if she didn't send 'em all to sleep till twelve hours arter the election was over. They took one man up to the booth, in a truck, fast asleep, by way of experiment, but it was no go—they wouldn't poll him; so they brought him back, and put him to bed again."

" Strange practices, these," said Mr. Pickwick ; half speaking to himself and half addressing Sam.

" Not half so strange as a miraculous circumstance as happened to my own father, at an election time, in this werry place, sir," replied Sam.

" What was that ?" inquired Mr. Pickwick.

" Why he drove a coach down here once," said Sam; " 'lection time came on, and he was engaged by vun party to bring down woters from London. Night afore he was a going to drive up, committee on t'other side sends for him quietly, and away he goes vith the messenger, who shows him in ;—large room—lots of gen'l'm'n—heaps of papers, pens and ink, and all that 'ere. ' Ah, Mr. Weller,' says the gen'l'm'n in the chair, ' glad to see you, sir; how are you ? '—' Werry well, thank'ee, sir,' says my father; ' I hope *you're* pretty middlin,' says he—' Pretty well, thank'ee, sir,' says the gen'l'm'n ; ' sit down, Mr. Weller—pray sit down, sir.' So my father sits down, and he and the gen'l'm'n looks werry hard at each other. ' You don't remember me ?' says the gen'l'm'n.— ' Can't say I do,' says my father—' Oh, I know you,' says the gen'l'm'n ; ' know'd you when you was a boy,' says he.—' Well, I don't remember you,' says my father—' That's very odd,' says the gen'l'm'n—' Werry,' says my father—' You must have a bad mem'ry, Mr. Weller,' says the gen'l'm'n—' Well, it is a wery bad 'un,' says my father—'I thought so,' says the gen'l'm'n. So then they pours him out a glass of wine, and gammons him about his driving, and gets him into a reg'lar good humour, and at last shoves a twenty pound note in his hand. 'It's a werry bad road between this and London,' says the gen'l'm'n.—'Here and there it *is* a heavy road,' says my father—''Specially near the canal, I think,' says the gen'l'm'n—'Nasty bit that 'ere,' says my father— 'Well, Mr. Weller,' says the gen'l'm'n, 'you're a wery good whip, and can do what you like with your horses, we know. We're all wery fond o' you, Mr. Weller, so in case you *should* have an accident when you're a bringing these here woters down, and *should* tip 'em over into the canal vithout hurtin' of 'em, this is for yourself,' says he—'Gen'l'm'n, you're wery kind,' says my father, 'and I'll drink your health in another glass of wine,' says he; which he did, and then buttons up the money, and bows himself out. You wouldn't believe, sir," continued Sam, with a look of inexpressible impudence at his master, "that on the wery day as he came down with them woters, his coach *was* upset on that 'ere wery spot, and ev'ry man on 'em was turned into the canal."

"And got out again?" inquired Mr. Pickwick, hastily.

"Why," replied Sam, very slowly, "I rather think one old gen'l'm'n was missin'; I know his hat was found, but I a'n't quite certain whether his head was in it or not. But what I look at, is the hex-traordinary, and wonderful coincidence, that arter what that gen'l'm'n said, my father's coach should be upset in that wery place, and on that wery day!"

"It is, no doubt, a very extraordinary circumstance indeed," said Mr. Pickwick. "But brush my hat, Sam, for I hear Mr. Winkle calling me to breakfast."

With these words Mr. Pickwick descended to the parlour, where he found breakfast laid, and the family already assembled. The meal was hastily despatched; each of the gentlemen's hats was decorated with an enormous blue favour, made up by the fair hands of Mrs. Pott herself; and as Mr.

Winkle had undertaken to escort that lady to a house-top, in the immediate vicinity of the hustings, Mr. Pickwick and Mr. Pott repaired alone to the Town Arms, from the back window of which, one of Mr. Slumkey's committee was addressing six small boys, and one girl, whom he dignified, at every second sentence, with the imposing title of "men of Eatanswill," whereat the six small boys aforesaid cheered prodigiously.

The stable-yard exhibited unequivocal symptoms of the glory and strength of the Eatanswill Blues. There was a regular army of blue flags, some with one handle, and some with two, exhibiting appropriate devices, in golden characters four feet high, and stout in proportion. There was a grand band of trumpets, bassoons and drums, marshalled four abreast, and earning their money, if ever men did, especially the drum beaters, who were very muscular. There were bodies of constables with blue staves, twenty committee-men with blue scarfs, and a mob of voters with blue cockades. There were electors on horseback, and electors a-foot. There was an open carriage and four, for the honourable Samuel Slumkey; and there were four carriages and pair, for his friends and supporters; and the flags were rustling, and the band was playing, and the constables were swearing, and the twenty committee-men were squabbling, and the mob were shouting, and the horses were backing, and the post-boys perspiring; and everybody, and everything, then and there assembled, was for the special use, behoof, honour, and renown, of the honourable Samuel Slumkey, of Slumkey Hall, one of the candidates for the representation of the Borough of Eatanswill, in the Commons House of Parliament of the United Kingdom.

Loud and long were the cheers, and mighty was the rustling of one of the blue flags, with " Liberty of the Press " inscribed thereon, when the sandy head of Mr. Pott was discerned in one of the windows, by the mob beneath; and tremendous was the enthusiasm when the honourable Samuel Slumkey himself, in top-boots, and a blue neckerchief, advanced and seized the hand of the said Pott, and melodramatically testified by gestures to the crowd, his ineffaceable obligations to the Eatanswill Gazette.

"Is everything ready?" said the honourable Samuel Slumkey to Mr. Perker.

"Everything, my dear sir," was the little man's reply.

"Nothing has been omitted, I hope?" said the honourable Samuel Slumkey.

"Nothing has been left undone, my dear sir—nothing whatever. There are twenty washed men at the street door for you to shake hands with; and six children in arms that you're to pat on the head, and inquire the age of; be particular about the children, my dear sir,—it has always a great effect, that sort of thing."

"I'll take care," said the honourable Samuel Slumkey.

"And, perhaps, my dear sir—" said the cautious little man, "perhaps if you *could*—I don't mean to say it's indispensable—but if you *could* manage to kiss one of 'em, it would produce a very great impression on the crowd."

"Wouldn't it have as good an effect if the proposer or seconder did that?" said the honourable Samuel Slumkey.

"Why, I am afraid it wouldn't,'' replied the agent; "if it were done by yourself, my dear sir, I think it would make you very popular."

"Very well," said the honourable Samuel Slumkey, with a resigned air, "then it must be done. That's all."

"Arrange the procession," cried the twenty committee-men.

Amidst the cheers of the assembled throng, the band, and the constables, and the committee-men, and the voters, and the horsemen, and the carriages, took their places—each of the two-horse vehicles being closely packed with as many gentlemen as could manage to stand upright in it; and that assigned to Mr. Perker, containing Mr. Pickwick, Mr. Tupman, Mr. Snodgrass, and about half a dozen of the committee beside.

There was a moment of awful suspense as the procession

waited for the honourable Samuel Slumkey to step into his carriage. Suddenly the crowd set up a great cheering.

"He has come out," said little Mr. Perker, greatly excited; the more so as their position did not enable them to see what was going forward.

Another cheer, much louder.

"He has shaken hands with the men," cried the little agent.

Another cheer, far more vehement.

"He has patted the babies on the head," said Mr. Perker, trembling with anxiety.

A roar of applause that rent the air.

"He has kissed one of 'em!" exclaimed the delighted little man.

A second roar.

"He has kissed another," gasped the excited manager.

A third roar.

"He's kissing 'em all!" screamed the enthusiastic little gentleman. And hailed by the deafening shouts of the multitude, the procession moved on.

How or by what means it became mixed up with the other procession, and how it was ever extricated from the confusion consequent thereupon, is more than we can undertake to describe, inasmuch as Mr. Pickwick's hat was knocked over his eyes, nose, and mouth, by one poke of a Buff flag-staff, very early in the proceedings. He describes himself as being surrounded on every side, when he could catch a glimpse of the scene, by angry and ferocious countenances, by a vast cloud of dust, and by a dense crowd of combatants. He represents himself as being forced from the carriage by some unseen power, and being personally engaged in a pugilistic encounter; but with whom, or how, or why, he is wholly unable to state. He then felt himself forced up some wooden steps by the persons from behind; and on removing his hat, found himself surrounded by his friends, in the very front of the left hand side of the hustings. The right was reserved for the Buff party, and the centre for the Mayor and his officers; one of whom—the fat crier of Eatanswill—was ringing an enormous bell, by way of commanding silence, while Mr. Horatio Fizkin, and the honourable Samuel Slumkey, with their hands upon their hearts, were bowing with the utmost affability to the troubled sea of heads that inundated the open space in front; and from whence arose a storm of groans, and shouts, and yells, and hootings, that would have done honour to an earthquake.

"There's Winkle," said Mr. Tupman, pulling his friend by the sleeve.

"Where?" said Mr. Pickwick, putting on his spectacles, which he had fortunately kept in his pocket hitherto.

"There," said Mr. Tupman, "on the top of that house." And there, sure enough, in the leaden gutter of a tiled roof, were Mr. Winkle and Mrs. Pott, comfortably seated in a couple of chairs, waving their handkerchiefs in token of recognition—a compliment which Mr. Pickwick returned by kissing his hand to the lady.

The proceedings had not yet commenced; and as an inactive crowd is generally disposed to be jocose, this very innocent action was sufficient to awaken their facetiousness.

"Oh you wicked old rascal," cried one voice, "looking arter the girls, are you?"

"Oh you wenerable sinner," cried another.

"Putting on his spectacles to look at a married 'ooman!" said a third.

"I see him a winkin' at her, with his wicked old eye," shouted a fourth.

"Look arter your wife, Pott," bellowed a fifth;—and then there was a roar of laughter.

As these taunts were accompanied with invidious comparisons between Mr. Pickwick and an aged ram, and several witticisms of the like nature; and as they moreover rather tended to convey reflections upon the honour of an innocent lady, Mr. Pickwick's indignation was excessive; but as silence was proclaimed at the moment, he contented himself by scorching the mob with a look of pity for their misguided minds, at which they laughed more boisterously than ever.

"Silence!" roared the mayor's attendants.

"Whiffin, proclaim silence," said the mayor, with an air of pomp befitting his lofty station. In obedience to this command the crier performed another concerto on the bell, whereupon a gentleman in the crowd called out "muffins;" which occasioned another laugh.

"Gentlemen," said the Mayor, at as loud a pitch as he could possibly force his voice to, "Gentlemen. Brother electors of the Borough of Eatanswill. We are met here to-day for the purpose of choosing a representative in the room of our late—"

Here the Mayor was interrupted by a voice in the crowd.

"Suc-cess to the Mayor!" cried the voice, "and may he never desert the nail and sarspan business, as he got his money by."

This allusion to the professional pursuits of the orator was received with a storm of delight, which, with a bell-accompaniment, rendered the remainder of his speech inaudible, with the exception of the concluding sentence, in which he thanked the meeting for the patient attention with which they had heard him throughout,—an expression of gratitude which elicited another burst of mirth, of about a quarter of an hour's duration.

Next, a tall thin gentleman, in a very stiff white neckerchief, after being repeatedly desired by the crowd to "send a boy home, to ask whether he hadn't left his woice under the pillow," begged to nominate a fit and proper person to represent them in Parliament. And when he said it was Horatio Fizkin, Esquire, of Fizkin Lodge, near Eatanswill, the Fizkinites applauded, and the Slumkeyites groaned, so long, and so loudly, that both he and the seconder might have sung comic songs in lieu of speaking, without anybody's being a bit the wiser.

The friends of Horatio Fizkin, Esquire, having had their

innings, a little choleric, pink-faced man stood forward to propose another fit and proper person to represent the electors of Eatanswill in Parliament; and very swimmingly the pink-faced gentleman would have gone on, if he had not been rather too choleric to entertain a sufficient perception of the fun of the crowd. But after a very few sentences of figurative eloquence, the pink-faced gentleman got from denouncing those who interrupted him in the mob, to exchanging defiances with the gentlemen on the hustings; whereupon arose an uproar which reduced him to the necessity of expressing his feelings by serious pantomime, which he did, and then left the stage to his seconder, who delivered a written speech of half an hour's length, and wouldn't be stopped, because he had sent it all to the Eatanswill Gazette, and the Eatanswill Gazette had already printed it, every word.

Then Horatio Fizkin, Esquire, of Fizkin Lodge, near Eatanswill, presented himself for the purpose of addressing the electors; which he no sooner did, than the band employed by the honourable Samuel Slumkey, commenced performing with a power to which their strength in the morning was a trifle; in return for which, the Buff crowd belaboured the heads and shoulders of the Blue crowd; on which the Blue crowd endeavoured to dispossess themselves of their very unpleasant neighbours the Buff crowd; and a scene of struggling, and pushing, and fighting, succeeded, to which we can no more do justice than the Mayor could, although he issued imperative orders to twelve constables to seize the ringleaders, who might amount in number to two hundred and fifty, or thereabouts. At all these encounters, Horatio Fizkin, Esquire, of Fizkin Lodge, and his friends, waxed fierce and furious; until at last Horatio Fizkin, Esquire, of Fizkin Lodge, begged to ask his opponent the honourable Samuel Slumkey, of Slumkey Hall, whether that band played by his consent; which question the honourable Samuel Slumkey declining to answer, Horatio Fizkin, Esquire, of Fizkin Lodge, shook his fist in the countenance of the honourable Samuel Slumkey,

The Election at Eatanswill

of Slumkey Hall; upon which the honourable Samuel Slumkey, his blood being up, defied Horatio Fizkin, Esquire, to mortal combat. At this violation of all known rules and precedents of order, the Mayor commanded another fantasia on the bell, and declared that he would bring before himself, both Horatio Fizkin, Esquire, of Fizkin Lodge, and the honourable Samuel Slumkey, of Slumkey Hall, and bind them over to keep the peace. Upon this terrific denunciation, the supporters of the two candidates interfered, and after the friends of each party had quarrelled in pairs, for three-quarters of an hour, Horatio Fizkin, Esquire, touched his hat to the honourable Samuel Slumkey: the honourable Samuel Slumkey touched his to Horatio Fizkin, Esquire: the band was stopped: the crowd were partially quieted: and Horatio Fizkin, Esquire, was permitted to proceed.

The speeches of the two candidates, though differing in every other respect, afforded a beautiful tribute to the merit and high worth of the electors of Eatanswill. Both expressed their opinion that a more independent, a more enlightened, a more public-spirited, a more noble-minded, a more disinterested set of men than those who had promised to vote for him, never existed on earth; each darkly hinted his suspicions that the electors in the opposite interest had certain swinish and besotted infirmities which rendered them unfit for the exercise of the important duties they were called upon to discharge. Fizkin expressed his readiness to do anything he was wanted; Slumkey, his determination to do nothing that was asked of him. Both said that the trade, the manufactures, the commerce, the prosperity of Eatanswill, would ever be dearer to their hearts than any earthly object; and each had it in his power to state, with the utmost confidence, that he was the man who would eventually be returned.

There was a show of hands; the Mayor decided in favour of the honourable Samuel Slumkey, of Slumkey Hall. Horatio Fizkin, Esquire, of Fizkin Lodge, demanded a poll, and a poll was fixed accordingly. Then a vote of thanks was moved to the Mayor for his able conduct in the chair; and the Mayor devoutly wishing that he had had a chair to display his able conduct in (for he had been standing during the whole proceedings), returned thanks. The processions re-formed, the carriages rolled slowly through the crowd, and its members screeched and shouted after them as their feelings or caprice dictated.

During the whole time of the polling, the town was in a perpetual fever of excitement. Everything was conducted on the most liberal and delightful scale. Exciseable articles were remarkably cheap at all the public-houses; and spring vans paraded the streets for the accommodation of voters who were seized with any temporary dizziness in the head—an epidemic which prevailed among the electors, during the contest, to a most alarming extent, and under the influence of which they might frequently be seen lying on the pavements in a state of utter insensibility. A small body of electors remained unpolled on the very last day. They were calculating and reflecting persons, who had not yet been convinced by the arguments of either party, although they had had frequent conferences with each. One hour before the close of the poll, Mr. Perker solicited the honour of a private interview with these intelligent, these noble, these patriotic men. It was granted. His arguments were brief, but satisfactory. They went in a body to the poll; and when they returned, the honourable Samuel Slumkey, of Slumkey Hall, was returned also.

CHAPTER XIV.

COMPRISING A BRIEF DESCRIPTION OF THE COMPANY AT THE
PEACOCK ASSEMBLED ; AND A TALE TOLD BY A BAGMAN.

It is pleasant to turn from contemplating the strife and turmoil of political existence, to the peaceful repose of private life. Although in reality no great partisan of either side, Mr. Pickwick was sufficiently fired with Mr. Pott's enthusiasm, to apply his whole time and attention to the proceedings, of which the last chapter affords a description compiled from his own memoranda. Nor while he was thus occupied was Mr. Winkle idle, his whole time being devoted to pleasant walks and short country excursions with Mrs. Pott, who never failed, when such an opportunity presented itself, to seek some relief from the tedious monotony she so constantly complained of. The two gentlemen being thus completely domesticated in the Editor's house, Mr. Tupman and Mr. Snodgrass were in a great measure cast upon their own resources. Taking but little interest in public affairs, they beguiled their time chiefly with such amusements as the Peacock afforded, which were limited to a bagatelle-board in the first floor, and a sequestered skittle-ground in the back yard. In the science and nicety of both these recreations, which are far more abstruse than ordinary men suppose, they were gradually initiated by Mr. Weller, who possessed a perfect knowledge of such pastimes. Thus, notwithstanding that they were in a great measure deprived of the comfort

211

and advantage of Mr. Pickwick's society, they were still enabled to beguile the time, and to prevent its hanging heavily on their hands.

It was in the evening, however, that the Peacock presented attractions which enabled the two friends to resist even the invitations of the gifted, though prosy, Pott. It was in the evening that the "commercial room" was filled with a social circle, whose characters and manners it was the delight of Mr. Tupman to observe; whose sayings and doings it was the habit of Mr. Snodgrass to note down.

Most people know what sort of places commercial rooms usually are. That of the Peacock differed in no material respect from the generality of such apartments; that is to say, it was a large bare-looking room, the furniture of which had no doubt been better when it was newer, with a spacious table in the centre, and a variety of smaller dittos in the corners: an extensive assortment of variously shaped chairs, and an old Turkey carpet, bearing about the same relative proportion to the size of the room, as a lady's pocket-handkerchief might to the floor of a watch-box. The walls were garnished with one or two large maps; and several weatherbeaten rough great coats, with complicated capes, dangled from a long row of pegs in one corner. The mantelshelf was ornamented with a wooden inkstand, containing one stump of a pen and half a wafer: a road-book and directory: a county history minus the cover: and the mortal remains of a trout in a glass coffin. The atmosphere was redolent of tobacco-smoke, the fumes of which had communicated a rather dingy hue to the whole room, and more especially to the dusty red curtains which shaded the windows. On the sideboard a variety of miscellaneous articles were huddled together, the most conspicuous of which were some very cloudy fishsauce cruets, a couple of driving-boxes, two or three whips, and as many travelling shawls, a tray of knives and forks, and the mustard.

Here it was that Mr. Tupman and Mr. Snodgrass were

seated on the evening after the conclusion of the election, with several other temporary inmates of the house, smoking and drinking.

"Well, gents," said a stout, hale personage of about forty, with only one eye—a very bright black eye, which twinkled with a roguish expression of fun and good humour, "our noble selves, gents. I always propose that toast to the company, and drink Mary to myself. Eh, Mary!"

"Get along with you, you wretch," said the hand-maiden, obviously not ill pleased with the compliment, however.

"Don't go away, Mary," said the black-eyed man.

"Let me alone, imperence," said the young lady.

"Never mind," said the one-eyed man, calling after the girl as she left the room. "I'll step out by and by, Mary. Keep your spirits up, dear." Here he went through the not very difficult process of winking upon the company with his solitary eye, to the enthusiastic delight of an elderly personage with a dirty face and a clay pipe.

"Rum creeters is women," said the dirty-faced man, after a pause.

"Ah! no mistake about that," said a very red-faced man, behind a cigar.

After this little bit of philosophy there was another pause.

"There's rummer things than women in this world though, mind you," said the man with the black eye, slowly filling a large Dutch pipe, with a most capacious bowl.

"Are you married?" inquired the dirty-faced man.

"Can't say I am."

"I thought not." Here the dirty-faced man fell into fits of mirth at his own retort, in which he was joined by a man of bland voice and placid countenance, who always made it a point to agree with everybody.

"Women, after all, gentlemen," said the enthusiastic Mr. Snodgrass, "are the great props and comforts of our existence."

"So they are," said the placid gentleman.

" When they're in a good humour," interposed the dirty-faced man.

" And that's very true," said the placid one.

" I repudiate that qualification," said Mr. Snodgrass, whose thoughts were fast reverting to Emily Wardle, " I repudiate it with disdain—with indignation. Show me the man who says anything against women, as women, and I boldly declare he is not a man." And Mr. Snodgrass took his cigar from his mouth, and struck the table violently with his clenched fist.

" That's good sound argument," said the placid man.

" Containing a position which I deny," interrupted he of the dirty countenance.

" And there's certainly a very great deal of truth in what you observe too, sir," said the placid gentleman.

" Your health, sir," said the bagman with the lonely eye, bestowing an approving nod on Mr. Snodgrass.

Mr. Snodgrass acknowledged the compliment.

" I always like to hear a good argument," continued the bagman, " a sharp one, like this; it's very improving; but this little argument about women brought to my mind a story I have heard an old uncle of mine tell, the recollection of which, just now, made me say there were rummer things than women to be met with, sometimes."

" I should like to hear that same story," said the red-faced man with the cigar.

" Should you?" was the only reply of the bagman, who continued to smoke with great vehemence.

" So should I," said Mr. Tupman, speaking for the first time. He was always anxious to increase his stock of experience.

" Should *you?* Well then, I'll tell it. No I won't. I know you won't believe it," said the man with the roguish eye, making that organ look more roguish than ever.

" If you say it's true, of course I shall," said Mr. Tupman.

" Well, upon that understanding I'll tell you," replied the traveller. " Did you ever hear of the great commercial house of Bilson and Slum? But it doesn't matter though, whether you did or not, because they retired from business long since. It's eighty years ago, since the circumstance happened to a traveller for that house, but he was a particular friend of my uncle's; and my uncle told the story to me. It's a queer name; but he used to call it

THE BAGMAN'S STORY,

and he used to tell it, something in this way.

"One winter's evening, about five o'clock, just as it began to grow dusk, a man in a gig might have been seen urging his tired horse along the road which leads across Marlborough Downs, in the direction of Bristol. I say he might have been seen, and I have no doubt he would have been, if anybody but a blind man had happened to pass that way; but the weather was so bad, and the night so cold and wet, that nothing was out but the water, and so the traveller jogged along in the middle of the road, lonesome and dreary enough. If any bagman of that day could have caught sight of the little neck-or-nothing sort of gig, with a clay-coloured body and red wheels, and the vixenish ill-tempered, fast-going bay mare, that looked like a cross between a butcher's horse and a two-penny post-office pony, he would have known at once, that this traveller could have been no other than Tom Smart, of the great house of Bilson and Slum, Cateaton Street, City. However, as there was no bagman to look on, nobody knew anything at all about the matter; and so Tom Smart and his clay-coloured gig with the red wheels, and the vixenish mare with the fast pace, went on together, keeping the secret among them: and nobody was a bit the wiser.

"There are many pleasanter places even in this dreary world, than Marlborough Downs when it blows hard; and if you throw in beside, a gloomy winter's evening, a miry and sloppy road, and a pelting fall of heavy rain, and try the effect, by way of experiment, in your own proper person, you will experience the full force of this observation.

"The wind blew—not up the road or down it, though that's bad enough, but sheer across it, sending the rain slanting down like the lines they used to rule in the copy-books at school, to make the boys slope well. For a moment it would die away, and the traveller would begin to delude himself into the belief that, exhausted with its previous fury, it had quietly lain itself down to rest, when, whoo! he would hear it growling and whistling in the distance, and on it would come rushing over the hill-tops, and sweeping along the plain, gathering sound and strength as it drew nearer, until it dashed with a heavy gust against horse and man, driving the sharp rain into their ears, and its cold damp breath into their very bones; and past them it would scour, far, far away, with a stunning roar, as if in ridicule of their weakness, and triumphant in the consciousness of its own strength and power.

"The bay mare splashed away, through the mud and water, with drooping ears; now and then tossing her head as if to express her disgust at this very ungentlemanly behaviour of the elements, but keeping a good pace notwithstanding, until a gust of wind, more furious than any that had yet assailed them, caused her to stop suddenly and plant her four feet firmly against the ground, to prevent her being blown over. It's a special mercy that she did this, for if she *had* been blown over, the vixenish mare was so light, and the gig was so light, and Tom Smart such a light weight into the bargain, that they must infallibly have all gone rolling over and over together, until they reached the confines of earth, or until the wind fell; and in either case the probability is, that neither the vixenish mare, nor the clay-coloured gig with the red wheels, nor Tom Smart, would ever have been fit for service again.

"'Well, damn my straps and whiskers,' says Tom Smart, (Tom sometimes had an unpleasant knack of swearing), 'Damn my straps and whiskers,' says Tom, 'if this ain't pleasant, blow me!'

SNUGLY HOUSED.

" You'll very likely ask me why, as Tom Smart had been pretty well blown already, he expressed this wish to be submitted to the same process again. I can't say—all I know is, that Tom Smart said so—or at least he always told my uncle he said so, and it's just the same thing.

"'Blow me,' says Tom Smart; and the mare neighed as if she were precisely of the same opinion.

"'Cheer up, old girl,' said Tom, patting the bay mare on the neck with the end of his whip. 'It won't do pushing on, such a night as this; the first house we come to we'll put up at, so the faster you go the sooner it's over. Soho, old girl—gently—gently.'

" Whether the vixenish mare was sufficiently well acquainted with the tones of Tom's voice to comprehend his meaning, or whether she found it colder standing still than moving on, of course I can't say. But I can say that Tom had no sooner finished speaking, than she pricked up her ears, and started forward at a speed which made the clay-coloured gig rattle till you would have supposed every one of the red spokes were going to fly out on the turf of Marlborough Downs; and even Tom, whip as he was, couldn't stop or check her pace, until she drew up, of her own accord, before a road-side inn on the right-hand side of the way, about half a quarter of a mile from the end of the Downs.

" Tom cast a hasty glance at the upper part of the house as he threw the reins to the hostler, and stuck the whip in the box. It was a strange old place, built of a kind of shingle, inlaid, as it were, with cross-beams, with gabled-topped windows projecting completely over the pathway, and a low door with a dark porch, and a couple of steep steps leading down into the house, instead of the modern fashion of half a dozen shallow ones leading up to it. It was a comfortable-looking place though, for there was a strong cheerful light in the bar-window, which shed a bright ray across the road, and even lighted up the hedge on the other side; and there was a red flickering light in the opposite window, one moment but

217

faintly discernible, and the next gleaming strongly through the drawn curtains, which intimated that a rousing fire was blazing within. Marking these little evidences with the eye of an experienced traveller, Tom dismounted with as much agility as his half-frozen limbs would permit, and entered the house.

"In less than five minutes' time, Tom was ensconced in the room opposite the bar—the very room where he had imagined the fire blazing—before a substantial matter-of-fact roaring fire, composed of something short of a bushel of coals, and wood enough to make half a dozen decent gooseberry bushes, piled half way up the chimney, and roaring and crackling with a sound that of itself would have warmed the heart of any reasonable man. This was comfortable, but this was not all, for a smartly dressed girl, with a bright eye and a neat ancle, was laying a very clean white cloth on the table; and as Tom sat with his slippered feet on the fender, and his back to the open door, he saw a charming prospect of the bar reflected in the glass over the chimney-piece, with delightful rows of green bottles and gold labels, together with jars of pickles and preserves, and cheeses and boiled hams, and rounds of beef, arranged on shelves in the most tempting and delicious array. Well, this was comfortable too; but even this was not all—for in the bar, seated at tea at the nicest possible little table, drawn close up before the brightest possible little fire, was a buxom widow of somewhere about eight and forty or thereabouts, with a face as comfortable as the bar, who was evidently the landlady of the house, and the supreme ruler over all these agreeable possessions. There was only one drawback to the beauty of the whole picture, and that was a tall man—a very tall man—in a brown coat and bright basket buttons, and black whiskers, and wavy black hair, who was seated at tea with the widow, and who it required no great penetration to discover was in a fair way of persuading her to be a widow no longer, but to confer upon him the privilege of sitting down in that bar, for and during the whole remainder of the term of his natural life.

HOT PUNCH.

"Tom Smart was by no means of an irritable or envious disposition, but somehow or other the tall man with the brown coat and the bright basket buttons did rouse what little gall he had in his composition, and did make him feel extremely indignant: the more especially as he could now and then observe, from his seat before the glass, certain little affectionate familiarities passing between the tall man and the widow, which sufficiently denoted that the tall man was as high in favour as he was in size. Tom was fond of hot punch—I may venture to say he was *very* fond of hot punch—and after he had seen the vixenish mare well fed and well littered down, and had eaten every bit of the nice little hot dinner which the widow tossed up for him with her own hands, he just ordered a tumbler of it, by way of experiment. Now, if there was one thing in the whole range of domestic art, which the widow could manufacture better than another, it was this identical article; and the first tumbler was adapted to Tom Smart's taste with such peculiar nicety, that he ordered a second with the least possible delay. Hot punch is a pleasant thing, gentlemen—an extremely pleasant thing under any circumstances—but in that snug old parlour, before the roaring fire, with the wind blowing outside till every timber in the old house creaked again, Tom Smart found it perfectly delightful. He ordered another tumbler, and then another—I am not quite certain whether he didn't order another after that—but the more he drank of the hot punch, the more he thought of the tall man.

"'Confound his impudence!' said Tom to himself, 'what business has he in that snug bar? Such an ugly villain too!' said Tom. 'If the widow had any taste, she might surely pick up some better fellow than that.' Here Tom's eye wandered from the glass on the chimney-piece, to the glass on the table; and as he felt himself become gradually sentimental, he emptied the fourth tumbler of punch and ordered a fifth.

"Tom Smart, gentlemen, had always been very much

attached to the public line. It had long been his ambition to stand in a bar of his own, in a green coat, knee-cords, and tops. He had a great notion of taking the chair at convivial dinners, and he had often thought how well he could preside in a room of his own in the talking way, and what a capital example he could set to his customers in the drinking department. All these things passed rapidly through Tom's mind as he sat drinking the hot punch by the roaring fire, and he felt very justly and properly indignant that the tall man should be in a fair way of keeping such an excellent house, while he, Tom Smart, was as far from it as ever. So, after deliberating over the last two tumblers, whether he hadn't a perfect right to pick a quarrel with the tall man for having contrived to get into the good graces of the buxom widow, Tom Smart at last arrived at the satisfactory conclusion that he was a very ill-used and persecuted individual, and had better go to bed.

"Up a wide and ancient staircase the smart girl preceded Tom, shading the chamber candle with her hand, to protect it from the currents of air which in such a rambling old place might have found plenty of room to disport themselves in, without blowing the candle out, but which did blow it out nevertheless; thus affording Tom's enemies an opportunity of asserting that it was he, and not the wind, who extinguished the candle, and that while he pretended to be blowing it alight again, he was in fact kissing the girl. Be this as it may, another light was obtained, and Tom was conducted through a maze of rooms, and a labyrinth of passages, to the apartment which had been prepared for his reception, where the girl bade him good night, and left him alone.

"It was a good large room with big closets, and a bed which might have served for a whole boarding-school, to say nothing of a couple of oaken presses that would have held the baggage of a small army; but what struck Tom's fancy most was a strange, grim-looking high-backed chair, carved in the most fantastic manner, with a flowered damask cushion, and the round knobs at the bottom of the legs carefully tied up in red cloth, as if it had got the gout in its toes. Of any other queer chair, Tom would only have thought it *was* a queer chair, and there would have been an end of the matter; but there was something about this particular chair, and yet he couldn't tell what it was, so odd and so unlike any other piece of furniture he had ever seen that it seemed to fascinate him. He sat down before the fire, and stared at the old chair for half an hour;—Deuce take the chair, it was such a strange old thing, he couldn't take his eyes off it.

"'Well,' said Tom, slowly undressing himself, and staring at the old chair all the while, which stood with a mysterious aspect by the bedside, 'I never saw such a rum concern as that in my days. Very odd,' said Tom, who had got rather sage with the hot punch, 'Very odd.' Tom shook his head with an air of profound wisdom, and looked at the chair again. He couldn't make anything of it though, so he got into bed, covered himself up warm, and fell asleep.

"In about half an hour, Tom woke up, with a start, from a confused dream of tall men and tumblers of punch: and the first object that presented itself to his waking imagination was the queer chair.

"'I won't look at it any more,' said Tom to himself, and he squeezed his eyelids together, and tried to persuade himself he was going to sleep again. No use; nothing but queer chairs danced before his eyes, kicking up their legs, jumping over each other's backs, and playing all kinds of antics.

"'I may as well see one real chair, as two or three complete sets of false ones,' said Tom, bringing out his head from under the bed-clothes. There it was, plainly discernible by the light of the fire, looking as provoking as ever.

"Tom gazed at the chair; and, suddenly as he looked at it, a most extraordinary change seemed to come over it. The carving of the back gradually assumed the lineaments and expression of an old shrivelled human face; the damask cushion became an antique, flapped waistcoat: the round knobs grew into a couple of feet, encased in red cloth slippers; and the old chair looked like a very ugly old man, of the previous century, with his arms a-kimbo. Tom sat up in bed, and rubbed his eyes to dispel the illusion. No. The chair was an ugly old gentleman; and what was more, he was winking at Tom Smart.

"Tom was naturally a headlong, careless sort of dog, and he had had five tumblers of hot punch into the bargain; so, although he was a little startled at first, he began to grow rather indignant when he saw the old gentleman winking and leering at him with such an impudent air. At length he resolved that he wouldn't stand it; and as the old face still kept winking away as fast as ever, Tom said, in a very angry tone:

"'What the devil are you winking at me for?'

"'Because I like it, Tom Smart,' said the chair; or the old gentleman, whichever you like to call him. He stopped winking though, when Tom spoke, and began grinning like a superannuated monkey.

"'How do you know my name, old nut-cracker face!' inquired Tom Smart, rather staggered;—though he pretended to carry it off so well.

"'Come, come, Tom,' said the old gentleman, 'that's not the way to address solid Spanish Mahogany. Dam'me, you couldn't treat me with less respect if I was veneered.' When the old gentleman said this, he looked so fierce that Tom began to be frightened.

"'I didn't mean to treat you with any disrespect, sir,' said Tom; in a much humbler tone than he had spoken in at first.

"'Well, well,' said the old fellow, 'perhaps not—perhaps not. Tom—'

"'Sir—'

"'I know everything about you, Tom; everything. You're very poor, Tom.'

"'I certainly am,' said Tom Smart. 'But how came you to know that?'

" ' Never mind that,' said the old gentleman; 'you're much too fond of punch, Tom.'

" Tom Smart was just on the point of protesting that he hadn't tasted a drop since his last birth-day, but when his eye encountered that of the old gentleman, he looked so knowing that Tom blushed, and was silent.

" ' Tom,' said the old gentleman, 'the widow's a fine woman —remarkably fine woman—eh, Tom ? ' Here the old fellow screwed up his eyes, cocked up one of his wasted little legs, and looked altogether so unpleasantly amorous, that Tom was quite disgusted with the levity of his behaviour;—at his time of life, too !

" ' I am her guardian, Tom,' said the old gentleman.

" ' Are you ? ' inquired Tom Smart.

" ' I knew her mother, Tom,' said the old fellow; 'and her grandmother. She was very fond of me—made me this waistcoat, Tom.'

" ' Did she ? ' said Tom Smart.

" ' And these shoes,' said the old fellow, lifting up one of the red-cloth mufflers; 'but don't mention it, Tom. I shouldn't like to have it known that she was so much attached to me. It might occasion some unpleasantness in the family.' When the old rascal said this, he looked so extremely impertinent, that, as Tom Smart afterwards declared, he could have sat upon him without remorse.

" ' I have been a great favourite among the women in my time, Tom,' said the profligate old debauchee; 'hundreds of fine women have sat in my lap for hours together. What do you think of that, you dog, eh ! ' The old gentleman was proceeding to recount some other exploits of his youth, when he was seized with such a violent fit of creaking that he was unable to proceed.

" ' Just serves you right, old boy,' thought Tom Smart; but he didn't say anything.

" ' Ah ! ' said the old fellow, 'I am a good deal troubled with this now. I am getting old, Tom, and have lost nearly all my rails. I have had an operation performed, too—a small piece let into my back—and I found it a severe trial, Tom.'

"'I dare say you did, sir,' said Tom Smart.

"'However,' said the old gentleman, 'that's not the point. Tom! I want you to marry the widow.'

"'Me, sir!' said Tom.

"'You;' said the old gentleman.

"'Bless your reverend locks,' said Tom—(he had a few scattered horse-hairs left), 'bless your reverend locks, she wouldn't have me.' And Tom sighed involuntarily, as he thought of the bar.

"'Wouldn't she?' said the old gentleman, firmly.

"'No, no,' said Tom; 'there's somebody else in the wind. A tall man—a confoundedly tall man—with black whiskers.'

"'Tom,' said the old gentleman; 'she will never have him.'

"'Won't she?' said Tom. 'If you stood in the bar, old gentleman, you'd tell another story.'

"'Pooh, pooh,' said the old gentleman. 'I know all about that.'

"'About what?' said Tom.

"'The kissing behind the door, and all that sort of thing, Tom,' said the old gentleman. And here he gave another impudent look, which made Tom very wroth, because as you all know, gentlemen, to hear an old fellow, who ought to know better, talking about these things, is very unpleasant—nothing more so.

"'I know all about that, Tom,' said the old gentleman. 'I have seen it done very often in my time, Tom, between more people than I should like to mention to you; but it never came to anything after all.'

"'You must have seen some queer things,' said Tom, with an inquisitive look.

"'You may say that, now,' replied the old fellow, with a very complicated wink. 'I am the last of my family, Tom,' said the old gentleman, with a melancholy sigh.

224

" ' Was it a large one?' inquired Tom Smart.

" ' There were twelve of us, Tom,' said the old gentleman;
'fine straight-backed, handsome fellows as you'd wish to see.
None of your modern abortions—all with arms, and with a
degree of polish, though I say it that should not, which would
have done your heart good to behold.'

" ' And what's become of the others, sir?' asked Tom Smart.

" The old gentleman applied his elbow to his eye as he
replied, ' Gone, Tom, gone. We had hard service, Tom, and
they hadn't all my constitution. They got rheumatic about
the legs and arms, and went into kitchens and other hospitals;
and one of 'em, with long service and hard usage, positively
lost his senses :—he got so crazy that he was obliged to be
burnt. Shocking thing that, Tom.'

" ' Dreadful!' said Tom Smart.

" The old fellow paused for a few minutes, apparently
struggling with his feelings of emotion, and then said:

" ' However, Tom, I am wandering from the point. This
tall man, Tom, is a rascally adventurer. The moment he
married the widow, he would sell off all the furniture, and
run away. What would be the consequence? She would be
deserted and reduced to ruin, and I should catch my death
of cold in some broker's shop.'

" ' Yes, but—'

" ' Don't interrupt me,' said the old gentleman. ' Of you,
Tom, I entertain a very different opinion; for I well know
that if you once settled yourself in a public house, you would
never leave it, as long as there was anything to drink within
its walls.'

" ' I am very much obliged to you for your good opinion,
sir,' said Tom Smart.

" ' Therefore,' resumed the old gentleman, in a dictatorial
tone; ' you shall have her, and he shall not.'

" ' What is to prevent it?' said Tom Smart, eagerly.

" ' This disclosure,' replied the old gentleman; ' he is already
married.'

225

"'How can I prove it?' said Tom, starting half out of bed.

"The old gentleman untucked his arm from his side, and having pointed to one of the oaken presses, immediately replaced it in its old position.

"'He little thinks,' said the old gentleman, 'that in the right hand pocket of a pair of trousers in that press, he has left a letter, entreating him to return to his disconsolate wife, with six—mark me, Tom—six babes, and all of them small ones.'

"As the old gentleman solemnly uttered these words, his features grew less and less distinct, and his figure more shadowy. A film came over Tom Smart's eyes. The old man seemed gradually blending into the chair, the damask waistcoat to resolve into a cushion, the red slippers to shrink into little red cloth bags. The light faded gently away, and Tom Smart fell back on his pillow, and dropped asleep.

"Morning aroused Tom from the lethargic slumber, into which he had fallen on the disappearance of the old man. He sat up in bed, and for some minutes vainly endeavoured to recall the events of the preceding night. Suddenly they rushed upon him. He looked at the chair; it was a fantastic and grim-looking piece of furniture, certainly, but it must have been a remarkably ingenious and lively imagination, that could have discovered any resemblance between it and an old man.

"'How are you, old boy?' said Tom. He was bolder in the daylight—most men are.

"The chair remained motionless, and spoke not a word.

"'Miserable morning,' said Tom. No. The chair would not be drawn into conversation.

"'Which press did you point to?—you can tell me that,' said Tom. Devil a word, gentlemen, the chair would say.

"'It's not much trouble to open it, anyhow,' said Tom, getting out of bed very deliberately. He walked up to one of the presses. The key was in the lock; he turned it, and opened the door. There *was* a pair of trousers there. He put his hand into the pocket, and drew forth the identical letter the old gentleman had described!

"'Queer sort of thing, this,' said Tom Smart; looking first at the chair and then at the press, and then at the letter, and then at the chair again. 'Very queer,' said Tom. But, as there was nothing in either, to lessen the queerness, he thought he might as well dress himself, and settle the tall man's business at once—just to put him out of his misery.

"Tom surveyed the rooms he passed through, on his way down stairs, with the scrutinising eye of a landlord; thinking it not impossible, that before long, they and their contents would be his property: The tall man was standing in the snug little bar, with his hands behind him, quite at home. He grinned vacantly at Tom. A casual observer might have supposed he did it, only to show his white teeth; but Tom Smart thought that a consciousness of triumph was passing through the place where the tall man's mind would have been, if he had had any. Tom laughed in his face; and summoned the landlady.

"'Good morning, ma'am,' said Tom Smart, closing the door of the little parlour as the widow entered.

"'Good morning, sir,' said the widow. 'What will you take for breakfast, sir?'

"Tom was thinking how he should open the case, so he made no answer.

"'There's a very nice ham,' said the widow, 'and a beautiful cold larded fowl. Shall I send 'em in, sir?'

"These words roused Tom from his reflections. His admiration of the widow increased as she spoke. Thoughtful creature! Comfortable provider!

"'Who is that gentleman in the bar, ma'am?' inquired Tom.

"'His name is Jinkins, sir,' said the widow, slightly blushing.

"'He's a tall man,' said Tom.

"'He is a very fine man, sir,' replied the widow, 'and a very nice gentleman.'

"'Ah!' said Tom.

"'Is there anything more you want, sir?' inquired the widow, rather puzzled by Tom's manner.

"'Why, yes,' said Tom. 'My dear ma'am, will you have the kindness to sit down for one moment?'

"The widow looked much amazed, but she sat down, and Tom sat down too, close beside her. I don't know how it happened, gentlemen—indeed my uncle used to tell me that Tom Smart said *he* didn't know how it happened either—but somehow or other the palm of Tom's hand fell upon the back of the widow's hand, and remained there while he spoke.

"'My dear ma'am,' said Tom Smart—he had always a great notion of committing the amiable—'My dear ma'am, you deserve a very excellent husband;—you do indeed.'

"'Lor, sir!' said the widow—as well she might: Tom's mode of commencing the conversation being rather unusual, not to say startling; the fact of his never having set eyes upon her before the previous night, being taken into consideration. 'Lor, sir!'

"'I scorn to flatter, my dear ma'am,' said Tom Smart. 'You deserve a very admirable husband, and whoever he is, he'll be a very lucky man.' As Tom said this his eye involuntarily wandered from the widow's face, to the comforts around him.

"The widow looked more puzzled than ever, and made an effort to rise. Tom gently pressed her hand, as if to detain her, and she kept her seat. Widows, gentlemen, are not usually timorous, as my uncle used to say.

"'I am sure I am very much obliged to you, sir, for your good opinion,' said the buxom landlady, half laughing; 'and if ever I marry again'—

"'*If*,' said Tom Smart, looking very shrewdly out of the right-hand corner of his left eye. '*If*'—

"'Well,' said the widow, laughing outright this time. '*When* I do, I hope I shall have as good a husband as you describe.'

"'Jinkins to wit,' said Tom.

"'Lor, sir!' exclaimed the widow.

"'Oh, don't tell me,' said Tom, 'I know him.'

"'I am sure nobody who knows him, knows anything bad of him,' said the widow, bridling up at the mysterious air with which Tom had spoken.

"'Hem!' said Tom Smart.

"The widow began to think it was high time to cry, so she took out her handkerchief, and inquired whether Tom wished to insult her: whether he thought it like a gentleman to take away the character of another gentleman behind his back: why, if he had got anything to say, he didn't say it to the man, like a man, instead of terrifying a poor weak woman in that way; and so forth.

"'I'll say it to him fast enough,' said Tom, 'only I want you to hear it first.'

"'What is it?' inquired the widow, looking intently in Tom's countenance.

"'I'll astonish you,' said Tom, putting his hand in his pocket.

"'If it is, that he wants money,' said the widow, 'I know that already, and you needn't trouble yourself.'

"'Pooh, nonsense, that's nothing,' said Tom Smart. '*I* want money. 'Tan't that.'

"'Oh, dear, what can it be?' exclaimed the poor widow.

"'Don't be frightened,' said Tom Smart. He slowly drew forth the letter, and unfolded it. 'You won't scream?' said Tom, doubtfully.

"'No, no,' replied the widow; 'let me see it.'

"'You won't go fainting away, or any of that nonsense?' said Tom.

"'No, no,' returned the widow, hastily.

"'And don't run out, and blow him up,' said Tom, 'because I'll do all that for you; you had better not exert yourself.'

"'Well, well,' said the widow, 'let me see it.'

"'I will,' replied Tom Smart; and, with these words, he placed the letter in the widow's hand.

"Gentlemen, I have heard my uncle say, that Tom Smart said the widow's lamentations when she heard the disclosure would have pierced a heart of stone. Tom was certainly very tender-hearted, but they pierced his, to the very core. The widow rocked herself to and fro, and wrung her hands.

"'Oh, the deception and villainy of man!' said the widow.

"'Frightful, my dear ma'am; but compose yourself,' said Tom Smart.

"'Oh, I can't compose myself,' shrieked the widow. 'I shall never find any one else I can love so much!'

"'Oh yes, you will, my dear soul,' said Tom Smart, letting fall a shower of the largest sized tears, in pity for the widow's misfortunes. Tom Smart, in the energy of his compassion, had put his arm round the widow's waist; and the widow, in a passion of grief, had clasped Tom's hand. She looked up in Tom's face, and smiled through her tears. Tom looked down in hers, and smiled through his.

"I never could find out, gentlemen, whether Tom did or did not kiss the widow at that particular moment. He used to tell my uncle he didn't, but I have my doubts about it. Between ourselves, gentlemen, I rather think he did.

"At all events, Tom kicked the very tall man out at the front door half an hour after, and married the widow a month after. And he used to drive about the country, with the clay-coloured gig with red wheels, and the vixenish mare with the fast pace, till he gave up business many years afterwards, and went to France with his wife; and then the old house was pulled down."

"Will you allow me to ask you," said the inquisitive old gentleman, "what became of the chair?"

"Why," replied the one-eyed bagman, "it was observed to creak very much on the day of the wedding; but Tom Smart couldn't say for certain whether it was with pleasure or bodily infirmity. He rather thought it was the latter, though, for it never spoke afterwards."

" Everybody believed the story, didn't they ? " said the dirty-faced man, re-filling his pipe.

" Except Tom's enemies," replied the bagman. " Some of 'em said Tom invented it altogether; and others said he was drunk, and fancied it, and got hold of the wrong trousers by mistake before he went to bed. But nobody ever minded what *they* said."

" Tom said it was all true ? "

" Every word."

" And your uncle ? "

" Every letter."

" They must have been very nice men, both of 'em ; " said the dirty-faced man.

" Yes, they were," replied the bagman ; " very nice men indeed ! "

CHAPTER XV.

IN WHICH IS GIVEN A FAITHFUL PORTRAITURE OF TWO DISTIN-
GUISHED PERSONS: AND AN ACCURATE DESCRIPTION OF A
PUBLIC BREAKFAST IN THEIR HOUSE AND GROUNDS; WHICH
PUBLIC BREAKFAST LEADS TO THE RECOGNITION OF AN OLD
ACQUAINTANCE, AND THE COMMENCEMENT OF ANOTHER
CHAPTER.

MR. PICKWICK's conscience had been somewhat reproaching him for his recent neglect of his friends at the Peacock; and he was just on the point of walking forth in quest of them, on the third morning after the election had terminated, when his faithful valet put into his hand a card, on which was engraved the following inscription:—

Mrs. Leo Hunter.

The Den.   Eatanswill.

" Person's a waitin'," said Sam, epigrammatically.

" Does the person want me, Sam?" inquired Mr. Pickwick.

" He wants you particklar; and no one else'll do, as the Devil's private secretary said ven he fetched avay Doctor Faustus," replied Mr. Weller.

" *He.*   Is it a gentleman?" said Mr. Pickwick.

" A wery good imitation o' one, if it an't," replied Mr. Weller.

" But this is a lady's card," said Mr. Pickwick.

" Given me by a gen'l'm'n, hows'ever," replied Sam, " and

232

he's a waitin' in the drawing-room—said he'd rather wait all day, than not see you."

Mr. Pickwick, on hearing this determination, descended to the drawing-room, where sat a grave man, who started up on his entrance, and said, with an air of profound respect:

"Mr. Pickwick, I presume?"

"The same."

"Allow me, sir, the honour of grasping your hand. Permit me, sir, to shake it," said the grave man.

"Certainly," said Mr. Pickwick.

The stranger shook the extended hand, and then continued.

"We have heard of your fame, sir. The noise of your antiquarian discussion has reached the ears of Mrs. Leo Hunter—my wife, sir; *I* am *Mr.* Leo Hunter"—the stranger paused, as if he expected that Mr. Pickwick would be overcome by the disclosure; but seeing that he remained perfectly calm, proceeded.

"My wife, sir—Mrs. Leo Hunter—is proud to number among her acquaintance all those who have rendered themselves celebrated by their works and talents. Permit me, sir, to place in a conspicuous part of the list the name of Mr. Pickwick, and his brother members of the club that derives its name from him."

"I shall be extremely happy to make the acquaintance of such a lady, sir," replied Mr. Pickwick.

"You *shall* make it, sir," said the grave man. "To-morrow morning, sir, we give a public breakfast—a *fête champetre*—to a great number of those who have rendered themselves celebrated by their works and talents. Permit Mrs. Leo Hunter, sir, to have the gratification of seeing you at the Den."

"With great pleasure," replied Mr. Pickwick.

"Mrs. Leo Hunter has many of these breakfasts, sir," resumed the new acquaintance—"'feasts of reason, sir, and flows of soul,' as somebody who wrote a sonnet to Mrs. Leo Hunter on her breakfasts, feelingly and originally observed."

233

"Was *he* celebrated for his works and talents?" inquired Mr. Pickwick.

"He was, sir," replied the grave man, "all Mrs. Leo Hunter's acquaintance are; it is her ambition, sir, to have no other acquaintance."

"It is a very noble ambition," said Mr. Pickwick.

"When I inform Mrs. Leo Hunter. that that remark fell from *your* lips, sir, she will indeed be proud," said the grave man. "You have a gentleman in your train, who has produced some beautiful little poems, I think, sir."

"My friend Mr. Snodgrass has a great taste for poetry," replied Mr. Pickwick.

"So has Mrs. Leo Hunter, sir. She doats on poetry, sir. She adores it; I may say that her whole soul and mind are wound up, and entwined with it. She has produced some delightful pieces, herself, sir. You may have met with her 'Ode to an Expiring Frog,' sir."

"I don't think I have," said Mr. Pickwick.

"You astonish me, sir," said Mr. Leo Hunter. "It created an immense sensation. It was signed with an 'L' and eight stars, and appeared originally in a Lady's Magazine. It commenced

> 'Can I view thee panting, lying
> On thy stomach, without sighing;
> Can I unmoved see thee dying
> On a log,
> Expiring frog!'"

"Beautiful!" said Mr. Pickwick.

"Fine," said Mr. Leo Hunter, "so simple."

"Very," said Mr. Pickwick.

"The next verse is still more touching. Shall I repeat it?"

"If you please," said Mr. Pickwick.

"It runs thus," said the grave man, still more gravely.

> 'Say, have fiends in shape of boys,
> With wild halloo, and brutal noise,
> Hunted thee from marshy joys,
> With a dog,
> Expiring frog!'"

" Finely expressed," said Mr. Pickwick.

" All point, sir," said Mr. Leo Hunter, " but you shall hear Mrs. Leo Hunter repeat it. *She* can do justice to it, sir. She will repeat it, in character, sir, to-morrow morning."

" In character ! "

" As Minerva. But I forgot—it's a fancy-dress breakfast."

" Dear me," said Mr. Pickwick, glancing at his own figure —" I can't possibly— "

" Can't, sir ; can't ! " exclaimed Mr. Leo Hunter. " Solomon Lucas, the Jew in the High Street, has thousands of fancy dresses. Consider, sir, how many appropriate characters are open for your selection. Plato, Zeno, Epicurus, Pythagoras —all founders of clubs."

" I know that," said Mr. Pickwick, " but as I cannot put myself in competition with those great men, I cannot presume to wear their dresses."

The grave man considered deeply, for a few seconds, and then said,

" On reflection, sir, I don't know whether it would not afford Mrs. Leo Hunter greater pleasure, if her guests saw a gentleman of your celebrity in his own costume, rather than in an assumed one. I may venture to promise an exception in your case, sir—yes, I am quite certain that on behalf of Mrs. Leo Hunter, I may venture to do so."

" In that case," said Mr. Pickwick, " I shall have great pleasure in coming."

" But I waste your time, sir," said the grave man, as if suddenly recollecting himself. " I know its value, sir. I will not detain you. I may tell Mrs. Leo Hunter, then, that she may confidently expect you and your distinguished friends ? Good morning, sir, I am proud to have beheld so eminent a personage—not a step, sir ; not a word." And without giving Mr. Pickwick time to offer remonstrance or denial, Mr. Leo Hunter stalked gravely away.

Mr. Pickwick took up his hat, and repaired to the Peacock

but Mr. Winkle had conveyed the intelligence of the fancy ball there, before him.

"Mrs. Pott's going," were the first words with which he saluted his leader.

"Is she?" said Mr. Pickwick.

"As Apollo," replied Mr. Winkle. "Only Pott objects to the tunic."

"He is right. He is quite right," said Mr. Pickwick emphatically.

"Yes;—so she's going to wear a white satin gown with gold spangles."

"They'll hardly know what she's meant for; will they?" inquired Mr. Snodgrass.

"Of course they will," replied Mr. Winkle indignantly. "They'll see her lyre, won't they?"

"True; I forgot that," said Mr. Snodgrass.

"I shall go as a Bandit," interrupted Mr. Tupman.

"What!" said Mr. Pickwick, with a sudden start.

"As a bandit," repeated Mr. Tupman, mildly.

"You don't mean to say," said Mr. Pickwick, gazing with solemn sternness at his friend, "You don't mean to say, Mr. Tupman, that it is your intention to put yourself into a green velvet jacket, with a two-inch tail?"

"Such *is* my intention, sir," replied Mr. Tupman warmly. "And why not, sir?"

"Because, sir," said Mr. Pickwick, considerably excited. "Because you are too old, sir."

"Too old!" exclaimed Mr. Tupman.

"And if any further ground of objection be wanting," continued Mr. Pickwick, "you are too fat, sir."

"Sir," said Mr. Tupman, his face suffused with a crimson glow. "This is an insult."

"Sir," replied Mr. Pickwick in the same tone, "It is not half the insult to you, that your appearance in my presence in a green velvet jacket, with a two-inch tail, would be to me."

PICKWICKIAN WARMTH.

"Sir," said Mr. Tupman, "you're a fellow."

"Sir," said Mr. Pickwick, "you're another!"

Mr. Tupman advanced a step or two, and glared at Mr. Pickwick. Mr. Pickwick returned the glare, concentrated into a focus by means of his spectacles, and breathed a bold defiance. Mr. Snodgrass and Mr. Winkle looked on, petrified at beholding such a scene between two such men.

"Sir," said Mr. Tupman, after a short pause, speaking in a low, deep voice, "you have called me old."

"I have," said Mr. Pickwick.

"And fat."

"I reiterate the charge."

"And a fellow."

"So you are!"

There was a fearful pause.

"My attachment to your person, sir," said Mr. Tupman, speaking in a voice tremulous with emotion, and tucking up his wristbands meanwhile, "is great—very great—but upon that person, I must take summary vengeance."

"Come on, sir!" replied Mr. Pickwick. Stimulated by the exciting nature of the dialogue, the heroic man actually threw himself into a paralytic attitude, confidently supposed by the two by-standers to have been intended as a posture of defence.

"What!" exclaimed Mr. Snodgrass, suddenly recovering the power of speech, of which intense astonishment had previously bereft him, and rushing between the two, at the imminent hazard of receiving an application on the temple from each, "What! Mr. Pickwick, with the eyes of the world upon you! Mr. Tupman! Who, in common with us all, derives a lustre from his undying name! For shame, gentlemen; for shame."

The unwonted lines which momentary passion had ruled in Mr. Pickwick's clear and open brow, gradually melted away, as his young friend spoke, like the marks of a black-lead pencil beneath the softening influence of India rubber. His

237

countenance had resumed its usual benign expression, ere he concluded.

"I have been hasty," said Mr. Pickwick, "very hasty. Tupman; your hand."

The dark shadow passed from Mr. Tupman's face, as he warmly grasped the hand of his friend.

"I have been hasty, too," said he.

"No, no," interrupted Mr. Pickwick, "the fault was mine. You will wear the green velvet jacket?"

"No, no," replied Mr. Tupman.

"To oblige me, you will," resumed Mr. Pickwick.

"Well, well, I will," said Mr. Tupman.

It was accordingly settled that Mr. Tupman, Mr. Winkle, and Mr. Snodgrass, should all wear fancy dresses. Thus Mr. Pickwick was led by the very warmth of his own good feelings to give his consent to a proceeding from which his better judgment would have recoiled—a more striking illustration of his amiable character could hardly have been conceived, even if the events recorded in these pages had been wholly imaginary.

Mr. Leo Hunter had not exaggerated the resources of Mr. Solomon Lucas. His wardrobe was extensive—very extensive —not strictly classical perhaps, nor quite new, nor did it contain any one garment made precisely after the fashion of any age or time, but everything was more or less spangled; and what *can* be prettier than spangles! It may be objected that they are not adapted to the daylight, but everybody knows that they would glitter if there were lamps; and nothing can be clearer than that if people give fancy balls in the day-time, and the dresses do not show quite as well as they would by night, the fault lies solely with the people who give the fancy balls, and is in no wise chargeable on the spangles. Such was the convincing reasoning of Mr. Solomon Lucas; and influenced by such arguments did Mr. Tupman, Mr. Winkle, and Mr. Snodgrass, engage to array themselves in costumes which his taste and experience induced him to recommend as admirably suited to the occasion.

FANCY COSTUMES.

A carriage was hired from the Town Arms, for the accommodation of the Pickwickians, and a chariot was ordered from the same repository, for the purpose of conveying Mr. and Mrs. Pott to Mrs. Leo Hunter's grounds, which Mr. Pott, as a delicate acknowledgment of having received an invitation, had already confidently predicted in the Eatanswill Gazette "would present a scene of varied and delicious enchantment—a bewildering coruscation of beauty and talent —a lavish and prodigal display of hospitality—above all, a degree of splendour softened by the most exquisite taste; and adornment refined with perfect harmony and the chastest good keeping—compared with which, the fabled gorgeousness of Eastern Fairy-land itself, would appear to be clothed in as many dark and murky colours, as must be the mind of the splenetic and unmanly being who could presume to taint with the venom of his envy, the preparations making by the virtuous and highly distinguished lady, at whose shrine this humble tribute of admiration was offered." This last was a piece of biting sarcasm against the Independent, who in consequence of not having been invited at all, had been through four numbers affecting to sneer at the whole affair, in his very largest type, with all the adjectives in capital letters.

The morning came: it was a pleasant sight to behold Mr. Tupman in full Brigand's costume, with a very tight jacket, sitting like a pincushion over his back and shoulders: the upper portion of his legs encased in the velvet shorts, and the lower part thereof swathed in the complicated bandages to which all Brigands are peculiarly attached. It was pleasing to see his open and ingenuous countenance, well mustachioed and corked, looking out from an open shirt collar; and to contemplate the sugar-loaf hat, decorated with ribbons of all colours, which he was compelled to carry on his knee, inasmuch as no known conveyance with a top to it would admit of any man's carrying it between his head and the roof. Equally humourous and agreeable was the appearance of Mr. Snodgrass in blue satin trunks and cloak, white silk tights and shoes,

239

and Grecian helmet: which everybody knows (and if they do not, Mr. Solomon Lucas did) to have been the regular, authentic, every-day costume of a Troubadour, from the earliest ages down to the time of their final disappearance from the face of the earth. All this was pleasant, but this was as nothing compared with the shouting of the populace when the carriage drew up, behind Mr. Pott's chariot, which chariot itself drew up at Mr. Pott's door, which door itself opened, and displayed the great Pott accoutred as a Russian officer of justice, with a tremendous knout in his hand—tastefully typical of the stern and mighty power of the Eatanswill Gazette, and the fearful lashings it bestowed on public offenders.

"Bravo!" shouted Mr. Tupman and Mr. Snodgrass from the passage, when they beheld the walking allegory.

"Bravo!" Mr. Pickwick was heard to exclaim, from the passage.

"Hoo—roar Pott!" shouted the populace. Amid these salutations, Mr. Pott, smiling with that kind of bland dignity which sufficiently testified that he felt his power, and knew how to exert it, got into the chariot.

Then there emerged from the house, Mrs. Pott, who would have looked very like Apollo if she hadn't had a gown on: conducted by Mr. Winkle, who in his light-red coat, could not possibly have been mistaken for anything but a sportsman, if he had not borne an equal resemblance to a general postman. Last of all came Mr. Pickwick, whom the boys applauded as loud as anybody, probably under the impression that his tights and gaiters were some remnants of the dark ages; and then the two vehicles proceeded towards Mrs. Leo Hunter's: Mr. Weller (who was to assist in waiting) being stationed on the box of that in which his master was seated.

Every one of the men, women, boys, girls, and babies, who were assembled to see the visitors in their fancy dresses, screamed with delight and ecstasy, when Mr. Pickwick, with the Brigand on one arm, and the Troubadour on the other,

Mrs. Leo Hunter's Fancy-Dress Déjeûné

walked solemnly up the entrance. Never were such shouts heard, as those which greeted Mr. Tupman's efforts to fix the sugar-loaf hat on his head, by way of entering the garden in style.

The preparations were on the most delightful scale; fully realising the prophetic Pott's anticipations about the gorgeousness of Eastern Fairy-land, and at once affording a sufficient contradiction to the malignant statements of the reptile Independent. The grounds were more than an acre and a quarter in extent, and they were filled with people! Never was such a blaze of beauty, and fashion, and literature. There was the young lady who "did" the poetry in the Eatanswill Gazette, in the garb of a sultana, leaning upon the arm of the young gentleman who "did" the review department, and who was appropriately habited in a field marshal's uniform— the boots excepted. There were hosts of these geniuses, and any reasonable person would have thought it honour enough to meet them. But more than these, there were half a dozen lions from London—authors, real authors, who had written whole books, and printed them afterwards—and here you might see 'em, walking about, like ordinary men, smiling, and talking—aye, and talking pretty considerable nonsense too, no doubt with the benign intention of rendering themselves intelligible to the common people about them. Moreover, there was a band of music in pasteboard caps; four something-ean singers in the costume of their country, and a dozen hired waiters in the costume of *their* country—and very dirty costume too. And above all, there was Mrs. Leo Hunter in the character of Minerva, receiving the company, and overflowing with pride and gratification at the notion of having called such distinguished individuals together.

"Mr. Pickwick, ma'am," said a servant, as that gentleman approached the presiding goddess, with his hat in his hand, and the Brigand and Troubadour on either arm.

"What! Where!" exclaimed Mrs. Leo Hunter, starting up, in an affected rapture of surprise.

241

"Here," said Mr. Pickwick.

"Is it possible that I have really the gratification of beholding Mr. Pickwick himself!" ejaculated Mrs. Leo Hunter.

"No other, ma'am," replied Mr. Pickwick, bowing very low. "Permit me to introduce my friends—Mr. Tupman—Mr. Winkle—Mr. Snodgrass—to the authoress of 'The Expiring Frog.'"

Very few people but those who have tried it, know what a difficult process it is, to bow in green velvet smalls, and a tight jacket, and high-crowned hat: or in blue satin trunks and white silks: or knee-cords and top-boots that were never made for the wearer, and have been fixed upon him without the remotest reference to the comparative dimensions of himself and the suit. Never were such distortions as Mr. Tupman's frame underwent in his efforts to appear easy and graceful—never was such ingenious posturing, as his fancy-dressed friends exhibited.

"Mr. Pickwick," said Mrs. Leo Hunter, "I must make you promise not to stir from my side the whole day. There are hundreds of people here, that I must positively introduce you to."

"You are very kind, ma'am," said Mr. Pickwick.

"In the first place, here are my little girls; I had almost forgotten them," said Minerva, carelessly pointing towards a couple of full-grown young ladies, of whom one might be about twenty, and the other a year or two older, and who were dressed in very juvenile costumes—whether to make them look young, or their mamma younger, Mr. Pickwick does not distinctly inform us.

"They are very beautiful," said Mr. Pickwick, as the juveniles turned away, after being presented

"They are very like their mamma, sir," said Mr. Pott, majestically.

"Oh you naughty man," exclaimed Mrs. Leo Hunter, playfully tapping the Editor's arm with her fan (Minerva with a fan!)

A DISTINGUISHED FOREIGNER.

"Why now, my dear Mrs. Hunter," said Mr. Pott, who was trumpeter in ordinary at the Den, "you *know* that when your picture was in the Exhibition of the Royal Academy, last year, everybody inquired whether it was intended for you, or your youngest daughter; for you were so much alike that there was no telling the difference between you."

"Well, and if they did, why need you repeat it, before strangers?" said Mrs. Leo Hunter, bestowing another tap on the slumbering lion of the Eatanswill Gazette.

"Count, Count," screamed Mrs. Leo Hunter to a well-whiskered individual in a foreign uniform, who was passing by.

"Ah! you want me?" said the Count, turning back.

"I want to introduce two very clever people to each other," said Mrs. Leo Hunter. "Mr. Pickwick, I have great pleasure in introducing you to Count Smorltork." She added in a hurried whisper to Mr. Pickwick—"the famous foreigner—gathering materials for his great work on England—hem!—Count Smorltork, Mr. Pickwick."

Mr. Pickwick saluted the Count with all the reverence due to so great a man, and the Count drew forth a set of tablets.

"What you say, Mrs. Hunt?" inquired the Count, smiling graciously on the gratified Mrs. Leo Hunter, "Pig Vig or Big Vig—what you call—Lawyer—eh? I see—that is it. Big Vig"—and the Count was proceeding to enter Mr. Pickwick in his tablets, as a gentleman of the long robe, who derived his name from the profession to which he belonged, when Mrs. Leo Hunter interposed.

"No, no, Count," said the lady, "Pick-wick."

"Ah, ah, I see," replied the Count. "Peek—christian name; Weeks—surname; good, ver good. Peek Weeks. How you do, Weeks?"

"Quite well, I thank you," replied Mr. Pickwick, with all his usual affability. "Have you been long in England?"

"Long—ver long time—fortnight—more."

"Do you stay here long?"

"One week."

"You will have enough to do," said Mr. Pickwick, smiling, "to gather all the materials you want, in that time."

"Eh, they are gathered," said the Count.

"Indeed!" said Mr. Pickwick.

"They are here," added the Count, tapping his forehead significantly. "Large book at home—full of notes—music, picture, science, poetry, poltic; all tings."

"The word politics, sir," said Mr. Pickwick, "comprises, in itself, a difficult study of no inconsiderable magnitude."

"Ah!" said the Count, drawing out the tablets again, "ver good—fine words to begin a chapter. Chapter forty-seven. Poltics. The word poltic surprises by himself—" And down went Mr. Pickwick's remark, in Count Smorltork's tablets, with such variations and additions as the Count's exuberant fancy suggested, or his imperfect knowledge of the language, occasioned.

"Count," said Mrs. Leo Hunter.

"Mrs. Hunt," replied the Count.

"This is Mr. Snodgrass, a friend of Mr. Pickwick's, and a poet."

"Stop," exclaimed the Count, bringing out the tablets once more. "Head, potry—chapter, literary friends—name, Snowgrass; ver good. Introduced to Snowgrass—great poet, friend of Peek Weeks—by Mrs. Hunt, which wrote other sweet poem —what is that name?—Fog—Perspiring Fog—ver good—ver good indeed." And the Count put up his tablets, and with sundry bows and acknowledgments walked away, thoroughly satisfied that he had made the most important and valuable additions to his stock of information.

"Wonderful man, Count Smorltork," said Mrs. Leo Hunter.

"Sound philosopher," said Mr. Pott.

"Clear-headed, strong-minded person," added Mr. Snodgrass.

A chorus of by-standers took up the shout of Count Smorltork's praise, shook their heads sagely, and unanimously cried "Very!"

ODE TO A FROG.

As the enthusiasm in Count Smorltork's favour ran very high, his praises might have been sung until the end of the festivities, if the four something-ean singers had not ranged themselves in front of a small apple-tree, to look picturesque, and commenced singing their national songs, which appeared by no means difficult of execution, inasmuch as the grand secret seemed to be, that three of the something-ean singers should grunt, while the fourth howled. This interesting performance having concluded amidst the loud plaudits of the whole company, a boy forthwith proceeded to entangle himself with the rails of a chair, and to jump over it, and crawl under it, and fall down with it, and do everything but sit upon it, and then to make a cravat of his legs, and tie them round his neck, and then to illustrate the ease with which a human being can be made to look like a magnified toad—all which feats yielded delight and satisfaction to the assembled spectators. After which, the voice of Mrs. Pott was heard to chirp faintly forth, something which courtesy interpreted into a song, which was all very classical, and strictly in character, because Apollo was himself a composer, and composers can very seldom sing their own music or anybody else's, either. This was succeeded by Mrs. Leo Hunter's recitation of her far-famed Ode to an Expiring Frog, which was encored once, and would have been encored twice, if the major part of the guests, who thought it was high time to get something to eat, had not said that it was perfectly shameful to take advantage of Mrs. Hunter's good nature. So although Mrs. Leo Hunter professed her perfect willingness to recite the ode again, her kind and considerate friends wouldn't hear of it on any account; and the refreshment room being thrown open, all the people who had ever been there before, scrambled in with all possible despatch: Mrs. Leo Hunter's usual course of proceeding, being, to issue cards for a hundred, and breakfast for fifty, or in other words to feed only the very particular lions, and let the smaller animals take care of themselves.

"Where is Mr. Pott?" said Mrs. Leo Hunter, as she placed the aforesaid lions around her.

"Here I am," said the editor, from the remotest end of the room; far beyond all hope of food, unless something was done for him by the hostess.

"Won't you come up here?"

"Oh pray don't mind him," said Mrs. Pott, in the most obliging voice—"you give yourself a great deal of unnecessary trouble, Mrs. Hunter. You'll do very well there, won't you —dear."

"Certainly—love," replied the unhappy Pott, with a grim smile. Alas for the knout! The nervous arm that wielded it, with such gigantic force, on public characters, was paralysed beneath the glance of the imperious Mrs. Pott.

Mrs. Leo Hunter looked round her in triumph. Count Smorltork was busily engaged in taking notes of the contents of the dishes; Mr. Tupman was doing the honours of the lobster salad to several lionesses, with a degree of grace which no Brigand ever exhibited before; Mr. Snodgrass having cut out the young gentleman who cut up the books for the Eatanswill Gazette, was engaged in an impassioned argument with the young lady who did the poetry: and Mr. Pickwick was making himself universally agreeable. Nothing seemed wanting to render the select circle complete, when Mr. Leo Hunter—whose department on these occasions, was to stand about in doorways, and talk to the less important people— suddenly called out—

"My dear; here's Mr. Charles Fitz-Marshall."

"Oh dear," said Mrs. Leo Hunter, "how anxiously I have been expecting him. Pray make room, to let Mr. Fitz-Marshall pass. Tell Mr. Fitz-Marshall, my dear, to come up to me directly, to be scolded for coming so late."

"Coming, my dear ma'am," cried a voice, "as quick as I can—crowds of people—full room—hard work—very."

Mr. Pickwick's knife and fork fell from his hand. He stared across the table at Mr. Tupman, who had dropped *his* knife and fork, and was looking as if he were about to sink into the ground without further notice.

"Ah!" cried the voice, as its owner pushed his way among the last five and twenty Turks, officers, cavaliers, and Charles the Seconds, that remained between him and the table, "regular mangle—Baker's patent—not a crease in my coat, after all this squeezing—might have 'got up my linen' as I came along—ha! ha! not a bad idea, that—queer thing to have it mangled when it's upon one, though—trying process —very."

With these broken words, a young man dressed as a naval officer made his way up to the table, and presented to the astonished Pickwickians, the identical form and features of Mr. Alfred Jingle.

The offender had barely time to take Mrs. Leo Hunter's proffered hand, when his eyes encountered the indignant orbs of Mr. Pickwick.

"Hallo!" said Jingle. "Quite forgot—no directions to postilion—give 'em at once—back in a minute."

"The servant, or Mr. Hunter will do it in a moment, Mr. Fitz-Marshall," said Mrs. Leo Hunter.

"No, no—I'll do it—shan't be long—back in no time," replied Jingle. With these words he disappeared among the crowd.

"Will you allow me to ask you, ma'am," said the excited Mr. Pickwick, rising from his seat, "who that young man is, and where he resides!"

"He is a gentleman of fortune, Mr. Pickwick," said Mrs. Leo Hunter, "to whom I very much want to introduce you. The Count will be delighted with him."

"Yes, yes," said Mr. Pickwick, hastily. "His residence—"

"Is at present at the Angel at Bury."

"At Bury?"

"At Bury St. Edmunds, not many miles from here. But dear me, Mr. Pickwick, you are not going to leave us: surely, Mr. Pickwick, you cannot think of going so soon."

But long before Mrs. Leo Hunter had finished speaking, Mr. Pickwick had plunged through the throng, and reached the garden, whither he was shortly afterwards joined by Mr. Tupman, who had followed his friend closely.

"It's of no use," said Mr. Tupman. "He has gone."

"I know it," said Mr. Pickwick, "and I will follow him."

"Follow him! Where?" inquired Mr. Tupman.

"To the Angel at Bury," replied Mr. Pickwick, speaking very quickly. "How do we know whom he is deceiving there? He deceived a worthy man once, and we were the innocent cause. He shall not do it again, if I can help it; I'll expose him! Where's my servant?"

"Here you are, sir," said Mr. Weller, emerging from a sequestered spot, where he had been engaged in discussing a bottle of Madeira, which he had abstracted from the breakfast-table, an hour or two before. "Here's your servant, sir. Proud o' the title, as the Living Skellinton said, ven they show'd him."

"Follow me instantly," said Mr. Pickwick. "Tupman, if I stay at Bury, you can join me there, when I write. Till then, good-bye!"

Remonstrances were useless. Mr. Pickwick was roused, and his mind was made up. Mr. Tupman returned to his companions; and in another hour had drowned all present recollection of Mr. Alfred Jingle, or Mr. Charles Fitz-Marshall, in an exhilarating quadrille and a bottle of champagne. By that time, Mr. Pickwick and Sam Weller, perched on the outside of a stage coach, were every succeeding minute placing a less and less distance between themselves and the good old town of Bury St. Edmunds.

CHAPTER XVI.

TOO FULL OF ADVENTURE TO BE BRIEFLY DESCRIBED.

THERE is no month in the whole year, in which nature wears a more beautiful appearance than in the month of August. Spring has many beauties, and May is a fresh and blooming month, but the charms of this time of year are enhanced by their contrast with the winter season. August has no such advantage. It comes when we remember nothing but clear skies, green fields and sweet-smelling flowers—when the recollection of snow, and ice, and bleak winds, has faded from our minds as completely as they have disappeared from the earth,—and yet what a pleasant time it is! Orchards and corn-fields ring with the hum of labour; trees bend beneath the thick clusters of rich fruit which bow their branches to the ground; and the corn, piled in graceful sheaves, or waving in every light breath that sweeps above it, as if it wooed the sickle, tinges the landscape with a golden hue. A mellow softness appears to hang over the whole earth; the influence of the season seems to extend itself to the very waggon, whose slow motion across the well-reaped field, is perceptible only to the eye, but strikes with no harsh sound upon the ear.

As the coach rolls swiftly past the fields and orchards which skirt the road, groups of women and children, piling the fruit in sieves, or gathering the scattered ears of corn, pause for an instant from their labour, and shading the sun-burnt face with a still browner hand, gaze upon the passengers with curious eyes, while some stout urchin, too small to work, but too mischievous to be left at home, scrambles over the side of the basket in which he has been deposited for security, and kicks and screams with delight. The reaper stops in his work, and stands with folded arms, looking at the vehicle as it whirls past; and the rough cart horses bestow a sleepy glance upon the smart coach team, which says, as plainly as a horse's glance can, "It's all very fine to look at, but slow going, over a heavy field, is better than warm work like that, upon a dusty road, after all." You cast a look behind you, as you turn a corner of the road. The women and children have resumed their labour : the reaper once more stoops to his work : the cart-horses have moved on : and all are again in motion.

The influence of a scene like this, was not lost upon the well-regulated mind of Mr. Pickwick. Intent upon the resolution he had formed, of exposing the real character of the nefarious Jingle, in any quarter in which he might be pursuing his fraudulent designs, he sat at first taciturn and contemplative, brooding over the means by which his purpose could be best attained. By degrees his attention grew more and more attracted by the objects around him; and at last he derived as much enjoyment from the ride, as if it had been undertaken for the pleasantest reason in the world.

"Delightful prospect, Sam," said Mr. Pickwick.

"Beats the chimley pots, sir," replied Mr. Weller, touching his hat.

"I suppose you have hardly seen anything but chimney-pots and bricks and mortar all your life, Sam," said Mr. Pickwick, smiling.

"I worn't always a boots, sir," said Mr. Weller, with a shake of the head. "I wos a wagginer's boy, once."

"When was that?" inquired Mr. Pickwick

"When I wos first pitched neck and crop into the world, to play at leap-frog with its troubles," replied Sam. "I wos a carrier's boy at startin': then a vagginer's, then a helper, then a boots. Now I'm a gen'l'm'n's servant. I shall be a gen'l'm'n myself one of these days, perhaps, with a pipe in my mouth, and a summer-house in the back garden. Who knows? *I* shouldn't be surprised, for one."

"You are quite a philosopher, Sam," said Mr. Pickwick.

"It runs in the family, I b'lieve, sir," replied Mr. Weller. "My father's wery much in that line, now. If my mother-in-law blows him up, he whistles. She flies in a passion, and breaks his pipe; he steps out, and gets another. Then she screams wery loud, and falls into 'sterics; and he smokes wery comfortably 'till she comes to agin. That's philosophy, sir, an't it?"

"A very good substitute for it, at all events," replied Mr. Pickwick, laughing. "It must have been of great service to you, in the course of your rambling life, Sam."

"Service, sir," exclaimed Sam. "You may say that. Arter I run away from the carrier, and afore I took up with the wagginer, I had unfurnished lodgin's for a fortnight."

"Unfurnished lodgings?" said Mr. Pickwick.

"Yes—the dry arches of Waterloo Bridge. Fine sleeping-place—within ten minutes' walk of all the public offices—only if there is any objection to it, it is that the sitivation's *rayther* too airy. I see some queer sights there."

"Ah, I suppose you did," said Mr. Pickwick, with an air of considerable interest.

"Sights, sir," resumed Mr. Weller, "as 'ud penetrate your benevolent heart, and come out on the other side. You don't see the reg'lar wagrants there; trust 'em, they knows better than that. Young beggars, male and female, as hasn't made a rise in their profession, takes up their quarters there sometimes; but it's generally the worn-out, starving, houseless creeturs as rolls themselves in the dark corners o' them lonesome places—poor creeturs as an't up to the twopenny rope."

"And, pray, Sam, what is the twopenny rope?" inquired Mr. Pickwick.

"The twopenny rope, sir," replied Mr. Weller, "is just a cheap lodgin' house, where the beds is twopence a night."

"What do they call a bed a rope for?" said Mr. Pickwick.

"Bless your innocence, sir, that a'nt it," replied Sam. "Wen the lady and gen'l'm'n as keeps the Hot-el first begun business they used to make the beds on the floor; but this wouldn't do at no price, 'cos instead o' taking a moderate two-penn'orth o' sleep, the lodgers used to lie there half the day. So now they has two ropes, 'bout six foot apart, and three from the floor, which goes right down the room; and the beds are made of slips of coarse sacking, stretched across 'em."

"Well," said Mr. Pickwick.

"Well," said Mr. Weller, "the adwantage o' the plan's hobvious. At six o'clock every mornin' they lets go the ropes at one end, and down falls all the lodgers. 'Consequence is, that being thoroughly waked, they get up wery quietly, and walk away! Beg your pardon, sir," said Sam, suddenly breaking off in his loquacious discourse. "Is this Bury St. Edmunds?"

"It is," replied Mr. Pickwick.

The coach rattled through the well-paved streets of a handsome little town, of thriving and cleanly appearance, and stopped before a large inn situated in a wide open street, nearly facing the old abbey.

"And this," said Mr. Pickwick, looking up, "is the Angel! We alight here, Sam. But some caution is necessary. Order a private room, and do not mention my name. You understand."

"Right as a trivet, sir," replied Mr. Weller, with a wink of intelligence; and having dragged Mr. Pickwick's portmanteau from the hind boot, into which it had been hastily thrown when they joined the coach at Eatanswill, Mr. Weller disappeared on his errand. A private room was speedily engaged; and into it Mr. Pickwick was ushered without delay.

"Now, Sam," said Mr. Pickwick, "the first thing to be done is to—"

"Order dinner, sir," interposed Mr. Weller. "It's wery late, sir."

"Ah, so it is," said Mr. Pickwick, looking at his watch. "You are right, Sam."

"And if I might adwise, sir," added Mr. Weller, "I'd just have a good night's rest arterwards, and not begin inquiring arter this here deep 'un 'till the mornin'. There's nothin' so refreshin' as sleep, sir, as the servant-girl said afore she drank the egg-cupful o' laudanum."

"I think you are right, Sam," said Mr. Pickwick. "But I must first ascertain that he is in the house, and not likely to go away."

"Leave that to me, sir," said Sam. "Let me order you a snug little dinner, and make any inquiries below while it's a getting ready; I could worm ev'ry secret out o' the boots's heart, in five minutes, sir."

"Do so," said Mr. Pickwick: and Mr. Weller at once retired.

In half an hour, Mr. Pickwick was seated at a very satisfactory dinner; and in three-quarters Mr. Weller returned with the intelligence that Mr. Charles Fitz-Marshall had ordered his private room to be retained for him, until further notice. He was going to spend the evening at some private house in the neighbourhood, had ordered the boots to sit up until his return, and had taken his servant with him.

"Now, sir," argued Mr. Weller, when he had concluded his report, "if I can get a talk with this here servant in the mornin', he'll tell me all his master's concerns."

"How do you know that?" interposed Mr. Pickwick.

"Bless your heart, sir, servants always do," replied Mr. Weller.

"Oh, ah, I forgot that," said Mr. Pickwick. "Well."

"Then you can arrange what's best to be done, sir, and we can act according."

As it appeared that this was the best arrangement that could be made, it was finally agreed upon. Mr. Weller, by his master's permission, retired to spend the evening in his own way; and was shortly afterwards elected, by the unanimous voice of the assembled company, into the tap-room chair, in which honourable post he acquitted himself so much to the satisfaction of the gentlemen-frequenters, that their roars of laughter and approbation penetrated to Mr. Pickwick's bed-room, and shortened the term of his natural rest by at least three hours.

Early on the ensuing morning, Mr. Weller was dispelling all the feverish remains of the previous evening's conviviality, through the instrumentality of a halfpenny shower-bath (having induced a young gentleman attached to the stable-department, by the offer of that coin, to pump over his head and face, until he was perfectly restored), when he was attracted by the appearance of a young fellow in mulberry-coloured livery, who was sitting on a bench in the yard, reading what appeared to be a hymn-book, with an air of deep abstraction, but who occasionally stole a glance at the individual under the pump, as if he took some interest in his proceedings, never-theless.

"You're a rum 'un to look at, you are!" thought Mr. Weller, the first time his eyes encountered the glance of the stranger in the mulberry suit: who had a large, sallow, ugly face, very sunken eyes, and a gigantic head, from which depended a quantity of lank black hair. "You're a rum 'un!" thought Mr. Weller; and thinking this, he went on washing himself, and thought no more about him.

Still the man kept glancing from his hymn-book to Sam, and from Sam to his hymn-book, as if he wanted to open a conversation. So at last, Sam, by way of giving him an opportunity, said with a familiar nod—

"How are you, governor?"

"I am happy to say, I am pretty well, sir," said the man, speaking with great deliberation, and closing the book. "I hope you are the same, sir?"

"Why, if I felt less like a walking brandy-bottle, I

shouldn't be quite so staggery this mornin'," replied Sam. "Are you stoppin' in this house, old 'un?"

The mulberry man replied in the affirmative.

"How was it, you worn't one of us, last night?" inquired Sam, scrubbing his face with the towel. "You seem one of the jolly sort—looks as conwivial as a live trout in a lime basket," added Mr. Weller, in an under tone.

"I was out last night, with my master," replied the stranger.

"What's his name?" inquired Mr. Weller, colouring up very red with sudden excitement, and the friction of the towel combined.

"Fitz-Marshall," said the mulberry man.

"Give us your hand," said Mr. Weller, advancing; "I should like to know you. I like your appearance, old fellow."

"Well, that is very strange," said the mulberry man, with great simplicity of manner. "I like your's so much, that I wanted to speak to you, from the very first moment I saw you under the pump."

"Did you though?"

"Upon my word. Now, isn't that curious?"

"Wery sing'ler," said Sam, inwardly congratulating himself upon the softness of the stranger. "What's your name, my patriarch?"

"Job."

"And a wery good name it is—only one I know, that ain't got a nickname to it. What's the other name?"

"Trotter," said the stranger. "What is yours!"

Sam bore in mind his master's caution, and replied.

"My name's Walker; my master's name's Wilkins. Will you take a drop o' somethin' this mornin', Mr. Trotter?"

Mr. Trotter acquiesced in this agreeable proposal: and having deposited his book in his coat-pocket, accompanied Mr. Weller to the tap, where they were soon occupied in discussing an exhilarating compound, formed by mixing together, in a pewter vessel, certain quantities of British Hollands, and the fragrant essence of the clove.

"And what sort of a place have you got?" inquired Sam, as he filled his companion's glass, for the second time.

"Bad," said Job, smacking his lips, "very bad."

"You don't mean that?" said Sam.

"I do, indeed. Worse than that, my master's going to be married."

"No."

"Yes; and worse than that, too, he's going to run away with an immense rich heiress, from boarding-school."

"What a dragon!" said Sam, refilling his companion's glass. "It's some boarding-school in this town, I suppose, a'nt it?"

Now, although this question was put in the most careless tone imaginable, Mr. Job Trotter plainly showed by gestures, that he perceived his new friend's anxiety to draw forth an answer to it. He emptied his glass, looked mysteriously at his companion, winked both of his small eyes, one after the other, and finally made a motion with his arm, as if he were working an imaginary pump-handle : thereby intimating that he (Mr. Trotter) considered himself as undergoing the process of being pumped, by Mr. Samuel Weller.

"No, no," said Mr. Trotter, in conclusion, "that's not to be told to everybody. That is a secret—a great secret, Mr. Walker."

As the mulberry man said this, he turned his glass upside down, as a means of reminding his companion that he had nothing left wherewith to slake his thirst. Sam observed the hint ; and feeling the delicate manner in which it was conveyed, ordered the pewter vessel to be refilled, whereat the small eyes of the mulberry man glistened.

"And so it's a secret?" said Sam.

"I should rather suspect it was," said the mulberry man, sipping his liquor, with a complacent face.

"I suppose your mas'r 's wery rich?" said Sam.

Mr. Trotter smiled, and holding his glass in his left hand, gave four distinct slaps on the pocket of his mulberry indescribables with his right, as if to intimate that his master might have done the same without alarming anybody much by the chinking of coin.

"Ah," said Sam, "that's the game, is it?"

The mulberry man nodded significantly.

"Well, and don't you think, old feller," remonstrated Mr. Weller, "that if you let your master take in this here young lady, you're a precious rascal?"

"I know that," said Job Trotter, turning upon his companion a countenance of deep contrition, and groaning slightly. "I know that, and that's what it is that preys upon my mind. But what am I to do?"

"Do!" said Sam; "di-wulge to the missis, and give up your master."

"Who'd believe me?" replied Job Trotter. "The young lady's considered the very picture of innocence and discretion. She'd deny it, and so would my master. Who'd believe me? I should lose my place, and get indicted for a conspiracy, or some such thing; that's all I should take by my motion."

"There's somethin' in that," said Sam, ruminating; "there's somethin' in that."

"If I knew any respectable gentleman who would take the matter up," continued Mr. Trotter, "I might have some hope of preventing the elopement; but there's the same difficulty, Mr. Walker, just the same. I know no gentleman in this strange place, and ten to one if I did, whether he would believe my story."

"Come this way," said Sam, suddenly jumping up, and grasping the mulberry man by the arm. "My mas'r 's the man you want, I see." And after a slight resistance on the part of Job Trotter, Sam led his newly-found friend to the apartment of Mr. Pickwick, to whom he presented him, together with a brief summary of the dialogue we have just repeated.

"I am very sorry to betray my master, sir," said Job

Trotter, applying to his eyes a pink checked pocket handkerchief about six inches square.

"The feeling does you a great deal of honour," replied Mr. Pickwick; "but it is your duty, nevertheless."

"I know it is my duty, sir," replied Job, with great emotion. "We should all try to discharge our duty, sir, and I humbly endeavour to discharge mine, sir; but it is a hard trial to betray a master, sir, whose clothes you wear, and whose bread you eat, even though he is a scoundrel, sir."

"You are a very good fellow," said Mr. Pickwick, much affected, "an honest fellow."

"Come, come," interposed Sam, who had witnessed Mr. Trotter's tears with considerable impatience, "blow this here water-cart bis'ness. It won't do no good, this won't."

"Sam," said Mr. Pickwick, reproachfully, "I am sorry to find that you have so little respect for this young man's feelings."

"His feelins is all wery well, sir," replied Mr. Weller; "and as they're so wery fine, and it's a pity he should lose 'em, I think he'd better keep 'em in his own buzzum, than let 'em ewaporate in hot water, 'specially as they do no good. Tears never yet wound up a clock, or worked a steam ingen'. The next time you go out to a smoking party, young fellow, fill your pipe with that 'ere reflection; and for the present just put that bit of pink gingham into your pocket. 'T'an't so handsome that you need keep waving it about, as if you was a tight-rope dancer."

"My man is in the right," said Mr. Pickwick, accosting Job, "although his mode of expressing his opinion is somewhat homely, and occasionally incomprehensible."

"He is, sir, very right," said Mr. Trotter, "and I will give way no longer."

"Very well," said Mr. Pickwick. "Now, where is this boarding-school?"

"It is a large, old, red-brick house, just outside the town, sir," replied Job Trotter

"And when," said Mr. Pickwick, "when is this villainous design to be carried into execution—when is this elopement to take place?"

"To-night, sir," replied Job.

"To-night!" exclaimed Mr. Pickwick.

"This very night, sir," replied Job Trotter. "That is what alarms me so much."

"Instant measures must be taken," said Mr. Pickwick. "I will see the lady who keeps the establishment immediately."

"I beg your pardon, sir," said Job, "but that course of proceeding will never do."

"Why not?" inquired Mr. Pickwick.

"My master, sir, is a very artful man."

"I know he is," said Mr. Pickwick.

"And he has so wound himself round the old lady's heart, sir," resumed Job, "that she would believe nothing to his prejudice, if you went down on your bare knees, and swore it; especially as you have no proof but the word of a servant, who, for anything she knows (and my master would be sure to say so), was discharged for some fault, and does this in revenge."

"What had better be done, then?" said Mr. Pickwick.

"Nothing but taking him in the very fact of eloping, will convince the old lady, sir," replied Job.

"All them old cats *will* run their heads agin mile-stones," observed Mr. Weller in a parenthesis.

"But this taking him in the very act of elopement, would be a very difficult thing to accomplish, I fear," said Mr. Pickwick.

"I don't know, sir," said Mr. Trotter, after a few moments' reflection. "I think it might be very easily done."

"How?" was Mr. Pickwick's inquiry.

"Why," replied Mr. Trotter, "my master and I, being in the confidence of the two servants, will be secreted in the kitchen at ten o'clock. When the family have retired to rest, we shall come out of the kitchen, and the young lady out of her bed-room. A post-chaise will be waiting, and away we go."

"Well?" said Mr. Pickwick.

"Well, sir, I have been thinking that if you were in waiting in the garden behind, alone——"

"Alone," said Mr. Pickwick. "Why alone?"

"I thought it very natural," replied Job, "that the old lady wouldn't like such an unpleasant discovery to be made before more persons than can possibly be helped. The young lady too, sir—consider her feelings."

"You are very right," said Mr. Pickwick. "The consideration evinces your delicacy of feeling. Go on; you are very right."

"Well sir, I have been thinking that if you were waiting in the back garden alone, and I was to let you in, at the door which opens into it, from the end of the passage, at exactly half-past eleven o'clock, you would be just in the very moment of time to assist me in frustrating the designs of this bad man, by whom I have been unfortunately ensnared." Here Mr. Trotter sighed deeply.

"Don't distress yourself on that account," said Mr. Pickwick, "if he had one grain of the delicacy of feeling which distinguishes you, humble as your station is, I should have some hopes of him."

Job Trotter bowed low; and in spite of Mr. Weller's previous remonstrance, the tears again rose to his eyes.

"I never see such a feller," said Sam. "Blessed if I don't think he's got a main in his head as is always turned on."

"Sam," said Mr. Pickwick, with great severity. "Hold your tongue."

"Werry well, sir," replied Mr. Weller.

"I don't like this plan," said Mr. Pickwick, after deep meditation. "Why cannot I communicate with the young lady's friends?"

"Because they live one hundred miles from here, sir," responded Job Trotter.

"That's a clincher," said Mr. Weller, aside.

"Then this garden," resumed Mr. Pickwick. "How am I to get into it?"

"The wall is very low, sir, and your servant will give you a leg up."

"My servant will give me a leg up," repeated Mr. Pickwick, mechanically. "You will be sure to be near this door that you speak of?"

"You cannot mistake it, sir; it's the only one that opens into the garden. Tap at it when you hear the clock strike, and I will open it instantly."

"I don't like the plan," said Mr. Pickwick; "but as I see no other, and as the happiness of this young lady's whole life is at stake, I adopt it. I shall be sure to be there."

Thus, for the second time, did Mr. Pickwick's innate good-feeling involve him in an enterprise from which he would most willingly have stood aloof.

"What is the name of the house?" inquired Mr. Pickwick.

"Westgate House, sir. You turn a little to the right when you get to the end of the town; it stands by itself, some little distance off the high road, with the name on a brass plate on the gate."

"I know it," said Mr. Pickwick. "I observed it once before, when I was in this town. You may depend upon me."

Mr. Trotter made another bow, and turned to depart, when Mr. Pickwick thrust a guinea into his hand.

"You're a fine fellow," said Mr. Pickwick, "and I admire your goodness of heart. No thanks. Remember—eleven o'clock."

"There is no fear of my forgetting it, sir," replied Job Trotter. With these words he left the room, followed by Sam.

"I say," said the latter, "not a bad notion that 'ere crying. I'd cry like a rain-water spout in a shower on such good terms. How do you do it?"

"It comes from the heart, Mr. Walker," replied Job, solemnly. "Good morning, sir."

"You're a soft customer, you are;—we've got it all out o' you, any how," thought Mr. Weller, as Job walked away.

We cannot state the precise nature of the thoughts which passed through Mr. Trotter's mind, because we don't know what they were.

The day wore on, evening came, and a little before ten o'clock Sam Weller reported that Mr. Jingle and Job had gone out together, that their luggage was packed up, and that they had ordered a chaise. The plot was evidently in execution, as Mr. Trotter had foretold.

Half-past ten o'clock arrived, and it was time for Mr. Pickwick to issue forth on his delicate errand. Resisting Sam's tender of his great-coat, in order that he might have no incumbrance in scaling the wall, he set forth, followed by his attendant.

There was a bright moon, but it was behind the clouds. It was a fine dry night, but it was most uncommonly dark. Paths, hedges, fields, houses, and trees, were enveloped in one deep shade. The atmosphere was hot and sultry, the summer lightning quivered faintly on the verge of the horizon, and was the only sight that varied the dull gloom in which everything was wrapped—sound there was none, except the distant barking of some restless house-dog.

They found the house, read the brass-plate, walked round the wall, and stopped at that portion of it which divided them from the bottom of the garden.

"You will return to the inn, Sam, when you have assisted me over," said Mr. Pickwick.

"Very well, sir."

"And you will sit up, 'till I return."

"Cert'nly, sir."

"Take hold of my leg; and, when I say 'Over,' raise me gently."

"All right, sir."

Having settled these preliminaries, Mr. Pickwick grasped the top of the wall, and gave the word "Over," which was very literally obeyed. Whether his body partook in some degree of the elasticity of his mind, or whether Mr. Weller's notions of a gentle push were of a somewhat rougher description than Mr. Pickwick's, the immediate effect of his assistance was to jerk that immortal gentleman completely over the wall on to the bed beneath, where, after crushing three gooseberry-bushes and a rose-tree, he finally alighted at full length.

"You ha'n't hurt yourself, I hope, sir?" said Sam, in a loud whisper, as soon as he recovered from the surprise consequent upon the mysterious disappearance of his master.

"I have not hurt *myself*, Sam, certainly," replied Mr. Pickwick, from the other side of the wall, "but I rather think that *you* have hurt me."

"I hope not, sir," said Sam.

"Never mind," said Mr. Pickwick, rising, "it's nothing but a few scratches. Go away, or we shall be overheard."

"Good-bye, sir."

"Good-bye."

With stealthy steps Sam Weller departed, leaving Mr. Pickwick alone in the garden.

Lights occasionally appeared in the different windows of the house, or glanced from the staircases, as if the inmates were retiring to rest. Not caring to go too near the door, until the appointed time, Mr. Pickwick crouched into an angle of the wall, and awaited its arrival.

It was a situation which might well have depressed the spirits of many a man. Mr. Pickwick, however, felt neither depression nor misgiving. He knew that his purpose was in the main a good one, and he placed implicit reliance on the high-minded Job. It was dull, certainly; not to say, dreary; but a contemplative man can always employ himself in meditation. Mr. Pickwick had meditated himself into a doze, when he was roused by the chimes of the neighbouring church ringing out the hour—half-past eleven.

'That is the time," thought Mr. Pickwick, getting cautiously on his feet. He looked up at the house. The lights had disappeared, and the shutters were closed—all in bed, no doubt. He walked on tip-toe to the door, and gave a gentle tap. Two or three minutes passing without any reply, he gave another tap rather louder, and then another rather louder than that.

At length the sound of feet was audible upon the stairs, and then the light of a candle shone through the key-hole of the door. There was a good deal of unchaining and unbolting, and the door was slowly opened.

Now the door opened outwards: and as the door opened wider and wider, Mr. Pickwick receded behind it, more and more. What was his astonishment when he just peeped out, by way of caution, to see that the person who had opened it was—not Job Trotter, but a servant-girl with a candle in her hand! Mr. Pickwick drew in his head again, with the swiftness displayed by that admirable melodramatic performer, Punch, when he lies in wait for the flat-headed comedian with the tin box of music.

"It must have been the cat, Sarah," said the girl, addressing herself to some one in the house. "Puss, puss, puss,—tit, tit, tit."

But no animal being decoyed by these blandishments, the girl slowly closed the door, and re-fastened it; leaving Mr. Pickwick drawn up straight against the wall.

"This is very curious," thought Mr. Pickwick. "They are sitting up beyond their usual hour, I suppose. Extremely unfortunate, that they should have chosen this night, of all others, for such a purpose—exceedingly." And with these thoughts, Mr. Pickwick cautiously retired to the angle of the wall in which he had been before ensconced; waiting until such time as he might deem it safe to repeat the signal.

He had not been here five minutes, when a vivid flash of lightning was followed by a loud peal of thunder that crashed and rolled away in the distance with a terrific noise—then came another flash of lightning, brighter than the other, and a second peal of thunder louder than the first; and then down came the rain, with a force and fury that swept everything before it.

Mr. Pickwick was perfectly aware that a tree is a very dangerous neighbour in a thunder-storm. He had a tree on his right, a tree on his left, a third before him, and a fourth behind. If he remained where he was, he might fall the victim of an accident; if he showed himself in the centre of the garden, he might be consigned to a constable;—once or twice he tried to scale the wall, but having no other legs this time, than those with which Nature had furnished him, the only effect of his struggles was to inflict a variety of very unpleasant gratings on his knees and shins, and to throw him into a state of the most profuse perspiration.

"What a dreadful situation," said Mr. Pickwick, pausing to wipe his brow after this exercise. He looked up at the house—all was dark. They must be gone to bed now. He would try the signal again.

He walked on tip-toe across the moist gravel, and tapped at the door. He held his breath, and listened at the key-hole. No reply: very odd. Another knock. He listened again. There was a low whispering inside, and then a voice cried—

"Who's there?"

"That's not Job," thought Mr. Pickwick, hastily drawing himself straight up against the wall again. "It's a woman."

He had scarcely had time to form this conclusion, when a window above stairs was thrown up, and three or four female voices repeated the query—"Who's there?"

Mr. Pickwick dared not move hand or foot. It was clear that the whole establishment was roused. He made up his mind to remain where he was, until the alarm had subsided: and then by a supernatural effort, to get over the wall, or perish in the attempt.

Like all Mr. Pickwick's determinations, this was the best that could be made under the circumstances; but, unfortunately, it was founded upon the assumption that they would not venture to open the door again. What was his discomfiture, when he heard the chain and bolts withdrawn, and saw the door slowly opening, wider and wider! He retreated into the corner, step by step; but do what he would, the interposition of his own person, prevented its being opened to its utmost width.

"Who's there?" screamed a numerous chorus of treble voices from the staircase inside, consisting of the spinster lady of the establishment, three teachers, five female servants, and thirty boarders, all half-dressed, and in a forest of curl-papers.

Of course Mr. Pickwick didn't say who *was* there; and then the burden of the chorus changed into—"Lor'! I am so frightened."

"Cook," said the lady abbess, who took care to be on the top stair, the very last of the group—"Cook, why don't you go a little way into the garden?"

"Please, ma'am, I don't like," responded the cook.

"Lor', what a stupid thing that cook is!" said the thirty boarders.

"Cook," said the lady abbess, with great dignity; "don't answer me, if you please. I insist upon your looking into the garden immediately."

Here the cook began to cry, and the house-maid said it was "a shame!" for which partisanship she received a month's warning on the spot.

"Do you hear, cook?" said the lady abbess, stamping her foot impatiently.

"Don't you hear your missis, cook?" said the three teachers.

"What an impudent thing, that cook is!" said the thirty boarders.

The unfortunate cook, thus strongly urged, advanced a step or two, and holding her candle just where it prevented her from seeing anything at all, declared there was nothing there, and it must have been the wind. The door was just going to be closed in consequence, when an inquisitive boarder, who had been peeping between the hinges, set up a fearful screaming, which called back the cook and the housemaid, and all the more adventurous, in no time.

"What is the matter with Miss Smithers?" said the lady abbess, as the aforesaid Miss Smithers proceeded to go into hysterics of four young lady power.

"Lor', Miss Smithers dear," said the other nine-and-twenty boarders.

"Oh, the man—the man—behind the door!" screamed Miss Smithers.

The lady abbess no sooner heard this appalling cry, than she retreated to her own bed-room, double-locked the door, and fainted away comfortably. The boarders, and the teachers, and the servants, fell back upon the stairs, and upon each other; and never was such a screaming, and fainting, and struggling, beheld. In the midst of the tumult Mr. Pickwick emerged from his concealment, and presented himself amongst them.

"Ladies—dear ladies," said Mr. Pickwick.

"Oh, he says we're dear," cried the oldest and ugliest teacher. "Oh, the wretch!"

"Ladies," roared Mr. Pickwick, rendered desperate by the danger of his situation. "Hear me. I am no robber. I want the lady of the house."

"Oh, what a ferocious monster!" screamed another teacher. "He wants Miss Tomkins."

Here there was a general scream.

"Ring the alarm bell, somebody!" cried a dozen voices.

"Don't—don't," shouted Mr. Pickwick. "Look at me. Do I look like a robber! My dear ladies—you may bind me hand and leg, or lock me up in a closet, if you like. Only hear what I have got to say—only hear me."

"How did you come in our garden?" faltered the housemaid.

"Call the lady of the house, and I'll tell her everything —everything:" said Mr. Pickwick, exerting his lungs to the utmost pitch. "Call her—only be quiet, and call her, and you shall hear everything."

It might have been Mr. Pickwick's appearance, or it might have been his manner, or it might have been the temptation —irresistible to a female mind—of hearing something at present enveloped in mystery, that reduced the more reasonable portion of the establishment (some four individuals) to a state of comparative quiet. By them it was proposed, as a test of Mr. Pickwick's sincerity, that he should immediately submit to personal restraint; and that gentleman having consented to hold a conference with Miss Tomkins, from the interior of a closet in which the day boarders hung their bonnets and sandwich-bags, he at once stepped into it of his own accord, and was securely locked in. This revived the others; and Miss Tomkins having been brought to, and brought down, the conference began.

"What did you do in my garden, Man?" said Miss Tomkins, in a faint voice.

"I came to warn you, that one of your young ladies was going to elope to-night," replied Mr. Pickwick, from the interior of the closet.

"Elope!" exclaimed Miss Tomkins, the three teachers, the thirty boarders, and the five servants. "Who with?"

"Your friend, Mr. Charles Fitz-Marshall."

"*My* friend! I don't know any such person."

"Well; Mr. Jingle, then."

"I never heard the name in my life."

"Then, I have been deceived, and deluded," said Mr. Pickwick. "I have been the victim of a conspiracy—a foul and base conspiracy. Send to the Angel, my dear ma'am, if you don't believe me. Send to the Angel for Mr. Pickwick's man-servant, I implore you, ma'am."

"He must be respectable—he keeps a man-servant," said Miss Tomkins to the writing and ciphering governess.

"It's my opinion, Miss Tomkins," said the writing and ciphering governess, "that his man-servant keeps him. *I* think he's a madman, Miss Tomkins, and the other's his keeper."

*The Unexpected "Breaking-up" of the Seminary
for Young Ladies*

RELEASE OF MR. PICKWICK.

"I think you are very right, Miss Gwynn," responded Miss Tomkins. "Let two of the servants repair to the Angel, and let the others remain here, to protect us."

So two of the servants were despatched to the Angel in search of Mr. Samuel Weller: and the remaining three stopped behind to protect Miss Tomkins, and the three teachers, and the thirty boarders. And Mr. Pickwick sat down in the closet, beneath a grove of sandwich bags, and awaited the return of the messengers, with all the philosophy and fortitude he could summon to his aid.

An hour and a half elapsed before they came back, and when they did come, Mr. Pickwick recognised, in addition to the voice of Mr. Samuel Weller, two other voices, the tones of which struck familiarly on his ear; but whose they were, he could not for the life of him call to mind.

A very brief conversation ensued. The door was unlocked. Mr. Pickwick stepped out of the closet, and found himself in the presence of the whole establishment of Westgate House, Mr. Samuel Weller, and—old Wardle, and his destined son-in-law, Mr. Trundle!

"My dear friend," said Mr. Pickwick, running forward and grasping Wardle's hand, "my dear friend, pray, for Heaven's sake, explain to this lady the unfortunate and dreadful situation in which I am placed. You must have heard it from my servant; say, at all events, my dear fellow, that I am neither a robber nor a madman."

"I have said so, my dear friend. I have said so already," replied Mr. Wardle, shaking the right hand of his friend, while Mr. Trundle shook the left.

"And whoever says, or has said, he is," interposed Mr. Weller, stepping forward, "says that which is not the truth, but so far from it, on the contrary, quite the rewerse. And if there's any number o' men on these here premises as has said so, I shall be wery happy to give 'em all a wery convincing proof o' their being mistaken, in this here wery room, if these wery respectable ladies 'll have the goodness to retire, and order 'em up, one at a time." Having delivered this defiance with great volubility, Mr. Weller struck his open palm emphatically with his clenched fist, and winked pleasantly on Miss Tomkins: the intensity of whose horror at his supposing it within the bounds of possibility that there could be any men on the premises of Westgate House Establishment for Young Ladies, it is impossible to describe.

Mr. Pickwick's explanation having already been partially made, was soon concluded. But neither in the course of his walk home with his friends, nor afterwards when seated before a blazing fire at the supper he so much needed, could a single observation be drawn from him. He seemed bewildered and amazed. Once, and only once, he turned round to Mr. Wardle, and said

"How did you come here?"

"Trundle and I came down here, for some good shooting on the first," replied Wardle. "We arrived to-night, and were astonished to hear from your servant that you were here too. But I am glad you are," said the old fellow, slapping him on the back. "I am glad you are. We shall have a jovial party on the first, and we'll give Winkle another chance—eh, old boy?"

Mr. Pickwick made no reply; he did not even ask after his friends at Dingley Dell, and shortly afterwards retired for the night, desiring Sam to fetch his candle when he rung.

The bell did ring in due course, and Mr. Weller presented himself.

"Sam," said Mr. Pickwick, looking out from under the bed-clothes.

"Sir," said Mr. Weller.

Mr. Pickwick paused, and Mr. Weller snuffed the candle.

"Sam," said Mr. Pickwick again, as if with a desperate effort.

"Sir," said Mr. Weller, once more.

"Where is that Trotter?"

"Job, sir?"

MR. PICKWICK CRESTFALLEN.

" Yes."

" Gone, sir."

" With his master, I suppose ? "

" Friend or master, or whatever he is, he's gone with him," replied Mr. Weller. " There's a pair on 'em, sir."

" Jingle suspected my design, and set that fellow on you, with this story, I suppose ? " said Mr. Pickwick, half choking.

" Just that, sir," replied Mr. Weller.

" It was all false, of course ? "

" All, sir," replied Mr. Weller. " Reg'lar do, sir; artful dodge."

" I don't think he'll escape us quite so easily the next time, Sam ? " said Mr. Pickwick.

" I don't think he will, sir."

" Whenever I meet that Jingle again, wherever it is," said Mr. Pickwick, raising himself in bed, and indenting his pillow with a tremendous blow, " I'll inflict personal chastisement on him, in addition to the exposure he so richly merits. I will, or my name is not Pickwick."

" And wenever I catches hold o' that there melan-cholly chap with the black hair," said Sam, " if I don't bring some real water into his eyes, for once in a way, my name a'nt Weller. Good night, sir ! "

271

CHAPTER XVII.

SHOWING THAT AN ATTACK OF RHEUMATISM, IN SOME CASES, ACTS
AS A QUICKENER TO INVENTIVE GENIUS.

The constitution of Mr. Pickwick, though able to sustain a very considerable amount of exertion and fatigue, was not proof against such a combination of attacks as he had undergone on the memorable night, recorded in the last chapter. The process of being washed in the night air, and rough-dried in a closet, is as dangerous as it is peculiar. Mr. Pickwick was laid up with an attack of rheumatism.

But although the bodily powers of the great man were thus impaired, his mental energies retained their pristine vigour. His spirits were elastic; his good humour was restored. Even the vexation consequent upon his recent adventure had vanished from his mind; and he could join in the hearty laughter which any allusion to it excited in Mr. Wardle, without anger and without embarrassment. Nay, more. During the two days Mr. Pickwick was confined to his bed, Sam was his constant attendant. On the first, he endeavoured to amuse his master by anecdote and conversation; on the second, Mr. Pickwick demanded his writing-desk, and pen and ink, and was deeply engaged during the whole day. On the third, being able to sit up in his bed-chamber, he despatched his valet with a message to Mr. Wardle and Mr. Trundle, intimating that if they would take their wine there, that evening, they would greatly oblige him. The invitation was most willingly accepted; and when they were seated over their wine, Mr. Pickwick with sundry blushes, produced the following little tale, as having been "edited" by himself, during his recent indisposition, from his notes of Mr. Weller's unsophisticated recital.

THE PARISH CLERK.
A TALE OF TRUE LOVE.

"Once upon a time in a very small country town, at a considerable distance from London, there lived a little man named Nathaniel Pipkin, who was the parish clerk of the little town, and lived in a little house in the little High Street, within ten minutes' walk of the little church; and who was to be found every day from nine till four, teaching a little learning to the little boys. Nathaniel Pipkin was a harmless, inoffensive, good-natured being, with a turned-up nose, and rather turned-in legs: a cast in his eye, and a halt in his gait; and he divided his time between the church and his school, verily believing that there existed not, on the face of the earth, so clever a man as the curate, so imposing an apartment as the vestry-room, or so well-ordered a seminary as his own. Once, and only once, in his life, Nathaniel Pipkin had seen a bishop—a real bishop, with his arms in lawn sleeves, and his head in a wig. He had seen him walk, and heard him talk, at a confirmation, on which momentous occasion Nathaniel Pipkin was so overcome with reverence and awe, when the aforesaid bishop laid his hand on his head, that he fainted right clean away, and was borne out of church in the arms of the beadle.

"This was a great event, a tremendous era, in Nathaniel Pipkin's life, and it was the only one that had ever occurred to ruffle the smooth current of his quiet existence, when happening one fine afternoon, in a fit of mental abstraction, to raise his eyes from the slate on which he was devising some tremendous problem in compound addition for an offending urchin to solve, they suddenly rested on the blooming countenance of

Maria Lobbs, the only daughter of old Lobbs, the great saddler over the way. Now, the eyes of Mr. Pipkin had rested on the pretty face of Maria Lobbs many a time and oft before, at church and elsewhere; but the eyes of Maria Lobbs had never looked so bright, the cheeks of Maria Lobbs had never looked so ruddy, as upon this particular occasion. No wonder then, that Nathaniel Pipkin was unable to take his eyes from the countenance of Miss Lobbs; no wonder that Miss Lobbs, finding herself stared at by a young man, withdrew her head from the window out of which she had been peeping, and shut the casement and pulled down the blind; no wonder that Nathaniel Pipkin, immediately thereafter, fell upon the young urchin who had previously offended, and cuffed and knocked him about, to his heart's content. All this was very natural, and there's nothing at all to wonder about it.

"It *is* matter of wonder, though, that any one of Mr. Nathaniel Pipkin's retiring disposition, nervous temperament, and most particularly diminutive income, should from this day forth, have dared to aspire to the hand and heart of the only daughter of the fiery old Lobbs—of old Lobbs the great saddler, who could have bought up the whole village at one stroke of his pen, and never felt the outlay—old Lobbs, who was well known to have heaps of money, invested in the bank at the nearest market town—old Lobbs, who was reported to have countless and inexhaustible treasures, hoarded up in the little iron safe with the big key-hole, over the chimney-piece in the back parlour—old Lobbs, who it was well known, on festive occasions garnished his board with a real silver tea-pot, cream ewer, and sugar-basin, which he was wont, in the pride of his heart, to boast should be his daughter's property when she found a man to her mind. I repeat it, to be matter of profound astonishment and intense wonder, that Nathaniel Pipkin should have had the temerity to cast his eyes in this direction. But love is blind: and Nathaniel had a cast in his eye: and perhaps these two circumstances, taken together, prevented his seeing the matter in its proper light.

"Now, if old Lobbs had entertained the most remote or distant idea of the state of the affections of Nathaniel Pipkin, he would just have razed the school-room to the ground, or exterminated its master from the surface of the earth, or committed some other outrage and atrocity of an equally ferocious and violent description; for he was a terrible old fellow, was Lobbs, when his pride was injured, or his blood was up. Swear! Such trains of oaths would come rolling and pealing over the way, sometimes, when he was denouncing the idleness of the bony apprentice with the thin legs, that Nathaniel Pipkin would shake in his shoes with horror, and the hair of the pupils' heads would stand on end with fright.

"Well! Day after day, when school was over, and the pupils gone, did Nathaniel Pipkin sit himself down at the front window, and while he feigned to be reading a book, throw sidelong glances over the way in search of the bright eyes of Maria Lobbs; and he hadn't sat there many days, before the bright eyes appeared at an upper window, apparently deeply engaged in reading too. This was delightful, and gladdening to the heart of Nathaniel Pipkin. It was something to sit there for hours together, and look upon that pretty face when the eyes were cast down; but when Maria Lobbs began to raise her eyes from her book, and dart their rays in the direction of Nathaniel Pipkin, his delight and admiration were perfectly boundless. At last, one day when he knew old Lobbs was out, Nathaniel Pipkin had the temerity to kiss his hand to Maria Lobbs; and Maria Lobbs, instead of shutting the window, and pulling down the blind, kissed *hers* to him, and smiled. Upon which, Nathaniel Pipkin determined, that, come what might, he would develop the state of his feelings, without further delay.

"A prettier foot, a gayer heart, a more dimpled face, or a smarter form, never bounded so lightly over the earth they graced, as did those of Maria Lobbs, the old saddler's daughter.

There was a roguish twinkle in her sparkling eyes, that would have made its way to far less susceptible bosoms than that of Nathaniel Pipkin; and there was such a joyous sound in her merry laugh, that the sternest misanthrope must have smiled to hear it. Even old Lobbs himself, in the very height of his ferocity, couldn't resist the coaxing of his pretty daughter; and when she, and her cousin Kate—an arch, impudent-looking, bewitching little person—made a dead set upon the old man together, as, to say the truth, they very often did, he could have refused them nothing, even had they asked for a portion of the countless and inexhaustible treasures, which were hidden from the light, in the iron safe.

"Nathaniel Pipkin's heart beat high within him, when he saw this enticing little couple some hundred yards before him one summer's evening, in the very field in which he had many a time strolled about till night-time, and pondered on the beauty of Maria Lobbs. But though he had often thought then, how briskly he would walk up to Maria Lobbs and tell her of his passion if he could only meet her, he felt now that she was unexpectedly before him, all the blood in his body mounting to his face, manifestly to the great detriment of his legs, which, deprived of their usual portion, trembled beneath him. When they stopped to gather a hedge-flower, or listen to a bird, Nathaniel Pipkin stopped too, and pretended to be absorbed in meditation, as indeed he really was; for he was thinking what on earth he should ever do, when they turned back, as they inevitably must in time, and meet him face to face. But though he was afraid to make up to them, he couldn't bear to lose sight of them; so when they walked faster, he walked faster, when they lingered he lingered, and when they stopped he stopped; and so they might have gone on, until the darkness prevented them, if Kate had not looked slyly back, and encouragingly beckoned Nathaniel to advance. There was something in Kate's manner that was not to be resisted, and so Nathaniel Pipkin complied with the invitation; and after a great deal of blushing on his part, and immoderate laughter on that of the wicked little cousin, Nathaniel Pipkin went down on his knees on the dewy grass, and declared his resolution to remain there for ever, unless he were permitted to rise the accepted lover of Maria Lobbs. Upon this, the merry laughter of Maria Lobbs rang through the calm evening air—without seeming to disturb it, though; it had such a pleasant sound —and the wicked little cousin laughed more immoderately than before, and Nathaniel Pipkin blushed deeper than ever. At length, Maria Lobbs being more strenuously urged by the love-worn little man, turned away her head, and whispered her cousin to say, or at all events Kate *did* say, that she felt much honoured by Mr. Pipkin's addresses; that her hand and heart were at her father's disposal; but that nobody could be insensible to Mr. Pipkin's merits. As all this was said with much gravity, and as Nathaniel Pipkin walked home with Maria Lobbs, and struggled for a kiss at parting, he went to bed a happy man, and dreamed all night long, of softening old Lobbs, opening the strong box, and marrying Maria.

"The next day, Nathaniel Pipkin saw old Lobbs go out upon his old grey pony, and after a great many signs at the window from the wicked little cousin, the object and meaning of which he could by no means understand, the bony apprentice with the thin legs came over to say that his master wasn't coming home all night, and that the ladies expected Mr. Pipkin to tea, at six o'clock precisely. How the lessons were got through that day, neither Nathaniel Pipkin nor his pupils knew any more than you do; but they were got through somehow, and, after the boys had gone, Nathaniel Pipkin took till full six o'clock to dress himself to his satisfaction. Not that it took long to select the garments he should wear, inasmuch as he had no choice about the matter; but the putting of them on to the best advantage, and the touching of them up previously, was a task of no inconsiderable difficulty or importance.

"There was a very snug little party, consisting of Maria Lobbs and her cousin Kate, and three or four romping, good-humoured, rosy-cheeked girls. Nathaniel Pipkin had ocular demonstration of the fact, that the rumours of old Lobbs's treasures were not exaggerated. There were the real solid silver tea-pot, cream-ewer, and sugar-basin, on the table, and real silver spoons to stir the tea with, and real china cups to drink it out of, and plates of the same, to hold the cakes and toast in. The only eye-sore in the whole place, was another cousin of Maria Lobbs's, and a brother of Kate, whom Maria Lobbs called 'Henry,' and who seemed to keep Maria Lobbs all to himself, up in one corner of the table. It's a delightful thing to see affection in families, but it may be carried rather too far, and Nathaniel Pipkin could not help thinking that Maria Lobbs must be very particularly fond of her relations, if she paid as much attention to all of them as to this individual cousin. After tea, too, when the wicked little cousin proposed a game at blind man's buff, it somehow or other happened that Nathaniel Pipkin was nearly always blind, and whenever he laid his hand upon the male cousin, he was sure to find that Maria Lobbs was not far off. And though the wicked little cousin and the other girls pinched him, and pulled his hair, and pushed chairs in his way, and all sorts of things, Maria Lobbs never seemed to come near him at all; and once—once—Nathaniel Pipkin could have sworn he heard the sound of a kiss, followed by a faint remonstrance from Maria Lobbs, and a half-suppressed laugh from her female friends. All this was odd—very odd —and there is no saying what Nathaniel Pipkin might or might not have done, in consequence, if his thoughts had not been suddenly directed into a new channel.

"The circumstance which directed his thoughts into a new channel was a loud knocking at the street-door, and the person who made this loud knocking at the street-door, was no other than old Lobbs himself, who had unexpectedly returned, and was hammering away like a coffin-maker: for he wanted his supper. The alarming intelligence was no sooner communicated by the bony apprentice with the thin legs, than the girls tripped up-stairs to Maria Lobbs's bed-room, and the male cousin and Nathaniel Pipkin were thrust into a couple of closets in the sitting-room, for want of any better places of concealment; and when Maria Lobbs and the wicked little cousin had stowed them away, and put the room to rights, they opened the street door to old Lobbs, who had never left off knocking since he first began.

"Now it did unfortunately happen that old Lobbs being very hungry was monstrous cross. Nathaniel Pipkin could hear him growling away like an old mastiff with a sore throat; and whenever the unfortunate apprentice with the thin legs came into the room, so surely did old Lobbs commence swearing at him in a most Saracenic and ferocious manner, though apparently with no other end or object than that of easing his bosom by the discharge of a few superfluous oaths. At length some supper, which had been warming up, was placed on the table, and then old Lobbs fell to, in regular style; and having made clear work of it in no time, kissed his daughter, and demanded his pipe.

"Nature had placed Nathaniel Pipkin's knees in very close juxtaposition, but when he heard old Lobbs demand his pipe, they knocked together, as if they were going to reduce each other to powder; for, depending from a couple of hooks, in the very closet in which he stood, was a large brown-stemmed, silver-bowled pipe, which pipe he himself had seen in the mouth of old Lobbs, regularly every afternoon and evening, for the last five years. The two girls went down-stairs for the pipe, and up-stairs for the pipe, and everywhere but where they knew the pipe was, and old Lobbs stormed away mean-while, in the most wonderful manner. At last he thought of the closet, and walked up to it. It was of no use a little man like Nathaniel Pipkin pulling the door inwards when a great strong fellow like old Lobbs was pulling it outwards. Old Lobbs gave it one tug and open it flew, disclosing

Nathaniel Pipkin standing bolt upright inside, and shaking with apprehension from head to foot. Bless us! what an appalling look old Lobbs gave him, as he dragged him out by the collar, and held him at arm's length.

"'Why, what the devil do you want here?' said old Lobbs, in a fearful voice.

"Nathaniel Pipkin could make no reply, so old Lobbs shook him backwards and forwards, for two or three minutes, by way of arranging his ideas for him.

"'What do you want here?' roared Lobbs, 'I suppose *you* have come after my daughter, now?'

"Old Lobbs merely said this as a sneer: for he did not believe that mortal presumption could have carried Nathaniel Pipkin so far. What was his indignation, when that poor man replied:

"'Yes, I did, Mr. Lobbs. I did come after your daughter. I love her, Mr. Lobbs.'

"'Why, you snivelling, wry-faced, puny villain,' gasped old Lobbs, paralysed by the atrocious confession; 'what do you mean by that? Say this to my face! Damme, I'll throttle you!'

"It is by no means improbable that old Lobbs would have carried this threat into execution, in the excess of his rage, if his arm had not been stayed by a very unexpected apparition, to wit, the male cousin, who, stepping out of his closet, and walking up to old Lobbs, said:

"'I cannot allow this harmless person, sir, who has been asked here in some girlish frolic, to take upon himself in a very noble manner, the fault (if fault it is) which I am guilty of, and am ready to avow. *I* love your daughter, sir; and *I* am here for the purpose of meeting her.'

"Old Lobbs opened his eyes very wide at this, but not wider than Nathaniel Pipkin.

"'You did?' said Lobbs: at last finding breath to speak.

"'I did.'

"'And I forbade you this house, long ago.'

THE WICKED LITTLE COUSIN.

"'You did, or I should not have been here, clandestinely, to-night.'

"I am sorry to record it, of old Lobbs, but I think he would have struck the cousin, if his pretty daughter, with her bright eyes swimming in tears, had not clung to his arm.

"'Don't stop him, Maria,' said the young man: 'if he has the will to strike me, let him. I would not hurt a hair of his grey head, for the riches of the world.'

"The old man cast down his eyes at this reproof, and they met those of his daughter. I have hinted once or twice before, that they were very bright eyes, and, though they were tearful now, their influence was by no means lessened. Old Lobbs turned his head away, as if to avoid being persuaded by them, when, as fortune would have it, he encountered the face of the wicked little cousin, who, half afraid for her brother, and half laughing at Nathaniel Pipkin, presented as bewitching an expression of countenance, with a touch of shyness in it too, as any man, old or young, need look upon. She drew her arm coaxingly through the old man's, and whispered something in his ear; and do what he would, old Lobbs couldn't help breaking out into a smile. while a tear stole down his cheek at the same time.

"Five minutes after this, the girls were brought down from the bed-room with a great deal of giggling and modesty; and while the young people were making themselves perfectly happy, old Lobbs got down the pipe, and smoked it: and it was a remarkable circumstance about that particular pipe of tobacco, that it was the most soothing and delightful one he ever smoked.

"Nathaniel Pipkin thought it best to keep his own counsel, and by so doing gradually rose into high favour with old Lobbs, who taught him to smoke in time; and they used to sit out in the garden on the fine evenings, for many years afterwards, smoking and drinking in great state. He soon recovered the effects of his attachment, for we find his name in the parish register, as a witness to the marriage of

Maria Lobbs to her cousin; and it also appears, by reference to other documents, that on the night of the wedding he was incarcerated in the village cage, for having, in a state of extreme intoxication, committed sundry excesses in the streets, in all of which he was aided and abetted by the bony apprentice with the thin legs."

CHAPTER XVIII.

For two days after the breakfast at Mrs. Hunter's the Pickwickians remained at Eatanswill, anxiously awaiting the arrival
of some intelligence from their revered leader. Mr. Tupman
and Mr. Snodgrass were once again left to their own means
of amusement; for Mr. Winkle, in compliance with a most
pressing invitation, continued to reside at Mr. Pott's house,
and to devote his time to the companionship of his amiable
lady. Nor was the occasional society of Mr. Pott himself,
wanting to complete their felicity. Deeply immersed in the
intensity of his speculations for the public weal and the
destruction of the Independent, it was not the habit of that
great man to descend from his mental pinnacle to the humble
level of ordinary minds. On this occasion, however, and as
if expressly in compliment to any follower of Mr. Pickwick's,
he unbent, relaxed, stepped down from his pedestal, and
walked upon the ground : benignly adapting his remarks to
the comprehension of the herd, and seeming in outward form,
if not in spirit, to be one of them.

Such having been the demeanour of this celebrated public
character towards Mr. Winkle, it will be readily imagined
that considerable surprise was depicted on the countenance
of the latter gentleman, when, as he was sitting alone in the
breakfast-room, the door was hastily thrown open, and as

hastily closed, on the entrance of Mr. Pott, who, stalking majestically towards him, and thrusting aside his proffered hand, ground his teeth, as if to put a sharper edge on what he was about to utter, and exclaimed, in a saw-like voice,—

"Serpent!"

"Sir!" exclaimed Mr. Winkle, starting from his chair.

"Serpent, sir," repeated Mr. Pott, raising his voice, and then suddenly depressing it; "I said, Serpent, sir—make the most of it."

When you have parted with a man, at two o'clock in the morning, on terms of the utmost good fellowship, and he meets you again, at half-past nine, and greets you as a serpent, it is not unreasonable to conclude that something of an unpleasant nature has occurred meanwhile. So Mr. Winkle thought. He returned Mr. Pott's gaze of stone, and in compliance with that gentleman's request, proceeded to make the most he could of the "serpent." The most, however, was nothing at all; so, after a profound silence of some minutes' duration, he said,—

"Serpent, sir! Serpent, Mr. Pott! What can you mean, sir?—this is pleasantry."

"Pleasantry, sir!" exclaimed Pott, with a motion of the hand, indicative of a strong desire to hurl the Britannia metal tea-pot at the head of his visitor. "Pleasantry, sir! ——but no, I will be calm; I will be calm, sir;" in proof of his calmness, Mr. Pott flung himself into a chair, and foamed at the mouth.

"My dear sir," interposed Mr. Winkle

"*Dear* sir!" replied Pott. "How dare you address me, as dear sir, sir? How dare you look me in the face and do it, sir?"

"Well, sir, if you come to that," responded Mr. Winkle, "how dare you look *me* in the face, and call me a serpent, sir?"

"Because you are one," replied Mr. Pott.

"Prove it, sir," said Mr. Winkle, warmly. "Prove it."

A malignant scowl passed over the profound face of the

editor, as he drew from his pocket, the Independent of that morning; and laying his finger on a particular paragraph, threw the journal across the table to Mr. Winkle.

That gentleman took it up, and read as follows:—

"Our obscure and filthy contemporary, in some disgusting observations on the recent election for this borough, has presumed to violate the hallowed sanctity of private life, and to refer, in a manner not to be misunderstood, to the personal affairs of our late candidate—aye, and notwithstanding his base defeat, we will add, our future member, Mr. Fizkin. What does our dastardly contemporary mean? What would the ruffian say, if we, setting at naught, like him, the decencies of social intercourse, were to raise the curtain which happily conceals HIS private life from general ridicule, not to say from general execration? What, if we were even to point out, and comment on, facts and circumstances, which are publicly notorious, and beheld by every one, but our mole-eyed contemporary—what if we were to print the following effusion, which we received while we were writing the commencement of this article, from a talented fellow-townsman and correspondent!

"'LINES TO A BRASS POT.

"'Oh Pott! if you'd known
How false she'd have grown,
When you heard the marriage bells tinkle;
You'd have done then, I vow,
What you cannot help now,
And handed her over to W * * * * *'"

"What," said Mr. Pott, solemnly: "what rhymes to 'tinkle,' villain?"

"What rhymes to tinkle?" said Mrs. Pott, whose entrance at the moment forestalled the reply. "What rhymes to tinkle? Why Winkle, I should conceive:" saying this, Mrs. Pott smiled sweetly on the disturbed Pickwickian, and extended her hand towards him. The agitated young man would have accepted it, in his confusion, had not Pott indignantly interposed.

"Back, ma'am—back!" said the editor. "Take his hand before my very face!"

"Mr. P.!" said his astonished lady.

"Wretched woman, look here," exclaimed the husband. "Look here, ma'am—'Lines to a brass Pot.' 'Brass pot;' —that's me, ma'am. 'False she'd have grown;'—that's you, ma'am—you." With this ebullition of rage, which was not unaccompanied with something like a tremble, at the expression of his wife's face, Mr. Pott dashed the current number of the Eatanswill Independent at her feet.

"Upon my word, sir," said the astonished Mrs. Pott, stooping to pick up the paper. "Upon my word, sir!"

Mr. Pott winced beneath the contemptuous gaze of his wife. He had made a desperate struggle to screw up his courage, but it was fast coming unscrewed again.

There appears nothing very tremendous in this little sentence, "Upon my word, sir," when it comes to be read; but the tone of voice in which it was delivered, and the look that accompanied it, both seeming to bear reference to some revenge to be thereafter visited upon the head of Pott, produced their full effect upon him. The most unskilful observer could have detected in his troubled countenance, a readiness to resign his Wellington boots to any efficient substitute who would have consented to stand in them at that moment.

Mrs. Pott read the paragraph, uttered a loud shriek, and threw herself at full length on the hearth-rug, screaming, and tapping it with the heels of her shoes, in a manner which could leave no doubt of the propriety of her feelings on the occasion.

"My dear," said the petrified Pott,—"I didn't say I believed it;—I——" but the unfortunate man's voice was drowned in the screaming of his partner.

"Mrs. Pott, let me entreat you, my dear ma'am, to compose yourself," said Mr. Winkle; but the shrieks and tappings were louder, and more frequent than ever.

"My dear," said Mr. Pott, "I'm very sorry. If you won't

consider your own health, consider me, my dear. We shall have a crowd round the house." But the more strenuously Mr. Pott entreated, the more vehemently the screams poured forth.

Very fortunately, however, attached to Mrs. Pott's person was a body-guard of one, a young lady whose ostensible employment was to preside over her toilet, but who rendered herself useful in a variety of ways, and in none more so than in the particular department of constantly aiding and abetting her mistress in every wish and inclination opposed to the desires of the unhappy Pott. The screams reached this young lady's ears in due course, and brought her into the room with a speed which threatened to derange, materially, the very exquisite arrangement of her cap and ringlets.

"Oh, my dear, dear mistress!" exclaimed the body-guard, kneeling frantically by the side of the prostrate Mrs. Pott. "Oh, my dear mistress, what is the matter?"

"Your master—your brutal master," murmured the patient.

Pott was evidently giving way

"It's a shame," said the body-guard, reproachfully. "I know he'll be the death of you, ma'am. Poor dear thing!"

He gave way more. The opposite party followed up the attack.

"Oh don't leave me—don't leave me, Goodwin," murmured Mrs. Pott, clutching at the wrist of the said Goodwin with an hysteric jerk. "You're the only person that's kind to me, Goodwin."

At this affecting appeal, Goodwin got up a little domestic tragedy of her own, and shed tears copiously.

"Never, ma'am—never," said Goodwin. "Oh, sir, you should be careful—you should indeed; you don't know what harm you may do missis; you'll be sorry for it one day, I know—I've always said so."

The unlucky Pott looked timidly on, but said nothing.

"Goodwin," said Mrs. Pott, in a soft voice.

"Ma'am," said Goodwin.

"If you only knew how I have loved that man——"

"Don't distress yourself by recollecting it, ma'am," said the body-guard.

Pott looked very frightened. It was time to finish him.

"And now," sobbed Mrs. Pott, "now, after all, to be treated in this way; to be reproached and insulted in the presence of a third party, and that party almost a stranger. But I will not submit to it! Goodwin," continued Mrs. Pott, raising herself in the arms of her attendant, "my brother, the Lieutenant, shall interfere. I'll be separated, Goodwin!"

"It would certainly serve him right, ma'am," said Goodwin.

Whatever thoughts the threat of a separation might have awakened in Mr. Pott's mind, he forebore to give utterance to them, and contented himself by saying, with great humility:

"My dear, will you hear me?"

A fresh train of sobs was the only reply, as Mrs. Pott grew more hysterical, requested to be informed why she was ever born, and required sundry other pieces of information of a similar description.

"My dear," remonstrated Mr. Pott, "do not give way to these sensitive feelings. I never believed that the paragraph had any foundation, my dear—impossible. I was only angry, my dear—I may say outrageous—with the Independent people for daring to insert it; that's all:" Mr. Pott cast an imploring look at the innocent cause of the mischief, as if to entreat him to say nothing about the serpent.

"And what steps, sir, do you mean to take to obtain redress?" inquired Mr. Winkle, gaining courage as he saw Pott losing it.

"Oh, Goodwin," observed Mrs. Pott, "does he mean to horsewhip the editor of the Independent—does he, Goodwin?"

"Hush, hush, ma'am; pray keep yourself quiet," replied the body-guard. "I dare say he will, if you wish it, ma'am."

"Certainly," said Pott, as his wife evinced decided symptoms of going off again. "Of course I shall."

"When, Goodwin—when?" said Mrs. Pott, still undecided about the going off.

"Immediately, of course," said Mr. Pott; "before the day is out."

"Oh, Goodwin," resumed Mrs. Pott, "it's the only way of meeting the slander, and setting me right with the world."

"Certainly, ma'am," replied Goodwin. "No man as is a man, ma'am, could refuse to do it."

So, as the hysterics were still hovering about, Mr. Pott said once more that he would do it; but Mrs. Pott was so overcome at the bare idea of having ever been suspected, that she was half-a-dozen times on the very verge of a relapse, and most unquestionably would have gone off, had it not been for the indefatigable efforts of the assiduous Goodwin, and repeated entreaties for pardon from the conquered Pott; and finally, when that unhappy individual had been frightened and snubbed down to his proper level, Mrs. Pott recovered, and they went to breakfast.

"You will not allow this base newspaper slander to shorten your stay here, Mr. Winkle?" said Mrs. Pott, smiling through the traces of her tears.

"I hope not," said Mr. Pott, actuated, as he spoke, by a wish that his visitor would choke himself with the morsel of dry toast which he was raising to his lips at the moment: and so terminate his stay effectually.

"I hope not."

"You are very good," said Mr. Winkle; "but a letter has been received from Mr. Pickwick—so I learn by a note from Mr. Tupman, which was brought up to my bed-room door, this morning—in which he requests us to join him at Bury to-day; and we are to leave by the coach at noon."

"But you will come back?" said Mrs. Pott.

"Oh, certainly," replied Mr. Winkle.

"You are quite sure?" said Mrs. Pott, stealing a tender look at her visitor.

"Quite," responded Mr. Winkle.

The breakfast passed off in silence, for each member of the party was brooding over his, or her, own personal grievances. Mrs. Pott was regretting the loss of a beau; Mr. Pott his rash pledge to horsewhip the Independent; Mr. Winkle his having innocently placed himself in so awkward a situation. Noon approached, and after many adieux and promises to return, he tore himself away.

"If he ever comes back, I'll poison him," thought Mr. Pott, as he turned into the little back office where he prepared his thunderbolts.

"If I ever do come back, and mix myself up with these people again," thought Mr. Winkle, as he wended his way to the Peacock, "I shall deserve to be horsewhipped myself —that's all."

His friends were ready, the coach was nearly so, and in half-an-hour they were proceeding on their journey, along the road over which Mr. Pickwick and Sam had so recently travelled, and of which, as we have already said something, we do not feel called upon to extract Mr. Snodgrass's poetical and beautiful description.

Mr. Weller was standing at the door of the Angel, ready to receive them, and by that gentleman they were ushered to the apartment of Mr. Pickwick, where, to the no small surprise of Mr. Winkle and Mr. Snodgrass, and the no small embarrassment of Mr. Tupman, they found old Wardle and Trundle.

"How are you?" said the old man, grasping Mr. Tupman's hand. "Don't hang back, or look sentimental about it; it can't be helped, old fellow. For her sake, I wish you'd had her; for your own, I'm very glad you have not. A young fellow like you will do better one of these days—eh?" With this consolation, Wardle slapped Mr. Tupman on the back, and laughed heartily.

"Well, and how are you, my fine fellows?" said the old gentleman, shaking hands with Mr. Winkle and Mr. Snodgrass at the same time. "I have just been telling Pickwick that we must have you all down at Christmas. We're going to have a wedding—a real wedding this time."

"A wedding!" exclaimed Mr. Snodgrass, turning very pale.

"Yes, a wedding. But don't be frightened," said the good-humoured old man; "it's only Trundle there, and Bella."

"Oh, is that all!" said Mr. Snodgrass, relieved from a painful doubt which had fallen heavily on his breast. "Give you joy, sir. How is Joe?"

"Very well," replied the old gentleman. "Sleepy as ever."

"And your mother, and the clergyman, and all of 'em?"

"Quite well."

"Where," said Mr. Tupman, with an effort—"where is— *she*, sir?" and he turned away his head, and covered his eyes with his hand.

"*She!*" said the old gentleman, with a knowing shake of the head. "Do you mean my single relative—eh?"

Mr. Tupman, by a nod, intimated that his question applied to the disappointed Rachael.

"Oh, she's gone away," said the old gentleman. "She's living at a relation's, far enough off. She couldn't bear to see the girls, so I let her go. But come! Here's the dinner. You must be hungry after your ride. *I* am, without any ride at all; so let us fall to."

Ample justice was done to the meal; and when they were seated round the table, after it had been disposed of, Mr. Pickwick, to the intense horror and indignation of his followers, related the adventure he had undergone, and the success which had attended the base artifices of the diabolical Jingle.

"And the attack of rheumatism which I caught in that garden," said Mr. Pickwick, in conclusion, "renders me lame at this moment."

"I, too, have had something of an adventure," said Mr. Winkle, with a smile; and at the request of Mr. Pickwick he detailed the malicious libel of the Eatanswill Independent, and the consequent excitement of their friend, the editor.

Mr. Pickwick's brow darkened during the recital. His friends observed it, and, when Mr. Winkle had concluded, maintained a profound silence. Mr. Pickwick struck the table emphatically with his clenched fist, and spoke as follows

"Is it not a wonderful circumstance," said Mr. Pickwick, "that we seem destined to enter no man's house without involving him in some degree of trouble? Does it not, I ask, bespeak the indiscretion, or, worse than that, the blackness of heart—that I should say so!—of my followers, that, beneath whatever roof they locate, they disturb the peace of mind and happiness of some confiding female? Is it not, I say——"

Mr. Pickwick would in all probability have gone on for some time, had not the entrance of Sam, with a letter, caused him to break off in his eloquent discourse. He passed his handkerchief across his forehead, took off his spectacles, wiped them, and put them on again; and his voice had recovered its wonted softness of tone when he said:

"What have you there, Sam?"

"Called at the Post-office just now, and found this here letter, as has laid there for two days," replied Mr. Weller. "It's sealed with a vafer, and directed in round hand."

"I don't know this hand," said Mr. Pickwick, opening the letter. "Mercy on us! what's this? It must be a jest; it —it—can't be true."

"What's the matter?" was the general inquiry.

"Nobody dead, is there?" said Wardle, alarmed at the horror in Mr. Pickwick's countenance.

Mr. Pickwick made no reply, but, pushing the letter across the table, and desiring Mr. Tupman to read it aloud, fell back in his chair with a look of vacant astonishment quite alarming to behold.

Mr. Tupman, with a trembling voice, read the letter, of which the following is a copy :—

MR. PICKWICK RECEIVES NOTICE OF WRIT.

Freeman's Court, Cornhill, August 28th, 1830.
Bardell against Pickwick.

Sir,

Having been instructed by Mrs. Martha Bardell to commence an action against you for a breach of promise of marriage, for which the plaintiff lays her damages at fifteen hundred pounds, we beg to inform you that a writ has been issued against you in this suit in the Court of Common Pleas; and request to know, by return of post, the name of your attorney in London, who will accept service thereof.

We are, Sir,
Your obedient servants,
Dodson and Fogg.

Mr. Samuel Pickwick.

There was something so impressive in the mute astonishment with which each man regarded his neighbour, and every man regarded Mr. Pickwick, that all seemed afraid to speak. The silence was at length broken by Mr. Tupman.

"Dodson and Fogg," he repeated mechanically.

"Bardell and Pickwick," said Mr. Snodgrass, musing.

"Peace of mind and happiness of confiding females," murmured Mr. Winkle, with an air of abstraction.

"It's a conspiracy," said Mr. Pickwick, at length recovering the power of speech; "a base conspiracy between these two grasping attorneys, Dodson and Fogg. Mrs. Bardell would never do it;—she hasn't the heart to do it;—she hasn't the case to do it. Ridiculous—ridiculous."

"Of her heart," said Wardle, with a smile, "you should certainly be the best judge. I don't wish to discourage you, but I should certainly say that, of her case, Dodson and Fogg are far better judges than any of us can be."

"It's a vile attempt to extort money," said Mr. Pickwick.

"I hope it is," said Wardle, with a short, dry cough.

"Who ever heard me address her in any way but that in which a lodger would address his landlady?" continued Mr.

293

Pickwick, with great vehemence. "Who ever saw me with her? Not even my friends here——"

"Except on one occasion," said Mr. Tupman.

Mr. Pickwick changed colour.

"Ah," said Mr. Wardle. "Well, that's important. There was nothing suspicious then, I suppose?"

Mr. Tupman glanced timidly at his leader. "Why," said he, "there was nothing suspicious; but—I don't know how it happened, mind—she certainly was reclining in his arms."

"Gracious powers!" ejaculated Mr. Pickwick, as the recollection of the scene in question struck forcibly upon him; "what a dreadful instance of the force of circumstances! So she was—so she was."

"And our friend was soothing her anguish," said Mr. Winkle, rather maliciously.

"So I was," said Mr. Pickwick. "I won't deny it. So I was."

"Hallo!" said Wardle; "for a case in which there's nothing suspicious, this looks rather queer—eh, Pickwick? Ah, sly dog—sly dog!" and he laughed till the glasses on the sideboard rang again.

"What a dreadful conjunction of appearances!" exclaimed Mr. Pickwick, resting his chin upon his hands. "Winkle—Tupman—I beg your pardon for the observations I made just now. We are all the victims of circumstances, and I the greatest." With this apology Mr. Pickwick buried his head in his hands, and ruminated; while Wardle measured out a regular circle of nods and winks, addressed to the other members of the company.

"I'll have it explained, though," said Mr. Pickwick, raising his head and hammering the table. "I'll see this Dodson and Fogg! I'll go to London to-morrow."

"Not to-morrow," said Wardle; "you're too lame."

"Well, then, next day."

"Next day is the first of September, and you're pledged to ride out with us, as far as Sir Geoffrey Manning's grounds, at all events, and to meet us at lunch, if you don't take the field."

"Well, then, the day after," said Mr. Pickwick; "Thursday. —Sam!"

"Sir," replied Mr. Weller.

"Take two places outside to London, on Thursday morning, for yourself and me."

"Wery well, sir."

Mr. Weller left the room, and departed slowly on his errand, with his hands in his pocket, and his eyes fixed on the ground.

"Rum feller, the hemperor," said Mr. Weller, as he walked slowly up the street. "Think o' his making up to that ere Mrs. Bardell—vith a little boy, too! Always the vay vith these here old 'uns hows'ever, as is such steady goers to look at. I didn't think he'd ha' done it, though—I didn't think he'd ha' done it!" Moralising in this strain, Mr. Samuel Weller bent his steps towards the booking-office.

CHAPTER XIX.

A PLEASANT DAY, WITH AN UNPLEASANT TERMINATION.

THE birds, who, happily for their own peace of mind and personal comfort, were in blissful ignorance of the preparations which had been making to astonish them, on the first of September, hailed it no doubt, as one of the pleasantest mornings they had seen that season. Many a young partridge who strutted complacently among the stubble, with all the finicking coxcombry of youth, and many an older one who watched his levity out of his little round eye, with the contemptuous air of a bird of wisdom and experience, alike unconscious of their approaching doom, basked in the fresh morning air with lively and blithesome feelings, and a few hours afterwards were laid low upon the earth. But we grow affecting: let us proceed.

In plain common-place matter-of-fact, then, it was a fine morning—so fine that you would scarcely have believed that the few months of an English summer had yet flown by. Hedges, fields, and trees, hill and moorland, presented to the eye their ever-varying shades of deep rich green; scarce a leaf had fallen, scarce a sprinkle of yellow mingled with the hues of summer, warned you that autumn had begun. The sky was cloudless, the sun shone out bright and warm; the songs of birds, and hum of myriads of summer insects, filled the air; and the cottage gardens, crowded with flowers of every rich and beautiful tint, sparkled, in the heavy dew, like beds of glittering jewels. Everything bore the stamp of summer, and none of its beautiful colours had yet faded from the die.

Such was the morning, when an open carriage, in which were three Pickwickians, (Mr. Snodgrass having preferred to remain at home,) Mr. Wardle, and Mr. Trundle, with Sam Weller on the box beside the driver, pulled up by a gate at the road-side, before which stood a tall, raw-boned gamekeeper, and a half-booted, leather-leggined boy : each bearing a bag of capacious dimensions, and accompanied by a brace of pointers.

"I say," whispered Mr. Winkle to Wardle, as the man let down the steps, "they don't suppose we're going to kill game enough to fill those bags, do they ? "

"Fill them ! " exclaimed old Wardle. "Bless you, yes ! You shall fill one, and I the other ; and when we've done with them, the pockets of our shooting-jackets will hold as much more."

Mr. Winkle dismounted without saying anything in reply to this observation ; but he thought within himself, that if the party remained in the open air, until he had filled one of the bags, they stood a considerable chance of catching colds in their heads.

"Hi, Juno, lass—hi, old girl ; down, Daph, down," said Wardle, caressing the dogs. "Sir Geoffrey still in Scotland, of course, Martin ? "

The tall gamekeeper replied in the affirmative, and looked with some surprise from Mr. Winkle, who was holding his gun as if he wished his coat pocket to save him the trouble of pulling the trigger, to Mr. Tupman, who was holding his as if he were afraid of it—as there is no earthly reason to doubt he really was.

"My friends are not much in the way of this sort of thing yet, Martin," said Wardle, noticing the look. "Live and learn, you know. They'll be good shots one of these days. I beg my friend Winkle's pardon, though ; he has had some practice."

Mr. Winkle smiled feebly over his blue neckerchief in

acknowledgment of the compliment, and got himself so mysteriously entangled with his gun, in his modest confusion, that if the piece had been loaded, he must inevitably have shot himself dead upon the spot.

"You mustn't handle your piece in that ere way, when you come to have the charge in it, sir," said the tall gamekeeper, gruffly, "or I'm damned if you won't make cold meat of some on us."

Mr. Winkle, thus admonished, abruptly altered its position, and in so doing, contrived to bring the barrel into pretty sharp contact with Mr. Weller's head.

"Hallo!" said Sam, picking up his hat, which had been knocked off, and rubbing his temple. "Hallo, sir! if you comes it this vay, you'll fill one o' them bags, and something to spare, at one fire."

Here the leather-leggined boy laughed very heartily, and then tried to look as if it was somebody else, whereat Mr. Winkle frowned majestically.

"Where did you tell the boy to meet us with the snack, Martin?" inquired Wardle.

"Side of One-tree Hill, at twelve o'clock, sir."

"That's not Sir Geoffrey's land, is it?"

"No, sir; but it's close by it. It's Captain Boldwig's land; but there'll be nobody to interrupt us, and there's a fine bit of turf there."

"Very well," said old Wardle. "Now the sooner we're off the better. Will you join us at twelve, then, Pickwick?"

Mr. Pickwick was particularly desirous to view the sport, the more especially as he was rather anxious in respect of Mr. Winkle's life and limbs. On so inviting a morning, too, it was very tantalising to turn back, and leave his friends to enjoy themselves. It was, therefore, with a very rueful air that he replied,

"Why, I suppose I must."

"An't the gentleman a shot, sir?" inquired the long gamekeeper.

"No," replied Wardle; "and he's lame besides."

"I should very much like to go," said Mr. Pickwick, "very much."

There was a short pause of commiseration.

"There's a barrow t'other side the hedge," said the boy. "If the gentleman's servant would wheel along the paths, he could keep nigh us, and we could lift it over the stiles, and that."

"The wery thing," said Mr. Weller, who was a party interested, inasmuch as he ardently longed to see the sport. "The wery thing. Well said, Smallcheck; I'll have it out in a minute."

But here a difficulty arose. The long gamekeeper resolutely protested against the introduction into a shooting party, of a gentleman in a barrow, as a gross violation of all established rules and precedents.

It was a great objection, but not an insurmountable one. The gamekeeper having been coaxed and feed, and having, moreover, eased his mind by "punching" the head of the inventive youth who had first suggested the use of the machine, Mr. Pickwick was placed in it, and off the party set; Wardle and the long gamekeeper leading the way, and Mr. Pickwick in the barrow, propelled by Sam, bringing up the rear.

"Stop, Sam," said Mr. Pickwick, when they had got half across the first field.

"What's the matter now?" said Wardle.

"I won't suffer this barrow to be moved another step," said Mr. Pickwick, resolutely, "unless Winkle carries that gun of his, in a different manner."

"How *am* I to carry it?" said the wretched Winkle.

"Carry it with the muzzle to the ground," replied Mr. Pickwick.

"It's so unsportsman-like," reasoned Winkle.

"I don't care whether it's unsportsman-like or not," replied Mr. Pickwick; "I am not going to be shot in a wheelbarrow, for the sake of appearances, to please anybody."

"I know the gentleman 'll put that ere charge into somebody afore he's done," growled the long man.

"Well, well—I don't mind," said poor Winkle, turning his gun-stock uppermost;—"there."

"Anythin' for a quiet life," said Mr. Weller; and on they went again.

"Stop!" said Mr. Pickwick, after they had gone a few yards further.

"What now?" said Wardle.

"That gun of Tupman's is not safe: I know it isn't," said Mr. Pickwick.

"Eh? What! not safe?" said Mr. Tupman, in a tone of great alarm.

"Not as you are carrying it," said Mr. Pickwick. "I am very sorry to make any further objection, but I cannot consent to go on, unless you carry it as Winkle does his."

"I think you had better, sir," said the long gamekeeper, "or you're quite as likely to lodge the charge in yourself as in anything else."

Mr. Tupman, with the most obliging haste, placed his piece in the position required, and the party moved on again; the two amateurs marching with reversed arms, like a couple of privates at a royal funeral.

The dogs suddenly came to a dead stop, and the party advancing stealthily a single pace, stopped too.

"What's the matter with the dogs' legs?" whispered Mr. Winkle. "How queer they're standing."

"Hush, can't you?" replied Wardle, softly. "Don't you see, they're making a point?"

"Making a point!" said Mr. Winkle, staring about him, as if he expected to discover some particular beauty in the landscape, which the sagacious animals were calling special attention to. "Making a point! What are they pointing at?"

"Keep your eyes open," said Wardle, not heeding the question in the excitement of the moment. "Now then."

MR. WINKLE IS EXCITED.

There was a sharp whirring-noise, that made Mr. Winkle start back as if he had been shot himself. Bang, bang, went a couple of guns;—the smoke swept quickly away over the field, and curled into the air.

"Where are they?" said Mr. Winkle, in a state of the highest excitement, turning round and round in all directions. "Where are they? Tell me when to fire. Where are they —where are they?"

"Where are they?" said Wardle, taking up a brace of birds which the dogs had deposited at his feet. "Why, here they are."

"No, no; I mean the others," said the bewildered Winkle.

"Far enough off, by this time," replied Wardle, coolly reloading his gun.

"We shall very likely be up with another covey in five minutes," said the long gamekeeper. "If the gentleman begins to fire now, perhaps he'll just get the shot out of the barrel by the time they rise."

"Ha! ha! ha!" roared Mr. Weller.

"Sam," said Mr. Pickwick, compassionating his follower's confusion and embarrassment.

"Sir."

"Don't laugh."

"Certainly not, sir." So, by way of indemnification, Mr. Weller contorted his features from behind the wheelbarrow, for the exclusive amusement of the boy with the leggings, who thereupon burst into a boisterous laugh, and was summarily cuffed by the long gamekeeper, who wanted a pretext for turning round, to hide his own merriment.

"Bravo, old fellow!" said Wardle to Mr. Tupman; "you fired that time, at all events."

"Oh yes," replied Mr. Tupman, with conscious pride. "I let it off."

"Well done. You'll hit something next time, if you look sharp. Very easy, ain't it?"

"Yes, it's very easy," said Mr. Tupman. "How it hurts

301

one's shoulder, though. It nearly knocked me backwards. I had no idea these small fire-arms kicked so."

"Ah," said the old gentleman, smiling; "you'll get used to it in time. Now then—all ready—all right with the barrow there?"

"All right, sir," replied Mr. Weller.

"Come along then."

"Hold hard, sir," said Sam, raising the barrow.

"Aye, aye," replied Mr. Pickwick; and on they went, as briskly as need be.

"Keep that barrow back now," cried Wardle when it had been hoisted over a stile into another field, and Mr. Pickwick had been deposited in it once more.

"All right, sir," replied Mr. Weller, pausing.

"Now, Winkle," said the old gentleman, "follow me softly, and don't be too late this time."

"Never fear," said Mr. Winkle. "Are they pointing?"

"No, no; not now. Quietly now, quietly." On they crept, and very quietly they would have advanced, if Mr. Winkle, in the performance of some very intricate evolutions with his gun, had not accidentally fired, at the most critical moment, over the boy's head, exactly in the very spot where the tall man's brain would have been, had he been there instead.

"Why, what on earth did you do that for?" said old Wardle, as the birds flew unharmed away.

"I never saw such a gun in my life," replied poor Mr. Winkle, looking at the lock, as if that would do any good. "It goes off of its own accord. It *will* do it."

"Will do it!" echoed Wardle, with something of irritation in his manner. "I wish it would kill something of its own accord."

"It'll do that afore long, sir," observed the tall man, in a low, prophetic voice.

"What do you mean by that observation, sir?" inquired Mr. Winkle, angrily.

"Never mind, sir, never mind," replied the long gamekeeper; "I've no family myself, sir; and this here boy's mother will get something handsome from Sir Geoffrey, if he's killed on his land. Load, again, sir, load again."

"Take away his gun," cried Mr. Pickwick from the barrow, horror-stricken at the long man's dark insinuations. "Take away his gun, do you hear, somebody?"

Nobody, however, volunteered to obey the command; and Mr. Winkle, after darting a rebellious glance at Mr. Pickwick, reloaded his gun, and proceeded onwards with the rest.

We are bound, on the authority of Mr. Pickwick, to state, that Mr. Tupman's mode of proceeding evinced far more of prudence and deliberation, than that adopted by Mr. Winkle. Still, this by no means detracts from the great authority of the latter gentleman, on all matters connected with the field; because, as Mr. Pickwick beautifully observes, it has somehow or other happened, from time immemorial, that many of the best and ablest philosophers, who have been perfect lights of science in matters of theory, have been wholly unable to reduce them to practice.

Mr. Tupman's process, like many of our most sublime discoveries, was extremely simple. With the quickness and penetration of a man of genius, he had at once observed that the two great points to be attained were—first, to discharge his piece without injury to himself, and, secondly, to do so, without danger to the by-standers;—obviously, the best thing to do, after surmounting the difficulty of firing at all, was to shut his eyes firmly, and fire into the air.

On one occasion, after performing this feat, Mr. Tupman, on opening his eyes, beheld a plump partridge in the act of falling wounded to the ground. He was on the point of congratulating Mr. Wardle on his invariable success, when that gentleman advanced towards him, and grasped him warmly by the hand.

"Tupman," said the old gentleman, "you singled out that particular bird?"

"No," said Mr. Tupman—"no."

"You did," said Wardle. "I saw you do it—I observed you pick him out—I noticed you, as you raised your piece to take aim; and I will say this, that the best shot in existence could not have done it more beautifully. You are an older hand at this, than I thought you, Tupman; you have been out before."

It was in vain for Mr. Tupman to protest, with a smile of self-denial that he never had. The very smile was taken as evidence to the contrary; and from that time forth, his reputation was established. It is not the only reputation that has been acquired as easily, nor are such fortunate circumstances confined to partridge-shooting.

Meanwhile, Mr. Winkle flashed, and blazed, and smoked away, without producing any material results worthy of being noted down; sometimes expending his charge in mid-air, and at others sending it skimming along so near the surface of the ground as to place the lives of the two dogs on a rather uncertain and precarious tenure. As a display of fancy shooting, it was extremely varied and curious; as an exhibition of firing with any precise object, it was, upon the whole, perhaps a failure. It is an established axiom, that "every bullet has its billet." If it apply in an equal degree to shot, those of Mr. Winkle were unfortunate foundlings, deprived of their natural rights, cast loose upon the world, and billeted nowhere.

"Well," said Wardle, walking up to the side of the barrow, and wiping the streams of perspiration from his jolly red face; "smoking day, isn't it?"

"It is, indeed," replied Mr. Pickwick. "The sun is tremendously hot, even to me. I don't know how you must feel it."

"Why," said the old gentleman, "pretty hot. It's past twelve, though. You see that green hill there?"

"Certainly."

"That's the place where we are to lunch; and, by Jove, there's the boy with the basket, punctual as clockwork!"

A CLEVER PIEMAN.

"So he is," said Mr. Pickwick, brightening up. "Good boy, that. I'll give him a shilling, presently. Now, then, Sam, wheel away."

"Hold on, sir," said Mr. Weller, invigorated with the prospect of refreshments. "Out of the vay, young leathers. If you walley my precious life don't upset me, as the gen'l'm'n said to the driver when they was a carryin' him to Tyburn." And quickening his pace to a sharp run, Mr. Weller wheeled his master nimbly to the green hill, shot him dexterously out by the very side of the basket, and proceeded to unpack it with the utmost dispatch.

"Weal pie," said Mr. Weller, soliloquising, as he arranged the eatables on the grass. "Wery good thing is weal pie, when you know the lady as made it, and is quite sure it an't kittens; and arter all though, where's the odds, when they're so like weal that the wery piemen themselves don't know the difference?"

"Don't they, Sam?" said Mr. Pickwick.

"Not they, sir," replied Mr. Weller, touching his hat. "I lodged in the same house vith a pieman once, sir, and a wery nice man he was—reg'lar clever chap, too—make pies out o' anything, he could. 'What a number o' cats you keep, Mr. Brooks,' says I, when I'd got intimate with him. 'Ah,' says he, 'I do—a good many,' says he. 'You must be wery fond o' cats,' says I. 'Other people is,' says he, a winkin' at me; 'they an't in season till the winter though,' says he. 'Not in season!' says I. 'No,' says he, 'fruits is in, cats is out.' 'Why, what do you mean?' says I. 'Mean?' says he. 'That I'll never be a party to the combination o' the butchers, to keep up the prices o' meat,' says he. 'Mr. Weller,' says he, a squeezing my hand wery hard, and vispering in my ear—'don't mention this here agin—but it's the seasonin' as does it. They're all made o' them noble animals,' says he, a pointin' to a wery nice little tabby kitten, 'and I seasons 'em for beefsteak, weal, or kidney, 'cordin to the demand. And more than that,' says he, 'I can make a

305

weal a beef-steak, or a beef-steak a kidney, or any one on 'em a mutton, at a minute's notice, just as the market changes, and appetites wary!"

"He must have been a very ingenious young man, that, Sam," said Mr. Pickwick, with a slight shudder.

"Just was, sir," replied Mr. Weller, continuing his occupation of emptying the basket, "and the pies was beautiful. Tongue; well that's a wery good thing when it an't a woman's. Bread—knuckle o' ham, reg'lar picter—cold beef in slices, wery good. What's in them stone jars, young touch-and-go?"

"Beer in this one," replied the boy, taking from his shoulder a couple of large stone bottles, fastened together by a leathern strap—"cold punch in t'other."

"And a wery good notion of a lunch it is, take it altogether," said Mr. Weller, surveying his arrangement of the repast with great satisfaction. "Now, gen'l'm'n, 'fall on,' as the English said to the French when they fixed bagginets."

It needed no second invitation to induce the party to yield full justice to the meal; and as little pressing did it require to induce Mr. Weller, the long gamekeeper, and the two boys, to station themselves on the grass, at a little distance, and do good execution upon a decent proportion of the viands. An old oak afforded a pleasant shelter to the group, and a rich prospect of arable and meadow land, intersected with luxuriant hedges, and richly ornamented with wood, lay spread out below them.

"This is delightful—thoroughly delightful!" said Mr. Pickwick, the skin of whose expressive countenance was rapidly peeling off, with exposure to the sun.

"So it is: so it is, old fellow," replied Wardle. "Come; a glass of punch!"

"With great pleasure," said Mr. Pickwick; the satisfaction of whose countenance, after drinking it, bore testimony to the sincerity of the reply.

"Good," said Mr. Pickwick, smacking his lips. "Very

good. I'll take another. Cool; very cool. Come, gentlemen," continued Mr. Pickwick, still retaining his hold upon the jar, "a toast. Our friends at Dingley Dell."

The toast was drunk with loud acclamations.

"I'll tell you what I shall do, to get up my shooting again," said Mr. Winkle, who was eating bread and ham with a pocket-knife. "I'll put a stuffed partridge on the top of a post, and practise at it, beginning at a short distance, and lengthening it by degrees. I understand it's capital practice."

"I know a gen'l'man, sir," said Mr. Weller, "as did that, and begun at two yards; but he never tried it on agin; for he blowed the bird right clean away at the first fire, and nobody ever seed a feather on him arterwards."

"Sam," said Mr. Pickwick.

"Sir," replied Mr. Weller.

"Have the goodness to reserve your anecdotes till they are called for."

"Cert'nly, sir."

Here Mr. Weller winked the eye which was not concealed by the beer-can he was raising to his lips with such exquisite-ness, that the two boys went into spontaneous convulsions, and even the long man condescended to smile.

"Well that certainly is most capital cold punch," said Mr. Pickwick, looking earnestly at the stone bottle; "and the day is extremely warm, and—Tupman, my dear friend, a glass of punch?"

"With the greatest delight," replied Mr. Tupman; and having drank that glass, Mr. Pickwick took another, just to see whether there was any orange peel in the punch, because orange peel always disagreed with him; and finding that there was not, Mr. Pickwick took another glass to the health of their absent friend, and then felt himself imperatively called upon to propose another in honour of the punch-compounder, unknown.

This constant succession of glasses produced considerable

effect upon Mr. Pickwick; his countenance beamed with the most sunny smiles, laughter played around his lips, and good-humoured merriment twinkled in his eye. Yielding by degrees to the influence of the exciting liquid, rendered more so by the heat, Mr. Pickwick expressed a strong desire to recollect a song which he had heard in his infancy, and the attempt proving abortive, sought to stimulate his memory with more glasses of punch, which appeared to have quite a contrary effect; for, from forgetting the words of the song, he began to forget how to articulate any words at all; and finally, after rising to his legs to address the company in an eloquent speech, he fell into the barrow, and fast asleep, simultaneously.

The basket having been repacked, and it being found perfectly impossible to awaken Mr. Pickwick from his torpor, some discussion took place whether it would be better for Mr. Weller to wheel his master back again, or to leave him where he was, until they should all be ready to return. The latter course was at length decided on; and as the further expedition was not to exceed an hour's duration, and as Mr. Weller begged very hard to be one of the party, it was determined to leave Mr. Pickwick asleep in the barrow, and to call for him on their return. So away they went, leaving Mr. Pickwick snoring most comfortably in the shade.

That Mr. Pickwick would have continued to snore in the shade until his friends came back, or, in default thereof, until the shades of evening had fallen on the landscape, there appears no reasonable cause to doubt; always supposing that he had been suffered to remain there in peace. But he was *not* suffered to remain there in peace. And this was what prevented him.

Captain Boldwig was a little fierce man in a stiff black neckerchief and blue surtout, who, when he did condescend to walk about his property, did it in company with a thick rattan stick with a brass ferrule, and a gardener and sub-gardener with meek faces, to whom (the gardeners, not the stick) Captain Boldwig gave his orders with all due grandeur and ferocity: for Captain Boldwig's wife's sister had married a Marquis, and the Captain's house was a villa, and his land "grounds," and it was all very high, and mighty, and great.

Mr. Pickwick had not been asleep half an hour when little Captain Boldwig, followed by the two gardeners, came striding along as fast as his size and importance would let him; and when he came near the oak tree, Captain Boldwig paused, and drew a long breath, and looked at the prospect as if he thought the prospect ought to be highly gratified at having him to take notice of it; and then he struck the ground emphatically with his stick, and summoned the head-gardener.

" Hunt," said Captain Boldwig.

" Yes, sir," said the gardener.

" Roll this place to-morrow morning—do you hear, Hunt?"

" Yes, sir."

" And take care that you keep me this place in good order—do you hear, Hunt?"

" Yes, sir."

" And remind me to have a board done about trespassers, and spring guns, and all that sort of thing, to keep the common people out. Do you hear, Hunt; do you hear?"

" I'll not forget it, sir."

" I beg your pardon, sir," said the other man, advancing, with his hand to his hat.

" Well, Wilkins, what's the matter with *you?*" said Captain Boldwig.

" I beg your pardon, sir—but I think there have been trespassers here to-day."

" Ha!" said the Captain, scowling around him.

" Yes, sir—they have been dining here, I think, sir."

" Why, confound their audacity, so they have," said Captain Boldwig, as the crumbs and fragments that were strewn upon the grass met his eye. "They have actually been devouring their food here. I wish I had the vagabonds here!" said the Captain, clenching the thick stick.

"I wish I had the vagabonds here," said the Captain, wrathfully.

"Beg your pardon, sir," said Wilkins, "but—"

"But what? Eh?" roared the Captain; and following the timid glance of Wilkins, his eyes encountered the wheelbarrow and Mr. Pickwick.

"Who are you, you rascal?" said the Captain, administering several pokes to Mr. Pickwick's body with the thick stick. "What's your name?"

"Cold punch," murmured Mr. Pickwick, as he sunk to sleep again.

"What?" demanded Captain Boldwig.

No reply.

"What did he say his name was?" asked the Captain.

"Punch, I think, sir," replied Wilkins.

"That's his impudence; that's his confounded impudence," said Captain Boldwig. "He's only feigning to be asleep now," said the Captain, in a high passion. "He's drunk; he's a drunken plebeian. Wheel him away, Wilkins, wheel him away directly."

"Where shall I wheel him to, sir?" inquired Wilkins, with great timidity.

"Wheel him to the Devil," replied Captain Boldwig.

"Very well, sir," said Wilkins.

"Stay," said the Captain.

Wilkins stopped accordingly.

"Wheel him," said the Captain, "wheel him to the pound; and let us see whether he calls himself Punch when he comes to himself. He shall not bully me, he shall not bully me. Wheel him away."

Away Mr. Pickwick was wheeled in compliance with this imperious mandate; and the great Captain Boldwig, swelling with indignation, proceeded on his walk.

Inexpressible was the astonishment of the little party when they returned, to find that Mr. Pickwick had disappeared, and taken the wheelbarrow with him. It was the most mysterious and unaccountable thing that was ever heard of. For a lame man to have got upon his legs without any previous notice, and walked off, would have been most extraordinary; but when it came to his wheeling a heavy barrow before him, by way of amusement, it grew positively miraculous. They searched every nook and corner round, together and separately; they shouted, whistled, laughed, called—and all with the same result. Mr. Pickwick was not to be found. After some hours of fruitless search, they arrived at the unwelcome conclusion that they must go home without him.

Meanwhile Mr. Pickwick had been wheeled to the Pound, and safely deposited therein, fast asleep in the wheelbarrow, to the immeasurable delight and satisfaction, not only of all the boys in the village, but three-fourths of the whole population, who had gathered round, in expectation of his waking. If their most intense gratification had been excited by seeing him wheeled in, how many hundredfold was their joy increased when, after a few indistinct cries of "Sam!" he sat up in the barrow, and gazed with indescribable astonishment on the faces before him.

A general shout was of course the signal of his having woke up; and his involuntary inquiry of "What's the matter?" occasioned another, louder than the first, if possible.

"Here's a game!" roared the populace.

"Where am I?" exclaimed Mr. Pickwick.

"In the Pound," replied the mob.

"How came I here? What was I doing? Where was I brought from?"

"Boldwig! Captain Boldwig!" was the only reply.

"Let me out," cried Mr. Pickwick. "Where's my servant? Where are my friends?"

"You an't got no friends. Hurrah!" Then there came a turnip, then a potato, and then an egg: with a few other little tokens of the playful disposition of the many-headed.

How long this scene might have lasted, or how much Mr. Pickwick might have suffered, no one can tell, had not a carriage, which was driving swiftly by, suddenly pulled up, from whence there descended old Wardle and Sam Weller, the former of whom, in far less time than it takes to write it, if not to read it, had made his way to Mr. Pickwick's side, and placed him in the vehicle, just as the latter had concluded the third and last round of a single combat with the town-beadle.

"Run to the Justice's!" cried a dozen voices.

"Ah, run avay," said Mr. Weller, jumping up on the box. "Give my compliments—Mr. Veller's compliments—to the Justice, and tell him I've spiled his beadle, and that, if he'll svear in a new 'un, I'll come back agin to-morrow and spile him. Drive on, old feller."

"I'll give directions for the commencement of an action for false imprisonment against this Captain Boldwig, directly I get to London," said Mr. Pickwick, as soon as the carriage turned out of the town.

"We were trespassing, it seems," said Wardle.

"I don't care," said Mr. Pickwick, "I'll bring the action."

"No, you won't," said Wardle.

"I will, by—" but as there was a humorous expression in Wardle's face, Mr. Pickwick checked himself, and said: "Why not?"

"Because," said old Wardle, half-bursting with laughter, "because they might turn round on some of us, and say we had taken too much cold punch."

Do what he would, a smile would come into Mr. Pickwick's face; the smile extended into a laugh; the laugh into a roar; the roar became general. So, to keep up their good humour, they stopped at the first roadside tavern they came to, and ordered a glass of brandy and water all round, with a magnum of extra strength for Mr. Samuel Weller.

Mr. Pickwick in the Pound

CHAPTER XX.

SHOWING HOW DODSON AND FOGG WERE MEN OF BUSINESS, AND
THEIR CLERKS MEN OF PLEASURE; AND HOW AN AFFECTING
INTERVIEW TOOK PLACE BETWEEN MR. WELLER AND HIS
LONG-LOST PARENT; SHOWING ALSO WHAT CHOICE SPIRITS
ASSEMBLED AT THE MAGPIE AND STUMP, AND WHAT A
CAPITAL CHAPTER THE NEXT ONE WILL BE.

IN the ground-floor front of a dingy house, at the very
furthest end of Freeman's Court, Cornhill, sat the four clerks
of Messrs. Dodson and Fogg, two of his Majesty's Attorneys
of the Courts of King's Bench and Common Pleas at Westminster, and solicitors of the High Court of Chancery: the
aforesaid clerks catching as favourable glimpses of Heaven's
light and Heaven's sun, in the course of their daily labours,
as a man might hope to do, were he placed at the bottom
of a reasonably deep well; and without the opportunity of
perceiving the stars in the day-time, which the latter secluded
situation affords.

The clerks' office of Messrs. Dodson and Fogg was a dark,
mouldy, earthy-smelling room, with a high wainscotted
partition to screen the clerks from the vulgar gaze: a couple
of old wooden chairs: a very loud-ticking clock: an almanack,
an umbrella-stand, a row of hat-pegs, and a few shelves, on
which were deposited several ticketed bundles of dirty papers,
some old deal boxes with paper labels, and sundry decayed
stone ink bottles of various shapes and sizes. There was

a glass door leading into the passage which formed the entrance to the court, and on the outer side of this glass door, Mr. Pickwick, closely followed by Sam Weller, presented himself on the Friday morning succeeding the occurrence, of which a faithful narration is given in the last chapter.

"Come in, can't you!" cried a voice from behind the partition, in reply to Mr. Pickwick's gentle tap at the door. And Mr. Pickwick and Sam entered accordingly.

"Mr. Dodson or Mr. Fogg at home, sir?" inquired Mr. Pickwick, gently, advancing, hat in hand, towards the partition.

"Mr. Dodson ain't at home, and Mr. Fogg's particularly engaged," replied the voice; and at the same time the head to which the voice belonged, with a pen behind its ear, looked over the partition, and at Mr. Pickwick.

It was a ragged head, the sandy hair of which, scrupulously parted on one side, and flattened down with pomatum, was twisted into little semi-circular tails round a flat face ornamented with a pair of small eyes, and garnished with a very dirty shirt collar, and a rusty black stock.

"Mr. Dodson ain't at home, and Mr. Fogg's particularly engaged," said the man to whom the head belonged.

"When will Mr. Dodson be back, sir?" inquired Mr. Pickwick.

"Can't say."

"Will it be long before Mr. Fogg is disengaged, sir?"

"Don't know."

Here the man proceeded to mend his pen with great deliberation, while another clerk, who was mixing a Seidlitz powder, under cover of the lid of his desk, laughed approvingly.

"I think I'll wait," said Mr. Pickwick. There was no reply; so Mr. Pickwick sat down unbidden, and listened to the loud ticking of the clock and the murmured conversation of the clerks.

"That was a game, wasn't it?" said one of the gentlemen,

in a brown coat and brass buttons, inky drabs, and bluchers, at the conclusion of some inaudible relation of his previous evening's adventures.

"Devilish good—devilish good," said the Seidlitz-powder man.

"Tom Cummins was in the chair," said the man with the brown coat; "It was half-past four when I got to Somers Town, and then I was so uncommon lushey, that I couldn't find the place where the latch-key went in, and was obliged to knock up the old 'ooman. I say, I wonder what old Fogg 'ud say, if he knew it. I should get the sack, I s'pose —eh?"

At this humorous notion, all the clerks laughed in concert.

"There was such a game with Fogg here, this mornin'," said the man in the brown coat, "while Jack was up stairs sorting the papers, and you two were gone to the stamp-office. Fogg was down here, opening the letters, when that chap as we issued the writ against at Camberwell, you know, came in—what's his name again?"

"Ramsey," said the clerk who had spoken to Mr. Pickwick.

"Ah, Ramsey—a precious seedy-looking customer. 'Well, sir,' says old Fogg, looking at him very fierce—you know his way—'well, sir, have you come to settle?' 'Yes, I have, sir,' said Ramsey, putting his hand in his pocket, and bringing out the money, 'the debt's two pound ten, and the costs three pound five, and here it is, sir;' and he sighed like bricks, as he lugged out the money, done up in a bit of blotting-paper. Old Fogg looked first at the money, and then at him, a⸱ d then he coughed in his rum way, so that I knew something was coming. 'You don't know there's a declaration filed, which increases the costs materially, I suppose?' said Fogg. 'You don't say that, sir,' said Ramsey, starting back; 'the time was only out last night, sir.' 'I do say it, though,' said Fogg, 'my clerk's just gone to file it. Hasn't Mr. Jackson gone to file that declaration in Bullman and Ramsey, Mr. Wicks?' Of course

I said yes, and then Fogg coughed again, and looked at Ramsey. 'My God!' said Ramsey; 'and here have I nearly driven myself mad, scraping this money together, and all to no purpose.' 'None at all,' said Fogg, coolly; 'so you had better go back and scrape some more together, and bring it here in time.' 'I can't get it, by God!' said Ramsey, striking the desk with his fist. 'Don't bully me, sir,' said Fogg, getting into a passion on purpose. 'I am not bullying you, sir,' said Ramsey. 'You are,' said Fogg; 'get out, sir; get out of this office, sir, and come back, sir, when you know how to behave yourself.' Well, Ramsey tried to speak, but Fogg wouldn't let him, so he put the money in his pocket, and sneaked out. The door was scarcely shut, when old Fogg turned round to me, with a sweet smile on his face, and drew the declaration out of his coat pocket. 'Here, Wicks,' says Fogg, 'take a cab, and go down to the Temple as quick as you can, and file that. The costs are quite safe, for he's a steady man with a large family, at a salary of five-and-twenty shillings a week, and if he gives us a warrant of attorney, as he must in the end, I know his employers will see it paid; so we may as well get all we can out of him, Mr. Wicks; it's a Christian act to do it, Mr. Wicks, for with his large family and small income, he'll be all the better for a good lesson against getting into debt,—won't he, Mr. Wicks, won't he?'—and he smiled so good-naturedly as he went away, that it was delightful to see him. 'He is a capital man of business,' said Wicks, in a tone of the deepest admiration, "capital, isn't he?"

The other three cordially subscribed to this opinion, and the anecdote afforded the most unlimited satisfaction.

"Nice men these here, sir," whispered Mr. Weller to his master; "wery nice notion of fun they has, sir."

Mr. Pickwick nodded assent, and coughed to attract the attention of the young gentlemen behind the partition, who, having now relaxed their minds by a little conversation among themselves, condescended to take some notice of the stranger.

"I wonder whether Fogg's disengaged now?" said Jackson.

"I'll see," said Wicks, dismounting leisurely from his stool. "What name shall I tell Mr. Fogg?"

"Pickwick," replied the illustrious subject of these memoirs.

Mr. Jackson departed up stairs on his errand, and immediately returned with a message that Mr. Fogg would see Mr. Pickwick in five minutes; and having delivered it, returned again to his desk.

"What did he say his name was?" whispered Wicks.

"Pickwick," replied Jackson; "it's the defendant in Bardell and Pickwick."

A sudden scraping of feet, mingled with the sound of suppressed laughter, was heard from behind the partition.

"They're a twiggin' of you, sir," whispered Mr. Weller.

"Twigging of me, Sam!" replied Mr. Pickwick; "what do you mean by twigging me?"

Mr. Weller replied by pointing with his thumb over his shoulder, and Mr. Pickwick, on looking up, became sensible of the pleasing fact, that all the four clerks, with countenances expressive of the utmost amusement, and with their heads thrust over the wooden screen, were minutely inspecting the figure and general appearance of the supposed trifler with female hearts, and disturber of female happiness. On his looking up, the row of heads suddenly disappeared, and the sound of pens travelling at a furious rate over paper, immediately succeeded.

A sudden ring at the bell which hung in the office, summoned Mr. Jackson to the apartment of Fogg, from whence he came back to say that he (Fogg) was ready to see Mr. Pickwick if he would step up stairs.

Up stairs Mr. Pickwick did step accordingly, leaving Sam Weller below. The room door of the one-pair back, bore inscribed in legible characters the imposing words "Mr. Fogg;" and, having tapped thereat, and been desired to come in, Jackson ushered Mr. Pickwick into the presence.

"Is Mr. Dodson in?" inquired Mr. Fogg.

"Just come in, sir," replied Jackson.

"Ask him to step here."

"Yes, sir." Exit Jackson.

"Take a seat, sir," said Fogg; "there is the paper, sir; my partner will be here directly, and we can converse about this matter, sir."

Mr. Pickwick took a seat and the paper, but instead of reading the latter, peeped over the top of it, and took a survey of the man of business, who was an elderly, pimply-faced, vegetable-diet sort of man, in a black coat, dark mixture trousers, and small black gaiters; a kind of being who seemed to be an essential part of the desk at which he was writing, and to have as much thought or sentiment.

After a few minutes' silence, Mr. Dodson, a plump, portly, stern-looking man, with a loud voice, appeared; and the conversation commenced.

"This is Mr. Pickwick," said Fogg.

"Ah! You are the defendant, sir, in Bardell and Pickwick?" said Dodson.

"I am, sir," replied Mr. Pickwick.

"Well, sir," said Dodson, "and what do you propose?"

"Ah!" said Fogg, thrusting his hands into his trousers' pockets, and throwing himself back in his chair, "what do you propose, Mr. Pickwick?"

"Hush, Fogg," said Dodson, "let me hear what Mr. Pickwick has to say."

"I came, gentlemen," said Mr. Pickwick, gazing placidly on the two partners, "I came here, gentlemen, to express the surprise with which I received your letter of the other day, and to inquire what grounds of action you can have against me."

"Grounds of—" Fogg had ejaculated this much, when he was stopped by Dodson.

"Mr. Fogg," said Dodson, "I am going to speak."

"I beg your pardon, Mr. Dodson," said Fogg.

"For the grounds of action, sir," continued Dodson, with moral elevation in his air, "you will consult your own conscience and your own feelings. We, sir, we, are guided entirely

318

Mr. Pickwick and Sam in the Attorney's Office

by the statement of our client. That statement, sir, may be true, or it may be false; it may be credible, or it may be incredible; but, if it be true, and if it be credible, I do not hesitate to say, sir, that our grounds of action, sir, are strong, and not to be shaken. You may be an unfortunate man, sir, or you may be a designing one; but if I were called upon, as a juryman upon my oath, sir, to express an opinion of your conduct, sir, I do not hesitate to assert that I should have but one opinion about it." Here Dodson drew himself up, with an air of offended virtue, and looked at Fogg, who thrust his hands further in his pockets, and, nodding his head sagely, said, in a tone of the fullest concurrence, "Most certainly."

"Well, sir," said Mr. Pickwick, with considerable pain depicted in his countenance, "you will permit me to assure you, that I am a most unfortunate man, so far as this case is concerned."

"I hope you are, sir," replied Dodson; "I trust you may be, sir. If you are really innocent of what is laid to your charge, you are more unfortunate than I had believed any man could possibly be. What do *you* say, Mr. Fogg?"

"I say precisely what you say," replied Fogg, with a smile of incredulity.

"The writ, sir, which commences the action," continued Dodson, "was issued regularly. Mr. Fogg, where is the *præcipe* book?"

"Here it is," said Fogg, handing over a square book, with a parchment cover.

"Here is the entry," resumed Dodson. "'Middlesex, Capias *Martha Bardell, widow,* v. *Samuel Pickwick.* Damages, £1500. Dodson and Fogg for the plaintiff, Aug. 28, 1830.' All regular, sir; perfectly." Dodson coughed and looked at Fogg, who said "Perfectly," also. And then they both looked at Mr. Pickwick.

"I am to understand, then," said Mr. Pickwick, "that it really is your intention to proceed with this action?"

"Understand, sir? That you certainly may," replied Dodson, with something as near a smile as his importance would allow.

"And that the damages are actually laid at fifteen hundred pounds?" said Mr. Pickwick.

"To which understanding you may add my assurance, that if we could have prevailed upon our client, they would have been laid at treble the amount, sir:" replied Dodson.

"I believe Mrs. Bardell specially said, however," observed Fogg, glancing at Dodson, "that she would not compromise for a farthing less."

"Unquestionably," replied Dodson, sternly. For the action was only just begun; and it wouldn't have done to let Mr. Pickwick compromise it then, even if he had been so disposed.

"As you offer no terms, sir," said Dodson, displaying a slip of parchment in his right hand, and affectionately pressing a paper copy of it, on Mr. Pickwick with his left, "I had better serve you with a copy of this writ, sir. Here is the original, sir."

"Very well, gentlemen, very well," said Mr. Pickwick, rising in person and wrath at the same time; "you shall hear from my solicitor, gentlemen."

"We shall be very happy to do so," said Fogg, rubbing his hands.

"Very," said Dodson, opening the door.

"And before I go, gentlemen," said the excited Mr. Pickwick, turning round on the landing, "permit me to say, that of all the disgraceful and rascally proceedings—"

"Stay, sir, stay," interposed Dodson, with great politeness. "Mr. Jackson! Mr. Wicks!"

"Sir," said the two clerks, appearing at the bottom of the stairs.

"I merely want you to hear what this gentleman says," replied Dodson. "Pray, go on, sir—disgraceful and rascally proceedings, I think you said?"

"I did," said Mr. Pickwick, thoroughly roused. "I said,

sir, that of all the disgraceful and rascally proceedings that ever were attempted, this is the most so. I repeat it, sir."

"You hear that, Mr. Wicks?" said Dodson.

"You won't forget these expressions, Mr. Jackson?" said Fogg.

"Perhaps you would like to call us swindlers, sir," said Dodson. "Pray do, sir, if you feel disposed; now pray do, sir."

"I do," said Mr. Pickwick. "You *are* swindlers."

"Very good," said Dodson. "You can hear down there, I hope, Mr. Wicks?"

"Oh yes, si ," said Wicks.

"You had better come up a step or two higher, if you can't," added Mr. Fogg. "Go on, sir; do go on. You had better call us thieves, sir; or perhaps you would like to assault one of us. Pray do it, sir, if you would; we will not make the smallest resistance. Pray do it, sir."

As Fogg put himself very temptingly within the reach of Mr. Pickwick's clenched fist, there is little doubt that that gentleman would have complied with his earnest entreaty, but for the interposition of Sam, who, hearing the dispute, emerged from the office, mounted the stairs, and seized his master by the arm.

"You just come avay," said Mr. Weller. "Battledore and shuttlecock's a wery good game, vhen you an't the shuttlecock and two lawyers the battledores, in which case it gets too excitin' to be pleasant. Come avay, sir. If you want to ease your mind by blowing up somebody, come out into the court and blow up me; but it's rayther too expensive work to be carried on here."

And without the slightest ceremony, Mr. Weller hauled his master down the stairs, and down the court, and having safely deposited him in Cornhill, fell behind, prepared to follow whithersoever he should lead.

Mr. Pickwick walked on abstractedly, crossed opposite the Mansion House, and bent his steps up Cheapside. Sam began to wonder where they were going, when his master turned round, and said:

"Sam, I will go immediately to Mr. Perker's."

"That's just exactly the wery place vere you ought to have gone last night, sir," replied Mr. Weller.

"I think it is, Sam," said Mr. Pickwick.

"I *know* it is," said Mr. Weller.

"Well, well, Sam," replied Mr. Pickwick, "we will go there at once, but first, as I have been rather ruffled, I should like a glass of brandy and water warm, Sam. Where can I have it, Sam?"

Mr. Weller's knowledge of London was extensive and peculiar. He replied, without the slightest consideration:

"Second court on the right hand side—last house but vun on the same side the vay—take the box as stands in the first fire-place, 'cos there an't no leg in the middle o' the table, wich all the others has, and it's wery inconwenient."

Mr. Pickwick observed his valet's directions implicitly, and bidding Sam follow him, entered the tavern he had pointed out, where the hot brandy and water was speedily placed before him; while Mr. Weller, seated at a respectful distance, though at the same table with his master, was accommodated with a pint of porter.

The room was one of a very homely description, and was apparently under the especial patronage of stage coachmen: for several gentlemen, who had all the appearance of belonging to that learned profession, were drinking and smoking in the different boxes. Among the number was one stout, red-faced, elderly man in particular, seated in an opposite box, who attracted Mr. Pickwick's attention. The stout man was smoking with great vehemence, but between every half-dozen puffs, he took his pipe from his mouth, and looked first at Mr. Weller and then at Mr. Pickwick. Then, he would bury in a quart pot, as much of his countenance as the dimensions of the quart pot admitted of its receiving, and take another look at Sam and Mr. Pickwick. Then he would take another half-dozen puffs with an air of profound meditation and look at them again. At last the stout man, putting up his legs on the seat, and leaning his back against the wall, began to puff at his pipe without leaving off at all, and to stare through the smoke at the new comers, as if he had made up his mind to see the most he could of them.

At first the evolutions of the stout man had escaped Mr. Weller's observation, but by degrees, as he saw Mr. Pickwick's eyes every now and then turning towards him, he began to gaze in the same direction, at the same time shading his eyes with his hand, as if he partially recognised the object before him, and wished to make quite sure of its identity. His doubts were speedily dispelled, however; for the stout man having blown a thick cloud from his pipe, a hoarse voice, like some strange effort of ventriloquism, emerged from beneath the capacious shawls which muffled his throat and chest, and slowly uttered these sounds—" Wy, Sammy!"

" Who's that, Sam?" inquired Mr. Pickwick.

" Why, I wouldn't ha' believed it, sir," replied Mr. Weller with astonished eyes. "It's the old 'un."

" Old one," said Mr. Pickwick. " What old one?"

" My father, sir," replied Mr. Weller. " How are you, my ancient?" With which beautiful ebullition of filial affection, Mr. Weller made room on the seat beside him, for the stout man, who advanced pipe in mouth and pot in hand, to greet him.

" Wy, Sammy," said the father, " I han't seen you, for two year and better."

" Nor more you have, old codger," replied the son. " How's mother in law?"

" Wy, I'll tell you what, Sammy," said Mr. Weller, senior, with much solemnity in his manner; " there never was a nicer woman as a widder, than that 'ere second wentur o' mine—a sweet creetur she was, Sammy; all I can say on her now, is, that as she was such an uncommon pleasant widder, it's a great pity she ever changed her con-dition. She don't act as a vife, Sammy."

"Don't she, though?" inquired Mr. Weller junior.

The elder Mr. Weller shook his head, as he replied with a sigh, "I've done it once too often, Sammy; I've done it once too often. Take example by your father, my boy, and be wery careful o' widders all your life, specially if they've kept a public-house, Sammy." Having delivered this parental advice with great pathos, Mr. Weller senior re-filled his pipe from a tin box he carried in his pocket, and, lighting his fresh pipe from the ashes of the old one, commenced smoking at a great rate.

"Beg your pardon, sir," he said, renewing the subject, and addressing Mr. Pickwick, after a considerable pause, "nothin' personal, I hope, sir; I hope you han't got a widder, sir."

"Not I," replied Mr. Pickwick, laughing; and while Mr. Pickwick laughed, Sam Weller informed his parent in a whisper, of the relation in which he stood towards that gentleman.

"Beg your pardon, sir," said Mr. Weller, senior, taking off his hat, "I hope you've no fault to find with Sammy, sir?"

"None whatever," said Mr. Pickwick.

"Wery glad to hear it, sir," replied the old man; "I took a good deal o' pains with his eddication, sir; let him run in the streets when he was wery young, and shift for his-self. It's the only way to make a boy sharp, sir."

"Rather a dangerous process, I should imagine," said Mr. Pickwick, with a smile.

"And not a wery sure one, neither," added Mr. Weller; "I got reg'larly done the other day."

"No!" said his father.

"I did," said the son; and he proceeded to relate, in as few words as possible, how he had fallen a ready dupe to the stratagems of Job Trotter.

Mr. Weller senior listened to the tale with the most profound attention, and, at its termination, said:

"Worn't one o' these chaps slim and tall, with long hair, and the gift o' the gab wery gallopin'?"

TWO OLD ACQUAINTANCES.

Mr. Pickwick did not quite understand the last item of description, but, comprehending the first, said "Yes" at a venture.

"T'other's a black-haired chap in mulberry livery, with a wery large head?"

"Yes, yes, he is," said Mr. Pickwick and Sam, with great earnestness.

"Then I know where they are, and that's all about it," said Mr. Weller; "they're at Ipswich, safe enough, them two."

"No!" said Mr. Pickwick.

"Fact," said Mr. Weller, "and I'll tell you how I know it. I work an Ipswich coach now and then for a friend o' mine. I worked down the wery day arter the night as you caught the rheumatiz, and at the Black Boy at Chelmsford—the wery place they'd come to—I took 'em up, right through to Ipswich, where the man servant—him in the mulberries—told me they was a goin' to put up for a long time."

"I'll follow him," said Mr. Pickwick; "we may as well see Ipswich as any other place. I'll follow him."

"You're quite certain it was them, governor?" inquired Mr. Weller, junior.

"Quite, Sammy, quite," replied his father, "for their appearance is wery sing'ler; besides that 'ere, I wondered to see the gen'lm'n so formiliar with his servant; and, more than that, as they sat in front, right behind the box, I heerd 'em laughing, and saying how they'd done old Fireworks."

"Old who?" said Mr. Pickwick.

"Old Fireworks, sir; by which, I've no doubt, they meant you, sir."

There is nothing positively vile or atrocious in the appellation of "old Fireworks," but still it is by no means a respectful or flattering designation. The recollection of all the wrongs he had sustained at Jingle's hands had crowded on Mr. Pickwick's mind, the moment Mr. Weller began to speak: it wanted but a feather to turn the scale, and "old Fireworks" did it.

325

"I'll follow him," said Mr. Pickwick, with an emphatic blow on the table.

"I shall work down to Ipswich the day arter to-morrow, sir," said Mr. Weller the elder, "from the Bull in Whitechapel; and if you really mean to go, you'd better go with me."

"So we had," said Mr. Pickwick; "very true; I can write to Bury, and tell them to meet me at Ipswich. We will go with you. But don't hurry away, Mr. Weller; won't you take anything?"

"You're wery good, sir," replied Mr. W., stopping short; "perhaps a small glass of brandy to drink your health, and success to Sammy, sir, wouldn't be amiss."

"Certainly not," replied Mr. Pickwick. "A glass of brandy here!" The brandy was brought: and Mr. Weller, after pulling his hair to Mr. Pickwick, and nodding to Sam, jerked it down his capacious throat as if it had been a small thimble-full.

"Well done, father," said Sam, "take care, old fellow, or you'll have a touch of your old complaint, the gout."

"I've found a sov'rin' cure for that, Sammy," said Mr. Weller, setting down the glass.

"A sovereign cure for the gout," said Mr. Pickwick, hastily producing his note-book—"what is it?"

"The gout, sir," replied Mr. Weller, "the gout is a complaint as arises from too much ease and comfort. If ever you're attacked with the gout, sir, jist you marry a widder as has got a good loud woice, with a decent notion of usin' it, and you'll never have the gout agin. It's a capital prescription, sir. I takes it reg'lar, and I can warrant it to drive away any illness as is caused by too much jollity." Having imparted this valuable secret, Mr. Weller drained his glass once more, produced a laboured wink, sighed deeply, and slowly retired.

"Well, what do you think of what your father says, Sam?" inquired Mr. Pickwick, with a smile.

"Think, sir!" replied Mr. Weller; "why, I think he's the

wictim o' connubiality, as Blue Beard's domestic chaplain said, with a tear of pity, ven he buried him."

There was no replying to this very apposite conclusion, and, therefore, Mr. Pickwick, after settling the reckoning, resumed his walk to Gray's Inn. By the time he reached its secluded groves, however, eight o'clock had struck, and the unbroken stream of gentlemen in muddy high-lows, soiled white hats, and rusty apparel, who were pouring towards the different avenues of egress, warned him that the majority of the offices had closed for that day.

After climbing two pairs of steep and dirty stairs, he found his anticipations were realised. Mr. Perker's "outer door" was closed; and the dead silence which followed Mr. Weller's repeated kicks thereat, announced that the officials had retired from business for the night.

"This is pleasant, Sam," said Mr. Pickwick; "I shouldn't lose an hour in seeing him; I shall not be able to get one wink of sleep to-night, I know, unless I have the satisfaction of reflecting that I have confided this matter to a professional man."

"Here's an old 'ooman comin' up-stairs, sir," replied Mr. Weller; "p'raps she knows where we can find somebody. Hallo, old lady, vere's Mr. Perker's people?"

"Mr. Perker's people," said a thin, miserable-looking old woman, stopping to recover breath after the ascent of the staircase, "Mr. Perker's people's gone, and I'm a goin' to do the office out."

"Are you Mr. Perker's servant?" inquired Mr. Pickwick.

"I am Mr. Perker's laundress," replied the old woman.

"Ah," said Mr. Pickwick, half aside to Sam, "it's a curious circumstance, Sam, that they call the old women in these inns, laundresses. I wonder what's that for."

"'Cos they has a mortal awersion to washing anythin', I suppose, sir," replied Mr. Weller.

"I shouldn't wonder," said Mr. Pickwick, looking at the old woman, whose appearance, as well as the condition of the

327

office, which she had by this time opened, indicated a rooted antipathy to the application of soap and water; "do you know where I can find Mr. Perker, my good woman?"

"No, I don't," replied the old woman, gruffly; "he's out o' town now."

"That's unfortunate," said Mr. Pickwick; "where's his clerk? Do you know?"

"Yes, I know where he is, but he won't thank me for telling you," replied the laundress.

"I have very particular business with him," said Mr. Pickwick.

"Won't it do in the morning?" said the woman.

"Not so well," replied Mr. Pickwick.

"Well," said the old woman, "if it was anything very particular, I was to say where he was, so I suppose there's no harm in telling. If you just go to the Magpie and Stump, and ask at the bar for Mr. Lowten, they'll show you in to him, and he's Mr. Perker's clerk."

With this direction, and having been furthermore informed that the hostelry in question was situated in a court, happy in the double advantage of being in the vicinity of Clare Market, and closely approximating to the back of New Inn, Mr. Pickwick and Sam descended the ricketty staircase in safety, and issued forth in quest of the Magpie and Stump.

This favoured tavern, sacred to the evening orgies of Mr. Lowten and his companions, was what ordinary people would designate a public-house. That the landlord was a man of a money-making turn, was sufficiently testified by the fact of a small bulk-head beneath the tap-room window, in size and shape not unlike a sedan-chair, being underlet to a mender of shoes: and that he was a being of a philanthropic mind, was evident from the protection he afforded to a pieman, who vended his delicacies without fear of interruption on the very door-step. In the lower windows, which were decorated with curtains of a saffron hue, dangled two or three printed cards, bearing reference to Devonshire cyder and

Dantzic spruce, while a large black board, announcing in white letters to an enlightened public that there were 500,000 barrels of double stout in the cellars of the establishment, left the mind in a state of not unpleasing doubt and uncertainty as to the precise direction in the bowels of the earth, in which this mighty cavern might be supposed to extend. When we add, that the weather-beaten sign-board bore the half-obliterated semblance of a magpie intently eyeing a crooked streak of brown paint, which the neighbours had been taught from infancy to consider as the "stump," we have said all that need be said of the exterior of the edifice.

On Mr. Pickwick's presenting himself at the bar, an elderly female emerged from behind a screen therein, and presented herself before him.

"Is Mr. Lowten here, ma'am?" inquired Mr. Pickwick.

"Yes he is, sir," replied the landlady. "Here, Charley, show the gentleman in, to Mr. Lowten."

"The gen'lm'n can't go in just now," said a shambling pot-boy, with a red head, "'cos Mr. Lowten's a singin' a comic song, and he'll put him out. He'll be done d'rectly, sir."

The red-headed pot-boy had scarcely finished speaking, when a most unanimous hammering of tables, and jingling of glasses, announced that the song had that instant terminated; and Mr. Pickwick, after desiring Sam to solace himself in the tap, suffered himself to be conducted into the presence of Mr. Lowten.

At the announcement of "gentleman to speak to you, sir," a puffy-faced young man, who filled the chair at the head of the table, looked with some surprise in the direction from whence the voice proceeded: and the surprise seemed to be by no means diminished, when his eyes rested on an individual whom he had never seen before.

"I beg your pardon, sir," said Mr. Pickwick, "and I am very sorry to disturb the other gentlemen, too, but I come on very particular business; and if you will suffer me to detain you at this end of the room for five minutes, I shall be very much obliged to you."

The puffy-faced young man rose, and drawing a chair close to Mr. Pickwick in an obscure corner of the room, listened attentively to his tale of woe.

"Ah," he said, when Mr. Pickwick had concluded, "Dodson and Fogg—sharp practice theirs—capital men of business, Dodson and Fogg, sir."

Mr. Pickwick admitted the sharp practice of Dodson and Fogg, and Lowten resumed.

"Perker ain't in town, and he won't be, neither, before the end of next week; but if you want the action defended, and will leave the copy with me, I can do all that's needful till he comes back."

"That's exactly what I came here for," said Mr. Pickwick, handing over the document. "If anything particular occurs, you can write to me at the post-office, Ipswich."

"That's all right," replied Mr. Perker's clerk; and then seeing Mr. Pickwick's eye wandering curiously towards the table, he added, "Will you join us, for half-an-hour or so? We are capital company here to-night. There's Samkin and Green's managing-clerk, and Smithers and Price's chancery, and Pimkin and Thomas's out o' door—sings a capital song, he does—and Jack Bamber, and ever so many more. You're come out of the country, I suppose. Would you like to join us?"

Mr. Pickwick could not resist so tempting an opportunity of studying human nature. He suffered himself to be led to the table, where, after having been introduced to the company in due form, he was accommodated with a seat near the chairman, and called for a glass of his favourite beverage.

A profound silence, quite contrary to Mr. Pickwick's expectation, succeeded.

"You don't find this sort of thing disagreeable, I hope, sir?" said his right hand neighbour, a gentleman in a checked shirt, and Mosaic studs, with a cigar in his mouth.

A CONVIVIAL ASSEMBLAGE.

"Not in the least," replied Mr. Pickwick, "I like it very much, although I am no smoker myself."

"I should be very sorry to say I wasn't," interposed another gentleman on the opposite side of the table. "It's board and lodging to me, is smoke."

Mr. Pickwick glanced at the speaker, and thought that if it were washing too, it would be all the better.

Here there was another pause. Mr. Pickwick was a stranger, and his coming had evidently cast a damp upon the party.

"Mr. Grundy's going to oblige the company with a song," said the chairman.

"No he ain't," said Mr. Grundy.

"Why not?" said the chairman.

"Because he can't," said Mr. Grundy.

"You had better say he won't," replied the chairman.

"Well, then, he won't," retorted Mr. Grundy. Mr. Grundy's positive refusal to gratify the company occasioned another silence.

"Won't anybody enliven us?" said the chairman, despondingly.

"Why don't you enliven us yourself, Mr. Chairman?" said a young man with a whisker, a squint, and an open shirt collar (dirty), from the bottom of the table.

"Hear! hear!" said the smoking gentleman in the Mosaic jewellery.

"Because I only know one song, and I have sung it already, and it's a fine of 'glasses round' to sing the same song twice in a night," replied the chairman.

This was an unanswerable reply, and silence prevailed again.

"I have been to-night, gentlemen," said Mr. Pickwick, hoping to start a subject which all the company could take a part in discussing, "I have been to-night in a place which you all know very well, doubtless, but which I have not been in before for some years, and know very little of; I mean Gray's Inn, gentlemen. Curious little nooks in a great place, like London, these old Inns are."

" By Jove," said the chairman, whispering across the table to Mr. Pickwick, "you have hit upon something that one of us, at least, would talk upon for ever. You'll draw old Jack Bamber out; he was never heard to talk about anything else but the Inns, and he has lived alone in them till he's half crazy."

The individual to whom Lowten alluded, was a little yellow high-shouldered man, whose countenance, from his habit of stooping forward when silent, Mr. Pickwick had not observed before. He wondered though, when the old man raised his shrivelled face, and bent his grey eye upon him, with a keen inquiring look, that such remarkable features could have escaped his attention for a moment. There was a fixed grim smile perpetually on his countenance; he leant his chin on a long skinny hand, with nails of extraordinary length; and as he inclined his head to one side, and looked keenly out from beneath his ragged grey eyebrows, there was a strange, wild slyness in his leer, quite repulsive to behold.

This was the figure that now started forward, and burst into an animated torrent of words. As this chapter has been a long one, however, and as the old man was a remarkable personage, it will be more respectful to him, and more convenient to us, to let him speak for himself in a fresh one.

CHAPTER XXI.

"AHA!" said the old man, a brief description of whose
manner and appearance concluded the last chapter, "Aha!
who was talking about the Inns?"

"I was, sir," replied Mr. Pickwick; "I was observing what
singular old places they are."

"*You!*" said the old man, contemptuously, "What do
you know of the time when young men shut themselves up
in those lonely rooms, and read and read, hour after hour,
and night after night, till their reason wandered beneath
their midnight studies; till their mental powers were exhausted;
till morning's light brought no freshness or health to them;
and they sank beneath the unnatural devotion of their youthful energies to their dry old books? Coming down to a
later time, and a very different day, what do *you* know of
the gradual sinking beneath consumption, or the quick wasting
of fever—the grand results of 'life' and dissipation—which
men have undergone in these same rooms? How many vain
pleaders for mercy, do you think have turned away heart-sick
from the lawyer's office, to find a resting-place in the Thames,
or a refuge in the gaol? They are no ordinary houses, those.
There is not a panel in the old wainscotting, but what, if it
were endowed with the powers of speech and memory, could
start from the wall, and tell its tale of horror—the romance

333

of life, sir, the romance of life! Common-place as they may seem now, I tell you they are strange old places, and I would rather hear many a legend with a terrific sounding name, than the true history of one old set of chambers."

There was something so odd in the old man's sudden energy, and the subject which had called it forth, that Mr. Pickwick was prepared with no observation in reply; and the old man checking his impetuosity, and resuming the leer, which had disappeared during his previous excitement, said:

"Look at them in another light: their most common-place and least romantic. What fine places of slow torture they are! Think of the needy man who has spent his all, beggared himself, and pinched his friends, to enter the profession, which will never yield him a morsel of bread. The waiting —the hope—the disappointment—the fear—the misery—the poverty—the blight on his hopes, and end to his career—the suicide perhaps, or the shabby, slipshod drunkard. Am I not right about them?" And the old man rubbed his hands, and leered as if in delight at having found another point of view in which to place his favourite subject.

Mr. Pickwick eyed the old man with great curiosity, and the remainder of the company smiled, and looked on in silence.

"Talk of your German universities," said the little old man. "Pooh, pooh! there's romance enough at home without going half a mile for it; only people never think of it."

"I never thought of the romance of this particular subject before, certainly," said Mr. Pickwick, laughing.

"To be sure you didn't," said the little old man, "of course not. As a friend of mine used to say to me, 'What is there in chambers, in particular?' 'Queer old places,' said I. 'Not at all,' said he. 'Lonely,' said I. 'Not a bit of it,' said he. He died one morning of apoplexy, as he was going to open his outer door. Fell with his head in his own letter-box, and there he lay for eighteen months. Every body thought he'd gone out of town."

"And how was he found at last?" inquired Mr. Pickwick.

THE ROMANCE OF LIFE.

"The benchers determined to have his door broken open, as he hadn't paid any rent for two years. So they did. Forced the lock; and a very dusty skeleton in a blue coat, black knee-shorts, and silks, fell forward in the arms of the porter who opened the door. Queer, that. Rather, perhaps?" The little old man put his head more on one side, and rubbed his hands with unspeakable glee.

"I know another case," said the little old man, when his chuckles had in some degree subsided. "It occurred in Clifford's Inn. Tenant of a top set—bad character—shut himself up in his bed-room closet, and took a dose of arsenic. The steward thought he had run away; opened the door, and put a bill up. Another man came, took the chambers, furnished them, and went to live there. Somehow or other he couldn't sleep—always restless and uncomfortable. 'Odd,' says he. 'I'll make the other room my bed-chamber, and this my sitting-room.' He made the change, and slept very well at night, but suddenly found that, somehow, he couldn't read in the evening: he got nervous and uncomfortable, and used to be always snuffing his candles and staring about him. 'I can't make this out,' said he, when he came home from the play one night, and was drinking a glass of cold grog, with his back to the wall, in order that he mightn't be able to fancy there was any one behind him—'I can't make it out,' said he; and just then his eyes rested on the little closet that had been always locked up, and a shudder ran through his whole frame from top to toe. 'I have felt this strange feeling before,' said he, 'I cannot help thinking there's something wrong about that closet.' He made a strong effort, plucked up his courage, shivered the lock with a blow or two of the poker, opened the door, and there, sure enough, standing bolt upright in the corner, was the last tenant, with a little bottle clasped firmly in his hand, and his face—well!" As the little old man concluded, he looked round on the attentive faces of his wondering auditory with a smile of grim delight.

"What strange things these are you tell us of, sir," said Mr. Pickwick, minutely scanning the old man's countenance, by the aid of his glasses.

"Strange!" said the little old man. "Nonsense; you think them strange, because you know nothing about it. They are funny, but not uncommon."

"Funny!" exclaimed Mr. Pickwick, involuntarily.

"Yes, funny, are they not?" replied the little old man, with a diabolical leer; and then, without pausing for an answer, he continued:

"I knew another man—let me see—forty years ago now —who took an old, damp, rotten set of chambers, in one of the most ancient Inns, that had been shut up and empty for years and years before. There were lots of old women's stories about the place, and it certainly was very far from being a cheerful one; but he was poor, and the rooms were cheap, and that would have been quite a sufficient reason for him, if they had been ten times worse than they really were. He was obliged to take some mouldering fixtures that were on the place, and, among the rest, was a great lumbering wooden press for papers, with large glass doors, and a green curtain inside; a pretty useless thing for him, for he had no papers to put in it; and as to his clothes, he carried them about with him, and that wasn't very hard work, either. Well, he had moved in all his furniture—it wasn't quite a truck-full—and had sprinkled it about the room, so as to make the four chairs look as much like a dozen as possible, and was sitting down before the fire at night, drinking the first glass of two gallons of whiskey he had ordered on credit, wondering whether it would ever be paid for, and if so, in how many years' time, when his eyes encountered the glass doors of the wooden press. 'Ah,' says he. 'If I hadn't been obliged to take that ugly article at the old broker's valuation, I might have got something comfortable for the money. I'll tell you what it is, old fellow,' he said, speaking aloud to the press, having nothing else to speak to: 'If it wouldn't cost more to break up your old carcase, than it would ever be worth afterwards, I'd have a fire out of you in less than no time.' He had hardly spoken the words, when a sound resembling a faint groan, appeared to issue from the interior of the case. It startled him at first, but thinking, on a moment's reflection, that it must be some young fellow in the next chamber, who had been dining out, he put his feet on the fender, and raised the poker to stir the fire. At that moment, the sound was repeated: and one of the glass doors slowly opening, disclosed a pale and emaciated figure in soiled and worn apparel, standing erect in the press. The figure was tall and thin, and the countenance expressive of care and anxiety; but there was something in the hue of the skin, and gaunt and unearthly appearance of the whole form, which no being of this world was ever seen to wear. 'Who are you?' said the new tenant, turning very pale: poising the poker in his hand, however, and taking a very decent aim at the countenance of the figure. 'Who are you?' 'Don't throw that poker at me,' replied the form; 'If you hurled it with ever so sure an aim, it would pass through me, without resistance, and expend its force on the wood behind. I am a spirit.' 'And, pray, what do you want here?' faltered the tenant. 'In this room,' replied the apparition, 'my worldly ruin was worked, and I and my children beggared. In this press, the papers in a long, long suit, which accumulated for years, were deposited. In this room, when I had died of grief, and long-deferred hope, two wily harpies divided the wealth for which I had contested during a wretched existence, and of which, at last, not one farthing was left for my unhappy descendants. I terrified them from the spot, and since that day have prowled by night—the only period at which I can re-visit the earth—about the scenes of my long-protracted misery. This apartment is mine: leave it to me.' 'If you insist upon making your appearance here,' said the tenant, who had had time to collect his presence of mind during this prosy statement of the ghost's, 'I shall give up possession with the greatest pleasure; but I should like to ask you one question, if you will allow me.' 'Say on,' said the apparition, sternly. 'Well,' said the tenant, 'I don't apply the observation personally to you, because it is equally applicable to most of the ghosts I ever heard of; but it does appear to me somewhat inconsistent, that when you have an opportunity of visiting the fairest spots of earth—for I suppose space is nothing to you—you should always return exactly to the very places where you have been most miserable.' 'Egad, that's very true; I never thought of that before,' said the ghost. 'You see, sir,' pursued the tenant, 'this is a very uncomfortable room. From the appearance of that press, I should be disposed to say that it is not wholly free from bugs; and I really think you might find much more comfortable quarters: to say nothing of the climate of London, which is extremely disagreeable.' 'You are very right, sir,' said the ghost, politely, 'it never struck me till now; I'll try change of air directly.' In fact, he began to vanish as he spoke: his legs, indeed, had quite disappeared. 'And if, sir,' said the tenant, calling after him, 'if you *would* have the goodness to suggest to the other ladies and gentlemen who are now engaged in haunting old empty houses, that they might be much more comfortable elsewhere, you will confer a very great benefit on society.' 'I will,' replied the ghost; 'we must be dull fellows, very dull fellows, indeed; I can't imagine how we can have been so stupid.' With these words, the spirit disappeared; and what is rather remarkable," added the old man, with a shrewd look round the table, " he never came back again."

" That ain't bad, if it's true," said the man in the Mosaic studs, lighting a fresh cigar.

" *If!* " exclaimed the old man, with a look of excessive contempt. " I suppose," he added, turning to Lowten, " he'll say next, that my story about the queer client we had, when I was in an attorney's office, is not true, either—I shouldn't wonder."

THE OLD MAN'S TALE.

"I shan't venture to say anything at all about it, seeing that I never heard the story," observed the owner of the Mosaic decorations.

"I wish you would repeat it, sir," said Mr. Pickwick.

"Ah, do," said Lowten, "nobody has heard it but me, and I have nearly forgotten it."

The old man looked round the table, and leered more horribly than ever, as if in triumph, at the attention which was depicted in every face. Then rubbing his chin with his hand, and looking up to the ceiling as if to recall the circumstances to his memory, he began as follows:

THE OLD MAN'S TALE ABOUT THE QUEER CLIENT.

"IT matters little," said the old man, "where, or how, I picked up this brief history. If I were to relate it in the order in which it reached me, I should commence in the middle, and when I had arrived at the conclusion, go back for a beginning. It is enough for me to say that some of its circumstances passed before my own eyes. For the remainder I know them to have happened, and there are some persons yet living, who will remember them but too well.

"In the Borough High Street, near Saint George's Church, and on the same side of the way, stands, as most people know, the smallest of our debtors' prisons, the Marshalsea. Although in later times it has been a very different place from the sink of filth and dirt it once was, even its improved condition holds out but little temptation to the extravagant, or consolation to the improvident. The condemned felon has as good a yard for air and exercise in Newgate, as the insolvent debtor in the Marshalsea Prison.*

"It may be my fancy, or it may be that I cannot separate the place from the old recollections associated with it, but this part of London I cannot bear. The street is broad, the shops are spacious, the noise of passing vehicles, the footsteps of a perpetual stream of people—all the busy sounds of traffic,

* Better. But this is past, in a better age, and the prison exists no longer.

resound in it from morn to midnight, but the streets around are mean and close; poverty and debauchery lie festering in the crowded alleys; want and misfortune are pent up in the narrow prison; an air of gloom and dreariness seems, in my eyes at least, to hang about the scene, and to impart to it a squalid and sickly hue.

"Many eyes, that have long since been closed in the grave, have looked round upon that scene lightly enough, when entering the gate of the old Marshalsea Prison for the first time: for despair seldom comes with the first severe shock of misfortune. A man has confidence in untried friends, he remembers the many offers of service so freely made by his boon companions when he wanted them not; he has hope—the hope of happy inexperience—and however he may bend beneath the first shock, it springs up in his bosom, and flourishes there for a brief space, until it droops beneath the blight of disappointment and neglect. How soon have those same eyes, deeply sunken in the head, glared from faces wasted with famine, and sallow from confinement, in days when it was no figure of speech to say that debtors rotted in prison, with no hope of release, and no prospect of liberty! The atrocity in its full extent no longer exists, but there is enough of it left to give rise to occurrences that make the heart bleed.

"Twenty years ago, that pavement was worn with the footsteps of a mother and child, who, day by day, so surely as the morning came, presented themselves at the prison gate; often after a night of restless misery and anxious thoughts, were they there, a full hour too soon, and then the young mother turning meekly away, would lead the child to the old bridge, and raising him in her arms to show him the glistening water, tinted with the light of the morning's sun, and stirring with all the bustling preparations for business and pleasure that the river presented at that early hour, endeavour to interest his thoughts in the objects before him. But she would quickly set him down, and hiding her face in her shawl, give vent to the tears that blinded her; for no expression of interest or amusement lighted up his thin and sickly face. His recollections were few enough, but they were all of one kind: all connected with the poverty and misery of his parents. Hour after hour had he sat on his mother's knee, and with childish sympathy watched the tears that stole down her face, and then crept quietly away into some dark corner, and sobbed himself to sleep. The hard realities of the world, with many of its worst privations—hunger and thirst, and cold and want—had all come home to him, from the first dawnings of reason; and though the form of childhood was there, its light heart, its merry laugh, and sparkling eyes, were wanting.

"The father and mother looked on upon this, and upon each other, with thoughts of agony they dared not breathe in words. The healthy, strong-made man, who could have borne almost any fatigue of active exertion, was wasting beneath the close confinement and unhealthy atmosphere of a crowded prison. The slight and delicate woman was sinking beneath the combined effects of bodily and mental illness. The child's young heart was breaking.

"Winter came, and with it weeks of cold and heavy rain. The poor girl had removed to a wretched apartment close to the spot of her husband's imprisonment; and though the change had been rendered necessary by their increasing poverty, she was happier now, for she was nearer him. For two months, she and her little companion watched the opening of the gate as usual. One day she failed to come, for the first time. Another morning arrived, and she came alone. The child was dead.

"They little know, who coldly talk of the poor man's bereavements, as a happy release from pain to the departed, and a merciful relief from expense to the survivor—they little know, I say, what the agony of those bereavements is. A silent look of affection and regard when all other eyes are turned coldly away—the consciousness that we possess the sympathy and affection of one being when all others have deserted us—is a hold, a stay, a comfort, in the deepest affliction, which no wealth could purchase, or power bestow. The child had sat at his parents' feet for hours together, with his little hands patiently folded in each other, and his thin wan face raised towards them. They had seen him pine away, from day to day; and though his brief existence had been a joyless one, and he was now removed to that peace and rest which, child as he was, he had never known in this world, they were his parents, and his loss sunk deep into their souls.

"It was plain to those who looked upon the mother's altered face, that death must soon close the scene of her adversity and trial. Her husband's fellow-prisoners shrunk from obtruding on his grief and misery, and left to himself alone the small room he had previously occupied in common with two companions. She shared it with him: and lingering on without pain, but without hope, her life ebbed slowly away.

"She had fainted one evening in her husband's arms, and he had borne her to the open window, to revive her with the air, when the light of the moon falling full upon her face, shewed him a change upon her features, which made him stagger beneath her weight, like a helpless infant.

"'Set me down, George,' she said faintly. He did so, and seating himself beside her, covered his face with his hands, and burst into tears.

"'It is very hard to leave you, George,' she said, 'but it is God's will, and you must bear it for my sake. Oh! how I thank Him for having taken our boy! He is happy, and in Heaven now. What would he have done here, without his mother!'

"'You shall not die, Mary, you shall not die!' said the husband, starting up. He paced hurriedly to and fro, striking his head with his clenched fists; then reseating himself beside her, and supporting her in his arms, added more calmly, 'Rouse yourself, my dear girl. Pray, pray do. You will revive yet.'

ALONE IN THE WORLD.

"'Never again, George; never again,' said the dying woman. 'Let them lay me by my poor boy now, but promise me, that if ever you leave this dreadful place, and should grow rich, you will have us removed to some quiet country churchyard, a long, long way off—very far from here—where we can rest in peace. Dear George, promise me you will.'

"'I do, I do,' said the man, throwing himself passionately on his knees before her. 'Speak to me, Mary, another word; one look—but one!'

"He ceased to speak: for the arm that clasped his neck, grew stiff and heavy. A deep sigh escaped from the wasted form before him; the lips moved, and a smile played upon the face; but the lips were pallid, and the smile faded into a rigid and ghastly stare. He was alone in the world.

"That night, in the silence and desolation of his miserable room, the wretched man knelt down by the dead body of his wife, and called on God to witness a terrible oath, that from that hour, he devoted himself to revenge her death and that of his child; that thenceforth to the last moment of his life, his whole energies should be directed to this one object; that his revenge should be protracted and terrible; that his hatred should be undying and inextinguishable; and should hunt its object through the world.

"The deepest despair, and passion scarcely human, had made such fierce ravages on his face and form, in that one night, that his companions in misfortune shrunk affrighted from him as he passed by. His eyes were bloodshot and heavy, his face a deadly white, and his body bent as if with age. He had bitten his under lip nearly through in the violence of his mental suffering, and the blood which had flowed from the wound had trickled down his chin, and stained his shirt and neckerchief. No tear, or sound of complaint escaped him: but the unsettled look, and disordered haste with which he paced up and down the yard, denoted the fever which was burning within.

"It was necessary that his wife's body should be removed

343

from the prison, without delay. He received the communication with perfect calmness, and acquiesced in its propriety. Nearly all the inmates of the prison had assembled to witness its removal; they fell back on either side when the widower appeared; he walked hurriedly forward, and stationed himself, alone, in a little railed area close to the lodge gate, from whence the crowd, with an instinctive feeling of delicacy, had retired. The rude coffin was borne slowly forward on men's shoulders. A dead silence pervaded the throng, broken only by the audible lamentations of the women, and the shuffling steps of the bearers on the stone pavement. They reached the spot where the bereaved husband stood: and stopped. He laid his hand upon the coffin, and mechanically adjusting the pall with which it was covered, motioned them onward. The turnkeys in the prison lobby took off their hats as it passed through, and in another moment the heavy gate closed behind it. He looked vacantly upon the crowd, and fell heavily to the ground.

"Although for many weeks after this, he was watched, night and day, in the wildest ravings of fever, neither the consciousness of his loss, nor the recollection of the vow he had made, ever left him for a moment. Scenes changed before his eyes, place succeeded place, and event followed event, in all the hurry of delirium; but they were all connected in some way with the great object of his mind. He was sailing over a boundless expanse of sea, with a blood-red sky above, and the angry waters, lashed into fury beneath, boiling and eddying up, on every side. There was another vessel before them, toiling and labouring in the howling storm: her canvas fluttering in ribbons from the mast, and her deck thronged with figures who were lashed to the sides, over which huge waves every instant burst, sweeping away some devoted creatures into the foaming sea. Onward they bore, amidst the roaring mass of water, with a speed and force which nothing could resist; and striking the stern of the foremost vessel, crushed her, beneath their keel. From the huge whirlpool which the sinking wreck occasioned, arose a shriek so loud and shrill—the death-cry of a hundred drowning creatures, blended into one fierce yell—that it rung far above the war-cry of the elements, and echoed, and re-echoed till it seemed to pierce air, sky, and ocean. But what was that —that old grey-head that rose above the water's surface, and with looks of agony, and screams for aid, buffeted with the waves! One look, and he had sprung from the vessel's side, and with vigorous strokes was swimming towards it. He reached it; he was close upon it. They were *his* features. The old man saw him coming, and vainly strove to elude his grasp. But he clasped him tight, and dragged him beneath the water. Down, down with him, fifty fathoms down; his struggles grew fainter and fainter, until they wholly ceased. He was dead; he had killed him, and had kept his oath.

" He was traversing the scorching sands of a mighty desert, barefoot and alone. The sand choked and blinded him; its fine thin grains entered the very pores of his skin, and irritated him almost to madness. Gigantic masses of the same material, carried forward by the wind, and shone through, by the burning sun, stalked in the distance like pillars of living fire. The bones of men, who had perished in the dreary waste, lay scattered at his feet; a fearful light fell on everything around; so far as the eye could reach, nothing but objects of dread and horror presented themselves. Vainly striving to utter a cry of terror, with his tongue cleaving to his mouth, he rushed madly forward. Armed with supernatural strength, he waded through the sand, until exhausted with fatigue and thirst, he fell senseless on the earth. What fragrant coolness revived him; what gushing sound was that? Water! It was indeed a well; and the clear fresh stream was running at his feet. He drank deeply of it, and throwing his aching limbs upon the bank, sunk into a delicious trance. The sound of approaching footsteps roused him. An old grey-headed man tottered forward to slake his burning thirst.

It was *he* again! He wound his arms round the old man's body, and held him back. He struggled, and shrieked for water, for but one drop of water to save his life! But he held the old man firmly, and watched his agonies with greedy eyes; and when his lifeless head fell forward on his bosom, he rolled the corpse from him with his feet.

"When the fever left him, and consciousness returned, he awoke to find himself rich and free: to hear that the parent who would have let him die in gaol—*would!* who *had* let those who were far dearer to him than his own existence, die of want and sickness of heart that medicine cannot cure—had been found dead on his bed of down. He had had all the heart to leave his son a beggar, but proud even of his health and strength, had put off the act till it was too late, and now might gnash his teeth in the other world, at the thought of the wealth his remissness had left him. He awoke to this, and he awoke to more. To recollect the purpose for which he lived, and to remember that his enemy was his wife's own father—the man who had cast him into prison, and who, when his daughter and her child sued at his feet for mercy, had spurned them from his door. Oh, how he cursed the weakness that prevented him from being up, and active, in his scheme of vengeance!

"He caused himself to be carried from the scene of his loss and misery, and conveyed to a quiet residence on the sea-coast; not in the hope of recovering his peace of mind or happiness, for both were fled for ever; but to restore his prostrate energies, and meditate on his darling object. And here, some evil spirit cast in his way the opportunity for his first, most horrible revenge.

"It was summer time; and wrapped in his gloomy thoughts, he would issue from his solitary lodgings early in the evening, and wandering along a narrow path beneath the cliffs, to a wild and lonely spot that had struck his fancy in his ramblings, seat himself on some fallen fragment of the rock, and burying his face in his hands, remain there for hours—

sometimes until night had completely closed in, and the long shadows of the frowning cliffs above his head cast a thick black darkness on every object near him.

"He was seated here, one calm evening in his old position, now and then raising his head to watch the flight of a sea-gull, or carry his eye along the glorious crimson path, which, commencing in the middle of the ocean, seemed to lead to its very verge where the sun was setting, when the profound stillness of the spot was broken by a loud cry for help; he listened, doubtful of his having heard aright, when the cry was repeated with even greater vehemence than before, and starting to his feet, he hastened in the direction whence it proceeded.

"The tale told itself at once: some scattered garments lay on the beach; a human head was just visible above the waves at a little distance from the shore; and an old man, wringing his hands in agony, was running to and fro, shrieking for assistance. The invalid, whose strength was now sufficiently restored, threw off his coat, and rushed towards the sea, with the intention of plunging in, and dragging the drowning man a-shore.

"'Hasten here, sir, in God's name; help, help, sir, for the love of Heaven. He is my son, sir, my only son!' said the old man, frantically, as he advanced to meet him. 'My only son, sir, and he is dying before his father's eyes!'

"At the first word the old man uttered, the stranger checked himself in his career, and, folding his arms, stood perfectly motionless.

"'Great God!' exclaimed the old man, recoiling. 'Heyling!'

"The stranger smiled, and was silent.

"'Heyling!' said the old man, wildly: 'My boy, Heyling, my dear boy, look, look!' gasping for breath, the miserable father pointed to the spot where the young man was struggling for life.

"'Hark!' said the old man. 'He cries once more. He is alive yet. Heyling, save him, save him!'

"The stranger smiled again, and remained immovable as a statue.

"'I have wronged you,' shrieked the old man, falling on his knees, and clasping his hands together. 'Be revenged; take my all, my life; cast me into the water at your feet, and, if human nature can repress a struggle, I will die, without stirring hand or foot. Do it, Heyling, do it, but save my boy, he is so young, Heyling, so young to die!'

"'Listen,' said the stranger, grasping the old man fiercely by the wrist: 'I will have life for life, and here is ONE. *My* child died, before his father's eyes, a far more agonising and painful death than that young slanderer of his sister's worth is meeting while I speak. You laughed—laughed in your daughter's face, where death had already set his hand—at our sufferings, then. What think you of them now? See there, see there!'

"As the stranger spoke, he pointed to the sea. A faint cry died away upon its surface: the last powerful struggle of the dying man agitated the rippling waves for a few seconds: and the spot where he had gone down into his early grave, was undistinguishable from the surrounding water.

"Three years had elapsed, when a gentleman alighted from a private carriage at the door of a London attorney, then well known as a man of no great nicety in his professional dealings: and requested a private interview on business of importance. Although evidently not past the prime of life, his face was pale, haggard, and dejected; and it did not require the acute perception of the man of business, to discern at a glance, that disease or suffering had done more to work a change in his appearance, than the mere hand of time could have accomplished in twice the period of his whole life.

"'I wish you to undertake some legal business for me,' said the stranger.

"The attorney bowed obsequiously, and glanced at a large

packet which the gentleman carried in his hand. His visitor observed the look, and proceeded.

"'It is no common business,' said he; 'nor have these papers reached my hands without long trouble and great expense.'

"The attorney cast a still more anxious look at the packet: and his visitor, untying the string that bound it, disclosed a quantity of promissory notes, with copies of deeds, and other documents.

"'Upon these papers,' said the client, 'the man whose name they bear, has raised, as you will see, large sums of money, for some years past. There was a tacit understanding between him and the men into whose hands they originally went—and from whom I have by degrees purchased the whole, for treble and quadruple their nominal value—that these loans should be from time to time renewed, until a given period had elapsed. Such an understanding is nowhere expressed. He has sustained many losses of late; and these obligations accumulating upon him at once, would crush him to the earth.'

"'The whole amount is many thousands of pounds,' said the attorney, looking over the papers.

"'It is,' said the client.

"'What are we to do?' inquired the man of business.

"'Do!' replied the client, with sudden vehemence. 'Put every engine of the law in force, every trick that ingenuity can devise and rascality execute; fair means and foul; the open oppression of the law, aided by all the craft of its most ingenious practitioners. I would have him die a harassing and lingering death. Ruin him, seize and sell his lands and goods, drive him from house and home, and drag him forth a beggar in his old age, to die in a common grave."

"'But the costs, my dear sir, the costs of all this,' reasoned the attorney, when he had recovered from his momentary surprise. 'If the defendant be a man of straw, who is to pay the costs, sir?'

"'Name any sum,' said the stranger, his hand trembling so violently with excitement, that he could scarcely hold the pen he seized as he spoke; 'Any sum, and it is yours. Don't be afraid to name it, man. I shall not think it dear, if you gain my object.'

"The attorney named a large sum, at hazard, as the advance he should require to secure himself against the possibility of loss; but more with the view of ascertaining how far his client was really disposed to go, than with any idea that he would comply with the demand. The stranger wrote a cheque upon his banker, for the whole amount, and left him.

"The draft was duly honoured, and the attorney, finding that his strange client might be safely relied upon, commenced his work in earnest. For more than two years afterwards, Mr. Heyling would sit whole days together, in the office, poring over the papers as they accumulated, and reading again and again, his eyes gleaming with joy, the letters of remonstrance, the prayers for a little delay, the representations of the certain ruin in which the opposite party must be involved, which poured in, as suit after suit, and process after process, was commenced. To all applications for a brief indulgence, there was but one reply—the money must be paid. Land, house, furniture, each in its turn, was taken under some one of the numerous executions which were issued; and the old man himself would have been immured in prison had he not escaped the vigilance of the officers, and fled.

"The implacable animosity of Heyling, so far from being satiated by the success of his persecution, increased a hundred-fold with the ruin he inflicted. On being informed of the old man's flight, his fury was unbounded. He gnashed his teeth with rage, tore the hair from his head, and assailed with horrid imprecations the men who had been entrusted with the writ. He was only restored to comparative calmness by repeated assurances of the certainty of discovering the fugitive. Agents were sent in quest of him, in all directions; every stratagem that could be invented was resorted to, for the purpose of discovering his place of retreat; but it was all in vain. Half a year had passed over, and he was still undiscovered.

"At length, late one night, Heyling, of whom nothing had been seen for many weeks before, appeared at his attorney's private residence, and sent up word that a gentleman wished to see him instantly. Before the attorney, who had recognised his voice from above stairs, could order the servant to admit him, he had rushed up the staircase, and entered the drawing-room pale and breathless. Having closed the door, to prevent being overheard, he sunk into a chair, and said, in a low voice:

"Hush! I have found him at last.'

"'No!' said the attorney. 'Well done, my dear sir; well done.'

"'He lies concealed in a wretched lodging in Camden Town,' said Heyling. 'Perhaps it is as well, we *did* lose sight of him, for he has been living alone there, in the most abject misery, all the time, and he is poor—very poor.'

"'Very good,' said the attorney. 'You will have the caption made to-morrow, of course?'

"'Yes,' replied Heyling. 'Stay! No! The next day. You are surprised at my wishing to postpone it,' he added, with a ghastly smile; 'but I had forgotten. The next day is an anniversary in his life: let it be done then.'

"'Very good,' said the attorney. 'Will you write down instructions for the officer?'

"'No; let him meet me here, at eight in the evening, and I will accompany him, myself.'

"They met on the appointed night, and, hiring a hackney coach, directed the driver to stop at that corner of the old Pancras Road, at which stands the parish workhouse. By the time they alighted there, it was quite dark; and, proceeding by the dead wall in front of the Veterinary Hospital, they entered a small by-street, which is, or was at that time, called Little College Street, and which, whatever it may be now, was in those days a desolate place enough, surrounded by little else than fields and ditches.

"Having drawn the travelling cap he had on half over his face, and muffled himself in his cloak, Heyling stopped before the meanest-looking house in the street, and knocked gently at the door. It was at once opened by a woman, who dropped a curtesy of recognition, and Heyling, whispering the officer to remain below, crept gently upstairs, and, opening the door of the front room, entered at once.

"The object of his search and his unrelenting animosity, now a decrepit old man, was seated at a bare deal table, on which stood a miserable candle. He started on the entrance of the stranger, and rose feebly to his feet.

"'What now, what now?' said the old man. 'What fresh misery is this? What do you want here?'

"'A word with *you*,' replied Heyling. As he spoke, he seated himself at the other end of the table, and, throwing off his cloak and cap, disclosed his features.

"The old man seemed instantly deprived of the power of speech. He fell backward in his chair, and, clasping his hands together, gazed on the apparition with a mingled look of abhorrence and fear.

"'This day six years,' said Heyling, 'I claimed the life you owed me for my child's. Beside the lifeless form of your daughter, old man, I swore to live a life of revenge. I have never swerved from my purpose for a moment's space; but if I had, one thought of her uncomplaining, suffering look, as she drooped away, or of the starving face of our innocent child, would have nerved me to my task. My first act of requital you well remember: this is my last.'

"The old man shivered, and his hands dropped powerless by his side.

"'I leave England to-morrow,' said Heyling, after a moment's pause. 'To-night I consign you to the living death to which you devoted her—a hopeless prison—'

"He raised his eyes to the old man's countenance, and

The Last Visit of Heyling to the Old Man

paused. He lifted the light to his face, set it gently down, and left the apartment.

"'You had better see to the old man,' he said to the woman, as he opened the door, and motioned the officer to follow him into the street. 'I think he is ill.' The woman closed the door, ran hastily up stairs, and found him lifeless.

"Beneath a plain grave-stone, in one of the most peaceful and secluded churchyards in Kent, where wild flowers mingle with the grass, and the soft landscape around forms the fairest spot in the garden of England, lie the bones of the young mother and her gentle child. But the ashes of the father do not mingle with theirs; nor, from that night forward, did the attorney ever gain the remotest clue to the subsequent history of his queer client."

As the old man concluded his tale, he advanced to a peg in one corner, and taking down his hat and coat, put them on with great deliberation; and, without saying another word, walked slowly away. As the gentleman with the Mosaic studs had fallen asleep, and the major part of the company were deeply occupied in the humorous process of dropping melted tallow-grease into his brandy and water, Mr. Pickwick departed unnoticed, and having settled his own score, and that of Mr. Weller, issued forth, in company with that gentleman, from beneath the portal of the Magpie and Stump.

CHAPTER XXII.

MR. PICKWICK JOURNEYS TO IPSWICH, AND MEETS WITH A
ROMANTIC ADVENTURE WITH A MIDDLE-AGED LADY IN
YELLOW CURL PAPERS.

"THAT 'ere your governor's luggage, Sammy?" inquired
Mr. Weller of his affectionate son, as he entered the yard of
the Bull inn, Whitechapel, with a travelling bag and a small
portmanteau.

"You might ha' made a worser guess than that, old feller,"
replied Mr. Weller the younger, setting down his burden
in the yard, and sitting himself down upon it afterwards.
"The Governor hisself'll be down here presently."

"He's a cabbin' it, I suppose?" said the father.

"Yes, he's a havin' two mile o' danger at eight-pence,"
responded the son. "How's mother-in-law this mornin'?"

"Queer, Sammy, queer," replied the elder Mr. Weller, with
impressive gravity. "She's been gettin' rayther in the
Methodistical order lately, Sammy; and she is uncommon
pious, to be sure. She's too good a creetur for me, Sammy.
I feel I don't deserve her."

"Ah," said Mr. Samuel, "that's wery self-denyin' o' you."

"Wery," replied his parent, with a sigh. "She's got hold
o' some inwention for grown-up people being born again,
Sammy; the new birth, I thinks they calls it. I should wery
much like to see that system in haction, Sammy. I should
wery much like to see your mother-in-law born again.
Wouldn't I put her out to nurse!"

A FRESH DEPARTURE.

"What do you think them women does t'other day," continued Mr. Weller, after a short pause, during which he had significantly struck the side of his nose with his fore-finger some half-dozen times. "What do you think they does, t'other day, Sammy?"

"Don't know," replied Sammy, "what?"

"Goes and gets up a grand tea drinkin' for a feller they calls their shepherd," said Mr. Weller. "I was a standing starin' in at the pictur shop down at our place, when I sees a little bill about it; 'tickets half-a-crown. All applications to be made to the committee. Secretary, Mrs. Weller;' and when I got home there was the committee a sittin' in our back parlour. Fourteen women; I wish you could ha' heard 'em, Sammy. There they was, a passin' resolutions, and wotin' supplies, and all sorts o' games. Well, what with your mother-in-law a worrying me to go, and what with my looking for'ard to seein' some queer starts if I did, I put my name down for a ticket; at six o'clock on the Friday evenin' I dresses myself out wery smart, and off I goes with the old 'ooman, and up we walks into a fust floor where there was tea things for thirty, and a whole lot o' women as begins whisperin' at one another, and lookin' at me, as if they'd never seen a rayther stout gen'lm'n of eight-and-fifty afore. By and bye, there comes a great bustle down stairs, and a lanky chap with a red nose and a white neckcloth rushes up, and sings out, 'Here's the shepherd a coming to wisit his faithful flock;' and in comes a fat chap in black, vith a great white face, a smilin' avay like clockwork. Such goin's on, Sammy! 'The kiss of peace,' says the shepherd; and then he kissed the women all round, and ven he'd done, the man vith the red nose began. I was just a thinkin' whether I hadn't better begin too— 'specially as there was a wery nice lady a sittin' next me— ven in comes the tea, and your mother-in-law, as had been makin' the kettle bile down stairs. At it they went, tooth and nail. Such a precious loud hymn, Sammy, while the tea was a brewing; such a grace, such eatin' and drinkin'! I wish you could ha' seen the shepherd walkin' into the ham and muffins. I never see such a chap to eat and drink; never. The red-nosed man warn't by no means the sort of person you'd like to grub by contract, but he was nothin' to the shepherd. Well; arter the tea was over, they sang another hymn, and then the shepherd began to preach: and wery well he did it, considerin' how heavy them muffins must have lied on his chest. Presently he pulls up, all of a sudden, and hollers out 'Where is the sinner; where is the mis'rable sinner?' Upon which, all the women looked at me, and began to groan as if they was a dying. I thought it was rather sing'ler, but hows'ever, I says nothing. Presently he pulls up again, and lookin' wery hard at me, says, 'Where is the sinner; where is the mis'rable sinner?' and all the women groans again, ten times louder than afore. I got rather wild at this, so I takes a step or two for'ard and says, 'My friend,' says I, 'did you apply that 'ere obserwation to me?' 'Stead of begging my pardon as any gen'lm'n would ha' done, he got more abusive than ever: called me a wessel, Sammy—a wessel of wrath—and all sorts o' names. So my blood being reg'larly up, I first give him two or three for himself, and then two or three more to hand over to the man with the red nose, and walked off. I wish you could ha' heard how the women screamed, Sammy, ven they picked up the shepherd from under the table——Hallo! here's the governor, the size of life."

As Mr. Weller spoke, Mr. Pickwick dismounted from a cab, and entered the yard.

"Fine mornin', sir," said Mr. Weller senior.

"Beautiful indeed," replied Mr. Pickwick.

"Beautiful indeed," echoed a red-haired man with an inquisitive nose and blue spectacles, who had unpacked himself from a cab at the same moment as Mr. Pickwick. "Going to Ipswich, sir?"

"I am," replied Mr. Pickwick.

"Extraordinary coincidence. So am I."

Mr. Pickwick bowed.

ANOTHER PASSENGER.

"Going outside?" said the red-haired man.

Mr. Pickwick bowed again.

"Bless my soul, how remarkable—I am going outside, too," said the red-haired man: "we are positively going together." And the red-haired man, who was an important-looking, sharp-nosed, mysterious-spoken personage, with a bird-like habit of giving his head a jerk every time he said anything, smiled as if he had made one of the strangest discoveries that ever fell to the lot of human wisdom.

"I am happy in the prospect of your company, sir," said Mr. Pickwick.

"Ah," said the new-comer, "it's a good thing for both of us, isn't it? Company, you see—company is—is—it's a very different thing from solitude—ain't it?"

"There's no denying that 'ere," said Mr. Weller, joining in the conversation, with an affable smile. "That's what I call a self-evident proposition, as the dog's-meat man said, when the house-maid told him he warn't a gentleman."

"Ah," said the red-haired man, surveying Mr. Weller from head to foot with a supercilious look. "Friend of yours, sir?"

"Not exactly a friend," replied Mr. Pickwick in a low tone. "The fact is, he is my servant, but I allow him to take a good many liberties; for, between ourselves, I flatter myself he is an original, and I am rather proud of him."

"Ah," said the red-haired man, "that, you see, is a matter of taste. I am not fond of anything original; I don't like it; don't see the necessity for it. What's your name, sir?"

"Here is my card, sir," replied Mr. Pickwick, much amused by the abruptness of the question, and the singular manner of the stranger.

"Ah," said the red-haired man, placing the card in his pocket-book, "Pickwick; very good. I like to know a man's name, it saves so much trouble. That's my card, sir, Magnus, you will perceive, sir—Magnus is my name. It's rather a good name, I think, sir?"

357

"A very good name, indeed," said Mr. Pickwick, wholly unable to repress a smile.

"Yes, I think it is," resumed Mr. Magnus. "There's a good name before it, too, you will observe. Permit me, sir —if you hold the card a little slanting, this way, you catch the light upon the up-stroke. There—Peter Magnus—sounds well, I think, sir."

"Very," said Mr. Pickwick.

"Curious circumstance about those initials, sir," said Mr. Magnus. "You will observe—P.M.—post meridian. In hasty notes to intimate acquaintance, I sometimes sign myself 'Afternoon.' It amuses my friends very much, Mr. Pickwick."

"It is calculated to afford them the highest gratification, I should conceive," said Mr. Pickwick, rather envying the ease with which Mr. Magnus's friends were entertained.

"Now, gen'lm'n," said the hostler, "coach is ready, if you please."

"Is all my luggage in?" inquired Mr. Magnus.

"All right, sir."

"Is the red bag in?"

"All right, sir."

"And the striped bag?"

"Fore boot, sir."

"And the brown-paper parcel?"

"Under the seat, sir."

"And the leather hat-box?"

"They're all in, sir."

"Now, will you get up?" said Mr. Pickwick.

"Excuse me," replied Magnus, standing on the wheel. "Excuse me, Mr. Pickwick. I cannot consent to get up, in this state of uncertainty. I am quite satisfied from that man's manner, that that leather hat-box is *not* in."

The solemn protestations of the hostler being wholly unavailing, the leather hat-box was obliged to be raked up from the lowest depth of the boot, to satisfy him that it had been safely packed; and after he had been assured on this head, he felt a solemn presentiment, first, that the red bag was mislaid, and next that the striped bag had been stolen, and then that the brown-paper parcel "had come untied." At length when he had received ocular demonstration of the groundless nature of each and every of these suspicions, he consented to climb up to the roof of the coach, observing that now he had taken every thing off his mind, he felt quite comfortable and happy.

"You're given to nervousness, an't you, sir?" inquired Mr. Weller senior, eyeing the stranger askance, as he mounted to his place.

"Yes; I always am rather, about these little matters," said the stranger, "but I am all right now—quite right."

"Well, that's a blessin'," said Mr. Weller. "Sammy, help your master up to the box: t'other leg, sir, that's it; give us your hand, sir. Up with you. You was a lighter weight when you was a boy, sir."

"True enough, that, Mr. Weller," said the breathless Mr. Pickwick, good humouredly, as he took his seat on the box beside him.

"Jump up in front, Sammy," said Mr. Weller. "Now Villam, run 'em out. Take care o' the archvay, gen'lm'n. 'Heads,' as the pieman says. That'll do, Villam. Let 'em alone." And away went the coach up Whitechapel, to the admiration of the whole population of that pretty-densely populated quarter.

"Not a wery nice neighbourhood this, sir," said Sam, with a touch of the hat, which always preceded his entering into conversation with his master.

"It is not indeed, Sam," replied Mr. Pickwick, surveying the crowded and filthy street through which they were passing.

"It's a wery remarkable circumstance, sir," said Sam, "that poverty and oysters always seems to go together."

"I don't understand you, Sam," said Mr. Pickwick.

"What I mean, sir," said Sam, "is, that the poorer a place is, the greater call there seems to be for oysters. Look

here, sir; here's a oyster stall to every half-dozen houses.
The street's lined vith 'em. Blessed if I don't think that ven
a man's wery poor, he rushes out of his lodgings, and eats
oysters in reg'lar desperation."

"To be sure he does," said Mr. Weller senior; "and it's
just the same vith pickled salmon!"

"Those are two very remarkable facts, which never occurred
to me before," said Mr. Pickwick. "The very first place we
stop at, I'll make a note of them."

By this time they had reached the turnpike at Mile End;
a profound silence prevailed until they had got two or three
miles further on, when Mr. Weller senior, turning suddenly
to Mr. Pickwick, said:

"Wery queer life is a pike-keeper's, sir."

"A what?" said Mr. Pickwick.

"A pike-keeper."

"What do you mean by a pike-keeper?" inquired Mr.
Peter Magnus.

"The old 'un means a turnpike keeper, gen'lm'n," observed
Mr. Samuel Weller, in explanation.

"Oh," said Mr. Pickwick, "I see. Yes; very curious life.
Very uncomfortable."

"They're all on 'em men as has met vith some disappointment in life," said Mr. Weller senior.

"Ay, ay?" said Mr. Pickwick.

"Yes. Consequence of vich, they retires from the world,
and shuts themselves up in pikes; partly vith the view of
being solitary, and partly to rewenge themselves on mankind,
by takin' tolls."

"Dear me," said Mr. Pickwick, "I never knew that before."

"Fact, sir," said Mr. Weller; "if they was gen'lm'n
you'd call 'em misanthropes, but as it is, they only takes to
pike-keepin'."

With such conversation, possessing the inestimable charm
of blending amusement with instruction, did Mr. Weller
beguile the tediousness of the journey, during the greater

part of the day. Topics of conversation were never wanting, for even when any pause occurred in Mr. Weller's loquacity, it was abundantly supplied by the desire evinced by Mr. Magnus to make himself acquainted with the whole of the personal history of his fellow-travellers, and his loudly-expressed anxiety at every stage, respecting the safety and well-being of the two bags, the leather hat-box, and the brown-paper parcel.

In the main street of Ipswich, on the left-hand side of the way, a short distance after you have passed through the open space fronting the Town Hall, stands an inn known far and wide by the appellation of The Great White Horse, rendered the more conspicuous by a stone statue of some rampacious animal with flowing mane and tail, distantly resembling an insane cart-horse, which is elevated above the principal door. The Great White Horse is famous in the neighbourhood, in the same degree as a prize ox, or county paper-chronicled turnip, or unwieldy pig—for its enormous size. Never were such labyrinths of uncarpeted passages, such clusters of mouldy, ill-lighted rooms, such huge numbers of small dens for eating or sleeping in, beneath any one roof, as are collected together between the four walls of the Great White Horse at Ipswich.

It was at the door of this overgrown tavern that the London coach stopped, at the same hour every evening; and it was from this same London coach, that Mr. Pickwick, Sam Weller, and Mr. Peter Magnus dismounted, on the particular evening to which this chapter of our history bears reference.

"Do you stop here, sir?" inquired Mr. Peter Magnus, when the striped bag, and the red bag, and the brown-paper parcel, and the leather hat-box, had all been deposited in the passage. "Do you stop here, sir?"

"I do," said Mr. Pickwick.

"Dear me," said Mr. Magnus, "I never knew anything like these extraordinary coincidences. Why, I stop here too. I hope we dine together?"

"With pleasure," replied Mr. Pickwick. "I am not quite certain whether I have any friends here or not, though. Is there any gentleman of the name of Tupman here, waiter?"

A corpulent man, with a fortnight's napkin under his arm, and coeval stockings on his legs, slowly desisted from his occupation of staring down the street, on this question being put to him by Mr. Pickwick; and, after minutely inspecting that gentleman's appearance, from the crown of his hat to the lowest button of his gaiters, replied emphatically:

"No."

"Nor any gentleman of the name of Snodgrass?" inquired Mr. Pickwick.

"No!"

"Nor Winkle?"

"No."

"My friends have not arrived to-day, sir," said Mr. Pickwick. "We will dine alone, then. Shew us a private room, waiter."

On this request being preferred, the corpulent man condescended to order the boots to bring in the gentleman's luggage; and preceding them down a long dark passage, ushered them into a large badly-furnished apartment, with a dirty grate, in which a small fire was making a wretched attempt to be cheerful, but was fast sinking beneath the dispiriting influence of the place. After the lapse of an hour, a bit of fish and a steak were served up to the travellers, and when the dinner was cleared away, Mr. Pickwick and Mr. Peter Magnus drew their chairs up to the fire, and having ordered a bottle of the worst possible port wine, at the highest possible price, for the good of the house, drank brandy and water for their own.

Mr. Peter Magnus was naturally of a very communicative disposition, and the brandy and water operated with wonderful effect in warming into life the deepest hidden secrets of his bosom. After sundry accounts of himself, his family, his connexions, his friends, his jokes, his business, and his brothers (most talkative men have a great deal to say about their brothers), Mr. Peter Magnus took a blue view of Mr. Pickwick through his coloured spectacles for several minutes, and then said, with an air of modesty:

"And what do you think—what *do* you think, Mr. Pickwick—I have come down here for?"

"Upon my word," said Mr. Pickwick, "it is wholly impossible for me to guess; on business, perhaps."

"Partly right, sir," replied Mr. Peter Magnus, "but partly wrong, at the same time: try again, Mr. Pickwick."

"Really," said Mr. Pickwick, "I must throw myself on your mercy, to tell me or not, as you may think best; for I should never guess, if I were to try all night."

"Why, then, he—he—he!" said Mr. Peter Magnus, with a bashful titter, "what should you think, Mr. Pickwick, if I had come down here, to make a proposal, sir, eh? He—he—he!"

"Think! That you are very likely to succeed," replied Mr. Pickwick, with one of his beaming smiles.

"Ah!" said Mr. Magnus. "But do you really think so, Mr. Pickwick? Do you, though?"

"Certainly," said Mr. Pickwick.

"No; but you're joking, though."

"I am not, indeed."

"Why, then," said Mr. Magnus, "to let you into a little secret, *I* think so too. I don't mind telling you, Mr. Pickwick, although I'm dreadful jealous by nature—horrid—that the lady is in this house." Here Mr. Magnus took off his spectacles, on purpose to wink, and then put them on again.

"That's what you were running out of the room for, before dinner, then, so often," said Mr. Pickwick, archly.

"Hush! Yes, you're right, that was it; not such a fool as to see her, though."

"No!"

"No; wouldn't do, you know, after having just come off a journey. Wait till to-morrow, sir; double the chance then. Mr. Pickwick, sir, there is a suit of clothes in that bag, and a hat in that box, which I expect, in the effect they will produce, will be invaluable to me, sir."

" Indeed!" said Mr. Pickwick.

" Yes; you must have observed my anxiety about them to-day. I do not believe that such another suit of clothes, and such a hat, could be bought for money, Mr. Pickwick."

Mr. Pickwick congratulated the fortunate owner of the irresistible garments, on their acquisition; and Mr. Peter Magnus remained for a few moments apparently absorbed in contemplation.

" She's a fine creature," said Mr. Magnus.

" Is she?" said Mr. Pickwick.

" Very," said Mr. Magnus, " very. She lives about twenty miles from here, Mr. Pickwick. I heard she would be here to-night and all to-morrow forenoon, and came down to seize the opportunity. I think an inn is a good sort of a place to propose to a single woman in, Mr. Pickwick. She is more likely to feel the loneliness of her situation in travelling, perhaps, than she would be at home. What do you think, Mr. Pickwick?"

" I think it very probable," replied that gentleman.

" I beg your pardon, Mr. Pickwick," said Mr. Peter Magnus, " but I am naturally rather curious; what may *you* have come down here for?"

" On a far less pleasant errand, sir," replied Mr. Pickwick, the colour mounting to his face at the recollection. " I have come down here, sir, to expose the treachery and falsehood of an individual, upon whose truth and honour I placed implicit reliance."

" Dear me," said Mr. Peter Magnus, " that's very unpleasant. It is a lady, I presume? Eh? ah! Sly, Mr. Pickwick, sly. Well, Mr. Pickwick, sir, I wouldn't probe your feelings for the world. Painful subjects, these, sir, very painful. Don't mind me, Mr. Pickwick, if you wish to give vent to your feelings. I know what it is to be jilted, sir; I have endured that sort of thing three or four times."

RETIRING TO REST.

"I am much obliged to you, for your condolence on what you presume to be my melancholy case," said Mr. Pickwick, winding up his watch, and laying it on the table, "but—"

"No, no," said Mr. Peter Magnus, "not a word more: it's a painful subject. I see, I see. What's the time, Mr. Pickwick?"

"Past twelve."

"Dear me, it's time to go to bed. It will never do, sitting here. I shall be pale to-morrow, Mr. Pickwick."

At the bare notion of such a calamity, Mr. Peter Magnus rang the bell for the chamber-maid; and the striped bag, the red bag, the leathern hat-box, and the brown-paper parcel, having been conveyed to his bed-room, he retired in company with a japanned candlestick, to one side of the house, while Mr. Pickwick, and another japanned candlestick, were conducted through a multitude of tortuous windings, to another.

"This is your room, sir," said the chamber-maid.

"Very well," replied Mr. Pickwick, looking round him. It was a tolerably large double-bedded room, with a fire; upon the whole, a more comfortable-looking apartment than Mr. Pickwick's short experience of the accommodations of the Great White Horse had led him to expect.

"Nobody sleeps in the other bed, of course," said Mr. Pickwick.

"Oh, no, sir."

"Very good. Tell my servant to bring me up some hot water at half-past eight in the morning, and that I shall not want him any more to-night."

"Yes, sir." And bidding Mr. Pickwick good night, the chamber-maid retired, and left him alone.

Mr. Pickwick sat himself down in a chair before the fire, and fell into a train of rambling meditations. First he thought of his friends, and wondered when they would join him; then his mind reverted to Mrs. Martha Bardell; and from that lady it wandered, by a natural process, to the dingy counting-house of Dodson and Fogg. From Dodson and Fogg's it flew off at a tangent, to the very centre of the history of the queer client; and then it came back to the Great White Horse at Ipswich, with sufficient clearness to convince Mr. Pickwick that he was falling asleep. So he roused himself, and began to undress, when he recollected he had left his watch on the table down stairs.

Now, this watch was a special favourite with Mr. Pickwick, having been carried about, beneath the shadow of his waist-coat, for a greater number of years than we feel called upon to state at present. The possibility of going to sleep, unless it were ticking gently beneath his pillow, or in the watch-pocket over his head, had never entered Mr. Pickwick's brain. So as it was pretty late now, and he was unwilling to ring his bell at that hour of the night, he slipped on his coat, of which he had just divested himself, and taking the japanned candlestick in his hand, walked quietly down stairs.

The more stairs Mr. Pickwick went down, the more stairs there seemed to be to descend, and again and again, when Mr. Pickwick got into some narrow passage, and began to congratulate himself on having gained the ground-floor, did another flight of stairs appear before his astonished eyes. At last he reached a stone hall, which he remembered to have seen when he entered the house. Passage after passage did he explore; room after room did he peep into; at length, as he was on the point of giving up the search in despair, he opened the door of the identical room in which he had spent the evening, and beheld his missing property on the table.

Mr. Pickwick seized the watch in triumph, and proceeded to re-trace his steps to his bed-chamber. If his progress downward had been attended with difficulties and uncertainty, his journey back was infinitely more perplexing. Rows of doors, garnished with boots of every shape, make, and size, branched off in every possible direction. A dozen times did he softly turn the handle of some bed-room door which resembled his own, when a gruff cry from within of "Who the devil's that?" or "What do you want here?" caused him to steal away, on tiptoe, with a perfectly marvellous celerity. He was reduced to the verge of despair, when an open door attracted his attention. He peeped in. Right at last! There were the two beds, whose situation he perfectly remembered, and the fire still burning. His candle, not a long one when he first received it, had flickered away in the drafts of air through which he had passed, and sank into the socket as he closed the door after him. "No matter," said Mr. Pickwick, "I can undress myself just as well by the light of the fire."

The bedsteads stood one on each side of the door; and on the inner side of each was a little path, terminating in a rush-bottomed chair, just wide enough to admit of a person's getting into, or out of bed, on that side, if he or she thought proper. Having carefully drawn the curtains of his bed on the outside, Mr. Pickwick sat down on the rush-bottomed chair, and leisurely divested himself of his shoes and gaiters. He then took off and folded up his coat, waistcoat, and neckcloth, and slowly drawing on his tasseled night-cap, secured it firmly on his head, by tying beneath his chin the strings which he always had attached to that article of dress. It was at this moment that the absurdity of his recent bewilderment struck upon his mind. Throwing himself back in the rush-bottomed chair, Mr. Pickwick laughed to himself so heartily, that it would have been quite delightful to any man of well-constituted mind to have watched the smiles that expanded his amiable features as they shone forth from beneath the night-cap.

"It is the best idea," said Mr. Pickwick to himself, smiling till he almost cracked the night-cap strings: "It is the best idea, my losing myself in this place, and wandering about those staircases, that I ever heard of. Droll, droll, very droll." Here Mr. Pickwick smiled again, a broader smile than before, and was about to continue the process of undressing, in the best possible humour, when he was suddenly stopped by a most unexpected interruption; to wit, the entrance into the room of some person with a candle, who, after locking the door, advanced to the dressing table, and set down the light upon it.

The smile that played on Mr. Pickwick's features was instantaneously lost in a look of the most unbounded and wonder-stricken surprise. The person, whoever it was, had come in so suddenly and with so little noise, that Mr. Pickwick had had no time to call out, or oppose their entrance. Who could it be? A robber? Some evil-minded person who had seen him come up stairs with a handsome watch in his hand, perhaps. What was he to do!

The only way in which Mr. Pickwick could catch a glimpse of his mysterious visitor with the least danger of being seen himself, was by creeping on to the bed, and peeping out from between the curtains on the opposite side. To this manœuvre he accordingly resorted. Keeping the curtains carefully closed with his hand, so that nothing more of him could be seen than his face and night-cap, and putting on his spectacles, he mustered up courage, and looked out.

Mr. Pickwick almost fainted with horror and dismay. Standing before the dressing-glass was a middle-aged lady, in yellow curl-papers, busily engaged in brushing what ladies call their " back-hair." However the unconscious middle-aged lady came into that room, it was quite clear that she contemplated remaining there for the night; for she had brought a rushlight and shade with her, which, with praiseworthy precaution against fire, she had stationed in a basin on the floor, where it was glimmering away, like a gigantic light-house in a particularly small piece of water.

"Bless my soul," thought Mr. Pickwick, "what a dreadful thing!"

"Hem!" said the lady; and in went Mr. Pickwick's head with automaton-like rapidity.

"I never met with anything so awful as this," thought

The Middle-Aged Lady in the Double-Bedded Room

poor Mr. Pickwick, the cold perspiration starting in drops upon his night-cap. "Never. This is fearful."

It was quite impossible to resist the urgent desire to see what was going forward. So out went Mr. Pickwick's head again. The prospect was worse than before. The middle-aged lady had finished arranging her hair; had carefully enveloped it in a muslin night-cap with a small plaited border; and was gazing pensively on the fire.

"This matter is growing alarming," reasoned Mr. Pickwick with himself. "I can't allow things to go on in this way. By the self-possession of that lady it is clear to me that I must have come into the wrong room. If I call out she'll alarm the house; but if I remain here the consequences will be still more frightful."

Mr. Pickwick, it is quite unnecessary to say, was one of the most modest and delicate-minded of mortals. The very idea of exhibiting his night-cap to a lady overpowered him, but he had tied those confounded strings in a knot, and, do what he would, he couldn't get it off. The disclosure must be made. There was only one other way of doing it. He shrunk behind the curtains, and called out very loudly:

"Ha—hum!"

That the lady started at this unexpected sound was evident, by her falling up against the rushlight shade; that she persuaded herself it must have been the effect of imagination was equally clear, for when Mr. Pickwick, under the impression that she had fainted away stone-dead from fright, ventured to peep out again, she was gazing pensively on the fire as before.

"Most extraordinary female this," thought Mr. Pickwick, popping in again. "Ha—hum!"

These last sounds, so like those in which, as legends inform us, the ferocious giant Blunderbore was in the habit of expressing his opinion that it was time to lay the cloth, were too distinctly audible to be again mistaken for the workings of fancy.

"Gracious Heaven!" said the middle-aged lady, "what's that?"

"It's—it's—only a gentleman, Ma'am," said Mr. Pickwick from behind the curtains.

"A gentleman!" said the lady with a terrific scream.

"It's all over!" thought Mr. Pickwick.

"A strange man!" shrieked the lady. Another instant and the house would be alarmed. Her garments rustled as she rushed towards the door.

"Ma'am," said Mr. Pickwick, thrusting out his head, in the extremity of his desperation, "Ma'am!"

Now, although Mr. Pickwick was not actuated by any definite object in putting out his head, it was instantaneously productive of a good effect. The lady, as we have already stated, was near the door. She must pass it, to reach the staircase, and she would most undoubtedly have done so by this time, had not the sudden apparition of Mr. Pickwick's night-cap driven her back into the remotest corner of the apartment, where she stood staring wildly at Mr. Pickwick, while Mr. Pickwick in his turn stared wildly at her.

"Wretch," said the lady, covering her eyes with her hands, "what do you want here?"

"Nothing, Ma'am; nothing, whatever, Ma'am;" said Mr. Pickwick earnestly.

"Nothing!" said the lady, looking up.

"Nothing, Ma'am, upon my honour," said Mr. Pickwick, nodding his head so energetically that the tassel of his night-cap danced again. "I am almost ready to sink, Ma'am, beneath the confusion of addressing a lady in my night-cap (here the lady hastily snatched off hers), but I can't get it off, Ma'am (here Mr. Pickwick gave it a tremendous tug, in proof of the statement). It is evident to me, Ma'am, now, that I have mistaken this bed-room for my own. I had not been here five minutes, Ma'am, when you suddenly entered it."

"If this improbable story be really true, sir," said the lady, sobbing violently, "you will leave it instantly."

POLITENESS UNDER DIFFICULTIES.

"I will, Ma'am, with the greatest pleasure," replied Mr. Pickwick.

"Instantly, sir," said the lady.

"Certainly, Ma'am," interposed Mr. Pickwick very quickly. "Certainly, Ma'am. I—I—am very sorry, Ma'am," said Mr. Pickwick, making his appearance at the bottom of the bed, "to have been the innocent occasion of this alarm and emotion; deeply sorry, Ma'am."

The lady pointed to the door. One excellent quality of Mr. Pickwick's character was beautifully displayed at this moment, under the most trying circumstances. Although he had hastily put on his hat over his night-cap, after the manner of the old patrol; although he carried his shoes and gaiters in his hand, and his coat and waistcoat over his arm; nothing could subdue his native politeness.

"I am exceedingly sorry, Ma'am," said Mr. Pickwick, bowing very low.

"If you are, sir, you will at once leave the room," said the lady.

"Immediately, Ma'am; this instant, Ma'am," said Mr. Pickwick, opening the door, and dropping both his shoes with a crash in so doing.

"I trust, Ma'am," resumed Mr. Pickwick, gathering up his shoes, and turning round to bow again : "I trust, Ma'am, that my unblemished character, and the devoted respect I entertain for your sex, will plead as some slight excuse for this"—But before Mr. Pickwick could conclude the sentence the lady had thrust him into the passage, and locked and bolted the door behind him.

Whatever grounds of self-congratulation Mr. Pickwick might have for having escaped so quietly from his late awkward situation, his present position was by no means enviable. He was alone, in an open passage, in a strange house, in the middle of the night, half dressed; it was not to be supposed that he could find his way in perfect darkness to a room which he had been wholly unable to discover with a light, and if he made the slightest noise in his fruitless attempts to do so, he stood every chance of being shot at, and perhaps killed, by some wakeful traveller. He had no resource but to remain where he was until daylight appeared. So after groping his way a few paces down the passage, and, to his infinite alarm, stumbling over several pairs of boots in so doing, Mr. Pickwick crouched into a little recess in the wall, to wait for morning as philosophically as he might.

He was not destined, however, to undergo this additional trial of patience: for he had not been long ensconced in his present concealment when, to his unspeakable horror, a man, bearing a light, appeared at the end of the passage. His horror was suddenly converted into joy, however, when he recognised the form of his faithful attendant. It was indeed Mr. Samuel Weller, who after sitting up thus late, in conversation with the Boots, who was sitting up for the mail, was now about to retire to rest.

"Sam," said Mr. Pickwick, suddenly appearing before him, "where's my bed-room?"

Mr. Weller stared at his master with the most emphatic surprise; and it was not until the question had been repeated three several times, that he turned round, and led the way to the long-sought apartment.

"Sam," said Mr. Pickwick as he got into bed, "I have made one of the most extraordinary mistakes to-night, that ever were heard of."

"Wery likely, sir," replied Mr. Weller drily.

"But of this I am determined, Sam," said Mr. Pickwick; "that if I were to stop in this house for six months, I would never trust myself about it, alone, again."

"That's the wery prudentest resolution as you could come to, sir," replied Mr. Weller. "You rayther want somebody to look arter you, sir, wen your judgment goes out a wisitin'."

"What do you mean by that, Sam?" said Mr. Pickwick. He raised himself in bed, and extended his hand, as if he were about to say something more; but suddenly checking himself, turned round, and bade his valet "Good night."

"Good night, sir," replied Mr. Weller. He paused when he got outside the door—shook his head—walked on—stopped —snuffed the candle—shook his head again—and finally proceeded slowly to his chamber, apparently buried in the profoundest meditation.

CHAPTER XXIII

IN WHICH MR. SAMUEL WELLER BEGINS TO DEVOTE HIS ENERGIES
TO THE RETURN MATCH BETWEEN HIMSELF AND MR. TROTTER.

In a small room in the vicinity of the stable-yard, betimes
in the morning, which was ushered in by Mr. Pickwick's
adventure with the middle-aged lady in the yellow curl-papers,
sat Mr. Weller senior, preparing himself for his journey to
London. He was sitting in an excellent attitude for having
his portrait taken.

It is very possible that at some earlier period of his
career, Mr. Weller's profile might have presented a bold and
determined outline. His face, however, had expanded under
the influence of good living, and a disposition remarkable
for resignation; and its bold fleshy curves had so far extended
beyond the limits originally assigned them, that unless you
took a full view of his countenance in front, it was difficult to
distinguish more than the extreme tip of a very rubicund
nose. His chin, from the same cause, had acquired the grave
and imposing form which is generally described by prefixing
the word "double" to that expressive feature; and his com-
plexion exhibited that peculiarly mottled combination of
colours which is only to be seen in gentlemen of his profession,
and in underdone roast beef. Round his neck he wore a
crimson travelling shawl, which merged into his chin by
such imperceptible gradations, that it was difficult to
distinguish the folds of the one, from the folds of the other.

Over this, he mounted a long waistcoat of a broad pink-striped pattern, and over that again, a wide-skirted green coat, ornamented with large brass buttons, whereof the two which garnished the waist, were so far apart, that no man had ever beheld them both, at the same time. His hair, which was short, sleek, and black, was just visible beneath the capacious brim of a low-crowned brown hat. His legs were encased in knee-cord breeches, and painted top-boots: and a copper watch-chain, terminating in one seal, and a key of the same material, dangled loosely from his capacious waistband.

We have said that Mr. Weller was engaged in preparing for his journey to London—he was taking sustenance, in fact. On the table before him, stood a pot of ale, a cold round of beef, and a very respectable-looking loaf, to each of which he distributed his favours in turn, with the most rigid impartiality. He had just cut a mighty slice from the latter, when the footsteps of somebody entering the room, caused him to raise his head; and he beheld his son.

"Mornin', Sammy!" said the father.

The son walked up to the pot of ale, and nodding significantly to his parent, took a long draught by way of reply.

"Werry good power o' suction, Sammy," said Mr. Weller the elder, looking into the pot, when his first-born had set it down half empty. "You'd ha' made an uncommon fine oyster, Sammy, if you'd been born in that station o' life."

"Yes, I des-say I should ha' managed to pick up a respectable livin'," replied Sam, applying himself to the cold beef, with considerable vigour.

"I'm werry sorry, Sammy," said the elder Mr. Weller, shaking up the ale, by describing small circles with the pot, preparatory to drinking. "I'm werry sorry, Sammy, to hear from your lips, as you let yourself be gammoned by that 'ere mulberry man. I always thought, up to three days ago, that the names of Veller and gammon could never come into contract, Sammy, never."

"Always exceptin' the case of a widder, of course," said Sam.

"Widders, Sammy," replied Mr. Weller, slightly changing colour. "Widders are 'ceptions to ev'ry rule. I *have* heerd how many ord'nary women, one widder's equal to, in pint o' comin' over you. I think it's five-and-twenty, but I don't rightly know vether it an't more."

"Well; that's pretty well," said Sam.

"Besides," continued Mr. Weller, not noticing the interruption, "that's a wery different thing. You know what the counsel said, Sammy, as defended the gen'lem'n as beat his wife with the poker, venever he got jolly. 'And arter all, my Lord,' says he, 'it's a amable weakness.' So I says respectin' widders, Sammy, and so you'll say, ven you gets as old as me."

"I ought to ha' know'd better, I know," said Sam.

"Ought to ha' know'd better!" repeated Mr. Weller, striking the table with his fist. "Ought to ha' know'd better! why, I know a young 'un as hasn't had half nor quarter your eddication—as hasn't slept about the markets, no, not six months—who'd ha' scorned to be let in, in such a vay; scorned it, Sammy." In the excitement of feeling produced by this agonising reflection, Mr. Weller rang the bell, and ordered an additional pint of ale.

"Well, it's no use talking about it now," said Sam. "It's over, and can't be helped, and that's one consolation, as they always says in Turkey, ven they cuts the wrong man's head off. It's my innings now, gov'rnor, and as soon as I catches hold o' this ere Trotter, I'll have a good 'un."

"I hope you will, Sammy. I hope you will," returned Mr. Weller. "Here's your health, Sammy, and may you speedily vipe off the disgrace as you've inflicted on the family name." In honour of this toast Mr. Weller imbibed at a draught, at least two-thirds of the newly-arrived pint, and handed it over to his son, to dispose of the remainder, which he instantaneously did.

PARENTAL ADVICE.

"And now, Sammy," said Mr. Weller, consulting the large double-faced silver watch that hung at the end of the copper chain. "Now it's time I was up at the office to get my vay-bill, and see the coach loaded; for coaches, Sammy, is like guns—they requires to be loaded with wery great care, afore they go off."

At this parental and professional joke, Mr. Weller junior smiled a filial smile. His revered parent continued in a solemn tone:

"I'm a goin' to leave you, Samivel my boy, and there's no telling ven I shall see you again. Your mother-in-law may ha' been too much for me, or a thousand things may have happened by the time you next hears any news o' the celebrated Mr. Veller o' the Bell Savage. The family name depends wery much upon you, Samivel, and I hope you'll do wot's right by it. Upon all little pints o' breedin', I know I may trust you as vell as if it was my own self. So I've only this here one little bit of adwice to give you. If ever you gets to up'ards o' fifty, and feels disposed to go a marryin' anybody—no matter who—jist you shut yourself up in your own room, if you've got one, and pison yourself off hand. Hangin's wulgar, so don't you have nothin' to say to that. Pison yourself, Samivel, my boy, pison yourself, and you'll be glad on it arterwards." With these affecting words, Mr. Weller looked stedfastly on his son, and turning slowly upon his heel, disappeared from his sight.

In the contemplative mood which these words had awakened, Mr. Samuel Weller walked forth from the Great White Horse when his father had left him; and bending his steps towards St. Clement's Church, endeavoured to dissipate his melancholy, by strolling among its ancient precincts. He had loitered about, for some time, when he found himself in a retired spot —a kind of court-yard of venerable appearance—which he discovered had no other outlet than the turning by which he had entered. He was about retracing his steps, when he was suddenly transfixed to the spot by a sudden appearance: and the mode and manner of this appearance, we now proceed to relate.

Mr. Samuel Weller had been staring up, at the old brick houses now and then, in his deep abstraction, bestowing a wink upon some healthy-looking servant girl as she drew up a blind, or threw open a bed-room window, when the green gate of a garden at the bottom of the yard opened, and a man having emerged therefrom, closed the green gate very carefully after him, and walked briskly towards the very spot where Mr. Weller was standing.

Now, taking this, as an isolated fact, unaccompanied by any attendant circumstances, there was nothing very extraordinary in it; because in many parts of the world, men do come out of gardens, close green gates after them, and even walk briskly away, without attracting any particular share of public observation. It is clear, therefore, that there must have been something in the man, or in his manner, or both, to attract Mr. Weller's particular notice. Whether there was, or not, we must leave the reader to determine, when we have faithfully recorded the behaviour of the individual in question.

When the man had shut the green gate after him, he walked, as we have said twice already, with a brisk pace up the court-yard; but he no sooner caught sight of Mr. Weller, than he faltered, and stopped, as if uncertain, for the moment, what course to adopt. As the green gate was closed behind him, and there was no other outlet but the one in front, however, he was not long in perceiving that he must pass Mr. Samuel Weller to get away. He therefore resumed his brisk pace, and advanced, staring straight before him. The most extraordinary thing about the man was, that he was contorting his face into the most fearful and astonishing grimaces that ever were beheld. Nature's handywork never was disguised with such extraordinary artificial carving, as the man had overlaid his countenance with in one moment.

"Well!" said Mr. Weller to himself, as the man approached. "This is wery odd. I could ha' swore it was him."

MR. JOB TROTTER AGAIN.

Up came the man, and his face became more frightfully distorted than ever, as he drew nearer.

"I could take my oath to that 'ere black hair, and mulberry suit," said Mr. Weller; "only I never see such a face as that, afore."

As Mr. Weller said this, the man's features assumed an unearthly twinge, perfectly hideous. He was obliged to pass very near Sam, however, and the scrutinising glance of that gentleman enabled him to detect, under all these appalling twists of feature, something too like the small eyes of Mr. Job Trotter, to be easily mistaken.

"Hallo, you sir!" shouted Sam, fiercely.

The stranger stopped.

"Hallo!" repeated Sam, still more gruffly.

The man with the horrible face, looked, with the greatest surprise, up the court, and down the court, and in at the windows of the houses—everywhere but at Sam Weller—and took another step forward, when he was brought to again, by another shout.

"Hallo, you sir!" said Sam, for the third time.

There was no pretending to mistake where the voice came from now, so the stranger, having no other resource, at last looked Sam Weller full in the face.

"It won't do, Job Trotter," said Sam. "Come! None o' that 'ere nonsense. You ain't so wery 'andsome that you can afford to throw avay many o' your good looks. Bring them 'ere eyes o' your'n back into their proper places, or I'll knock 'em out of your head. D'ye hear?"

As Mr. Weller appeared fully disposed to act up to the spirit of this address, Mr. Trotter gradually allowed his face to resume its natural expression; and then giving a start of joy, exclaimed, "What do I see? Mr. Walker!"

"Ah," replied Sam. "You're wery glad to see me, ain't you?"

"Glad!" exclaimed Job Trotter; "oh, Mr. Walker, if you had but known how I have looked forward to this meeting!

379

It is too much, Mr. Walker; I cannot bear it, indeed I cannot." And with these words, Mr. Trotter burst into a regular inundation of tears, and, flinging his arms around those of Mr. Weller, embraced him closely, in an ecstasy of joy.

"Get off!" cried Sam, indignant at this process, and vainly endeavouring to extricate himself from the grasp of his enthusiastic acquaintance. "Get off, I tell you. What are you crying over me for, you portable ingine?"

"Because I am so glad to see you," replied Job Trotter, gradually releasing Mr. Weller, as the first symptoms of his pugnacity disappeared. "Oh, Mr. Walker, this is too much."

"Too much!" echoed Sam, "I think it is too much—rayther! Now what have you got to say to me, eh?"

Mr. Trotter made no reply; for the little pink pocket handkerchief was in full force.

"What have you got to say to me, afore I knock your head off?" repeated Mr. Weller, in a threatening manner.

"Eh!" said Mr. Trotter, with a look of virtuous surprise.

"What have you got to say to me?"

"I, Mr. Walker!"

"Don't call me Valker; my name's Veller; you know that vell enough. What have you got to say to me?"

"Bless you, Mr. Walker—Weller I mean—a great many things, if you will come away somewhere, where we can talk comfortably. If you knew how I have looked for you, Mr. Weller—"

"Wery hard, indeed, I s'pose?" said Sam, drily.

"Very, very, sir," replied Mr. Trotter, without moving a muscle of his face. "But shake hands, Mr. Weller."

Sam eyed his companion for a few seconds, and then, as if actuated by a sudden impulse, complied with his request.

"How," said Job Trotter, as they walked away, "How is your dear, good master? Oh, he is a worthy gentleman, Mr. Weller! I hope he didn't catch cold, that dreadful night, sir."

A TALK WITH THE MULBERRY MAN.

There was a momentary look of deep slyness in Job Trotter's eye, as he said this, which ran a thrill through Mr. Weller's clenched fist as he burnt with a desire to make a demonstration on his ribs. Sam constrained himself, however, and replied that his master was extremely well.

"Oh, I am so glad," replied Mr. Trotter, "is he here?"

"Is your'n?" asked Sam, by way of reply.

"Oh, yes, he is here, and I grieve to say, Mr. Weller, he is going on, worse than ever."

"Ah, ah?" said Sam.

"Oh, shocking—terrible!"

"At a boarding-school?" said Sam.

"No, not at a boarding-school," replied Job Trotter, with the same sly look which Sam had noticed before; "Not at a boarding-school."

"At the house with the green gate?" said Sam, eyeing his companion closely.

"No, no—oh, not there," replied Job, with a quickness very unusual to him, "not there."

"What was *you* a doin' there?" asked Sam, with a sharp glance. "Got inside the gate by accident, perhaps?"

"Why, Mr. Weller," replied Job, "I don't mind telling you my little secrets, because, you know, we took such a fancy for each other when we first met. You recollect how pleasant we were that morning?"

"Oh yes," said Sam, impatiently. "I remember. Well."

"Well," replied Job, speaking with great precision, and in the low tone of a man who communicates an important secret; "in that house with the green gate, Mr. Weller, they keep a good many servants."

"So I should think, from the look on it," interposed Sam.

"Yes," continued Mr. Trotter, "and one of them is a cook, who has saved up a little money, Mr. Weller, and is desirous, if she can establish herself in life, to open a little shop in the chandlery way, you see."

"Yes."

"Yes, Mr. Weller. Well, sir, I met her at a chapel that I go to; a very neat little chapel in this town, Mr. Weller, where they sing the number four collection of hymns, which I generally carry about with me, in a little book, which you may perhaps have seen in my hand—and I got a little intimate with her, Mr. Weller, and from that, an acquaintance sprung up between us, and I may venture to say, Mr. Weller, that I am to be the chandler."

"Ah, and a wery amiable chandler you'll make," replied Sam, eyeing Job with a side look of intense dislike.

"The great advantage of this, Mr. Weller," continued Job, his eyes filling with tears as he spoke, "will be, that I shall be able to leave my present disgraceful service with that bad man, and to devote myself to a better and more virtuous life; more like the way in which I was brought up, Mr. Weller."

"You must ha' been wery nicely brought up," said Sam.

"Oh, very, Mr. Weller, very," replied Job. At the recollection of the purity of his youthful days, Mr. Trotter pulled forth the pink handkerchief, and wept copiously.

"You must ha' been an uncommon nice boy, to go to school vith," said Sam.

"I was, sir," replied Job, heaving a deep sigh. "I was the idol of the place."

"Ah," said Sam, "I don't wonder at it. What a comfort you must ha' been to your blessed mother."

At these words, Mr. Job Trotter inserted an end of the pink handkerchief into the corner of each eye, one after the other, and began to weep copiously.

"Wot's the matter vith the man," said Sam, indignantly. "Chelsea water-works is nothin' to you. What are you melting vith now? The consciousness o' villainy?"

"I cannot keep my feelings down, Mr. Weller," said Job, after a short pause. "To think that my master should have suspected the conversation I had with yours, and so dragged me away in a post-chaise, and after persuading the sweet young lady to say she knew nothing of him, and bribing the school-mistress to do the same, deserted her for a better speculation! Oh! Mr. Weller, it makes me shudder."

"Oh, that was the vay, was it?" said Mr. Weller.

"To be sure it was," replied Job.

"Vell," said Sam, as they had now arrived near the Hotel, "I vant to have a little bit o' talk with you, Job; so if you're not partickler engaged, I should like to see you at the Great White Horse to-night, somewheres about eight o'clock."

"I shall be sure to come," said Job.

"Yes, you'd better," replied Sam, with a very meaning look, "or else I shall perhaps be asking arter you, at the other side of the green gate, and then I might cut you out, you know."

"I shall be sure to be with you, sir," said Mr. Trotter; and wringing Sam's hand with the utmost fervour, he walked away.

"Take care, Job Trotter, take care," said Sam, looking after him, "or I shall be one too many for you this time. I shall, indeed." Having uttered this soliloquy, and looked after Job till he was to be seen no more, Mr. Weller made the best of his way to his master's bed-room.

"It's all in training, sir," said Sam.

"What's in training, Sam?" inquired Mr. Pickwick.

"I have found 'em out, sir," said Sam.

"Found out who?"

"That 'ere queer customer, and the melan-cholly chap with the black hair."

"Impossible, Sam!" said Mr. Pickwick, with the greatest energy. "Where are they, Sam; where are they?"

"Hush, hush!" replied Mr. Weller; and as he assisted Mr. Pickwick to dress, he detailed the plan of action on which he proposed to enter.

"But when is this to be done, Sam?" inquired Mr. Pickwick.

"All in good time, sir," replied Sam.

Whether it was done in good time, or not, will be seen hereafter.

CHAPTER XXIV.

WHEREIN MR. PETER MAGNUS GROWS JEALOUS, AND THE MIDDLE-
AGED LADY APPREHENSIVE, WHICH BRINGS THE PICKWICKIANS
WITHIN THE GRASP OF THE LAW.

WHEN Mr. Pickwick descended to the room in which he and
Mr. Peter Magnus had spent the preceding evening, he found
that gentleman with the major part of the contents of the
two bags, the leathern hat-box, and the brown-paper parcel,
displayed to all possible advantage on his person, while he
himself was pacing up and down the room in a state of the
utmost excitement and agitation.

"Good morning, sir," said Mr. Peter Magnus. "What do
you think of this, sir?"

"Very effective indeed," replied Mr. Pickwick, surveying the
garments of Mr. Peter Magnus with a good-natured smile.

"Yes, I think it'll do," said Mr. Magnus. "Mr. Pickwick,
sir, I have sent up my card."

"Have you?" said Mr. Pickwick.

"And the waiter brought back word, that she would see
me at eleven—at eleven, sir; it only wants a quarter now."

"Very near the time," said Mr. Pickwick.

"Yes, it is rather near," replied Mr. Magnus, "rather too
near to be pleasant—eh! Mr. Pickwick, sir?"

"Confidence is a great thing in these cases," observed Mr.
Pickwick.

"I believe it is, sir," said Mr. Peter Magnus. "I am very

confident, sir. Really, Mr. Pickwick, I do not see why a man should feel any fear in such a case as this, sir. What is it, sir? There's nothing to be ashamed of; it's a matter of mutual accommodation, nothing more. Husband on one side, wife on the other. That's my view of the matter, Mr. Pickwick."

"It is a very philosophical one," replied Mr. Pickwick. "But breakfast is waiting, Mr. Magnus. Come."

Down they sat to breakfast, but it was evident, notwithstanding the boasting of Mr. Peter Magnus, that he laboured under a very considerable degree of nervousness, of which loss of appetite, a propensity to upset the tea-things, a spectral attempt at drollery, and an irresistible inclination to look at the clock, every other second, were among the principal symptoms.

"He—he—he," tittered Mr. Magnus, affecting cheerfulness, and gasping with agitation. "It only wants two minutes, Mr. Pickwick. Am I pale, sir?"

"Not very," replied Mr. Pickwick.

There was a brief pause.

"I beg your pardon, Mr. Pickwick; but have you ever done this sort of thing in your time?" said Mr. Magnus.

"You mean proposing?" said Mr. Pickwick.

"Yes."

"Never," said Mr. Pickwick, with great energy, "never."

"You have no idea, then, how it's best to begin?" said Mr. Magnus.

"Why," said Mr. Pickwick, "I may have formed some ideas upon the subject, but, as I have never submitted them to the test of experience, I should be sorry if you were induced to regulate your proceedings by them."

"I should feel very much obliged to you, for any advice, sir," said Mr. Magnus, taking another look at the clock: the hand of which was verging on the five minutes past.

"Well, sir," said Mr. Pickwick, with the profound solemnity with which that great man could, when he pleased, render

385

his remarks so deeply impressive: "I should commence, sir, with a tribute to the lady's beauty and excellent qualities; from them, sir, I should diverge to my own unworthiness."

"Very good," said Mr. Magnus.

"Unworthiness for *her* only, mind, sir," resumed Mr. Pickwick; "for to shew that I was not wholly unworthy, sir, I should take a brief review of my past life, and present condition. I should argue, by analogy, that to anybody else, I must be a very desirable object. I should then expatiate on the warmth of my love, and the depth of my devotion. Perhaps I might then be tempted to seize her hand."

"Yes, I see," said Mr. Magnus; "that would be a very great point."

"I should then, sir," continued Mr. Pickwick, growing warmer as the subject presented itself in more glowing colours before him: "I should then, sir, come to the plain and simple question, 'Will you have me?' I think I am justified in assuming that upon this, she would turn away her head."

"You think that may be taken for granted?" said Mr. Magnus; "because if she did not do that at the right place, it would be embarrassing."

"I think she would," said Mr. Pickwick. "Upon this, sir, I should squeeze her hand, and I think—I *think*, Mr. Magnus—that after I had done that, supposing there was no refusal, I should gently draw away the handkerchief, which my slight knowledge of human nature leads me to suppose the lady would be applying to her eyes at the moment, and steal a respectful kiss. I think I should kiss her, Mr. Magnus; and at this particular point, I am decidedly of opinion that if the lady were going to take me at all, she would murmur into my ears a bashful acceptance."

Mr. Magnus started; gazed on Mr. Pickwick's intelligent face, for a short time in silence; and then (the dial pointing to the ten minutes past) shook him warmly by the hand, and rushed desperately from the room.

Mr. Pickwick had taken a few strides to and fro; and the small hand of the clock following the latter part of his example, had arrived at the figure which indicates the half hour, when the door suddenly opened. He turned round to meet Mr. Peter Magnus, and encountered, in his stead, the joyous face of Mr. Tupman, the serene countenance of Mr. Winkle, and the intellectual lineaments of Mr. Snodgrass. As Mr. Pickwick greeted them, Mr. Peter Magnus tripped into the room.

"My friends, the gentleman I was speaking of—Mr. Magnus," said Mr. Pickwick.

"Your servant, gentlemen," said Mr. Magnus, evidently in a high state of excitement; "Mr. Pickwick, allow me to speak to you, one moment, sir."

As he said this, Mr. Magnus harnessed his forefinger to Mr. Pickwick's button-hole, and, drawing him to a window recess, said:

"Congratulate me, Mr. Pickwick; I followed your advice to the very letter."

"And it was all correct, was it?" inquired Mr. Pickwick.

"It was, sir. Could not possibly have been better," replied Mr. Magnus. "Mr. Pickwick, she is mine."

"I congratulate you with all my heart," replied Mr. Pickwick, warmly shaking his new friend by the hand.

"You must see her, sir," said Mr. Magnus; "this way, if you please. Excuse us for one instant, gentlemen." Hurrying on in this way, Mr. Peter Magnus drew Mr. Pickwick from the room. He paused at the next door in the passage, and tapped gently thereat.

"Come in," said a female voice. And in they went.

"Miss Witherfield," said Mr. Magnus, "Allow me to introduce my very particular friend, Mr. Pickwick. Mr. Pickwick, I beg to make you known to Miss Witherfield."

The lady was at the upper end of the room. As Mr. Pickwick bowed, he took his spectacles from his waistcoat pocket, and put them on; a process which he had no sooner gone through, than, uttering an exclamation of surprise, Mr. Pickwick retreated several paces, and the lady, with a half-suppressed scream, hid her face in her hands, and dropped into a chair; whereupon Mr. Peter Magnus was stricken motionless on the spot, and gazed from one to the other, with a countenance expressive of the extremities of horror and surprise.

This certainly was, to all appearance, very unaccountable behaviour; but the fact is, that Mr. Pickwick no sooner put on his spectacles, than he at once recognised in the future Mrs. Magnus the lady into whose room he had so unwarrantably intruded on the previous night; and the spectacles had no sooner crossed Mr. Pickwick's nose, than the lady at once identified the countenance which she had seen surrounded by all the horrors of a night-cap. So the lady screamed, and Mr. Pickwick started.

"Mr. Pickwick!" exclaimed Mr. Magnus, lost in astonishment, "What is the meaning of this, sir? What is the meaning of it, sir?" added Mr. Magnus, in a threatening, and a louder tone.

"Sir," said Mr. Pickwick, somewhat indignant at the very sudden manner in which Mr. Peter Magnus had conjugated himself into the imperative mood, "I decline answering that question."

"You decline it, sir?" said Mr. Magnus.

"I do, sir," replied Mr. Pickwick: "I object to saying anything which may compromise that lady, or awaken unpleasant recollections in her breast, without her consent and permission."

"Miss Witherfield," said Mr. Peter Magnus, "do you know this person?"

"Know him!" repeated the middle-aged lady, hesitating.

"Yes, know him, ma'am. I said know him," replied Mr. Magnus, with ferocity.

"I have seen him," replied the middle-aged lady.

"Where?" inquired Mr. Magnus, "where?"

"'That," said the middle-aged lady, rising from her seat, and averting her head, "that I would not reveal for worlds."

"I understand you, ma'am," said Mr. Pickwick, "and respect your delicacy; it shall never be revealed by *me*, depend upon it."

"Upon my word, ma'am," said Mr. Magnus, "considering the situation in which I am placed with regard to yourself, you carry this matter off with tolerable coolness—tolerable coolness, ma'am."

"Cruel Mr. Magnus!" said the middle-aged lady; here she wept very copiously indeed.

"Address your observations to me, sir," interposed Mr. Pickwick; "I alone am to blame, if anybody be."

"Oh! you alone are to blame, are you, sir?" said Mr. Magnus; "I—I—see through this, sir. You repent of your determination now, do you?"

"My determination!" said Mr. Pickwick.

"Your determination, sir. Oh! don't stare at me, sir," said Mr. Magnus; "I recollect your words last night, sir. You came down here, sir, to expose the treachery and false-hood of an individual on whose truth and honour you had placed implicit reliance—eh?" Here Mr. Peter Magnus indulged in a prolonged sneer; and taking off his green spectacles—which he probably found superfluous in his fit of jealousy—rolled his little eyes about, in a manner frightful to behold.

"Eh?" said Mr. Magnus; and then he repeated the sneer with increased effect. "But you shall answer it, sir."

"Answer what?" said Mr. Pickwick.

"Never mind, sir," replied Mr. Magnus, striding up and down the room. "Never mind."

There must be something very comprehensive in this phrase of "Never mind," for we do not recollect to have ever witnessed a quarrel in the street, at a theatre, public room, or else-where, in which it has not been the standard reply to all belligerent inquiries. "Do you call yourself a gentleman, sir ? "—" Never mind, sir." " Did I offer to say anything to the young woman, sir ? "—" Never mind, sir ? " " Do you want your head knocked up against that wall, sir ? "— " Never mind, sir." It is observable, too, that there would appear to be some hidden taunt in this universal " Never mind," which rouses more indignation in the bosom of the individual addressed, than the most lavish abuse could possibly awaken.

We do not mean to assert that the application of this brevity to himself, struck exactly that indignation to Mr. Pickwick's soul, which it would infallibly have roused in a vulgar breast. We merely record the fact that Mr. Pickwick opened the room door, and abruptly called out, " Tupman, come here ! "

Mr. Tupman immediately presented himself, with a look of very considerable surprise.

" Tupman," said Mr. Pickwick, " a secret of some delicacy, in which that lady is concerned, is the cause of a difference which has just arisen between this gentleman and myself. When I assure him, in your presence, that it has no relation to himself, and is not in any way connected with his affairs, I need hardly beg you to take notice that if he continue to dispute it, he expresses a doubt of my veracity, which I shall consider extremely insulting." As Mr. Pickwick said this, he looked encyclopædias at Mr. Peter Magnus.

Mr. Pickwick's upright and honourable bearing, coupled with that force and energy of speech which so eminently distinguished him, would have carried conviction to any reasonable mind ; but unfortunately at that particular moment, the mind of Mr. Peter Magnus was in anything but reasonable order. Consequently, instead of receiving Mr. Pickwick's explanation as he ought to have done, he forthwith proceeded to work himself into a red-hot, scorching, consuming, passion, and to talk about what was due to his own feelings, and all that sort of thing : adding force to his declamation by striding to and fro, and pulling his hair—

amusements which he would vary occasionally, by shaking his fist in Mr. Pickwick's philanthropic countenance.

Mr. Pickwick, in his turn, conscious of his own innocence and rectitude, and irritated by having unfortunately involved the middle-aged lady in such an unpleasant affair, was not so quietly disposed as was his wont. The consequence was, that words ran high, and voices higher; and at length Mr. Magnus told Mr. Pickwick he should hear from him; to which Mr. Pickwick replied, with laudable politeness, that the sooner he heard from him the better; whereupon the middle-aged lady rushed in terror from the room, out of which Mr. Tupman dragged Mr. Pickwick, leaving Mr. Peter Magnus to himself and meditation.

If the middle-aged lady had mingled much with the busy world, or had profited at all by the manners and customs of those who make the laws and set the fashions, she would have known that this sort of ferocity is the most harmless thing in nature; but as she had lived for the most part in the country, and never read the parliamentary debates, she was little versed in these particular refinements of civilised life. Accordingly, when she had gained her bed-chamber, bolted herself in, and begun to meditate on the scene she had just witnessed, the most terrific pictures of slaughter and destruction presented themselves to her imagination; among which, a full-length portrait of Mr. Peter Magnus borne home by four men, with the embellishment of a whole barrel-full of bullets in his left side, was among the very least. The more the middle-aged lady meditated, the more terrified she became; and at length she determined to repair to the house of the principal magistrate of the town, and request him to secure the persons of Mr. Pickwick and Mr. Tupman without delay.

To this decision the middle-aged lady was impelled by a variety of considerations, the chief of which, was the incontestable proof it would afford of her devotion to Mr. Peter Magnus, and her anxiety for his safety. She was too well acquainted with his jealous temperament to venture the slightest allusion to the real cause of her agitation on beholding Mr. Pickwick; and she trusted to her own influence and power of persuasion with the little man, to quell his boisterous jealousy, supposing that Mr. Pickwick were removed, and no fresh quarrel could arise. Filled with these reflections, the middle-aged lady arrayed herself in her bonnet and shawl, and repaired to the Mayor's dwelling straightway.

Now George Nupkins, Esquire, the principal magistrate aforesaid, was as grand a personage as the fastest walker would find out, between sunrise and sunset, on the twenty-first of June, which being, according to the almanacs, the longest day in the whole year, would naturally afford him the longest period for his search. On this particular morning, Mr. Nupkins was in a state of the utmost excitement and irritation, for there had been a rebellion in the town; all the day-scholars at the largest day-school had conspired to break the windows of an obnoxious apple-seller, and had hooted the beadle, and pelted the constabulary—an elderly gentleman in top-boots, who had been called out to repress the tumult, and who had been a peace-officer, man and boy, for half a century at least. And Mr. Nupkins was sitting in his easy chair, frowning with majesty, and boiling with rage, when a lady was announced on pressing, private, and particular business. Mr. Nupkins looked calmly terrible, and commanded that the lady should be shown in: which command, like all the mandates of emperors, and magistrates, and other great potentates of the earth, was forthwith obeyed; and Miss Witherfield, interestingly agitated, was ushered in accordingly.

"Muzzle!" said the magistrate.

Muzzle was an undersized footman, with a long body and short legs.

"Muzzle!"

"Yes, your worship."

"Place a chair, and leave the room."

"Yes, your worship."

THE DIGNITY OF THE BENCH.

"Now, ma'am, will you state your business?" said the magistrate.

"It is of a very painful kind, sir," said Miss Witherfield.

"Very likely, ma'am," said the magistrate. "Compose your feelings, ma'am." Here Mr. Nupkins looked benignant. "And then tell me what legal business brings you here, ma'am." Here the magistrate triumphed over the man; and he looked stern again.

"It is very distressing to me, sir, to give this information," said Miss Witherfield, "but I fear a duel is going to be fought here."

"Here, ma'am?" said the magistrate. "Where, ma'am?"

"In Ipswich."

"In Ipswich, ma'am! A duel in Ipswich!" said the magistrate, perfectly aghast at the notion. "Impossible, ma'am; nothing of the kind can be contemplated in this town, I am persuaded. Bless my soul, ma'am, are you aware of the activity of our local magistracy? Do you happen to have heard, ma'am, that I rushed into a prize-ring on the fourth of May last, attended by only sixty special constables; and, at the hazard of falling a sacrifice to the angry passions of an infuriated multitude, prohibited a pugilistic contest between the Middlesex Dumpling and the Suffolk Bantam? A duel in Ipswich, ma'am! I don't think—I do *not* think," said the magistrate, reasoning with himself, "that any two men can have had the hardihood to plan such a breach of the peace, in this town."

"My information is unfortunately but too correct," said the middle-aged lady, "I was present at the quarrel."

"It's a most extraordinary thing," said the astounded magistrate. "Muzzle!"

"Yes, your worship."

"Send Mr. Jinks here, directly! Instantly."

"Yes, your worship."

Muzzle retired; and a pale, sharp-nosed, half-fed, shabbily-clad clerk, of middle age, entered the room.

"Mr. Jinks," said the magistrate. "Mr. Jinks."

"Sir," said Mr. Jinks.

"This lady, Mr. Jinks, has come here, to give information of an intended duel in this town."

Mr. Jinks not knowing exactly what to do, smiled a dependent's smile.

"What are you laughing at, Mr. Jinks?" said the magistrate.

Mr. Jinks looked serious, instantly.

"Mr. Jinks," said the magistrate, "you're a fool."

Mr. Jinks looked humbly at the great man, and bit the top of his pen.

"You may see something very comical in this information, sir; but I can tell you this, Mr. Jinks; that you have very little to laugh at," said the magistrate.

The hungry-looking Jinks sighed, as if he were quite aware of the fact of his having very little indeed, to be merry about; and, being ordered to take the lady's information, shambled to a seat, and proceeded to write it down.

"This man, Pickwick, is the principal, I understand," said the magistrate, when the statement was finished.

"He is," said the middle-aged lady.

"And the other rioter—what's his name, Mr. Jinks?"

"Tupman, sir."

"Tupman is the second?"

"Yes."

"The other principal you say, has absconded, ma'am?"

"Yes," replied Miss Witherfield, with a short cough.

"Very well," said the magistrate. "These are two cut-throats from London, who have come down here to destroy his Majesty's population: thinking that at this distance from the capital, the arm of the law is weak and paralysed. They shall be made an example of. Draw up the warrants, Mr. Jinks. Muzzle!"

"Yes, your worship."

"Is Grummer down stairs?"

" Yes, your worship."

" Send him up."

The obsequious Muzzle retired, and presently returned, introducing the elderly gentleman in the top-boots, who was chiefly remarkable for a bottle-nose, a hoarse voice, a snuff-coloured surtout, and a wandering eye.

" Grummer," said the magistrate.

" Your wash-up."

" Is the town quiet now ? "

" Pretty well, your wash-up," replied Grummer. " Pop'lar feeling has in a measure subsided, consekens o' the boys having dispersed to cricket."

" Nothing but vigorous measures will do in these times, Grummer," said the magistrate, in a determined manner. " If the authority of the king's officers is set at nought, we must have the riot act read. If the civil power cannot protect these windows, Grummer, the military must protect the civil power, and the windows too. I believe that is a maxim of the constitution, Mr. Jinks ? '

" Certainly, sir," said Jinks.

" Very good," said the magistrate, signing the warrants. " Grummer, you will bring these persons before me, this afternoon. You will find them at the Great White Horse. You recollect the case of the Middlesex Dumpling and the Suffolk Bantam, Grummer ? "

Mr. Grummer intimated, by a retrospective shake of the head, that he should never forget it—as indeed it was not likely he would, so long as it continued to be cited daily

" This is even more unconstitutional," said the magistrate ; " this is even a greater breach of the peace, and a grosser infringement of his Majesty's prerogative. I believe duelling is one of his Majesty's most undoubted prerogatives, Mr. Jinks ? "

" Expressly stipulated in Magna Charta, sir," said Mr. Jinks.

" One of the brightest jewels in the British crown, wrung

from his Majesty by the Barons, I believe, Mr. Jinks?" said the magistrate.

"Just so, sir," replied Mr. Jinks.

"Very well," said the magistrate, drawing himself up proudly, "it shall not be violated in this portion of his dominions. Grummer, procure assistance, and execute these warrants with as little delay as possible. Muzzle!"

"Yes, your worship."

"Show the lady out."

Miss Witherfield retired, deeply impressed with the magistrate's learning and research; Mr. Nupkins retired to lunch; Mr. Jinks retired within himself—that being the only retirement he had, except the sofa-bedstead in the small parlour which was occupied by his landlady's family in the daytime—and Mr. Grummer retired, to wipe out, by his mode of discharging his present commission, the insult which had been fastened upon himself, and the other representative of his Majesty—the beadle—in the course of the morning.

While these resolute and determined preparations for the conservation of the King's peace, were pending, Mr. Pickwick and his friends, wholly unconscious of the mighty events in progress, had sat quietly down to dinner; and very talkative and companionable they all were. Mr. Pickwick was in the very act of relating his adventure of the preceding night, to the great amusement of his followers, Mr. Tupman especially, when the door opened, and a somewhat forbidding countenance peeped into the room. The eyes in the forbidding countenance looked very earnestly at Mr. Pickwick, for several seconds, and were to all appearance satisfied with their investigation; for the body to which the forbidding countenance belonged, slowly brought itself into the apartment, and presented the form of an elderly individual in top-boots—not to keep the reader any longer in suspense, in short, the eyes were the wandering eyes of Mr. Grummer, and the body was the body of the same gentleman.

Mr. Grummer's mode of proceeding was professional, but

peculiar. His first act was to bolt the door on the inside; his second, to polish his head and countenance very carefully with a cotton handkerchief; his third, to place his hat, with the cotton handkerchief in it, on the nearest chair; and his fourth, to produce from the breast-pocket of his coat a short truncheon, surmounted by a brazen crown, with which he beckoned to Mr. Pickwick with a grave and ghost-like air.

Mr. Snodgrass was the first to break the astonished silence. He looked steadily at Mr. Grummer for a brief space, and then said emphatically: "This is a private room, sir. A private room."

Mr. Grummer shook his head, and replied, "No room's private to his Majesty when the street door's once passed. That's law. Some people maintains that an Englishman's house is his castle. That's gammon."

The Pickwickians gazed on each other with wondering eyes.

"Which is Mr. Tupman?" inquired Mr. Grummer. He had an intuitive perception of Mr. Pickwick; he knew *him* at once.

"My name's Tupman," said that gentleman.

"My name's Law," said Mr. Grummer.

"What?" said Mr. Tupman.

"Law," replied Mr. Grummer, "law, civil power, and exekative; them's my titles; here's my authority. Blank Tupman, blank Pickvick—against the peace of our sufferin Lord the King—stattit in that case made and purwided—and all regular. I apprehend you Pickvick! Tupman—the aforesaid."

"What do you mean by this insolence?" said Mr. Tupman, starting up: "Leave the room!"

"Halloo," said Mr. Grummer, retreating very expeditiously to the door, and opening it an inch or two, "Dubbley."

"Well," said a deep voice from the passage.

"Come for'ard, Dubbley."

At the word of command, a dirty-faced man, something over six feet high, and stout in proportion, squeezed himself

397

through the half-open door (making his face very red in the process), and entered the room.

"Is the other specials outside, Dubbley?" inquired Mr. Grummer.

Mr. Dubbley, who was a man of few words, nodded assent.

"Order in the diwision under your charge, Dubbley," said Mr. Grummer.

Mr. Dubbley did as he was desired; and half a dozen men, each with a short truncheon and a brass crown, flocked into the room. Mr. Grummer pocketed his staff, and looked at Mr. Dubbley; Mr. Dubbley pocketed *his* staff and looked at the division; the division pocketed *their* staves and looked at Messrs. Tupman and Pickwick.

Mr. Pickwick and his followers rose as one man.

"What is the meaning of this atrocious intrusion upon my privacy?" said Mr. Pickwick.

"Who dares apprehend me?" said Mr. Tupman.

"What do you want here, scoundrels?" said Mr. Snodgrass.

Mr. Winkle said nothing, but he fixed his eyes on Grummer, and bestowed a look upon him, which, if he had had any feeling, must have pierced his brain. As it was, however, it had no visible effect upon him whatever.

When the executive perceived that Mr. Pickwick and his friends were disposed to resist the authority of the law, they very significantly turned up their coat sleeves, as if knocking them down in the first instance, and taking them up afterwards, were a mere professional act which had only to be thought of, to be done, as a matter of course. This demonstration was not lost upon Mr. Pickwick. He conferred a few moments with Mr. Tupman apart, and then signified his readiness to proceed to the Mayor's residence, merely begging the parties then and there assembled, to take notice, that it was his firm intention to resent this monstrous invasion of his privileges as an Englishman, the instant he was at liberty; whereat the parties then and there assembled laughed very heartily, with the single exception of Mr. Grummer, who seemed to consider that any slight cast upon the divine right of magistrates, was a species of blasphemy, not to be tolerated.

But when Mr. Pickwick had signified his readiness to bow to the laws of his country; and just when the waiters, and hostlers, and chamber-maids, and post-boys, who had anticipated a delightful commotion from his threatened obstinacy, began to turn away, disappointed and disgusted, a difficulty arose which had not been foreseen. With every sentiment of veneration for the constituted authorities, Mr. Pickwick resolutely protested against making his appearance in the public streets, surrounded and guarded by the officers of justice, like a common criminal. Mr. Grummer, in the then disturbed state of public feeling (for it was half-holiday, and the boys had not yet gone home), as resolutely protested against walking on the opposite side of the way, and taking Mr. Pickwick's parole that he would go straight to the magistrate's; and both Mr. Pickwick and Mr. Tupman as strenuously objected to the expense of a post-coach, which was the only respectable conveyance that could be obtained. The dispute ran high, and the dilemma lasted long; and just as the executive were on the point of overcoming Mr. Pickwick's objection to walking to the magistrate's, by the trite expedient of carrying him thither, it was recollected that there stood in the inn yard, an old sedan chair, which having been originally built for a gouty gentleman with funded property, would hold Mr. Pickwick and Mr. Tupman, at least as conveniently as a modern post-chaise. The chair was hired, and brought into the hall; Mr. Pickwick and Mr. Tupman squeezed themselves inside, and pulled down the blinds; a couple of chairmen were speedily found; and the procession started in grand order. The specials surrounded the body of the vehicle; Mr. Grummer and Mr. Dubbley marched triumphantly in front; Mr. Snodgrass and Mr. Winkle walked arm-in-arm behind; and the unsoaped of Ipswich brought up the rear.

The shopkeepers of the town, although they had a very

indistinct notion of the nature of the offence, could not but be much edified and gratified by this spectacle. Here was the strong arm of the law, coming down with twenty gold-beater force, upon two offenders from the metropolis itself; the mighty engine was directed by their own magistrate, and worked by their own officers; and both the criminals by their united efforts, were securely shut up, in the narrow compass of one sedan-chair. Many were the expressions of approval and admiration which greeted Mr. Grummer, as he headed the cavalcade, staff in hand; loud and long were the shouts raised by the unsoaped; and amidst these united testimonials of public approbation, the procession moved slowly and majestically along.

Mr. Weller, habited in his morning jacket with the black calico sleeves, was returning in a rather desponding state from an unsuccessful survey of the mysterious house with the green gate, when, raising his eyes, he beheld a crowd pouring down the street, surrounding an object which had very much the appearance of a sedan-chair. Willing to divert his thoughts from the failure of his enterprise, he stepped aside to see the crowd pass; and finding that they were cheering away, very much to their own satisfaction, forthwith began (by way of raising his spirits) to cheer too, with all his might and main.

Mr. Grummer passed, and Mr. Dubbley passed, and the sedan passed, and the body-guard of specials passed, and Sam was still responding to the enthusiastic cheers of the mob, and waving his hat about as if he were in the very last extreme of the wildest joy (though, of course, he had not the faintest idea of the matter in hand), when he was suddenly stopped by the unexpected appearance of Mr. Winkle and Mr. Snodgrass.

"What's the row, gen'l'm'n?" cried Sam. "Who have they got in this here watch-box in mournin'?

Both gentlemen replied together, but their words were lost in the tumult.

"Who?" cried Sam again.

Once more was a joint reply returned; and, though the words were inaudible, Sam saw by the motion of the two pairs of lips that they had uttered the magic word "Pickwick."

This was enough. In another minute Mr. Weller had made his way through the crowd, stopped the chairmen, and confronted the portly Grummer.

"Hallo, old gen'l'm'n!" said Sam. "Who have you got in this here conwayance?"

"Stand back," said Mr. Grummer, whose dignity, like the dignity of a great many other men, had been wondrously augmented by a little popularity.

"Knock him down, if he don't," said Mr. Dubbley.

"I'm wery much obliged to you, old gen'l'm'n," replied Sam, "for consulting my conwenience, and I'm still more obliged to the other gen'l'm'n, who looks as if he'd just escaped from a giant's carrywan, for his wery 'ansome suggestion; but I should perfer your givin' me a answer to my question, if it's all the same to you.—How are you, sir?" This last observation was addressed with a patronising air to Mr. Pickwick, who was peeping through the front window.

Mr. Grummer, perfectly speechless with indignation, dragged the truncheon with the brass crown from its particular pocket, and flourished it before Sam's eyes.

"Ah," said Sam, "it's wery pretty, 'specially the crown, which is uncommon like the real one."

"Stand back!" said the outraged Mr. Grummer. By way of adding force to the command, he thrust the brass emblem of royalty into Sam's neckcloth with one hand, and seized Sam's collar with the other: a compliment which Mr. Weller returned by knocking him down out of hand: having previously, with the utmost consideration, knocked down a chairman for him to lie upon.

Whether Mr. Winkle was seized with a temporary attack of that species of insanity which originates in a sense of injury, or animated by this display of Mr. Weller's valour, is uncertain; but certain it is, that he no sooner saw Mr.

Grummer fall than he made a terrific onslaught on a small
boy who stood next him; whereupon Mr. Snodgrass, in a
truly christian spirit, and in order that he might take no one
unawares, announced in a very loud tone that he was going
to begin, and proceeded to take off his coat with the utmost
deliberation. He was immediately surrounded and secured;
and it is but common justice both to him and Mr. Winkle
to say, that they did not make the slightest attempt to
rescue either themselves or Mr. Weller: who, after a most
vigorous resistance, was overpowered by numbers and taken
prisoner. The procession then re-formed; the chairmen
resumed their stations; and the march was re-commenced.

Mr. Pickwick's indignation during the whole of this
proceeding was beyond all bounds. He could just see Sam
upsetting the specials, and flying about in every direction;
and that was all he could see, for the sedan doors wouldn't
open, and the blinds wouldn't pull up. At length, with the
assistance of Mr. Tupman, he managed to push open the
roof; and mounting on the seat, and steadying himself as well
as he could, by placing his hand on that gentleman's shoulder,
Mr. Pickwick proceeded to address the multitude; to dwell
upon the unjustifiable manner in which he had been treated;
and to call upon them to take notice that his servant had
been first assaulted. In this order they reached the magistrate's
house; the chairmen trotting, the prisoners following, Mr.
Pickwick oratorising, and the crowd shouting.

Mr. Weller Attacks the Executive of Ipswich

CHAPTER XXV.

SHOWING, AMONG A VARIETY OF PLEASANT MATTERS, HOW
MAJESTIC AND IMPARTIAL MR. NUPKINS WAS; AND HOW
MR. WELLER RETURNED MR. JOB TROTTER'S SHUTTLECOCK
AS HEAVILY AS IT CAME. WITH ANOTHER MATTER, WHICH
WILL BE FOUND IN ITS PLACE.

VIOLENT was Mr. Weller's indignation as he was borne along;
numerous were the allusions to the personal appearance and
demeanour of Mr. Grummer and his companion: and valorous
were the defiances to any six of the gentlemen present: in
which he vented his dissatisfaction. Mr. Snodgrass and Mr.
Winkle listened with gloomy respect to the torrent of eloquence
which their leader poured forth from the sedan-chair, and the
rapid course of which not all Mr. Tupman's earnest entreaties
to have the lid of the vehicle closed, were able to check for an
instant. But Mr. Weller's anger quickly gave way to curiosity
when the procession turned down the identical court-yard in
which he had met with the runaway Job Trotter: and curiosity
was exchanged for a feeling of the most gleeful astonishment,
when the all-important Mr. Grummer, commanding the
sedan-bearers to halt, advanced with dignified and porte tous
steps to the very green gate from which Job Trotter had
emerged, and gave a mighty pull at the bell-handle which
hung at the side thereof. The ring was answered by a very
smart and pretty-faced servant-girl, who, after holding up her
hands in astonishment at the rebellious appearance of the

403

prisoners, and the impassioned language of Mr. Pickwick, summoned Mr Muzzle. Mr. Muzzle opened one half of the carriage gate, to admit the sedan, the captured ones, and the specials; and immediately slammed it in the faces of the mob, who, indignant at being excluded, and anxious to see what followed, relieved their feelings by kicking at the gate and ringing the bell, for an hour or two afterwards. In this amusement they all took part by turns, except three or four fortunate individuals, who, having discovered a grating in the gate which commanded a view of nothing, stared through it with the indefatigable perseverance with which people will flatten their noses against the front windows of a chemist's shop, when a drunken man, who has been run over by a dog-cart in the street, is undergoing a surgical inspection in the back-parlour.

At the foot of a flight of steps, leading to the house door, which was guarded on either side by an American aloe in a green tub, the sedan-chair stopped. Mr. Pickwick and his friends were conducted into the hall, whence, having been previously announced by Muzzle, and ordered in by Mr. Nupkins, they were ushered into the worshipful presence of that public-spirited officer.

The scene was an impressive one, well calculated to strike terror to the hearts of culprits, and to impress them with an adequate idea of the stern majesty of the law. In front of a big book-case, in a big chair, behind a big table, and before a big volume, sat Mr. Nupkins, looking a full size larger than any one of them, big as they were. The table was adorned with piles of papers: and above the further end of it, appeared the head and shoulders of Mr. Jinks, who was busily engaged in looking as busy as possible. The party having all entered, Muzzle carefully closed the door, and placed himself behind his master's chair to await his orders. Mr. Nupkins threw himself back, with thrilling solemnity, and scrutinised the faces of his unwilling visitors.

" Now, Grummer, who is that person?" said Mr. Nupkins,

pointing to Mr. Pickwick, who, as the spokesman of his friends, stood hat in hand, bowing with the utmost politeness and respect.

"This here's Pickvick, your wash-up," said Grummer.

"Come, none o' that 'ere, old Strike-a-light," interposed Mr. Weller, elbowing himself into the front rank. "Beg your pardon, sir, but this here officer o' yourn in the gambooge tops, 'ull never earn a decent livin' as a master o' the ceremonies any vere. This here, sir," continued Mr. Weller, thrusting Grummer aside, and addressing the magistrate with pleasant familiarity, "This here is S. Pickvick, Esquire; this here's Mr. Tupman; that 'ere's Mr. Snodgrass; and furder on, next him on the t'other side, Mr. Winkle—all wery nice genl'm'n, sir, as you'll be wery happy to have the acquaintance on; so the sooner you commits these here officers o' yourn to the tread-mill for a month or two, the sooner we shall begin to be on a pleasant understanding. Business first, pleasure arterwards, as King Richard the Third said wen he stabbed the t'other king in the Tower, afore he smothered the babbies."

At the conclusion of this address, Mr. Weller brushed his hat with his right elbow, and nodded benignly to Jinks, who had heard him throughout, with unspeakable awe.

"Who is this man, Grummer?" said the magistrate.

"Wery desp'rate ch'racter, your wash-up," replied Grummer. "He attempted to rescue the prisoners, and assaulted the officers; so we took him into custody, and brought him here."

"You did quite right," replied the magistrate. "He is evidently a desperate ruffian."

"He is my servant, sir," said Mr. Pickwick, angrily.

"Oh! he is your servant, is he?" said Mr. Nupkins. "A conspiracy to defeat the ends of justice, and murder its officers. Pickwick's servant. Put that down, Mr. Jinks."

Mr. Jinks did so.

"What's your name, fellow?" thundered Mr. Nupkins.

"Veller," replied Sam.

"A very good name for the Newgate Calendar," said Mr. Nupkins.

This was a joke; so Jinks, Grummer, Dubbley, all the specials, and Muzzle, went into fits of laughter of five minutes' duration.

"Put down his name, Mr. Jinks," said the magistrate.

"Two L's, old feller," said Sam.

Here an unfortunate special laughed again, whereupon the magistrate threatened to commit him, instantly. It is a dangerous thing to laugh at the wrong man, in these cases.

"Where do you live?" said the magistrate.

"Vare-ever I can," replied Sam.

"Put down that, Mr. Jinks," said the magistrate, who was fast rising into a rage.

"Score it under," said Sam.

"He is a vagabond, Mr. Jinks," said the magistrate. "He is a vagabond on his own statement; is he not, Mr. Jinks?"

"Certainly, sir."

"Then I'll commit him. I'll commit him as such," said Mr. Nupkins.

"This is a wery impartial country for justice," said Sam. "There ain't a magistrate goin' as don't commit himself, twice as often as he commits other people."

At this sally another special laughed, and then tried to look so supernaturally solemn, that the magistrate detected him immediately.

"Grummer," said Mr. Nupkins, reddening with passion, "how dare you select such an inefficient and disreputable person for a special constable, as that man? How dare you do it, sir?"

"I am very sorry, your wash-up," stammered Grummer.

"Very sorry!" said the furious magistrate. "You shall repent of this neglect of duty, Mr. Grummer; you shall be made an example of. Take that fellow's staff away. He's drunk. You're drunk, fellow."

"I am not drunk, your worship," said the man.

"You *are* drunk," returned the magistrate. "How dare you say you are not drunk, sir, when I say you are? Doesn't he smell of spirits, Grummer?"

"Horrid, your wash-up," replied Grummer, who had a vague impression that there was a smell of rum somewhere.

"I knew he did," said Mr. Nupkins. "I saw he was drunk when he first came into the room, by his excited eye. Did you observe his excited eye, Mr. Jinks?"

"Certainly, sir."

"I haven't touched a drop of spirits this morning," said the man, who was as sober a fellow as need be.

"How dare you tell me a falsehood?" said Mr. Nupkins. "Isn't he drunk at this moment, Mr. Jinks?"

"Certainly, sir," replied Jinks.

"Mr. Jinks," said the magistrate, "I shall commit that man, for contempt. Make out his committal, Mr. Jinks."

And committed the special would have been, only Jinks, who was the magistrate's adviser (having had a legal education of three years in a country attorney's office), whispered the magistrate that he thought it wouldn't do; so the magistrate made a speech, and said, that in consideration of the special's family, he would merely reprimand and discharge him. Accordingly, the special was abused, vehemently, for a quarter of an hour, and sent about his business: and Grummer, Dubbley, Muzzle, and all the other specials murmured their admiration of the magnanimity of Mr. Nupkins.

"Now, Mr. Jinks," said the magistrate, "swear Grummer."

Grummer was sworn directly; but as Grummer wandered, and Mr. Nupkins' dinner was nearly ready, Mr. Nupkins cut the matter short, by putting leading questions to Grummer, which Grummer answered as nearly in the affirmative as he could. So the examination went off, all very smooth and comfortable, and two assaults were proved against Mr. Weller, and a threat against Mr. Winkle, and a push against Mr. Snodgrass. When all this was done to the magistrate's satisfaction, the magistrate and Mr. Jinks consulted in whispers.

407

The consultation having lasted about ten minutes, Mr. Jinks retired to his end of the table; and the magistrate, with a preparatory cough, drew himself up in his chair, and was proceeding to commence his address, when Mr. Pickwick interposed.

"I beg your pardon, sir, for interrupting you," said Mr. Pickwick; "but before you proceed to express, and act upon, any opinion you may have formed on the statements which have been made here, I must claim my right to be heard, so far as I am personally concerned."

"Hold your tongue, sir," said the magistrate, peremptorily.

"I must submit to you, sir," said Mr. Pickwick.

"Hold your tongue, sir," interposed the magistrate, "or I shall order an officer to remove you."

"You may order your officers to do whatever you please, sir," said Mr. Pickwick; "and I have no doubt, from the specimen I have had of the subordination preserved amongst them, that whatever you order, they will execute, sir; but I shall take the liberty, sir, of claiming my right to be heard, until I am removed by force."

"Pickvick and principle!" exclaimed Mr. Weller, in a very audible voice.

"Sam, be quiet," said Mr. Pickwick.

"Dumb as a drum vith a hole in it, sir," replied Sam.

Mr. Nupkins looked at Mr. Pickwick with a gaze of intense astonishment, at his displaying such unwonted temerity; and was apparently about to return a very angry reply, when Mr. Jinks pulled him by the sleeve, and whispered something in his ear. To this, the magistrate returned a half-audible answer, and then the whispering was renewed. Jinks was evidently remonstrating.

At length the magistrate, gulping down, with a very bad grace, his disinclination to hear anything more, turned to Mr. Pickwick, and said sharply: "What do you want to say?"

"First," said Mr. Pickwick, sending a look through his

spectacles, under which even Nupkins quailed. "First, I wish to know what I and my friend have been brought here for?'

"Must I tell him?" whispered the magistrate to Jinks.

"I think you had better, sir," whispered Jinks to the magistrate.

"An information has been sworn before me," said the magistrate, "that it is apprehended you are going to fight a duel, and that the other man, Tupman, is your aider and abettor in it. Therefore—eh, Mr. Jinks?"

"Certainly, sir."

"Therefore, I call upon you both, to—I think that's the course, Mr. Jinks?"

"Certainly, sir."

"To—to—what, Mr. Jinks?' said the magistrate, pettishly.

"To find bail, sir."

"Yes. Therefore, I call upon you both—as I was about to say, when I was interrupted by my clerk—to find bail."

"Good bail," whispered Mr. Jinks.

"I shall require good bail," said the magistrate.

"Town's-people," whispered Jinks.

"They must be town's-people," said the magistrate.

"Fifty pounds each," whispered Jinks, "and householders, of course."

"I shall require two sureties of fifty pounds each," said the magistrate aloud, with great dignity, "and they must be householders, of course."

"But, bless my heart, sir," said Mr. Pickwick, who, together with Mr. Tupman, was all amazement and indignation; "we are perfect strangers in this town. I have as little knowledge of any householders here, as I have intention of fighting a duel with anybody."

"I dare say," replied the magistrate, "I dare say—don't you, Mr. Jinks?"

"Certainly, sir."

"Have you anything more to say?" inquired the magistrate. Mr. Pickwick *had* a great deal more to say, which he would

409

no doubt have said, very little to his own advantage, or the magistrate's satisfaction, if he had not, the moment he ceased speaking, been pulled by the sleeve by Mr. Weller, with whom he was immediately engaged in so earnest a conversation, that he suffered the magistrate's inquiry to pass wholly unnoticed. Mr. Nupkins was not the man to ask a question of the kind twice over; and so, with another preparatory cough, he proceeded, amidst the reverential and admiring silence of the constables, to pronounce his decision.

He should fine Weller two pounds for the first assault, and three pounds for the second. He should fine Winkle two pounds, and Snodgrass one pound, besides requiring them to enter into their own recognizances to keep the peace towards all his Majesty's subjects, and especially towards his liege servant, Daniel Grummer. Pickwick and Tupman he had already held to bail.

Immediately on the magistrate ceasing to speak, Mr. Pickwick, with a smile mantling on his again good-humoured countenance, stepped forward, and said :

" I beg the magistrate's pardon, but may I request a few minutes' private conversation with him, on a matter of deep importance to himself ? "

" What ? " said the magistrate.

Mr. Pickwick repeated his request.

" This is a most extraordinary request," said the magistrate. " A private interview ? "

" A private interview," replied Mr. Pickwick, firmly ; " only, as a part of the information which I wish to communicate is derived from my servant, I should wish him to be present."

The magistrate looked at Mr. Jinks; Mr. Jinks looked at the magistrate ; the officers looked at each other in amazement. Mr. Nupkins turned suddenly pale. Could the man Weller, in a moment of remorse, have divulged some secret conspiracy for his assassination ? It was a dreadful thought. He was a public man: and he turned paler, as he thought of Julius Cæsar and Mr. Perceval.

ADJOURNMENT TO THE PRIVATE ROOM.

The magistrate looked at Mr. Pickwick again, and beckoned Mr. Jinks.

"What do you think of this request, Mr. Jinks?" murmured Mr. Nupkins.

Mr. Jinks, who didn't exactly know what to think of it, and was afraid he might offend, smiled feebly, after a dubious fashion, and, screwing up the corners of his mouth, shook his head slowly from side to side.

"Mr. Jinks," said the magistrate, gravely, "you are an ass."

At this little expression of opinion, Mr. Jinks smiled again —rather more feebly than before—and edged himself by degrees, back into his own corner.

Mr. Nupkins debated the matter within himself for a few seconds, and then, rising from his chair, and requesting Mr. Pickwick and Sam to follow him, led the way into a small room which opened into the justice parlour. Desiring Mr. Pickwick to walk to the upper end of the little apartment, and holding his hand upon the half-closed door, that he might be able to effect an immediate escape, in case there was the least tendency to a display of hostilities, Mr. Nupkins expressed his readiness to hear the communication, whatever it might be.

"I will come to the point at once, sir," said Mr. Pickwick; "it affects yourself, and your credit, materially. I have every reason to believe, sir, that you are harbouring in your house, a gross impostor!"

"Two," interrupted Sam. "Mulberry agin all natur, for tears and willainny!"

"Sam," said Mr. Pickwick, "if I am to render myself intelligible to this gentleman, I must beg you to control your feelings."

"Wery sorry, sir,' replied Mr. Weller; "but when I think o' that ere Job, I can't help opening the walve a inch or two."

"In one word, sir," said Mr. Pickwick, "is my servant right in suspecting that a certain Captain Fitz-Marshall is in the habit of visiting here? Because," added Mr. Pickwick, as he saw that Mr. Nupkins was about to offer a very indignant interruption, "because, if he be, I know that person to be a—"

"Hush, hush," said Mr. Nupkins, closing the door. "Know him to be what, sir?"

"An unprincipled adventurer—a dishonourable character—a man who preys upon society, and makes easily-deceived people his dupes, sir; his absurd, his foolish, his wretched dupes, sir," said the excited Mr. Pickwick.

"Dear me," said Mr. Nupkins, turning very red, and altering his whole manner directly. "Dear me, Mr. —"

"Pickvick," said Sam.

"Pickwick," said the magistrate, "dear me, Mr. Pickwick —pray take a seat—you cannot mean this? Captain Fitz-Marshall?"

"Don't call him a cap'en," said Sam, "nor Fitz-Marshall neither; he ain't neither one nor t'other. He's a strolling actor, he is, and his name's Jingle; and if ever there was a wolf in a mulberry suit, that ere Job Trotter 's him."

"It is very true, sir," said Mr. Pickwick, replying to the magistrate's look of amazement; "my only business in this town, is to expose the person of whom we now speak."

Mr. Pickwick proceeded to pour into the horror-stricken ear of Mr. Nupkins, an abridged account of Mr. Jingle's atrocities. He related how he had first met him; how he had eloped with Miss Wardle; how he had cheerfully resigned the lady for a pecuniary consideration; how he had entrapped himself into a lady's boarding-school at midnight; and how he (Mr. Pickwick) now felt it his duty to expose his assumption of his present name and rank.

As the narrative proceeded, all the warm blood in the body of Mr. Nupkins tingled up into the very tips of his ears. He had picked up the captain at a neighbouring race-course. Charmed with his long list of aristocratic acquaintance, his extensive travel, and his fashionable demeanour, Mrs. Nupkins and Miss Nupkins had exhibited Captain Fitz-Marshall, and quoted Captain Fitz-Marshall, and hurled Captain Fitz-Marshall at the devoted heads of their select circle of acquaintance, until their bosom friends, Mrs. Porkenham and the Miss Porkenhams, and Mr. Sidney Porkenham, were ready to burst with jealousy and despair. And now, to hear, after all, that he was a needy adventurer, a strolling player, and if not a swindler, something so very like it, that it was hard to tell the difference! Heavens! What would the Porkenhams say! What would be the triumph of Mr. Sidney Porkenham when he found that his addresses had been slighted for such a rival! How should he, Nupkins, meet the eye of old Porkenham at the next Quarter Sessions! And what a handle would it be for the opposition magisterial party, if the story got abroad!

"But after all," said Mr. Nupkins, brightening for a moment, after a long pause; "after all, this is a mere statement. Captain Fitz-Marshall is a man of very engaging manners, and, I dare say, has many enemies. What proof have you of the truth of these representations?"

"Confront me with him," said Mr. Pickwick, "that is all I ask, and all I require. Confront him with me and my friends here; you will want no further proof."

"Why," said Mr. Nupkins, "that might be very easily done, for he will be here to-night, and then there would be no occasion to make the matter public, just—just—for the young man's own sake, you know. I—I—should like to consult Mrs. Nupkins on the propriety of the step, in the first instance, though. At all events, Mr. Pickwick, we must despatch this legal business before we can do anything else. Pray step back into the next room."

Into the next room they went.

"Grummer," said the magistrate, in an awful voice.

"Your wash-up," replied Grummer, with the smile of a favourite.

"Come, come, sir," said the magistrate, sternly, "don't let me see any of this levity here. It is very unbecoming, and

413

I can assure you that you have very little to smile at. Was the account you gave me just now strictly true? Now be careful, sir?"

"Your wash-up," stammered Grummer, "I—"

"Oh, you are confused, are you?" said the magistrate. "Mr. Jinks, you observe this confusion?"

"Certainly, sir," replied Jinks.

"Now," said the magistrate, "repeat your statement, Grummer, and again I warn you to be careful. Mr. Jinks, take his words down."

The unfortunate Grummer proceeded to re-state his complaint, but, what between Mr. Jinks's taking down his words, and the magistrate's taking them up; his natural tendency to rambling, and his extreme confusion; he managed to get involved, in something under three minutes, in such a mass of entanglement and contradiction, that Mr. Nupkins at once declared he didn't believe him. So the fines were remitted, and Mr. Jinks found a couple of bail in no time. And all these solemn proceedings having been satisfactorily concluded, Mr. Grummer was ignominiously ordered out—an awful instance of the instability of human greatness, and the uncertain tenure of great men's favour.

Mrs. Nupkins was a majestic female in a pink gauze turban and a light brown wig. Miss Nupkins possessed all her mamma's haughtiness without the turban, and all her ill-nature without the wig; and whenever the exercise of these two amiable qualities involved mother and daughter in some unpleasant dilemma, as they not unfrequently did, they both concurred in laying the blame on the shoulders of Mr. Nupkins. Accordingly, when Mr. Nupkins sought Mrs. Nupkins, and detailed the communication which had been made by Mr. Pickwick, Mrs. Nupkins suddenly recollected that she had always expected something of the kind; that she had always said it would be so; that her advice was never taken; that she really did not know what Mr. Nupkins supposed she was; and so forth.

CLEARLY MR. NUPKINS'S FAULT.

"The idea!" said Miss Nupkins, forcing a tear of very scanty proportions into the corner of each eye; "the idea of my being made such a fool of!"

"Ah! you may thank your papa, my dear," said Mrs. Nupkins; "how have I implored and begged that man to inquire into the Captain's family connections; how have I urged and entreated him to take some decisive step! I am quite certain nobody would believe it—quite."

"But, my dear," said Mr. Nupkins.

"Don't talk to me, you aggravating thing, don't!" said Mrs. Nupkins.

"My love," said Mr. Nupkins, "you professed yourself very fond of Captain Fitz-Marshall. You have constantly asked him here, my dear, and you have lost no opportunity of introducing him elsewhere."

"Didn't I say so, Henrietta?" cried Mrs. Nupkins, appealing to her daughter, with the air of a much-injured female. "Didn't I say that your papa would turn round and lay all this at my door? Didn't I say so?" Here Mrs. Nupkins sobbed.

"Oh pa!" remonstrated Miss Nupkins. And here she sobbed too.

"Isn't it too much, when he has brought all this disgrace and ridicule upon us, to taunt *me* with being the cause of it?" exclaimed Mrs. Nupkins.

"How can we ever show ourselves in society!" said Miss Nupkins.

"How can we face the Porkenhams!" cried Mrs. Nupkins.

"Or the Griggs's!" cried Miss Nupkins.

"Or the Slummintowkens!" cried Mrs. Nupkins. "But what does your papa care! What is it to *him*!" At this dreadful reflection, Mrs. Nupkins wept with mental anguish, and Miss Nupkins followed on the same side.

Mrs. Nupkins's tears continued to gush forth, with great velocity, until she had gained a little time to think the matter over: when she decided, in her own mind, that the best thing to do would be to ask Mr. Pickwick and his friends to remain until the Captain's arrival, and then to give Mr. Pickwick the opportunity he sought. If it appeared that he had spoken truly, the Captain could be turned out of the house without noising the matter abroad, and they could easily account to the Porkenhams for his disappearance, by saying that he had been appointed, through the Court influence of his family, to the Governor-Generalship of Sierra Leone, or Saugur Point, or any other of those salubrious climates which enchant Europeans so much that, when they once get there, they can hardly ever prevail upon themselves to come back again.

When Mrs. Nupkins dried up her tears, Miss Nupkins dried up *hers*, and Mr. Nupkins was very glad to settle the matter as Mrs. Nupkins had proposed. So Mr. Pickwick and his friends, having washed off all marks of their late encounter, were introduced to the ladies, and soon afterwards to their dinner; and Mr. Weller, whom the magistrate with his peculiar sagacity had discovered in half an hour to be one of the finest fellows alive, was consigned to the care and guardianship of Mr. Muzzle, who was specially enjoined to take him below, and make much of him.

"How de do, sir?" said Mr. Muzzle, as he conducted Mr. Weller down the kitchen stairs.

"Why, no con-siderable change has taken place in the state of my system, since I see you cocked up behind your governor's chair in the parlour, a little vile ago," replied Sam.

"You will excuse my not taking more notice of you then," said Mr. Muzzle. "You see, master hadn't introduced us, then. Lord, how fond he is of you, Mr. Weller, to be sure!"

"Ah," said Sam, "what a pleasant chap he is!"

"Ain't he?" replied Mr. Muzzle.

"So much humour," said Sam.

"And such a man to speak," said Mr. Muzzle. "How his ideas flow, don't they?"

"Wonderful," replied Sam; "they come's a pouring out, knocking each other's heads so fast, that they seems to stun one another; you hardly know what he's arter, do you?"

"That's the great merit of his style of speaking," rejoined Mr. Muzzle. "Take care of the last step, Mr. Weller. Would you like to wash your hands, sir, before we join the ladies? Here's a sink, with the water laid on, sir, and a clean jack towel behind the door."

"Ah! perhaps I may as well have a rinse," replied Mr. Weller, applying plenty of yellow soap to the towel, and rubbing away, till his face shone again. "How many ladies are there?"

"Only two in our kitchen," said Mr. Muzzle, "cook and 'ousemaid. We keep a boy to do the dirty work, and a gal besides, but they dine in the washus."

"Oh, they dines in the washus, do they?" said Mr. Weller.

"Yes," replied Mr. Muzzle, "we tried 'em at our table when they first come, but we couldn't keep 'em. The gal's manners is dreadful vulgar; and the boy breathes so very hard while he's eating, that we found it impossible to sit at table with him."

"Young grampus!" said Mr. Weller.

"Oh, dreadful," rejoined Mr. Muzzle; "but that is the worst of country service, Mr. Weller; the juniors is always so very savage. This way, sir, if you please; this way."

Preceding Mr. Weller, with the utmost politeness, Mr. Muzzle conducted him into the kitchen.

"Mary," said Mr. Muzzle to the pretty servant-girl, "this is Mr. Weller: a gentleman as master has sent down, to be made as comfortable as possible."

"And your master's a knowin' hand, and has just sent me to the right place," said Mr. Weller, with a glance of admiration at Mary. "If I wos master o' this here house, I should alvays find the materials for comfort vere Mary wos."

"Lor, Mr. Weller!" said Mary, blushing.

"Well, I never!" ejaculated the cook.

"Bless me, cook, I forgot you," said Mr. Muzzle. "Mr. Weller, let me introduce you."

"How are you, ma'am," said Mr. Weller. "Werry glad to

417

see you, indeed, and hope our acquaintance may be a long 'un, as the gen'lm'n said to the fi' pun' note."

When this ceremony of introduction had been gone through, the cook and Mary retired into the back kitchen to titter, for ten minutes; then returning, all giggles and blushes, they sat down to dinner.

Mr. Weller's easy manners and conversational powers had such irresistible influence with his new friends, that before the dinner was half over, they were on footing of perfect intimacy, and in possession of a full account of the delinquency of Job Trotter.

"I never could a-bear that Job," said Mary.

"No more you never ought to, my dear," replied Mr. Weller.

"Why not?" inquired Mary.

"Cos ugliness and svindlin' never ought to be formiliar vith elegance and wirtew," replied Mr. Weller. "Ought they, Mr. Muzzle?"

"Not by no means," replied that gentleman.

Here Mary laughed, and said the cook had made her; and the cook laughed, and said she hadn't.

"I han't got a glass," said Mary.

"Drink with me, my dear," said Mr. Weller. "Put your lips to this here tumbler, and then I can kiss you by deputy."

"For shame, Mr. Weller!" said Mary.

"What's a shame, my dear?"

"Talkin' in that way."

"Nonsense; it ain't no harm. It's natur; ain't it, cook?"

"Don't ask me imperence," replied the cook in a high state of delight: and hereupon the cook and Mary laughed again, till what between the beer, and the cold meat, and the laughter combined, the latter young lady was brought to the verge of choking—an alarming crisis from which she was only recovered by sundry pats on the back, and other necessary attentions, most delicately administered by Mr. Samuel Weller.

In the midst of all this jollity and conviviality, a loud ring was heard at the garden-gate: to which the young gentleman

418

who took his meals in the wash-house, immediately responded. Mr. Weller was in the height of his attentions to the pretty house-maid; Mr. Muzzle was busy doing the honours of the table; and the cook had just paused to laugh, in the very act of raising a huge morsel to her lips; when the kitchen-door opened, and in walked Mr. Job Trotter.

We have said in walked Mr. Job Trotter, but the statement is not distinguished by our usual scrupulous adherence to fact. The door opened and Mr. Trotter appeared. He *would* have walked in, and was in the very act of doing so, indeed, when catching sight of Mr. Weller, he involuntarily shrank back a pace or two, and stood gazing on the unexpected scene before him, perfectly motionless with amazement and terror.

"Here he is!" said Sam, rising with great glee. "Why we were that wery moment a speaking o' you. How are you? Where *have* you been? Come in."

Laying his hand on the mulberry collar of the unresisting Job, Mr. Weller dragged him into the kitchen; and, locking the door, handed the key to Mr. Muzzle, who very coolly buttoned it up in a side-pocket.

"Well, here's a game!' cried Sam. "Only think o' my master havin' the pleasure o' meeting your'n, up stairs, and me havin' the joy o' meetin' you down here. How *are* yor gettin' on, and how *is* the chandlery bis'ness likely to do? Well, I am so glad to see you. How happy you look. It's quite a treat to see you; ain't it, Mr. Muzzle?"

"Quite," said Mr. Muzzle.

"So cheerful he is!" said Sam.

"In such good spirits!" said Muzzle.

"And so glad to see *us*—that makes it so much more comfortable," said Sam. "Sit down; sit down."

Mr. Trotter suffered himself to be forced into a chair by the fireside. He cast his small eyes, first on Mr. Weller, and then on Mr. Muzzle, but said nothing.

"Well, now," said Sam, "afore these here ladies, I should jest like to ask you, as a sort of curiosity, wether you don't con-sider yourself as nice and well-behaved a young gen'lm'n as ever used a pink check pocket-handkerchief, and the number four collection?"

"And as was ever a-going to be married to a cook," said that lady, indignantly. "The willin!"

"And leave off his evil ways, and set up in the chandlery line, arterwards," said the house-maid.

"Now, I'll tell you what it is, young man," said Mr. Muzzle, solemnly, enraged at the last two allusions, "this here lady (pointing to the cook) keeps company with me; and when you presume, sir, to talk of keeping chandlers' shops with her, you injure me in one of the most delicatest points in which one man can injure another. Do you understand me, sir?"

Here Mr. Muzzle, who had a great notion of his eloquence, in which he imitated his master, paused for a reply.

But Mr. Trotter made no reply. So Mr. Muzzle proceeded in a solemn manner:

"It's very probable, sir, that you won't be wanted up stairs for several minutes, sir, because *my* master is at this moment particularly engaged in settling the hash of *your* master, sir; and therefore you'll have leisure, sir, for a little private talk with me, sir. Do you understand me, sir?"

Mr. Muzzle again paused for a reply; and again Mr. Trotter disappointed him.

"Well, then," said Mr. Muzzle, "I'm very sorry to have to explain myself before ladies, but the urgency of the case will be my excuse. The back kitchen's empty, sir. If you will step in there, sir, Mr. Weller will see fair, and we can have mutual satisfaction 'till the bell rings. Follow me, sir!"

As Mr. Muzzle uttered these words, he took a step or two towards the door; and by way of saving time, began to pull off his coat as he walked along.

Now, the cook no sooner heard the concluding words of this desperate challenge, and saw Mr. Muzzle about to put it into execution, than she uttered a loud and piercing shriek,

Job Trotter Encounters Sam in Mr. Muzzle's Kitchen

and rushing on Mr. Job Trotter, who rose from his chair on the instant, tore and buffeted his large flat face, with an energy peculiar to excited females, and twining her hands in his long black hair, tore therefrom about enough to make five or six dozen of the very largest-sized mourning-rings. Having accomplished this feat with all the ardour which her devoted love for Mr. Muzzle inspired, she staggered back; and being a lady of very excitable and delicate feelings, she instantly fell under the dresser, and fainted away.

At this moment, the bell rang.

"That's for you, Job Trotter," said Sam; and before Mr. Trotter could offer remonstrance or reply—even before he had time to stanch the wounds inflicted by the insensible lady—Sam seized one arm and Mr. Muzzle the other; and one pulling before, and the other pushing behind, they conveyed him up stairs, and into the parlour.

It was an impressive tableau. Alfred Jingle, Esquire, alias Captain Fitz-Marshall, was standing near the door with his hat in his hand, and a smile on his face, wholly unmoved by his very unpleasant situation. Confronting him, stood Mr. Pickwick, who had evidently been inculcating some high moral lesson; for his left hand was beneath his coat tail, and his right extended in air, as was his wont when delivering himself of an impressive address. At a little distance, stood Mr. Tupman with indignant countenance, carefully held back by his two younger friends; at the further end of the room were Mr. Nupkins, Mrs. Nupkins, and Miss Nupkins, gloomily grand, and savagely vexed.

"What prevents me," said Mr. Nupkins, with magisterial dignity, as Job was brought in: "what prevents me from detaining these men as rogues and impostors? It is a foolish mercy. What prevents me?"

"Pride, old fellow, pride," replied Jingle, quite at his ease. "Wouldn't do—no go—caught a captain, eh?—ha! ha! very good—husband for daughter—biter bit—make it public—not for worlds—look stupid—very!"

"Wretch," said Mrs. Nupkins, "we scorn your base insinuations."

"I always hated him," added Henrietta.

"Oh, of course," said Jingle. "Tall young man—old lover —Sidney Porkenham—rich—fine fellow—not so rich as captain, though?—turn him away—off with him—anything for captain —nothing like captain anywhere—all the girls—raving mad —eh, Job?"

Here Mr. Jingle laughed very heartily; and Job, rubbing his hands with delight, uttered the first sound he had given vent to, since he entered the house—a low noiseless chuckle, which seemed to intimate that he enjoyed his laugh too much, to let any of it escape in sound.

"Mr. Nupkins," said the elder lady, "this is not a fit conversation for the servants to overhear. Let these wretches be removed."

"Certainly, my dear," said Mr. Nupkins. "Muzzle!"

"Your worship."

"Open the front door."

"Yes, your worship."

"Leave the house!" said Mr. Nupkins, waving his hand emphatically.

Jingle smiled, and moved towards the door.

"Stay!" said Mr. Pickwick.

Jingle stopped.

"I might," said Mr. Pickwick, "have taken a much greater revenge for the treatment I have experienced at your hands, and that of your hypocritical friend there."

Job Trotter bowed with great politeness, and laid his hand upon his heart.

"I say," said Mr. Pickwick, growing gradually angry, "that I might have taken a greater revenge, but I content myself with exposing you, which I consider a duty I owe to society. This is a leniency, sir, which I hope you will remember."

When Mr. Pickwick arrived at this point, Job Trotter,

with facetious gravity applied his hand to his ear, as if desirous not to lose a syllable he uttered.

"And I have only to add, sir," said Mr. Pickwick, now thoroughly angry, "that I consider you a rascal, and a—a ruffian—and—and worse than any man I ever saw, or heard of, except that pious and sanctified vagabond in the mulberry livery."

"Ha! ha!" said Jingle, "good fellow, Pickwick—fine heart —stout old boy—but must *not* be passionate—bad thing, very—bye, bye—see you again some day—keep up your spirits—now, Job—trot!"

With these words, Mr. Jingle stuck on his hat in the old fashion, and strode out of the room. Job Trotter paused, looked round, smiled, and then with a bow of mock solemnity to Mr. Pickwick, and a wink to Mr. Weller, the audacious slyness of which baffles all description, followed the footsteps of his hopeful master.

"Sam," said Mr. Pickwick, as Mr. Weller was following.

"Sir."

"Stay here."

Mr. Weller seemed uncertain.

"Stay here," repeated Mr. Pickwick.

"Mayn't I polish that ere Job off, in the front garden?" said Mr. Weller.

"Certainly not," replied Mr. Pickwick.

"Mayn't I kick him out o' the gate, sir?" said Mr. Weller.

"Not on any account," replied his master.

For the first time since his engagement, Mr. Weller looked, for a moment, discontented and unhappy. But his countenance immediately cleared up; for the wily Mr. Muzzle, by concealing himself behind the street door, and rushing violently out, at the right instant, contrived with great dexterity to overturn both Mr. Jingle and his attendant, down the flight of steps, into the American aloe tubs that stood beneath.

"Having discharged my duty, sir," said Mr. Pickwick to Mr. Nupkins, "I will, with my friends, bid you farewell.

While we thank you for such hospitality as we have received, permit me to assure you, in our joint names, that we should not have accepted it, or have consented to extricate ourselves in this way, from our previous dilemma, had we not been impelled by a strong sense of duty. We return to London to-morrow. Your secret is safe with us."

Having thus entered his protest against their treatment of the morning, Mr. Pickwick bowed low to the ladies, and notwithstanding the solicitations of the family, left the room with his friends.

"Get your hat, Sam," said Mr. Pickwick.

"It's below stairs, sir," said Sam, and he ran down after it.

Now, there was nobody in the kitchen, but the pretty house-maid; and as Sam's hat was mislaid, he had to look for it; and the pretty house-maid lighted him. They had to look all over the place for the hat. The pretty house-maid, in her anxiety to find it, went down on her knees, and turned over all the things that were heaped together in a little corner by the door. It was an awkward corner. You couldn't get at it without shutting the door first.

"Here it is," said the pretty house-maid. "This is it, ain't it?"

"Let me look," said Sam.

The pretty house-maid had stood the candle on the floor; as it gave a very dim light, Sam was obliged to go down on *his* knees before he could see whether it really was his own hat or not. It was a remarkably small corner, and so—it was nobody's fault but the man's who built the house—Sam and the pretty house-maid were necessarily very close together.

"Yes, this is it," said Sam. "Good bye!"

"Good bye!" said the pretty house-maid.

"Good bye!" said Sam; and as he said it, he dropped the hat that had cost so much trouble in looking for.

"How awkward you are," said the pretty house-maid. "You'll lose it again, if you don't take care."

So, just to prevent his losing it again, she put it on for him.

SOMETHING BEHIND THE DOOR.

Whether it was that the pretty house-maid's face looked prettier still, when it was raised towards Sam's, or whether it was the accidental consequence of their being so near to each other, is matter of uncertainty to this day; but Sam kissed her.

"You don't mean to say you did that on purpose," said the pretty house-maid, blushing.

"No, I didn't then," said Sam; "but I will now."

So he kissed her again.

"Sam!" said Mr. Pickwick, calling over the banisters.

"Coming, sir," replied Sam, running up stairs.

"How long you have been!" said Mr. Pickwick.

"There was something behind the door, sir, which perwented our getting it open, for ever so long, sir," replied Sam.

And this was the first passage of Mr. Weller's first love.

CHAPTER XXVI.

HAVING accomplished the main end and object of his journey, by the exposure of Jingle, Mr. Pickwick resolved on immediately returning to London, with the view of becoming acquainted with the proceedings which had been taken against him, in the mean time, by Messrs. Dodson and Fogg. Acting upon this resolution with all the energy and decision of his character, he mounted to the back seat of the first coach which left Ipswich on the morning after the memorable occurrences detailed at length in the two preceding chapters; and accompanied by his three friends, and Mr. Samuel Weller, arrived in the metropolis, in perfect health and safety, the same evening.

Here, the friends, for a short time, separated. Messrs. Tupman, Winkle, and Snodgrass repaired to their several homes to make such preparations as might be requisite for their forthcoming visit to Dingley Dell; and Mr. Pickwick and Sam took up their present abode in very good, old-fashioned, and comfortable quarters: to wit, the George and Vulture Tavern and Hotel, George Yard, Lombard Street.

Mr. Pickwick had dined, finished his second pint of particular port, pulled his silk handkerchief over his head, put his feet on the fender, and thrown himself back in an easy chair, when the entrance of Mr. Weller with his carpet bag, aroused him from his tranquil meditations.

MR. PICKWICK'S ARRANGEMENTS.

"Sam," said Mr. Pickwick.

"Sir," said Mr. Weller.

"I have just been thinking, Sam," said Mr. Pickwick, "that having left a good many things at Mrs. Bardell's, in Goswell Street, I ought to arrange for taking them away, before I leave town again."

"Wery good, sir," replied Mr. Weller.

"I could send them to Mr. Tupman's, for the present, Sam," continued Mr. Pickwick, "but before we take them away, it is necessary that they should be looked up, and put together. I wish you would step up to Goswell Street, Sam, and arrange about it."

"At once, sir?" inquired Mr. Weller.

"At once," replied Mr. Pickwick. "And stay, Sam," added Mr. Pickwick, pulling out his purse, "There is some rent to pay. The quarter is not due till Christmas, but you may pay it, and have done with it. A month's notice terminates my tenancy. Here it is, written out. Give it, and tell Mrs. Bardell she may put a bill up, as soon as she likes."

"Wery good, sir," replied Mr. Weller; "anythin' more, sir?"

"Nothing more, Sam."

Mr. Weller stepped slowly to the door, as if he expected something more; slowly opened it, slowly stepped out, and had slowly closed it within a couple of inches, when Mr. Pickwick called out,

"Sam."

"Sir," said Mr. Weller, stepping quickly back, and closing the door behind him.

"I have no objection, Sam, to your endeavouring to ascertain how Mrs. Bardell herself seems disposed towards me, and whether it is really probable that this vile and groundless action is to be carried to extremity. I say I do not object to your doing this, if you wish it, Sam," said Mr. Pickwick.

Sam gave a short nod of intelligence, and left the room.

Mr. Pickwick drew the silk handkerchief once more over his head, and composed himself for a nap. Mr. Weller promptly walked forth, to execute his commission.

It was nearly nine o'clock when he reached Goswell Street. A couple of candles were burning in the little front parlour. and a couple of caps were reflected on the window-blind. Mrs. Bardell had got company.

Mr. Weller knocked at the door, and after a pretty long interval—occupied by the party without, in whistling a tune, and by the party within, in persuading a refractory flat candle to allow itself to be lighted—a pair of small boots pattered over the floor-cloth, and Master Bardell presented himself.

"Well, young townskip," said Sam, "how's mother?"

"She's pretty well," replied Master Bardell, "so am I."

"Well, that's a mercy," said Sam; "tell her I want to speak to her, will you, my hinfant fernomenon?"

Master Bardell, thus adjured, placed the refractory flat candle on the bottom stair, and vanished into the front parlour with his message.

The two caps, reflected on the window-blind, were the respective head-dresses of a couple of Mrs. Bardell's most particular acquaintance, who had just stepped in, to have a quiet cup of tea, and a little warm supper of a couple of sets of pettitoes and some toasted cheese. The cheese was simmering and browning away, most delightfully, in a little Dutch oven before the fire; the pettitoes were getting on deliciously in a little tin saucepan on the hob; and Mrs. Bardell and her two friends were getting on very well, also, in a little quiet conversation about and concerning all their particular friends and acquaintance; when Master Bardell came back from answering the door, and delivered the message intrusted to him by Mr. Samuel Weller.

"Mr. Pickwick's servant!" said Mrs. Bardell, turning pale.

"Bless my soul!" said Mrs. Cluppins.

"Well, I raly would not ha' believed it, unless I had ha' happened to ha' been here!" said Mrs. Sanders.

MR. WELLER VISITS MRS. BARDELL.

Mrs. Cluppins was a little brisk, busy-looking woman; Mrs. Sanders was a big, fat, heavy-faced personage; and the two were the company.

Mrs. Bardell felt it proper to be agitated; and as none of the three exactly knew whether, under existing circumstances, any communication, otherwise than through Dodson and Fogg, ought to be held with Mr. Pickwick's servant, they were all rather taken by surprise. In this state of indecision, obviously the first thing to be done, was to thump the boy for finding Mr. Weller at the door. So his mother thumped him, and he cried melodiously.

"Hold your noise—do—you naughty creetur!" said Mrs. Bardell.

"Yes; don't worrit your poor mother," said Mrs. Sanders.

"She's quite enough to worrit her, as it is, without you, Tommy," said Mrs. Cluppins, with sympathising resignation.

"Ah! worse luck, poor lamb!" said Mrs. Sanders.

At all which moral reflections, Master Bardell howled the louder.

"Now, what *shall* I do?" said Mrs. Bardell to Mrs. Cluppins.

"*I* think you ought to see him," replied Mrs. Cluppins. "But on no account without a witness."

"*I* think two witnesses would be more lawful," said Mrs. Sanders, who, like the other friend, was bursting with curiosity.

"Perhaps he'd better come in here," said Mrs. Bardell.

"To be sure," replied Mrs. Cluppins, eagerly catching at the idea; "Walk in, young man; and shut the street door first, please."

Mr. Weller immediately took the hint; and presenting himself in the parlour, explained his business to Mrs. Bardell thus:

"Werry sorry to 'casion any personal inconwenience, ma'am, as the house-breaker said to the old lady when he put her on the fire; but as me and my governor's only jest come to town, and is jest going away agin, it can't be helped, you see."

"Of course, the young man can't help the faults of his master," said Mrs. Cluppins, much struck by Mr. Weller's appearance and conversation.

"Certainly not," chimed in Mrs. Sanders, who, from certain wistful glances at the little tin saucepan, seemed to be engaged in a mental calculation of the probable extent of the pettitoes, in the event of Sam's being asked to stop supper.

"So all I've come about, is jest this here," said Sam, disregarding the interruption; "First, to give my governor's notice—there it is. Secondly, to pay the rent—here it is. Thirdly, to say as all his things is to be put together, and give to anybody as we sends for 'em. Fourthly, that you may let the place as soon as you like—and that's all."

"Whatever has happened," said Mrs. Bardell, "I always have said, and always will say, that in every respect but one, Mr. Pickwick has always behaved himself like a perfect gentleman. His money always was as good as the bank: always.'

As Mrs. Bardell said this, she applied her handkerchief to her eyes, and went out of the room to get the receipt.

Sam well knew that he had only to remain quiet, and the women were sure to talk; so he looked alternately at the tin saucepan, the toasted cheese, the wall, and the ceiling, in profound silence.

"Poor dear!" said Mrs. Cluppins.

"Ah, poor thing!" replied Mrs. Sanders.

Sam said nothing. He saw they were coming to the subject.

"I rally cannot contain myself," said Mrs. Cluppins, "when I think of such perjury. I don't wish to say anything to make you uncomfortable, young man, but your master's an old brute, and I wish I had him here to tell him so."

"I wish you had," said Sam.

"To see how dreadful she takes on, going moping about, and taking no pleasure in nothing, except when her friends

430

comes in, out of charity, to sit with her, and make her comfortable," resumed Mrs. Cluppins, glancing at the tin saucepan and the Dutch oven, "it's shocking!"

"Barbareous," said Mrs. Sanders.

"And your master, young man! A gentleman with money, as could never feel the expense of a wife, no more than nothing," continued Mrs. Cluppins, with great volubility; "why there ain't the faintest shade of an excuse for his behaviour! Why don't he marry her?"

"Ah," said Sam, "to be sure; that's the question."

"Question, indeed," retorted Mrs. Cluppins; "she'd question him, if she'd my spirit. Hows'ever, there *is* law for us women, mis'rable creeturs as they'd make us, if they could; and that your master will find out, young man, to his cost, afore he's six months older."

At this consolatory reflection, Mrs. Cluppins bridled up, and smiled at Mrs. Sanders, who smiled back again.

"The action's going on, and no mistake," thought Sam, as Mrs. Bardell re-entered with the receipt.

"Here's the receipt, Mr. Weller," said Mrs. Bardell, "and here's the change, and I hope you'll take a little drop of something to keep the cold out, if it's only for old acquaintance' sake, Mr. Weller."

Sam saw the advantage he should gain, and at once acquiesced; whereupon Mrs. Bardell produced, from a small closet, a black bottle and a wine glass; and so great was her abstraction, in her deep mental affliction, that, after filling Mr. Weller's glass, she brought out three more wine glasses, and filled them too.

"Lauk, Mrs. Bardell," said Mrs. Cluppins, "see what you've been and done!"

"Well, that is a good one!" ejaculated Mrs. Sanders.

"Ah, my poor head!" said Mrs. Bardell, with a faint smile.

Sam understood all this, of course, so he said at once, that he never could drink before supper, unless a lady drank with him. A great deal of laughing ensued, and Mrs. Sanders

431

volunteered to humour him, so she took a slight sip out of her glass. Then, Sam said it must go all round, so they all took a slight sip. Then, little Mrs. Cluppins proposed as a toast, "Success to Bardell agin Pickwick;" and then the ladies emptied their glasses in honour of the sentiment, and got very talkative directly.

"I suppose you've heard what's going forward, Mr. Weller?" said Mrs. Bardell.

"I've heerd somethin' on it," replied Sam.

"It's a terrible thing to be dragged before the public, in that way, Mr. Weller," said Mrs. Bardell; "but I see now, that it's the only thing I ought to do, and my lawyers, Mr. Dodson and Fogg, tell me, that with the evidence as we shall call, we must succeed. I don't know what I should do, Mr. Weller, if I didn't."

The mere idea of Mrs. Bardell's failing in her action, affected Mrs. Sanders so deeply, that she was under the necessity of re-filling and re-emptying her glass immediately; feeling, as she said afterwards, that if she hadn't had the presence of mind to do so, she must have dropped.

"Ven is it expected to come on?" inquired Sam.

"Either in February or March," replied Mrs. Bardell.

"What a number of witnesses there'll be, won't there?" said Mrs. Cluppins.

"Ah, won't there!" replied Mrs. Sanders.

"And won't Mr. Dodson and Fogg be wild if the plaintiff shouldn't get it?" added Mrs. Cluppins, "when they do it all on speculation!'

"Ah! won't they!" said Mrs. Sanders.

"But the plaintiff must get it," resumed Mrs. Cluppins.

"I hope so," said Mrs. Bardell.

"Oh, there can't be any doubt about it," rejoined Mrs. Sanders.

"Vell,' said Sam, rising and setting down his glass, "All I can say is, that I wish you *may* get it."

"Thank'ee, Mr. Weller," said Mrs. Bardell fervently,

"And of them Dodson and Foggs, as does these sort o' things on spec," continued Mr. Weller, "as well as for the other kind and gen'rous people o' the same purfession, as sets people by the ears, free gratis for nothin', and sets their clerks to work to find out little disputes among their neighbours and acquaintances as vants settlin' by means o' law-suits—all I can say o' them is, that I vish they had the revard I'd give 'em."

"Ah, I wish they had the reward that every kind and generous heart would be inclined to bestow upon them!" said the gratified Mrs. Bardell.

"Amen to that," replied Sam, "and a fat and happy livin' they'd get out of it! Wish you good night, ladies."

To the great relief of Mrs. Sanders, Sam was allowed to depart without any reference, on the part of the hostess, to the pettitoes and toasted cheese: to which the ladies, with such juvenile assistance as Master Bardell could afford, soon afterwards rendered the amplest justice—indeed they wholly vanished before their strenuous exertions.

Mr. Weller went his way back to the George and Vulture, and faithfully recounted to his master, such indications of the sharp practice of Dodson and Fogg, as he had contrived to pick up in his visit to Mrs. Bardell's. An interview with Mr. Perker, next day, more than confirmed Mr. Weller's statement; and Mr. Pickwick was fain to prepare for his Christmas visit to Dingley Dell, with the pleasant anticipation that some two or three months afterwards, an action brought against him for damages sustained by reason of a breach of promise of marriage, would be publicly tried in the Court of Common Pleas: the plaintiff having all the advantages derivable, not only from the force of circumstances, but from the sharp practice of Dodson and Fogg to boot.

CHAPTER XXVII.

THERE still remaining an interval of two days before the time agreed upon for the departure of the Pickwickians to Dingley Dell, Mr. Weller sat himself down in a back room at the George and Vulture, after eating an early dinner, to muse on the best way of disposing of his time. It was a remarkably fine day; and he had not turned the matter over in his mind ten minutes, when he was suddenly stricken filial and affectionate; and it occurred to him so strongly that he ought to go down and· see his father, and pay his duty to his mother-in-law, that he was lost in astonishment at his own remissness in never thinking of this moral obligation before. Anxious to atone for his past neglect without another hour's delay, he straightway walked up stairs to Mr. Pickwick, and requested leave of absence for this laudable purpose.

"Certainly, Sam, certainly," said Mr. Pickwick, his eyes glistening with delight at this manifestation of filial feeling on the part of his attendant; "certainly, Sam."

Mr. Weller made a grateful bow.

"I am very glad to see that you have so high a sense of your duties as a son, Sam," said Mr. Pickwick.

"I always had, sir," replied Mr. Weller.

"That's a very gratifying reflection, Sam," said Mr. Pickwick, approvingly.

PILGRIMAGE TO DORKING.

"Wery, sir," replied Mr. Weller; "if ever I wanted anythin' o' my father, I always asked for it in a wery 'spectful and obligin' manner. If he didn't give it me, I took it, for fear I should be led to do anythin' wrong, through not havin' it. I saved him a world o' trouble in this vay, sir."

"That's not precisely what I meant, Sam," said Mr. Pickwick, shaking his head, with a slight smile.

"All good feelin', sir—the wery best intentions, as the gen'lm'n said ven he run away from his wife 'cos she seemed unhappy with him," replied Mr. Weller.

"You may go, Sam," said Mr. Pickwick.

"Thank'ee, sir," replied Mr. Weller; and having made his best bow, and put on his best clothes, Sam planted himself on the top of the Arundel coach, and journeyed on to Dorking.

The Marquis of Granby in Mrs. Weller's time was quite a model of a road-side public-house of the better class—just large enough to be convenient, and small enough to be snug. On the opposite side of the road was a large sign-board on a high post, representing the head and shoulders of a gentleman with an apoplectic countenance, in a red coat with deep blue facings, and a touch of the same blue over his three-cornered hat, for a sky. Over that again were a pair of flags; beneath the last button of his coat were a couple of cannon; and the whole formed an expressive and undoubted likeness of the Marquis of Granby of glorious memory.

The bar window displayed a choice collection of geranium plants, and a well-dusted row of spirit phials. The open shutters bore a variety of golden inscriptions, eulogistic of good beds and neat wines; and the choice group of countrymen and hostlers lounging about the stable-door and horse-trough, afforded presumptive proof of the excellent quality of the ale and spirits which were sold within. Sam Weller paused, when he dismounted from the coach, to note all these little indications of a thriving business, with the eye of an experienced traveller; and having done so, stepped in at once, highly satisfied with everything he had observed.

"Now, then!" said a shrill female voice the instant Sam thrust his head in at the door, "what do you want, young man?"

Sam looked round in the direction whence the voice proceeded. It came from a rather stout lady of comfortable appearance, who was seated beside the fire-place in the bar, blowing the fire to make the kettle boil for tea. She was not alone; for on the other side of the fire-place, sitting bolt upright in a high-backed chair, was a man in thread-bare black clothes, with a back almost as long and stiff as that of the chair itself, who caught Sam's most particular and especial attention at once.

He was a prim-faced, red-nosed man, with a long, thin countenance, and a semi-rattlesnake sort of eye—rather sharp, but decidedly bad. He wore very short trousers, and black-cotton stockings, which, like the rest of his apparel, were particularly rusty. His looks were starched, but his white neckerchief was not, and its long limp ends straggled over his closely-buttoned waistcoat in a very uncouth and unpicturesque fashion. A pair of old, worn beaver gloves, a broad-brimmed hat, and a faded green umbrella, with plenty of whalebone sticking through the bottom, as if to counterbalance the want of a handle at the top, lay on a chair beside him, and, being disposed in a very tidy and careful manner, seemed to imply that the red-nosed man, whoever he was, had no intention of going away in a hurry.

To do the red-nosed man justice, he would have been very far from wise if he had entertained any such intention; for, to judge from all appearances, he must have been possessed of a most desirable circle of acquaintance, if he could have reasonably expected to be more comfortable anywhere else. The fire was blazing brightly under the influence of the bellows, and the kettle was singing gaily under the influence of both. A small tray of tea-things was arranged on the table, a plate of hot buttered toast was gently simmering before the fire, and the red-nosed man himself was busily engaged in converting a large slice of bread into the same agreeable edible, through the instrumentality of a long brass toasting-fork. Beside him stood a glass of reeking hot pine-apple rum and water, with a slice of lemon in it; and every time the red-nosed man stopped to bring the round of toast to his eye, with the view of ascertaining how it got on, he imbibed a drop or two of the hot pine-apple rum and water, and smiled upon the rather stout lady, as she blew the fire.

Sam was so lost in the contemplation of this comfortable scene, that he suffered the first inquiry of the rather stout lady to pass unheeded. It was not until it had been twice repeated, each time in a shriller tone, that he became conscious of the impropriety of his behaviour.

"Governor in?" inquired Sam, in reply to the question.

"No, he isn't," replied Mrs. Weller; for the rather stout lady was no other than the quondam relict and sole executrix of the dead-and-gone Mr. Clarke; "No, he isn't, and I don't expect him, either."

"I suppose he's a drivin' up to-day?" said Sam.

"He may be, or he may not," replied Mrs. Weller, buttering the round of toast which the red-nosed man had just finished. "I don't know, and, what's more, I don't care. Ask a blessin', Mr. Stiggins."

The red-nosed man did as he was desired, and instantly commenced on the toast with fierce voracity.

The appearance of the red-nosed man had induced Sam, at first sight, to more than half suspect that he was the deputy shepherd of whom his estimable parent had spoken. The moment he saw him eat, all doubt on the subject was removed, and he perceived at once that if he purposed to take up his temporary quarters where he was, he must make his footing good without delay. He therefore commenced proceedings by putting his arm over the half-door of the bar, coolly unbolting it, and leisurely walking in.

"Mother-in-law," said Sam, "how are you?"

"Why, I do believe he is a Weller!" said Mrs. W., raising

her eyes to Sam's face, with no very gratified expression of countenance.

"I rayther think he is," said the imperturbable Sam; "and I hope this here reverend gen'lm'n 'll excuse me saying that I wish I was *the* Weller as owns you, mother-in-law."

This was a double-barrelled compliment. It implied that Mrs. Weller was a most agreeable female, and also that Mr. Stiggins had a clerical appearance. It made a visible impression at once; and Sam followed up his advantage by kissing his mother-in-law.

"Get along with you!" said Mrs. Weller, pushing him away.

"For shame, young man!" said the gentleman with the red nose.

"No offence, sir, no offence," replied Sam; "you're wery right, though; it ain't the right sort o' thing, wen mothers-in-law is young and good looking, is it, sir?"

"It's all vanity," said Mr. Stiggins.

"Ah, so it is," said Mrs. Weller, setting her cap to rights. Sam thought it was, too, but he held his peace.

The deputy shepherd seemed by no means best pleased with Sam's arrival; and when the first effervescence of the compliment had subsided, even Mrs. Weller looked as if she could have spared him without the smallest inconvenience. However, there he was; and as he couldn't be decently turned out, they all three sat down to tea.

"And how's father?" said Sam.

At this inquiry, Mrs. Weller raised her hands, and turned up her eyes, as if the subject were too painful to be alluded to.

Mr. Stiggins groaned.

"What's the matter with that 'ere gen'lm'n?" inquired Sam.

"He's shocked at the way your father goes on in," replied Mrs. Weller.

"Oh, he is, is he?" said Sam.

"And with too good reason," added Mrs. Weller, gravely.

Mr. Stiggins took up a fresh piece of toast, and groaned heavily.

"He is a dreadful reprobate," said Mrs. Weller.

"A man of wrath!" exclaimed Mr. Stiggins. He took a large semi-circular bite out of the toast, and groaned again.

Sam felt very strongly disposed to give the reverend Mr. Stiggins something to groan for, but he repressed his inclination, and merely asked, "What's the old 'un up to, now?"

"Up to, indeed!" said Mrs. Weller. "Oh, he has a hard heart. Night after night does this excellent man—don't frown, Mr. Stiggins: I *will* say you *are* an excellent man—come and sit here, for hours together, and it has not the least effect upon him."

"Well, that is odd," said Sam; "it 'ud have a wery considerable effect upon me, if I wos in his place; I know that."

"The fact is, my young friend," said Mr. Stiggins, solemnly, "he has an obderrate bosom. Oh, my young friend, who else could have resisted the pleading of sixteen of our fairest sisters, and withstood their exhortations to subscribe to our noble society for providing the infant negroes in the West Indies with flannel waistcoats and moral pocket handkerchiefs?"

"What's a moral pocket ankercher?" said Sam; "I never see one o' them articles o' furniter."

"Those which combine amusement with instruction, my young friend," replied Mr. Stiggins: "blending select tales with wood-cuts."

"Oh, I know," said Sam; "them as hangs up in the linendrapers' shops, with beggars' petitions and all that 'ere upon 'em?"

Mr. Stiggins began a third round of toast, and nodded assent.

"And he wouldn't be persuaded by the ladies, wouldn't he?" said Sam.

"Sat and smoked his pipe, and said the infant negroes were—what did he say the infant negroes were?" said Mrs. Weller.

"Little humbugs," replied Mr. Stiggins, deeply affected.

"Said the infant negroes were little humbugs," repeated Mrs. Weller. And they both groaned at the atrocious conduct of the old gentleman.

A great many more iniquities of a similar nature might have been disclosed, only the toast being all eaten, the tea having got very weak, and Sam holding out no indications of meaning to go, Mr. Stiggins suddenly recollected that he had a most pressing appointment with the shepherd, and took himself off accordingly.

The tea-things had been scarcely put away, and the hearth swept up, when the London coach deposited Mr. Weller senior at the door; his legs deposited him in the bar; and his eyes showed him his son.

"What, Sammy!" exclaimed the father.

"What, old Nobs!" ejaculated the son. And they shook hands heartily.

"Werry glad to see you, Sammy," said the elder Mr. Weller, "though how you've managed to get over your mother-in-law, is a mystery to me. I only vish you'd write me out the receipt, that's all."

"Hush!" said Sam, "she's at home, old feller."

"She ain't vithin hearin'," replied Mr. Weller; "she always goes and blows up, down stairs, for a couple of hours arter tea; so we 'll just give ourselves a damp, Sammy."

Saying this, Mr. Weller mixed two glasses of spirits and water, and produced a couple of pipes. The father and son sitting down opposite each other: Sam on one side of the fire, in the high-backed chair, and Mr. Weller senior on the other, in an easy ditto: they proceeded to enjoy themselves with all due gravity.

"Anybody been here, Sammy?" asked Mr. Weller senior, drily, after a long silence.

Sam nodded an expressive assent.

"Red-nosed chap?" inquired Mr. Weller.

Sam nodded again.

"Amiable man that 'ere, Sammy," said Mr. Weller, smoking violently.

"Seems so," observed Sam.

"Good hand at accounts," said Mr. Weller.

"Is he?" said Sam.

"Borrows eighteenpence on Monday, and comes on Tuesday for a shillin' to make it up half a crown; calls again on Vensday for another half crown to make it five shillin's; and goes on, doubling, till he gets it up to a five pund note in no time, like them sums in the 'rithmetic book 'bout the nails in the horse's shoes, Sammy."

Sam intimated by a nod that he recollected the problem alluded to by his parent.

"So you vouldn't subscribe to the flannel veskits?" said Sam, after another interval of smoking.

"Cert'nly not," replied Mr. Weller; "what's the good o' flannel veskits to the young niggers abroad? But I'll tell you what it is, Sammy," said Mr. Weller, lowering his voice, and bending across the fire-place; "I'd come down wery handsome towards strait veskits for some people at home."

As Mr. Weller said this, he slowly recovered his former position, and winked at his first-born, in a profound manner.

"It cert'nly seems a queer start to send out pocket ankerchers to people as don't know the use on 'em," observed Sam.

"They're alvays a doin' some gammon of that sort, Sammy," replied his father. "T'other Sunday I wos walkin' up the road, wen who should I see, a standin' at a chapel-door, with a blue soup-plate in her hand, but your mother-in-law! I werily believe there was change for a couple o' suv'rins in it, then, Sammy, all in ha'pence; and as the people come out, they rattled the pennies in it, till you'd ha' thought that no mortal plate as ever was baked, could ha' stood the wear and tear. What d'ye think it was all for?"

"For another tea-drinkin', perhaps," said Sam.

"Not a bit on it," replied the father; "for the shepherd's water-rate, Sammy."

"The shepherd's water-rate!" said Sam.

"Ay," replied Mr. Weller, "there was three quarters owin', and the shepherd hadn't paid a farden, not he—perhaps it might be on account that the water warn't o' much use to him, for it's wery little o' that tap he drinks, Sammy, wery; he knows a trick worth a good half dozen of that, he does. Hows'ever, it warn't paid, and so they cuts the water off. Down goes the shepherd to chapel, gives out as he's a persecuted saint, and says he hopes the heart of the turncock as cut the water off, 'll be softened, and turned in the right vay: but he rayther thinks he's booked for somethin' uncomfortable. Upon this, the women calls a meetin', sings a hymn, wotes your mother-in-law into the chair, wolunteers a collection next Sunday, and hands it all over to the shepherd. And if he ain't got enough out on 'em, Sammy, to make him free of the water company for life," said Mr. Weller, in conclusion, "I'm one Dutchman, and you're another, and that's all about it."

Mr. Weller smoked for some minutes in silence, and then resumed:

"The worst o' these here shepherds is, my boy, that they reg'larly turns the heads of all the young ladies, about here. Lord bless their little hearts, they thinks it's all right, and don't know no better; but they're the wictims o' gammon, Samivel, they're the wictims o' gammon."

"I s'pose they are," said Sam.

"Nothin' else," said Mr. Weller, shaking his head gravely; "and wot aggrawates me, Samivel, is to see 'em a wastin' all their time and labour in making clothes for copper-coloured people as don't want 'em, and taking no notice of flesh-coloured Christians as do. If I'd my vay, Samivel, I'd just stick some o' these here lazy shepherds behind a heavy wheelbarrow, and run 'em up and down a fourteen-inch-wide

442

plank all day. That 'ud shake the nonsense out of 'em, if anythin' vould."

Mr. Weller having delivered this gentle recipe with strong emphasis, eked out by a variety of nods and contortions of the eye, emptied his glass at a draught, and knocked the ashes out of his pipe, with native dignity.

He was engaged in this operation, when a shrill voice was heard in the passage.

"Here's your dear relation, Sammy," said Mr. Weller; and Mrs. W. hurried into the room.

"Oh, you've come back, have you!" said Mrs. Weller.

"Yes, my dear," replied Mr. Weller, filling a fresh pipe.

"Has Mr. Stiggins been back?" said Mrs. Weller.

"No, my dear, he hasn't," replied Mr. Weller, lighting the pipe by the ingenious process of holding to the bowl thereof, between the tongs, a red-hot coal from the adjacent fire; "and what's more, my dear, I shall manage to surwive it, if he don't come back at all."

"Ugh, you wretch!" said Mrs. Weller.

"Thank'ee, my love," said Mr. Weller.

"Come, come, father," said Sam, "none o' these little lovins afore strangers. Here's the reverend gen'lm'n a comin' in now."

At this announcement, Mrs. Weller hastily wiped off the tears which she had just begun to force on; and Mr. W. drew his chair sullenly into the chimney corner.

Mr. Stiggins was easily prevailed on, to take another glass of the hot pine-apple rum and water, and a second, and a third, and then to refresh himself with a slight supper, previous to beginning again. He sat on the same side as Mr. Weller senior; and every time he could contrive to do so, unseen by his wife, that gentleman indicated to his son the hidden emotions of his bosom, by shaking his fist over the deputy shepherd's head: a process which afforded his son the most unmingled delight and satisfaction, the more especially as Mr. Stiggins went on, quietly drinking the hot pine-apple rum and water, wholly unconscious of what was going on.

The major part of the conversation was confined to Mrs. Weller and the reverend Mr. Stiggins; and the topics principally descanted on, were the virtues of the shepherd, the worthiness of his flock, and the high crimes and misdemeanours of everybody beside; dissertations which the elder Mr. Weller occasionally interrupted by half-suppressed references to a gentleman of the name of Walker, and other running commentaries of the same kind.

At length Mr. Stiggins, with several most indubitable symptoms of having quite as much pine-apple rum and water about him, as he could comfortably accommodate, took his hat, and his leave: and Sam was, immediately afterwards, shown to bed by his father. The respectable old gentleman wrung his hand fervently, and seemed disposed to address some observation to his son; but on Mrs. Weller advancing towards him, he appeared to relinquish that intention, and abruptly bade him good night.

Sam was up betimes next day, and having partaken of a hasty breakfast, prepared to return to London. He had scarcely set foot without the house, when his father stood before him.

"Goin', Sammy?" inquired Mr. Weller.

"Off at once," replied Sam.

"I vish you could muffle that 'ere Stiggins, and take him with you," said Mr. Weller.

"I am ashamed on you!" said Sam, reproachfully; "what do you let him show his red nose in the Markis o' Granby at all, for?"

Mr. Weller the elder fixed on his son an earnest look, and replied, "'Cause I'm a married man, Samivel, 'cause I'm a married man. Wen you're a married man, Samivel, you'll understand a good many things as you don't understand now; but vether it's worth while goin' through so much, to learn so little, as the charity-boy said ven he got to the end of the alphabet, is a matter o' taste. *I* rayther think it isn't."

"Well," said Sam, "good bye."

"Tar, tar, Sammy," replied his father.

"I've only got to say this here," said Sam, stopping short, "that if *I* was the properiator o' the Markis o' Granby, and that 'ere Stiggins came and made toast in *my* bar, I'd—"

"What?" interposed Mr. Weller, with great anxiety. "What?"

"—Pison his rum and water," said Sam.

"No!" said Mr. Weller, shaking his son eagerly by the hand, "would you raly, Sammy; would you, though?"

"I would," said Sam. "I wouldn't be too hard upon him at first. I'd drop him in the water-butt, and put the lid on; and if I found he was insensible to kindness, I'd try the other persvasion."

The elder Mr. Weller bestowed a look of deep, unspeakable admiration on his son: and, having once more grasped his hand, walked slowly away, revolving in his mind the numerous reflections to which his advice had given rise.

Sam looked after him, until he turned a corner of the road: and then set forward on his walk to London. He meditated, at first, on the probable consequences of his own advice, and the likelihood and unlikelihood of his father's adopting it. He dismissed the subject from his mind, however, with the consolatory reflection that time alone would show; and this is the reflection we would impress upon the reader.

CHAPTER XXVIII.

A GOOD-HUMOURED CHRISTMAS CHAPTER, CONTAINING AN ACCOUNT
OF A WEDDING, AND SOME OTHER SPORTS BESIDE: WHICH
ALTHOUGH IN THEIR WAY, EVEN AS GOOD CUSTOMS AS
MARRIAGE ITSELF, ARE NOT QUITE SO RELIGIOUSLY KEPT
UP, IN THESE DEGENERATE TIMES.

As brisk as bees, if not altogether as light as fairies, did
the four Pickwickians assemble on the morning of the twenty-
second day of December, in the year of grace in which these,
their faithfully-recorded adventures, were undertaken and
accomplished. Christmas was close at hand, in all his bluff
and hearty honesty; it was the season of hospitality, merriment, and open-heartedness; the old year was preparing, like
an ancient philosopher, to call his friends around him, and
amidst the sound of feasting and revelry to pass gently and
calmly away. Gay and merry was the time, and gay and
merry were at least four of the numerous hearts that were
gladdened by its coming.

And numerous indeed are the hearts to which Christmas
brings a brief season of happiness and enjoyment. How many
families, whose members have been dispersed and scattered
far and wide, in the restless struggles of life, are then re-
united, and meet once again in that happy state of companionship and mutual good-will, which is a source of such pure
and unalloyed delight, and one so incompatible with the
cares and sorrows of the world, that the religious belief of

446

the most civilised nations, and the rude traditions of the roughest savages, alike number it among the first joys of a future condition of existence, provided for the blest and happy! How many old recollections, and how many dormant sympathies, does Christmas time awaken!

We write these words now, many miles distant from the spot at which, year after year, we met on that day, a merry and joyous circle. Many of the hearts that throbbed so gaily then, have ceased to beat; many of the looks that shone so brightly then, have ceased to glow; the hands we grasped have grown cold; the eyes we sought have hid their lustre in the grave; and yet the old house, the room, the merry voices and smiling faces, the jest, the laugh, the most minute and trivial circumstances connected with those happy meetings, crowd upon our mind at each recurrence of the season, as if the last assemblage had been but yesterday! Happy, happy Christmas, that can win us back to the delusions of our childish days; that can recall to the old man the pleasures of his youth; that can transport the sailor and the traveller, thousands of miles away, back to his own fire-side and his quiet home!

But we are so taken up and occupied with the good qualities of this saint Christmas, that we are keeping Mr. Pickwick and his friends waiting in the cold on the outside of the Muggleton coach, which they have just attained, well wrapped up in great-coats, shawls, and comforters. The portmanteaus and carpet-bags have been stowed away, and Mr. Weller and the guard are endeavouring to insinuate into the fore-boot a huge cod-fish several sizes too large for it—which is snugly packed up, in a long brown basket, with a layer of straw over the top, and which has been left to the last, in order that he may repose in safety on the half-dozen barrels of real native oysters, all the property of Mr. Pickwick, which have been arranged in regular order at the bottom of the receptacle. The interest displayed in Mr. Pickwick's countenance is most intense, as Mr. Weller and the guard try to squeeze the cod-fish into the boot, first head first, and then tail first, and then top upward, and then bottom upward, and then side-ways, and then long-ways, all of which artifices the implacable cod-fish sturdily resists, until the guard accidentally hits him in the very middle of the basket, whereupon he suddenly disappears into the boot, and with him, the head and shoulders of the guard himself, who, not calculating upon so sudden a cessation of the passive resistance of the cod-fish, experiences a very unexpected shock, to the unsmotherable delight of all the porters and bystanders. Upon this, Mr. Pickwick smiles with great good-humour, and drawing a shilling from his waistcoat pocket, begs the guard, as he picks himself out of the boot, to drink his health in a glass of hot brandy and water; at which the guard smiles too, and Messrs. Snodgrass, Winkle, and Tupman, all smile in company. The guard and Mr. Weller disappear for five minutes: most probably to get the hot brandy and water, for they smell very strongly of it, when they return, the coachman mounts to the box, Mr. Weller jumps up behind, the Pickwickians pull their coats round their legs and their shawls over their noses, the helpers pull the horse-cloths off, the coachman shouts out a cheery "All right," and away they go.

They have rumbled through the streets, and jolted over the stones, and at length reach the wide and open country. The wheels skim over the hard and frosty ground: and the horses, bursting into a canter at a smart crack of the whip, step along the road as if the load behind them: coach, passengers, cod-fish, oyster barrels, and all: were but a feather at their heels. They have descended a gentle slope, and enter upon a level, as compact and dry as a solid block of marble, two miles long. Another crack of the whip, and on they speed, at a smart gallop: the horses tossing their heads and rattling the harness, as if in exhilaration at the rapidity of the motion: while the coachman, holding whip and reins in one hand, takes off his hat with the other, and resting it on his knees, pulls out his handkerchief, and wipes his forehead:

partly because he has a habit of doing it, and partly because it's as well to show the passengers how cool he is, and what an easy thing it is to drive four-in-hand, when you have had as much practice as he has. Having done this very leisurely (otherwise the effect would be materially impaired), he replaces his handkerchief, pulls on his hat, adjusts his gloves, squares his elbows, cracks the whip again, and on they speed, more merrily than before.

A few small houses, scattered on either side of the road, betoken the entrance to some town or village. The lively notes of the guard's key-bugle vibrate in the clear cold air, and wake up the old gentleman inside, who, carefully letting down the window-sash half-way, and standing sentry over the air, takes a short peep out, and then carefully pulling it up again, informs the other inside that they're going to change directly; on which the other inside wakes himself up, and determines to postpone his next nap until after the stoppage. Again the bugle sounds lustily forth, and rouses the cottager's wife and children, who peep out at the house-door, and watch the coach till it turns the corner, when they once more crouch round the blazing fire, and throw on another log of wood against father comes home; while father himself, a full mile off, has just exchanged a friendly nod with the coachman, and turned round to take a good long stare at the vehicle as it whirls away.

And now the bugle plays a lively air as the coach rattles through the ill-paved streets of a country-town; and the coachman, undoing the buckle which keeps his ribands together, prepares to throw them off the moment he stops. Mr. Pickwick emerges from his coat collar, and looks about him with great curiosity; perceiving which, the coachman informs Mr. Pickwick of the name of the town, and tells him it was market-day yesterday, both of which pieces of information Mr. Pickwick retails to his fellow-passengers; whereupon they emerge from their coat collars too, and look about them also. Mr. Winkle, who sits at the extreme edge, with one leg dangling in the air, is nearly precipitated into the street, as the coach twists round the sharp corner by the cheesemonger's shop, and turns into the market-place; and before Mr. Snodgrass, who sits next to him, has recovered from his alarm, they pull up at the inn yard, where the fresh horses, with cloths on, are already waiting. The coachman throws down the reins and gets down himself, and the other outside passengers drop down also: except those who have no great confidence in their ability to get up again: and they remain where they are, and stamp their feet against the coach to warm them—looking, with longing eyes and red noses, at the bright fire in the inn bar, and the sprigs of holly with red berries which ornament the window.

But the guard has delivered at the corn-dealer's shop the brown paper packet he took out of the little pouch which hangs over his shoulder by a leathern strap; and has seen the horses carefully put to; and has thrown on the pavement the saddle which was brought from London on the coach-roof; and has assisted in the conference between the coachman and the hostler about the grey mare that hurt her off-fore-leg last Tuesday; and he and Mr. Weller are all right behind, and the coachman is all right in front, and the old gentleman inside, who has kept the window down full two inches all this time, has pulled it up again, and the cloths are off, and they are all ready for starting, except the "two stout gentle-men," whom the coachman inquires after with some impatience. Hereupon the coachman, and the guard, and Sam Weller, and Mr. Winkle, and Mr. Snodgrass, and all the hostlers, and every one of the idlers, who are more in number than all the others put together, shout for the missing gentlemen as loud as they can bawl. A distant response is heard from the yard, and Mr. Pickwick and Mr. Tupman come running down it, quite out of breath, for they have been having a glass of ale a-piece, and Mr. Pickwick's fingers are so cold that he has been full five minutes before he could find the sixpence to pay for it. The coachman shouts an admonitory

"Now then, gen'lm'n!" the guard re-echoes it; the old gentleman inside thinks it a very extraordinary thing that people *will* get down when they know there isn't time for it; Mr. Pickwick struggles up on one side, Mr. Tupman on the other; Mr. Winkle cries "All right;" and off they start. Shawls are pulled up, coat collars are re-adjusted, the pavement ceases, the houses disappear, and they are once again dashing along the open road, with the fresh clear air blowing in their faces, and gladdening their very hearts within them.

Such was the progress of Mr. Pickwick and his friends by the Muggleton Telegraph, on their way to Dingley Dell; and at three o'clock that afternoon they all stood, high and dry, safe and sound, hale and hearty, upon the steps of the Blue Lion, having taken on the road quite enough of ale and brandy to enable them to bid defiance to the frost that was binding up the earth in its iron fetters, and weaving its beautiful net-work upon the trees and hedges. Mr. Pickwick was busily engaged in counting the barrels of oysters and superintending the disinterment of the cod-fish, when he felt himself gently pulled by the skirts of the coat. Looking round, he discovered that the individual who resorted to this mode of catching his attention was no other than Mr. Wardle's favourite page, better known to the readers of this unvarnished history, by the distinguishing appellation of the fat boy.

"Aha!" said Mr. Pickwick.

"Aha!" said the fat boy.

As he said it, he glanced from the cod-fish to the oyster-barrels, and chuckled joyously. He was fatter than ever.

"Well, you look rosy enough, my young friend," said Mr. Pickwick.

"I've been asleep, right in front of the tap-room fire," replied the fat boy, who had heated himself to the colour of a new chimney-pot, in the course of an hour's nap. "Master sent me over with the shay-cart, to carry your luggage up

451

to the house. He'd ha' sent some saddle-horses, but he thought you'd rather walk, being a cold day."

"Yes, yes," said Mr. Pickwick, hastily, for he remembered how they had travelled over nearly the same ground on a previous occasion. "Yes, we would rather walk. Here, Sam!"

"Sir," said Mr. Weller.

"Help Mr. Wardle's servant to put the packages into the cart, and then ride on with him. We will walk forward at once."

Having given this direction, and settled with the coachman, Mr. Pickwick and his three friends struck into the footpath across the fields, and walked briskly away, leaving Mr. Weller and the fat boy confronted together for the first time. Sam looked at the fat boy with great astonishment, but without saying a word; and began to stow the luggage rapidly away in the cart, while the fat boy stood quietly by, and seemed to think it a very interesting sort of thing to see Mr. Weller working by himself.

"There," said Sam, throwing in the last carpet-bag. "There they are!"

"Yes," said the fat boy, in a very satisfied tone, "there they are."

"Vell, young twenty stun," said Sam, "you're a nice specimen of a prize boy, you are!"

"Thank'ee," said the fat boy.

"You ain't got nothin' on your mind as makes you fret yourself, have you?" inquired Sam.

"Not as I knows on," replied the fat boy.

"I should rayther ha' thought, to look at you, that you was a labourin' under an unrequited attachment to some young 'ooman," said Sam.

The fat boy shook his head.

"Vell," said Sam, "I'm glad to hear it. Do you ever drink anythin'?"

"I likes eating, better," replied the boy.

"Ah," said Sam, "I should ha' s'posed that; but what I mean is, should you like a drop of anythin' as 'd warm you? but I s'pose you never was cold, with all them elastic fixtures, was you?"

"Sometimes," replied the boy; "and I likes a drop of something, when it's good."

"Oh, you do, do you?" said Sam, "come this way, then!"

The Blue Lion tap was soon gained, and the fat boy swallowed a glass of liquor without so much as winking; a feat which considerably advanced him in Mr. Weller's good opinion. Mr. Weller having transacted a similar piece of business on his own account, they got into the cart.

"Can you drive?" said the fat boy.

"I should rayther think so," replied Sam.

"There, then," said the fat boy, putting the reins in his hand, and pointing up a lane, "it's as straight as you can go; you can't miss it."

With these words, the fat boy laid himself affectionately down by the side of the cod-fish: and placing an oyster-barrel under his head for a pillow, fell asleep instantaneously.

"Well," said Sam, "of all the cool boys ever I set my eyes on, this here young gen'l'm'n is the coolest. Come, wake up, young dropsy!"

But as young dropsy evinced no symptoms of returning animation, Sam Weller sat himself down in front of the cart, and starting the old horse with a jerk of the rein, jogged steadily on, towards Manor Farm.

Meanwhile, Mr. Pickwick and his friends having walked their blood into active circulation, proceeded cheerfully on. The paths were hard; the grass was crisp and frosty; the air had a fine, dry, bracing coldness; and the rapid approach of the grey twilight (slate-coloured is a better term in frosty weather) made them look forward with pleasant anticipation to the comforts which awaited them at their hospitable entertainer's. It was the sort of afternoon that might induce a couple of elderly gentlemen, in a lonely field, to take off their great-coats and play at leap-frog in pure lightness of heart and gaiety; and we firmly believe that had Mr. Tupman at that moment proffered "a back," Mr. Pickwick would have accepted his offer with the utmost avidity.

However, Mr. Tupman did not volunteer any such accommodation, and the friends walked on, conversing merrily. As they turned into a lane they had to cross, the sound of many voices burst upon their ears; and before they had even had time to form a guess to whom they belonged, they walked into the very centre of the party who were expecting their arrival—a fact which was first notified to the Pickwickians, by the loud "Hurrah," which burst from old Wardle's lips, when they appeared in sight.

First, there was Wardle himself, looking, if possible, more jolly than ever; then there were Bella and her faithful Trundle; and, lastly, there were Emily and some eight or ten young ladies, who had all come down to the wedding, which was to take place next day, and who were in as happy and important a state as young ladies usually are, on such momentous occasions; and they were, one and all, startling the fields and lanes, far and wide, with their frolic and laughter.

The ceremony of introduction, under such circumstances, was very soon performed, or we should rather say that the introduction was soon over, without any ceremony at all. In two minutes thereafter, Mr. Pickwick was joking with the young ladies who wouldn't come over the stile while he looked —or who, having pretty feet and unexceptionable ankles, preferred standing on the top-rail for five minutes or so, declaring that they were too frightened to move—with as much ease and absence of reserve or constraint, as if he had known them for life. It is worthy of remark, too, that Mr. Snodgrass offered Emily far more assistance than the absolute terrors of the stile (although it was full three feet high, and had only a couple of stepping-stones) would seem to require; while one black-eyed young lady in a very nice little pair of boots with fur round the top, was observed to scream very loudly, when Mr. Winkle offered to help her over.

All this was very snug and pleasant. And when the difficulties of the stile were at last surmounted, and they once more entered on the open field, old Wardle informed Mr. Pickwick how they had all been down in a body to inspect the furniture and fittings-up of the house, which the young couple were to tenant, after the Christmas holidays; at which communication Bella and Trundle both coloured up, as red as the fat boy after the tap-room fire; and the young lady with the black eyes and the fur round the boots, whispered something in Emily's ear, and then glanced archly at Mr. Snodgrass: to which Emily responded that she was a foolish girl, but turned very red, notwithstanding; and Mr. Snodgrass, who was as modest as all great geniuses usually are, felt the crimson rising to the crown of his head, and devoutly wished in the inmost recesses of his own heart that the young lady aforesaid, with her black eyes, and her archness, and her boots with the fur round the top, were all comfortably deposited in the adjacent county.

But if they were social and happy outside the house, what was the warmth and cordiality of their reception when they reached the farm! The very servants grinned with pleasure at sight of Mr. Pickwick; and Emma bestowed a half-demure, half-impudent, and all pretty, look of recognition, on Mr. Tupman, which was enough to make the statue of Bonaparte in the passage, unfold his arms, and clasp her within them.

The old lady was seated in customary state in the front parlour, but she was rather cross, and, by consequence, most particularly deaf. She never went out herself, and like a great many other old ladies of the same stamp, she was apt to consider it an act of domestic treason, if anybody else took the liberty of doing what she couldn't. So, bless her old soul, she sat as upright as she could, in her great chair, and looked as fierce as might be—and that was benevolent after all.

"Mother," said Wardle, "Mr. Pickwick. You recollect him?"

"Never mind," replied the old lady with great dignity. "Don't trouble Mr. Pickwick about an old creetur like me. Nobody cares about me now, and it's very nat'ral they shouldn't." Here the old lady tossed her head, and smoothed down her lavender-coloured silk dress, with trembling hands.

"Come, come, ma'am," said Mr. Pickwick, "I can't let you cut an old friend in this way. I have come down expressly to have a long talk, and another rubber with you; and we'll show these boys and girls how to dance a minuet, before they're eight-and-forty hours older."

The old lady was rapidly giving way, but she did not like to do it all at once; so she only said, "Ah! I can't hear him!"

"Nonsense, mother," said Wardle. "Come, come, don't be cross, there's a good soul. Recollect Bella; come, you must keep her spirits up, poor girl."

The good old lady heard this, for her lip quivered as her son said it. But age has its little infirmities of temper, and she was not quite brought round yet. So, she smoothed down the lavender-coloured dress again, and turning to Mr. Pickwick said, "Ah, Mr. Pickwick, young people was very different, when I was a girl."

"No doubt of that, ma'am," said Mr. Pickwick, "and that's the reason why I would make much of the few that have any traces of the old stock,"—and saying this, Mr. Pickwick gently pulled Bella towards him, and bestowing a kiss upon her forehead, bade her sit down on the little stool at her grandmother's feet. Whether the expression of her countenance, as it was raised towards the old lady's face, called up a thought of old times, or whether the old lady was touched by Mr. Pickwick's affectionate good nature, or whatever was the cause, she was fairly melted; so she threw herself on her grand-daughter's neck, and all the little ill-humour evaporated in a gush of silent tears.

THE WEDDING MORNING

A happy party they were, that night. Sedate and solemn were the score of rubbers in which Mr. Pickwick and the old lady played together; uproarious was the mirth of the round table. Long after the ladies had retired, did the hot elder wine, well qualified with brandy and spice, go round, and round, and round again; and sound was the sleep and pleasant were the dreams that followed. It is a remarkable fact that those of Mr. Snodgrass bore constant reference to Emily Wardle; and that the principal figure in Mr. Winkle's visions was a young lady with black eyes, an arch smile, and a pair of remarkably nice boots with fur round the tops.

Mr. Pickwick was awakened, early in the morning, by a hum of voices and a pattering of feet, sufficient to rouse even the fat boy from his heavy slumbers. He sat up in bed and listened. The female servants and female visitors were running constantly to and fro; and there were such multitudinous demands for hot water, such repeated outcries for needles and thread, and so many half-suppressed entreaties of "Oh, do come and tie me, there's a dear!" that Mr. Pickwick in his innocence began to imagine that something dreadful must have occurred: when he grew more awake, and remembered the wedding. The occasion being an important one he dressed himself with peculiar care, and descended to the breakfast room.

There were all the female servants in a bran new uniform of pink muslin gowns with white bows in their caps, running about the house in a state of excitement and agitation which it would be impossible to describe. The old lady was dressed out in a brocaded gown which had not seen the light for twenty years, saving and excepting such truant rays as had stolen through the chinks in the box in which it had been lain by, during the whole time. Mr. Trundle was in high feather and spirits, but a little nervous withal. The hearty old landlord was trying to look very cheerful and unconcerned, but failing signally in the attempt. All the girls were in tears and white muslin, except a select two or three who were

457

being honoured with a private view of the bride and brides-
maids, up stairs. All the Pickwickians were in most blooming
array; and there was a terrific roaring on the grass in front
of the house, occasioned by all the men, boys, and hobblede-
hoys attached to the farm, each of whom had got a white
bow in his button-hole, and all of whom were cheering with
might and main: being incited thereunto, and stimulated
therein, by the precept and example of Mr. Samuel Weller,
who had managed to become mighty popular already, and
was as much at home as if he had been born on the land.

A wedding is a licensed subject to joke upon, but there
really is no great joke in the matter after all;—we speak
merely of the ceremony, and beg it to be distinctly understood
that we indulge in no hidden sarcasm upon a married life.
Mixed up with the pleasure and joy of the occasion, are the
many regrets at quitting home, the tears of parting between
parent and child, the consciousness of leaving the dearest
and kindest friends of the happiest portion of human life, to
encounter its cares and troubles with others still untried and
little known: natural feelings which we would not render this
chapter mournful by describing, and which we should be still
more unwilling to be supposed to ridicule.

Let us briefly say, then, that the ceremony was performed
by the old clergyman, in the parish church of Dingley Dell,
and that Mr. Pickwick's name is attached to the register,
still preserved in the vestry thereof; that the young lady
with the black eyes signed her name in a very unsteady and
tremulous manner; that Emily's signature, as the other
bridesmaid, is nearly illegible; that it all went off in very
admirable style; that the young ladies generally thought it
far less shocking than they had expected; and that although
the owner of the black eyes and the arch smile informed Mr.
Winkle that she was sure she could never submit to anything
so dreadful, we have the very best reasons for thinking she
was mistaken. To all this, we may add, that Mr. Pickwick
was the first who saluted the bride, and that in so doing,

he threw over her neck a rich gold watch and chain, which no mortal eyes but the jeweller's had ever beheld before. Then, the old church bell rang as gaily as it could, and they all returned to breakfast.

" Vere does the mince pies go, young opium eater ? " said Mr. Weller to the fat boy, as he assisted in laying out such articles of consumption as had not been duly arranged on the previous night.

The fat boy pointed to the destination of the pies.

" Wery good," said Sam, " stick a bit o' Christmas in 'em. T'other dish opposite. There ; now we look compact and comfortable, as the father said ven he cut his little boy's head off, to cure him o' squintin'."

As Mr. Weller made the comparison, he fell back a step or two, to give full effect to it, and surveyed the preparations with the utmost satisfaction.

" Wardle," said Mr. Pickwick, almost as soon as they were all seated, " a glass of wine, in honour of this happy occasion ! "

" I shall be delighted, my boy," said Wardle. " Joe— damn that boy, he's gone to sleep."

" No, I ain't, sir," replied the fat boy, starting up from a remote corner, where, like the patron saint of fat boys— the immortal Horner—he had been devouring a Christmas pie : though not with the coolness and deliberation which characterised that young gentleman's proceedings.

" Fill Mr. Pickwick's glass."

" Yes, sir."

The fat boy filled Mr. Pickwick's glass, and then retired behind his master's chair, from whence he watched the play of the knives and forks, and the progress of the choice morsels from the dishes to the mouths of the company, with a kind of dark and gloomy joy that was most impressive.

" God bless you, old fellow ! " said Mr. Pickwick.

" Same to you, my boy," replied Wardle ; and they pledged each other, heartily.

459

"Mrs. Wardle," said Mr. Pickwick, "we old folks must have a glass of wine together, in honour of this joyful event."

The old lady was in a state of great grandeur just then, for she was sitting at the top of the table in the brocaded gown, with her newly-married granddaughter on one side and Mr. Pickwick on the other, to do the carving. Mr. Pickwick had not spoken in a very loud tone, but she understood him at once, and drank off a full glass of wine to his long life and happiness; after which the worthy old soul launched forth into a minute and particular account of her own wedding, with a dissertation on the fashion of wearing high-heeled shoes, and some particulars concerning the life and adventures of the beautiful Lady Tollimglower, deceased: at all of which the old lady herself laughed very heartily indeed, and so did the young ladies too, for they were wondering among themselves what on earth grandma was talking about. When they laughed, the old lady laughed ten times more heartily, and said that these always had been considered capital stories: which caused them all to laugh again, and put the old lady into the very best of humours. Then, the cake was cut, and passed through the ring; the young ladies saved pieces to put under their pillows to dream of their future husbands on; and a great deal of blushing and merriment was thereby occasioned.

"Mr. Miller," said Mr. Pickwick to his old acquaintance the hard-headed gentleman, "a glass of wine?"

"With great satisfaction, Mr. Pickwick," replied the hard-headed gentleman, solemnly.

"You'll take me in?" said the benevolent old clergyman.

"And me," interposed his wife.

"And me, and me," said a couple of poor relations at the bottom of the table, who had eaten and drank very heartily, and laughed at everything.

Mr. Pickwick expressed his heartfelt delight at every additional suggestion; and his eyes beamed with hilarity and cheerfulness.

THE TOAST OF THE DAY.

"Ladies and gentlemen," said Mr. Pickwick, suddenly rising.

"Hear, hear! Hear, hear! Hear, hear!" cried Mr. Weller, in the excitement of his feelings.

"Call in all the servants," cried old Wardle, interposing to prevent the public rebuke which Mr. Weller would otherwise most indubitably have received from his master. "Give them a glass of wine each, to drink the toast in. Now, Pickwick."

Amidst the silence of the company, the whispering of the women servants, and the awkward embarrassment of the men, Mr. Pickwick proceeded.

"Ladies and gentlemen—no, I won't say ladies and gentlemen, I'll call you my friends, my dear friends, if the ladies will allow me to take so great a liberty "——

Here Mr. Pickwick was interrupted by immense applause from the ladies, echoed by the gentlemen, during which the owner of the eyes was distinctly heard to state that she could kiss that dear Mr. Pickwick. Whereupon Mr. Winkle gallantly inquired if it couldn't be done by deputy : to which the young lady with the black eyes replied, "Go away"—and accompanied the request with a look which said as plainly as a look could do——" if you can."

"My dear friends," resumed Mr. Pickwick, "I am going to propose the health of the bride and bridegroom—God bless 'em (cheers and tears). My young friend, Trundle, I believe to be a very excellent and manly fellow; and his wife I know to be a very amiable and lovely girl, well qualified to transfer to another sphere of action the happiness which for twenty years she has diffused around her, in her father's house. (Here, the fat boy burst forth into stentorian blubberings, and was led forth by the coat collar, by Mr. Weller.) I wish," added Mr. Pickwick, "I wish I was young enough to be her sister's husband (cheers), but, failing that, I am happy to be old enough to be her father; for, being so, I shall not be suspected of any latent designs when I say, that I admire, esteem, and love them both (cheers and sobs). The bride's father, our good friend there, is a noble person, and I am proud to know him (great uproar). He is a kind, excellent, independent-spirited, fine-hearted, hospitable, liberal man (enthusiastic shouts from the poor relations, at all the adjectives; and especially at the two last). That his daughter may enjoy all the happiness, even he can desire; and that he may derive 'from the contemplation of her felicity all the gratification of heart and peace of mind which he so well deserves, is, I am persuaded, our united wish. So, let us drink their healths, and wish them prolonged life, and every blessing! "

Mr. Pickwick concluded amidst a whirlwind of applause; and once more were the lungs of the supernumeraries, under Mr. Weller's command, brought into active and efficient operation. Mr. Wardle proposed Mr. Pickwick; Mr. Pickwick proposed the old lady. Mr. Snodgrass proposed Mr. Wardle; Mr. Wardle proposed Mr. Snodgrass. One of the poor relations proposed Mr. Tupman, and the other poor relation proposed Mr. Winkle; all was happiness and festivity, until the mysterious disappearance of both the poor relations beneath the table, warned the party that it was time to adjourn.

At dinner they met again, after a five-and-twenty mile walk, undertaken by the males at Wardle's recommendation, to get rid of the effects of the wine at breakfast. The poor relations had kept in bed all day, with the view of attaining the same happy consummation, but, as they had been unsuccessful, they stopped there. Mr. Weller kept the domestics in a state of perpetual hilarity; and the fat boy divided his time into small alternate allotments of eating and sleeping.

The dinner was as hearty an affair as the breakfast, and was quite as noisy, without the tears. Then came the dessert and some more toasts. Then came the tea and coffee; and then, the ball.

The best sitting room at Manor Farm was a good, long, dark-panelled room with a high chimney-piece, and a capacious chimney, up which you could have driven one of the new patent cabs, wheels and all. At the upper end of the room, seated in a shady bower of holly and evergreens, were the two best fiddlers, and the only harp, in all Muggleton. In all sorts of recesses, and on all kinds of brackets, stood massive old silver candlesticks with four branches each. The carpet was up, the candles burnt bright, the fire blazed and crackled on the hearth, and merry voices and light-hearted laughter rang through the room. If any of the old English yeomen had turned into fairies when they died, it was just the place in which they would have held their revels.

If anything could have added to the interest of this agreeable scene, it would have been the remarkable fact of Mr. Pickwick's appearing without his gaiters, for the first time within the memory of his oldest friends.

"You mean to dance?" said Wardle.

"Of course I do," replied Mr. Pickwick. "Don't you see I am dressed for the purpose?" Mr. Pickwick called attention to his speckled silk stockings, and smartly tied pumps.

"*You* in silk stockings!" exclaimed Mr. Tupman jocosely.

"And why not, sir—why not?" said Mr. Pickwick, turning warmly upon him.

"Oh, of course there is no reason why you shouldn't wear them," responded Mr. Tupman.

"I imagine not, sir, I imagine not," said Mr. Pickwick in a very peremptory tone.

Mr. Tupman had contemplated a laugh, but he found it was a serious matter; so he looked grave, and said they were a pretty pattern.

"I hope they are," said Mr. Pickwick fixing his eyes upon his friend. "You see nothing extraordinary in the stockings, *as* stockings, I trust, sir?"

"Certainly not. Oh, certainly not," replied Mr. Tupman. He walked away; and Mr. Pickwick's countenance resumed its customary benign expression.

"We are all ready, I believe," said Mr. Pickwick, who was stationed with the old lady at the top of the dance, and had already made four false starts, in his excessive anxiety to commence.

"Then begin at once," said Wardle. "Now!"

Up struck the two fiddles and the one harp, and off went Mr. Pickwick into hands across, when there was a general clapping of hands, and a cry of "Stop, stop!"

"What's the matter!" said Mr. Pickwick, who was only brought to, by the fiddles and harp desisting, and could have been stopped by no other earthly power, if the house had been on fire.

"Where's Arabella Allen?" cried a dozen voices.

"And Winkle?" added Mr. Tupman.

"Here we are!" exclaimed that gentleman, emerging with his pretty companion from the corner; as he did so, it would have been hard to tell which was the redder in the face, he or the young lady with the black eyes.

"What an extraordinary thing it is, Winkle," said Mr. Pickwick, rather pettishly, "that you couldn't have taken your place before.

"Not at all extraordinary," said Mr. Winkle.

"Well," said Mr. Pickwick, with a very expressive smile, as his eyes rested on Arabella, "well, I don't know that it *was* extraordinary, either, after all."

However, there was no time to think more about the matter, for the fiddles and harp began in real earnest. Away went Mr. Pickwick—hands across—down the middle to the very end of the room, and half-way up the chimney, back again to the door—poussette everywhere—loud stamp on the ground —ready for the next couple—off again—all the figure over once more—another stamp to beat out the time—next couple, and the next, and the next again—never was such going! At last, after they had reached the bottom of the dance, and full fourteen couple after the old lady had retired in an exhausted state, and the clergyman's wife had been substituted in her stead, did that gentleman, when there was no demand whatever on his exertions, keep perpetually dancing in his place, to keep time to the music: smiling on his partner all the while with a blandness of demeanour which baffles all description.

Long before Mr. Pickwick was weary of dancing, the newly-married couple had retired from the scene. There was a glorious supper down-stairs, notwithstanding, and a good long sitting after it; and when Mr. Pickwick awoke, late the next morning, he had a confused recollection of having, severally and confidentially, invited somewhere about five-and-forty people to dine with him at the George and Vulture, the very first time they came to London; which Mr. Pickwick rightly considered a pretty certain indication of his having taken something besides exercise, on the previous night.

"And so your family has games in the kitchen to-night, my dear, has they?" inquired Sam of Emma.

"Yes, Mr. Weller," replied Emma; "we always have on Christmas eve. Master wouldn't neglect to keep it up on any account."

"Your master's a wery pretty notion of keepin' anythin' up, my dear," said Mr. Weller; "I never see such a sensible sort of man as he is, or such a reg'lar gen'l'm'n."

"Oh, that he is!" said the fat boy, joining in the conversation; "don't he breed nice pork!" The fat youth gave a semi-cannibalic leer at Mr. Weller, as he thought of the roast legs and gravy.

"Oh, you've woke up, at last, have you?" said Sam.

The fat boy nodded.

"I'll tell you what it is, young boa constructer," said Mr. Weller, impressively; "if you don't sleep a little less, and exercise a little more, wen you comes to be a man you'll lay yourself open to the same sort of personal inconwenience as was inflicted on the old gen'l'm'n as wore the pigtail."

"What did they do to him?" inquired the fat boy, in a faltering voice.

"I'm a-goin' to tell you," replied Mr. Weller; "he was one o' the largest patterns as was ever turned out—reg'lar fat man, as hadn't caught a glimpse of his own shoes for five-and-forty-year."

"Lor!" exclaimed Emma.

"No, that he hadn't, my dear," said Mr. Weller; "and if you'd put an exact model of his own legs on the dinin' table afore him, he wouldn't ha' known 'em. Well, he always walks to his office with a wery handsome gold watch-chain hanging out, about a foot and a quarter, and a gold watch in his fob pocket as was worth—I'm afraid to say how much, but as much as a watch can be—a large, heavy, round manafacter, as stout for a watch, as he was for a man, and with a big face in proportion. 'You'd better not carry that 'ere watch,' says the old gen'l'm'n's friends, 'you'll be robbed on it,' says they. 'Shall I?' says he. 'Yes, you will,' says they. 'Vell,' says he, 'I should like to see the thief as could get this here watch out, for I'm blest if *I* ever can, it's such a tight fit,' says he; 'and venever I wants to know what's o'clock, I'm obliged to stare into the bakers' shops,' he says. Well, then he laughs as hearty as if he was a goin' to pieces, and out he walks agin' with his powdered head and pigtail, and rolls down the Strand vith the chain hangin' out furder than ever, and the great round watch almost bustin' through his grey kersey smalls. There warn't a pickpocket in all London as didn't take a pull at that chain, but the chain 'ud never break, and the watch 'ud never come out, so they soon got tired o' dragging such a heavy old gen'l'm'n along the pavement, and he'd go home and laugh till the pigtail wibrated like the penderlum of a Dutch clock. At last, one day the old gen'l'm'n was a rollin' along, and he sees a pickpocket as he know'd by sight, a-comin' up, arm in arm vith a little boy vith a wery large head. 'Here's a game,' says the old gen'l'm'n to himself, 'they're a-goin' to have another try, but it won't do!' So he begins a-chucklin' wery hearty, wen, all of a sudden, the little boy leaves hold of the pickpocket's arm, and rushes headforemost straight into the old gen'l'm'n's stomach, and for a moment doubles him right up

466

vith the pain. 'Murder!' says the old gen'l'm'n. 'All right, sir,' says the pickpocket, a wisperin' in his ear. And wen he come straight agin, the watch and chain was gone, and what's worse than that, the old gen'l'm'n's digestion was all wrong ever artervards, to the wery last day of his life; so just you look about you, young feller, and take care you don't get too fat."

As Mr. Weller concluded this moral tale, with which the fat boy appeared much affected, they all three repaired to the large kitchen, in which the family were by this time assembled, according to annual custom on Christmas eve, observed by old Wardle's forefathers from time immemorial.

From the centre of the ceiling of this kitchen, old Wardle had just suspended, with his own hands, a huge branch of mistletoe, and this same branch of mistletoe instantaneously gave rise to a scene of general and delightful struggling and confusion; in the midst of which, Mr. Pickwick, with a gallantry that would have done honour to a descendant of Lady Tollimglower herself, took the old lady by the hand, led her beneath the mystic branch, and saluted her in all courtesy and decorum. The old lady submitted to this piece of practical politeness with all the dignity which befitted so important and serious a solemnity, but the younger ladies, not being so thoroughly imbued with a superstitious veneration for the custom: or imagining that the value of a salute is very much enhanced if it cost a little trouble to obtain it: screamed and struggled, and ran into corners, and threatened and remonstrated, and did everything but leave the room, until some of the less adventurous gentlemen were on the point of desisting, when they all at once found it useless to resist any longer, and submitted to be kissed with a good grace. Mr. Winkle kissed the young lady with the black eyes, and Mr. Snodgrass kissed Emily, and Mr. Weller, not being particular about the form of being under the mistletoe, kissed Emma and the other female servants, just as he caught them. As to the poor relations, they kissed everybody, not

467

even excepting the plainer portions of the young-lady visitors, who, in their excessive confusion, ran right under the mistletoe, as soon as it was hung up, without knowing it! Wardle stood with his back to the fire, surveying the whole scene, with the utmost satisfaction; and the fat boy took the opportunity of appropriating to his own use, and summarily devouring, a particularly fine mince-pie, that had been carefully put by for somebody else.

Now, the screaming had subsided, and faces were in a glow, and curls in a tangle, and Mr. Pickwick, after kissing the old lady as before mentioned, was standing under the mistletoe, looking with a very pleased countenance on all that was passing around him, when the young lady with the black eyes, after a little whispering with the other young ladies, made a sudden dart forward, and, putting her arm round Mr. Pickwick's neck, saluted him affectionately on the left cheek; and before Mr. Pickwick distinctly knew what was the matter, he was surrounded by the whole body, and kissed by every one of them.

It was a pleasant thing to see Mr. Pickwick in the centre of the group, now pulled this way, and then that, and first kissed on the chin, and then on the nose, and then on the spectacles: and to hear the peals of laughter which were raised on every side; but it was a still more pleasant thing to see Mr. Pickwick, blinded shortly afterwards with a silk handkerchief, falling up against the wall, and scrambling into corners, and going through all the mysteries of blind-man's buff, with the utmost relish for the game, until at last he caught one of the poor relations, and then had to evade the blind-man himself, which he did with a nimbleness and agility that elicited the admiration and applause of all beholders. The poor relations caught the people who they thought would like it, and, when the game flagged, got caught themselves. When they were all tired of blind-man's buff, there was a great game at snap-dragon, and when fingers enough were burned with that, and all the raisins were gone, they sat down by the huge

Christmas Eve at Mr. Wardle's

A CHRISTMAS CAROL.

fire of blazing logs to a substantial supper, and a mighty bowl of wassail, something smaller than an ordinary wash-house copper, in which the hot apples were hissing and bubbling with a rich look, and a jolly sound, that were perfectly irresistible.

"This," said Mr. Pickwick, looking round him, "this is, indeed, comfort."

"Our invariable custom." replied Mr. Wardle. "Everybody sits down with us on Christmas eve, as you see them now—servants and all; and here we wait, until the clock strikes twelve, to usher Christmas in, and beguile the time with forfeits and old stories. Trundle, my boy, rake up the fire."

Up flew the bright sparks in myriads as the logs were stirred. The deep red blaze sent forth a rich glow, that penetrated into the furthest corner of the room, and cast its cheerful tint on every face.

"Come," said Wardle, "a song—a Christmas song! I'll give you one, in default of a better."

"Bravo!" said Mr. Pickwick.

"Fill up," cried Wardle. "It will be two hours, good, before you see the bottom of the bowl through the deep rich colour of the wassail; fill up all round, and now for the song."

Thus saying, the merry old gentleman, in a good, round, sturdy voice, commenced without more ado:

A CHRISTMAS CAROL.

I CARE not for Spring; on his fickle wing
Let the blossoms and buds be borne:
He woos them amain with his treacherous rain,
And he scatters them ere the morn.
An inconstant elf, he knows not himself,
Nor his own changing mind an hour,
He'll smile in your face, and, with wry grimace,
He'll wither your youngest flower.

Let the Summer sun to his bright home run,
He shall never be sought by me;
When he's dimmed by a cloud I can laugh aloud,
And care not how sulky he be!
For his darling child is the madness wild
That sports in fierce fever's train;
And when love is too strong, it don't last long,
As many have found to their pain.

A mild harvest night, by the tranquil light
Of the modest and gentle moon,
Has a far sweeter sheen, for me, I ween,
Than the broad and unblushing noon.
But every leaf awakens my grief,
As it lieth beneath the tree;
So let Autumn air be never so fair,
It by no means agrees with me.

But my song I troll out, for CHRISTMAS stout,
The hearty, the true, and the bold;
A bumper I drain, and with might and main
Give three cheers for this Christmas old!
We'll usher him in with a merry din
That shall gladden his joyous heart,
And we'll keep him up, while there's bite or sup,
And in fellowship good, we'll part.

In his fine honest pride, he scorns to hide,
One jot of his hard-weather scars;
They're no disgrace, for there's much the same trace
On the cheeks of our bravest tars.
Then again I sing 'till the roof doth ring,
And it echoes from wall to wall—
To the stout old wight, fair welcome to-night,
As the King of the Seasons all!

This song was tumultuously applauded—for friends and dependents make a capital audience—and the poor relations, especially, were in perfect ecstasies of rapture. Again was the fire replenished, and again went the wassail round.

"How it snows!" said one of the men, in a low tone.

"Snows, does it?" said Wardle.

"Rough, cold night, sir," replied the man; "and there's a wind got up, that drifts it across the fields, in a thick white cloud."

"What does Jem say?" inquired the old lady. "There ain't anything the matter, is there?"

"No, no, mother," replied Wardle; "he says there's a snow-drift, and a wind that's piercing cold. I should know that, by the way it rumbles in the chimney."

"Ah!" said the old lady, "there was just such a wind, and just such a fall of snow, a good many years back, I recollect—just five years before your poor father died. It was a Christmas eve, too; and I remember that on that very night he told us the story about the goblins that carried away old Gabriel Grub."

"The story about what?" said Mr. Pickwick.

"Oh, nothing, nothing," replied Wardle. "About an old sexton, that the good people down here suppose to have been carried away by goblins."

"Suppose!" ejaculated the old lady. "Is there any body hardy enough to disbelieve it? Suppose! Haven't you heard ever since you were a child, that he *was* carried away by the goblins, and don't you know he was?"

"Very well, mother, he was, if you like," said Wardle, laughing. "He *was* carried away by goblins, Pickwick; and there's an end of the matter."

"No, no," said Mr. Pickwick, "not an end of it, I assure you; for I must hear how, and why, and all about it."

Wardle smiled, as every head was bent forward to hear; and filling out the wassail with no stinted hand, nodded a health to Mr. Pickwick, and began as follows:

But bless our editorial heart, what a long chapter we have been betrayed into! We had quite forgotten all such petty restrictions as chapters, we solemnly declare. So here goes, to give the goblin a fair start in a new one! A clear stage and no favour for the goblins, ladies and gentlemen, if you please.

CHAPTER XXIX.

THE STORY OF THE GOBLINS WHO STOLE A SEXTON.

"In an old abbey town, down in this part of the country, a long, long while ago—so long, that the story must be a true one, because our great grandfathers implicitly believed it—there officiated as sexton and grave-digger in the churchyard, one Gabriel Grub. It by no means follows that because a man is a sexton, and constantly surrounded by the emblems of mortality, therefore he should be a morose and melancholy man; your undertakers are the merriest fellows in the world; and I once had the honour of being on intimate terms with a mute, who in private life, and off duty, was as comical and jocose a little fellow as ever chirped out a devil-may-care song, without a hitch in his memory, or drained off the contents of a good stiff glass without stopping for breath. But, notwithstanding these precedents to the contrary, Gabriel Grub was an ill-conditioned, cross-grained, surly fellow—a morose and lonely man, who consorted with nobody but himself, and an old wicker bottle which fitted into his large deep waistcoat pocket—and who eyed each merry face, as it passed him by, with such a deep scowl of malice and ill-humour, as it was difficult to meet, without feeling something the worse for.

"A little before twilight, one Christmas Eve, Gabriel shouldered his spade, lighted his lantern, and betook himself towards the old churchyard; for he had got a grave to finish by next morning, and, feeling very low, he thought it might

raise his spirits, perhaps, if he went on with his work at once.
As he went his way, up the ancient street, he saw the cheerful
light of the blazing fires gleam through the old casements,
and heard the loud laugh and the cheerful shouts of those
who were assembled around them; he marked the bustling
preparations for next day's cheer, and smelt the numerous
savoury odours consequent thereupon, as they steamed up
from the kitchen windows in clouds. All this was gall and
wormwood to the heart of Gabriel Grub; and when groups
of children bounded out of the houses, tripped across the
road, and were met, before they could knock at the opposite
door, by half a dozen curly-headed little rascals who crowded
round them as they flocked up-stairs to spend the evening
in their Christmas games, Gabriel smiled grimly, and clutched
the handle of his spade with a firmer grasp, as he thought
of measles, scarlet-fever, thrush, hooping-cough, and a good
many other sources of consolation besides.

"In this happy frame of mind, Gabriel strode along:
returning a short, sullen growl to the good-humoured greetings of such of his neighbours as now and then passed him:
until he turned into the dark lane which led to the churchyard. Now, Gabriel had been looking forward to reaching
the dark lane, because it was, generally speaking, a nice,
gloomy, mournful place, into which the towns-people did not
much care to go, except in broad day-light, and when the
sun was shining; consequently, he was not a little indignant
to hear a young urchin roaring out some jolly song about a
merry Christmas, in this very sanctuary, which had been
called Coffin Lane ever since the days of the old abbey, and
the time of the shaven-headed monks. As Gabriel walked
on, and the voice drew nearer, he found it proceeded from a
small boy, who was hurrying along, to join one of the little
parties in the old street, and who, partly to keep himself
company, and partly to prepare himself for the occasion, was
shouting out the song at the highest pitch of his lungs. So
Gabriel waited until the boy came up, and then dodged him

into a corner, and rapped him over the head with his lantern five or six times, to teach him to modulate his voice. And as the boy hurried away with his hand to his head, singing quite a different sort of tune, Gabriel Grub chuckled very heartily to himself, and entered the churchyard: locking the gate behind him.

"He took off his coat, put down his lantern, and getting into the unfinished grave, worked at it for an hour or so. with right good will. But the earth was hardened with the frost, and it was no very easy matter to break it up, and shovel it out; and although there was a moon, it was a very young one, and shed little light upon the grave, which was in the shadow of the church. At any other time, these obstacles would have made Gabriel Grub very moody and miserable, but he was so well pleased with having stopped the small boy's singing, that he took little heed of the scanty progress he had made, and looked down into the grave, when he had finished work for the night, with grim satisfaction: murmuring as he gathered up his things:

> Brave lodgings for one, brave lodgings for one,
> A few feet of cold earth, when life is done;
> A stone at the head, a stone at the feet,
> A rich, juicy meal for the worms to eat;
> Rank grass over head, and damp clay around,
> Brave lodgings for one, these, in holy ground!

"'Ho! ho!' laughed Gabriel Grub, as he sat himself down on a flat tombstone which was a favourite resting-place of his; and drew forth his wicker bottle. 'A coffin at Christmas! A Christmas Box. Ho! ho! ho!'

"'Ho! ho! ho!' repeated a voice which sounded close behind him.

"Gabriel paused, in some alarm, in the act of raising the wicker bottle to his lips: and looked round. The bottom of the oldest grave about him, was not more still and quiet, than the churchyard in the pale moonlight. The cold hoar-frost glistened on the tombstones, and sparkled like rows of gems, among the stone carvings of the old church. The snow lay hard and crisp upon the ground; and spread over the thickly-strewn mounds of earth so white and smooth a cover that it seemed as if corpses lay there, hidden only by their winding sheets. Not the faintest rustle broke the profound tranquillity of the solemn scene. Sound itself appeared to be frozen up, all was so cold and still.

"'It was the echoes,' said Gabriel Grub, raising the bottle to his lips again.

"'It was *not*,' said a deep voice.

"Gabriel started up, and stood rooted to the spot with astonishment and terror; for his eyes rested on a form that made his blood run cold.

"Seated on an upright tombstone, close to him, was a strange unearthly figure, whom Gabriel felt at once, was no being of this world. His long fantastic legs which might have reached the ground, were cocked up, and crossed after a quaint, fantastic fashion; his sinewy arms were bare; and his hands rested on his knees. On his short round body, he wore a close covering, ornamented with small slashes; a short cloak dangled at his back; the collar was cut into curious peaks, which served the goblin in lieu of ruff or neckerchief; and his shoes curled up at his toes into long points. On his head, he wore a broad-brimmed sugar-loaf hat, garnished with a single feather. The hat was covered with the white frost; and the goblin looked as if he had sat on the same tombstone very comfortably, for two or three hundred years. He was sitting perfectly still; his tongue was put out, as if in derision; and he was grinning at Gabriel Grub with such a grin as only a goblin could call up.

"'It was *not* the echoes,' said the goblin.

"Gabriel Grub was paralysed, and could make no reply.

"'What do you do here on Christmas Eve?' said the goblin sternly.

"'I came to dig a grave, sir,' stammered Gabriel Grub.

"'What man wanders among graves and churchyards on such a night as this?' cried the goblin.

"'Gabriel Grub! Gabriel Grub!' screamed a wild chorus of voices that seemed to fill the churchyard. Gabriel looked fearfully round—nothing was to be seen.

"'What have you got in that bottle?' said the goblin.

"'Hollands, sir,' replied the sexton, trembling more than ever; for he had bought it of the smugglers, and he thought that perhaps his questioner might be in the excise department of the goblins.

"'Who drinks Hollands alone, and in a churchyard, on such a night as this?' said the goblin.

"'Gabriel Grub! Gabriel Grub!' exclaimed the wild voices again.

"The goblin leered maliciously at the terrified sexton, and then raising his voice, exclaimed:

"'And who, then, is our fair and lawful prize?'

"To this inquiry the invisible chorus replied, in a strain that sounded like the voices of many choristers singing to the mighty swell of the old church organ—a strain that seemed borne to the sexton's ears upon a wild wind, and to die away as it passed onward; but the burden of the reply was still the same, 'Gabriel Grub! Gabriel Grub!'

"The goblin grinned a broader grin than before, as he said, 'Well, Gabriel, what do you say to this?'

"The sexton gasped for breath.

"'What do you think of this, Gabriel?' said the goblin, kicking up his feet in the air on either side of the tombstone, and looking at the turned-up points with as much complacency as if he had been contemplating the most fashionable pair of Wellingtons in all Bond Street.

"'It's—it's—very curious, sir,' replied the sexton, half dead with fright; 'very curious, and very pretty, but I think I'll go back and finish my work, sir, if you please.'

"'Work!' said the goblin, 'what work?'

"'The grave, sir; making the grave,' stammered the sexton.

"'Oh, the grave, eh?' said the goblin; 'who makes graves

The Goblin and the Sexton

at a time when all other men are merry, and takes a pleasure in it?'

"Again the mysterious voices replied, 'Gabriel Grub! Gabriel Grub!'

"'I'm afraid my friends want you, Gabriel,' said the goblin, thrusting his tongue further into his cheek than ever—and a most astonishing tongue it was—'I'm afraid my friends want you, Gabriel,' said the goblin.

"'Under favour, sir,' replied the horror-stricken sexton, 'I don't think they can, sir; they don't know me, sir; I don't think the gentlemen have ever seen me, sir.'

"'Oh yes they have,' replied the goblin; 'we know the man with the sulky face and grim scowl, that came down the street to-night, throwing his evil looks at the children, and grasping his burying spade the tighter. We know the man who struck the boy in the envious malice of his heart, because the boy could be merry, and he could not. We know him, we know him.'

"Here, the goblin gave a loud shrill laugh, which the echoes returned twenty-fold: and throwing his legs up in the air, stood upon his head, or rather upon the very point of his sugar-loaf hat, on the narrow edge of the tomb-stone: whence he threw a somerset with extraordinary agility, right to the sexton's feet, at which he planted himself in the attitude in which tailors generally sit upon the shop-board.

"'I—I—am afraid I must leave you, sir,' said the sexton, making an effort to move.

"'Leave us!' said the goblin, 'Gabriel Grub going to leave us. Ho! ho! ho!'

"As the goblin laughed, the sexton observed, for one instant, a brilliant illumination within the windows of the church, as if the whole building were lighted up; it disappeared, the organ pealed forth a lively air, and whole troops of goblins, the very counterpart of the first one, poured into the church-yard, and began playing at leap-frog with the tomb-stones: never stopping for an instant to take breath, but 'overing' the highest among them, one after the other, with the utmost marvellous dexterity. The first goblin was a most astonishing leaper, and none of the others could come near him; even in the extremity of his terror the sexton could not help observing, that while his friends were content to leap over the common-sized gravestones, the first one took the family vaults, iron railings and all, with as much ease as if they had been so many street posts.

"At last the game reached to a most exciting pitch; the organ played quicker and quicker; and the goblins leaped faster and faster: coiling themselves up, rolling head over heels upon the ground, and bounding over the tombstones like foot-balls. The sexton's brain whirled round with the rapidity of the motion he beheld, and his legs reeled beneath him, as the spirits flew before his eyes: when the goblin king, suddenly darting towards him, laid his hand upon his collar, and sank with him through the earth.

"When Gabriel Grub had had time to fetch his breath, which the rapidity of his descent had for the moment taken away, he found himself in what appeared to be a large cavern, surrounded on all sides by crowds of goblins, ugly and grim; in the centre of the room, on an elevated seat, was stationed his friend of the churchyard; and close beside him stood Gabriel Grub himself, without power of motion.

"'Cold to-night,' said the king of the goblins, 'very cold. A glass of something warm, here!'

"At this command, half a dozen officious goblins, with a perpetual smile upon their faces, whom Gabriel Grub imagined to be courtiers, on that account, hastily disappeared, and presently returned with a goblet of liquid fire, which they presented to the king.

"'Ah!' cried the goblin, whose cheeks and throat were transparent, as he tossed down the flame, 'This warms one, indeed! Bring a bumper of the same, for Mr. Grub.'

"It was in vain for the unfortunate sexton to protest that

he was not in the habit of taking anything warm at night; one of the goblins held him while another poured the blazing liquid down his throat; the whole assembly screeched with laughter as he coughed and choked, and wiped away the tears which gushed plentifully from his eyes, after swallowing the burning draught.

"'And now,' said the king, fantastically poking the taper corner of his sugar-loaf hat into the sexton's eye, and thereby occasioning him the most exquisite pain: 'And now, show the man of misery and gloom, a few of the pictures from our own great storehouse!'

"As the goblin said this, a thick cloud which obscured the remoter end of the cavern, rolled gradually away, and disclosed, apparently at a great distance, a small and scantily furnished, but neat and clean apartment. A crowd of little children were gathered round a bright fire, clinging to their mother's gown, and gambolling around her chair. The mother occasionally rose, and drew aside the window-curtain, as if to look for some expected object: a frugal meal was ready spread upon the table; and an elbow chair was placed near the fire. A knock was heard at the door: the mother opened it, and the children crowded round her, and clapped their hands for joy, as their father entered. He was wet and weary, and shook the snow from his garments, as the children crowded round him, and seizing his cloak, hat, stick, and gloves, with busy zeal, ran with them from the room. Then, as he sat down to his meal before the fire, the children climbed about his knee, and the mother sat by his side, and all seemed happiness and comfort.

"But a change came upon the view, almost imperceptibly. The scene was altered to a small bed-room, where the fairest and youngest child lay dying; the roses had fled from his cheek, and the light from his eye; and even as the sexton looked upon him with an interest he had never felt or known before, he died. His young brothers and sisters crowded round his little bed, and seized his tiny hand, so cold and heavy;

but they shrunk back from its touch, and looked with awe on his infant face; for calm and tranquil as it was, and sleeping in rest and peace as the beautiful child seemed to be, they saw that he was dead, and they knew that he was an Angel looking down upon, and blessing them, from a bright and happy Heaven.

"Again the light cloud passed across the picture, and again the subject changed. The father and mother were old and helpless now, and the number of those about them was diminished more than half; but content and cheerfulness sat on every face, and beamed in every eye, as they crowded round the fireside, and told and listened to old stories of earlier and bygone days. Slowly and peacefully, the father sank into the grave, and, soon after, the sharer of all his cares and troubles followed him to a place of rest. The few, who yet survived them, knelt by their tomb, and watered the green turf which covered it, with their tears; then rose, and turned away: sadly and mournfully, but not with bitter cries, or despairing lamentations, for they knew that they should one day meet again; and once more they mixed with the busy world, and their content and cheerfulness were restored. The cloud settled upon the picture, and concealed it from the sexton's view.

"'What do you think of *that*?' said the goblin, turning his large face towards Gabriel Grub.

"Gabriel murmured out something about its being very pretty, and looked somewhat ashamed, as the goblin bent his fiery eyes upon him.

"'*You* a miserable man!' said the goblin, in a tone of excessive contempt. 'You!' He appeared disposed to add more, but indignation choked his utterance, so he lifted up one of his very pliable legs, and flourishing it above his head a little, to insure his aim, administered a good sound kick to Gabriel Grub; immediately after which, all the goblins in waiting, crowded round the wretched sexton, and kicked him without mercy: according to the established and invariable custom of courtiers upon earth, who kick whom royalty kicks, and hug whom royalty hugs.

"'Show him some more!' said the king of the goblins.

"At these words, the cloud was dispelled, and a rich and beautiful landscape was disclosed to view—there is just such another, to this day, within half a mile of the old abbey town. The sun shone from out the clear blue sky, the water sparkled beneath his rays, and the trees looked greener, and the flowers more gay, beneath his cheering influence. The water rippled on, with a pleasant sound; the trees rustled in the light wind that murmured among their leaves; the birds sang upon the boughs; and the lark carolled on high her welcome to the morning. Yes, it was morning; the bright, balmy morning of summer; the minutest leaf, the smallest blade of grass, was instinct with life. The ant crept forth to her daily toil, the butterfly fluttered and basked in the warm rays of the sun; myriads of insects spread their transparent wings, and revelled in their brief but happy existence. Man walked forth, elated with the scene; and all was brightness and splendour.

"'*You* a miserable man!' said the king of the goblins, in a more contemptuous tone than before. And again the king of the goblins gave his leg a flourish; again it descended on the shoulders of the sexton; and again the attendant goblins imitated the example of their chief.

"Many a time the cloud went and came, and many a lesson it taught to Gabriel Grub, who, although his shoulders smarted with pain from the frequent applications of the goblin's feet, looked on with an interest that nothing could diminish. He saw that men who worked hard, and earned their scanty bread with lives of labour, were cheerful and happy; and that to the most ignorant, the sweet face of nature was a never-failing source of cheerfulness and joy. He saw those who had been delicately nurtured, and tenderly brought up, cheerful under privations, and superior to suffering that would have crushed many of a rougher grain, because they bore within their own bosoms the materials of happiness, contentment, and peace. He saw that women, the tenderest and most fragile of all God's creatures, were the oftenest superior to sorrow, adversity, and distress; and he saw that it was because they bore, in their own hearts, an inexhaustible well-spring of affection and devotion. Above all, he saw that men like himself who snarled at the mirth and cheerfulness of others, were the foulest weeds on the fair surface of the earth; and setting all the good of the world against the evil, he came to the conclusion that it was a very decent and respectable sort of world after all. No sooner had he formed it, than the cloud which closed over the last picture, seemed to settle on his senses, and lull him to repose. One by one, the goblins faded from his sight; and as the last one disappeared, he sunk to sleep.

"The day had broken when Gabriel Grub awoke, and found himself lying, at full length on the flat grave-stone in the churchyard, with the wicker bottle lying empty by his side, and his coat, spade, and lantern, all well whitened by the last night's frost, scattered on the ground. The stone on which he had first seen the goblin seated, stood bolt upright before him, and the grave at which he had worked, the night before, was not far off. At first, he began to doubt the reality of his adventures, but the acute pain in his shoulders when he attempted to rise, assured him that the kicking of the goblins was certainly not ideal. He was staggered again, by observing no traces of footsteps in the snow on which the goblins had played at leap-frog with the grave-stones, but he speedily accounted for this circumstance when he remembered that, being spirits, they would leave no visible impression behind them. So, Gabriel Grub got on his feet as well as he could, for the pain in his back; and brushing the frost off his coat, put it on, and turned his face towards the town.

"But he was an altered man, and he could not bear the thought of returning to a place where his repentance would

be scoffed at, and his reformation disbelieved. He hesitated
for a few moments; and then turned away to wander where
he might, and seek his bread elsewhere.

"The lantern, the spade, and the wicker bottle, were found,
that day, in the churchyard. There were a great many speculations about the sexton's fate, at first, but it was speedily
determined that he had been carried away by the goblins;
and there were not wanting some very credible witnesses
who had distinctly seen him whisked through the air on the
back of a chestnut horse blind of one eye, with the hind-
quarters of a lion, and the tail of a bear. At length
all this was devoutly believed; and the new sexton used
to exhibit to the curious, for a trifling emolument, a good-
sized piece of the church weathercock which had been accidentally kicked off by the aforesaid horse in his aërial flight,
and picked up by himself in the churchyard, a year or two
afterwards.

"Unfortunately, these stories were somewhat disturbed by
the unlooked-for re-appearance of Gabriel Grub himself, some
ten years afterwards, a ragged, contented, rheumatic old man.
He told his story to the clergyman, and also to the mayor;
and in course of time it began to be received, as a matter of
history, in which form it has continued down to this very
day. The believers in the weathercock tale, having misplaced
their confidence once, were not easily prevailed upon to part
with it again, so they looked as wise as they could, shrugged
their shoulders, touched their foreheads, and murmured something about Gabriel Grub having drunk all the Hollands,
and then fallen asleep on the flat tombstone; and they
affected to explain what he supposed he had witnessed in
the goblin's cavern, by saying that he had seen the world,
and grown wiser. But this opinion, which was by no means
a popular one at any time, gradually died off; and be the
matter how it may, as Gabriel Grub was afflicted with rheumatism to the end of his days, this story has at least one
moral, if it teach no better one—and that is, that if a man

turn sulky and drink by himself at Christmas time, he may make up his mind to be not a bit the better for it: let the spirits be never so good, or let them be even as many degrees beyond proof, as those which Gabriel Grub saw in the goblin's cavern."

This book, designed
by William B. Taylor,
is a production
of Heron Books, London

Printed in Switzerland